The Price of Innocence

By

Gil Howard

authorHOUSE®

AuthorHouse™
1663 Liberty Drive, Suite 200
Bloomington, IN 47403
www.authorhouse.com
Phone: 1-800-839-8640

First published by AuthorHouse 6/18/2008

ISBN: 978-1-4343-8327-3 (sc)
ISBN: 978-1-4343-8326-6 (hc)

Library of Congress Control Number: 2008903646

Printed in the United States of America
Bloomington, Indiana

This book is printed on acid-free paper.

You may enjoy these other
novels by Gil Howard:

The Chaos Chip (1999)
Fury in the Shadow (2005)

This novel is dedicated

to my wife Nola T. Zitzelsberger
who spent endless hours reading and
who devoted her sharp insights to critiquing plot;

and to my friend Barbara Salem
whose research as to costume
and other matters was immeasurably helpful.

Prologue

It has been argued that true *evil* does not exist. Those who pursue that argument suggest that the word is a mere abstract noun like so many other abstract nouns, such as honor and integrity. They assert that tagging some person or group as *evil* is a mere value judgment with which intelligent people might disagree.

Murdock McCabe is not so sure. When people whom he respects and the woman he loves, fall into the hands of utterly ruthless people to whom rape, murder, and the destruction of the reputations of eminently honorable people are casual tools, he becomes even harder to convince.

It's written that the sword of justice has no scabbard.[1] That sword is too often parried by people utterly devoid of either honor or integrity. Murdock is determined to blunt the parry. With a team of trusted men and women of hard-nosed integrity and honor, he seeks the truth—the ultimate enemy of *evil*.

Regrettably, in such a clash, everyone cannot come out unscathed.

---

[1] Joseph De Maistre, *Les Soirées de Saint Petersbourg,* 1821

1

Munich, Bavaria, Germany
Thursday, March 2, 9:30 a.m.

Grace paused before the double glass doors with the logo of Veritus Investigations International etched on both. She buttoned her coat, turned up her collar, wrapped her cashmere scarf tightly around her neck, and tucked it inside her coat. Munich was in the grip of another blizzard, not unlike those she had often experienced in her native Iowa. With trepidation, she stepped outside and leaned into a frigid wind.

Born and raised in Spirit Lake, Iowa, Grace was an intelligent, fresh looking woman in her mid-thirties, and spirited; her character was firm but caring. A plucky sauciness, often with a sting in its tail, often punctured conceit or hypocrisy in others. She had her father's mind cultivated, brilliant and daring. She loved him deeply. He had been a huge influence on her life. Since she'd started school, they had constantly debated. Whatever position she took, he played the devil's advocate, challenging her intellectually, exposing the flip side of every coin, and compelling her to argue the opposing view. Her mother had been killed by a drunk driver when she was eight. He had raised her. All men were measured against him.

Passing the Alter Hof, she turned the corner into the full force of the wind. Few automobiles were moving. An ambulance struggled tentatively, and snaked its way among a labyrinth of vehicles stranded in awkward positions. Snow swirled into mini-blizzards, occasionally reducing visibility to zero. Few pedestrians, even those cursed with hard-headed German determination, had had the audacity to brave a sidewalk buried under fourteen inches. The headquarters of the Bavarian State Police was five cold blocks distant, but walking was more practical than attempting to drive. She passed the *Augustinerkloster*. It won't be long now, she thought, just another four blocks. She laughed at her optimism and tugged her woolen hat further down over her ears.

Grace was one of Veritus's most promising acquisitions. Upon graduating with honors from Michigan State University with a major in criminal justice, she had served an eight-year stint as an investigator for the Michigan State Police. Tiring of the seamy side of human experience, she yearned for the less seamy. That goal fit Veritus. This international private investigation agency targeted such mundane things as insurance fraud and the hidden wealth of ex-husbands. Veritus had not only offered better pay, but also greater opportunity for advancement and for foreign travel. They made an offer. She eagerly grasped it.

The first six years she worked at their office in Buffalo, New York. Two years ago a position opened in Munich, the capital of the German state of Bavaria. She was offered the position. She would replace one of Veritus's top agents, Murdock McCabe. He had been promoted to station chief and placed in charge of the Veritus office in Portland, Oregon. She had never traveled to Europe and eagerly accepted it.

She was the only soul on the sidewalk. That pleased her. She was tougher than most. It would take more than a mere blizzard to stop her.

A few days ago Murdock McCabe had phoned her. He had obtained permission from her station chief, Ernst Müller, for her to assist him with a criminal investigation. Their client was José Enrique Perez-Krieger, a Chilean businessman and one of the wealthiest men in the world. He and his son, Ricardo, lived on Grand Cayman Island, a British protectorate in the Caribbean Sea, south of Cuba and north of Honduras. Ricardo had been charged with rape. He swore that he was innocent. In her experience, that wasn't unusual. The alleged victim, Gretchen Weidner, had been visiting Grand Cayman Island as a tourist. She resided in Landshut, a city in Bavaria—the southern most of the German states. Grace's assignment was to develop a background report on her. She was curious about Murdock McCabe. Ernst had mentioned that McCabe was thought by many to be destined for the highest position in Veritus. Perez-Krieger was Veritus's premier client. He had expressly asked for McCabe to supervise the investigation. McCabe had expressly chosen her because of her police background.

Grace liked the sound of Murdock. It wasn't just his telephone voice. He had a positive can-do attitude balanced with intelligence, perceptivity, and sincerity. He reminded her of her dad. Not many men did. A woman in the office described him as a six-foot-three, broad-shouldered, trim, red-haired hunk. Success in this investigation might produce more than one advantage.

Her appointment was with Rudi Benzinger, the director of criminal investigations for the Bavarian State Police and a friend of Murdock's. She was familiar with Benzinger's reputation. Not only was he a highly competent investigator and able administrator, he was a no-nonsense straight shooter. When Veritus became involved in a criminal matter, company policy dictated that the police were notified. Normally, contact was made at a lower level. Benzinger seemed overkill. Veritus made few unnecessary moves. There had to be a good reason that McCabe had asked her to talk to him personally; something more than just friendship.

As she opened the door at state police headquarters, a blast of wind pushed her through. She stopped just inside. Even though she was an avid skier and accustomed to cold weather, she was relieved to be inside. Shaking the snow off her coat and boots, she noticed a woman in a neatly pressed brown uniform standing near her. Her name tag read Ingrid.

"You're Grace Bauer," the woman said. "We met briefly when I visited your office four months ago. You probably don't remember."

She didn't, but she nodded in recognition and shook her hand.

Ingrid escorted her to an elevator and pushed a button for the fifth floor. When they arrived, Ingrid guided her into an anteroom. An exceedingly bountiful woman was seated behind a hefty oak desk. Her intimidating size, uncommonly muscular arms, braided dirty-blonde hair knotted into a tight bun, and the coldest gray eyes Grace had ever seen, commanded respect. A uniform was unnecessary. Without a word the woman waved her hand in the direction of a chair. As Grace prepared to seat herself, Ingrid leaned close to her. Nodding toward the woman, she whispered, "Don't mind her. She's okay." Pointing toward a door, she added, "That's the powder room. You may want to comb your hair. You have time." Grace thanked her and took the advice.

* * *

Rudi Benzinger had been born and raised in Landshut, a city an hour's drive northeast along the Isar River. He knew the city well. For nearly twenty years, he had served at the state police post there. There were no local police in Bavaria. Fifteen years ago a promotion caused him to move to Munich, the state capital.

In medieval times, Landshut had been the capital of the princely state of Lower Bavaria. Until 1918 Bavaria had been a separate kingdom within the German empire. The Wittenberg family had ruled it for over a thousand years. Rudi had a deep sense of place and of Bavarian history. He was proud of it—except, of course, for the fact the Nazis had risen to power there.

Standing before a window with a mug of steaming hot coffee, he stared outside at the winter scene. *It's a splendid morning,* he thought. He loved the clean, sharp beauty of each new snowfall. He took a sip. His office was comfortable. Its furnishings and general ambience exuded power. It affirmed that he was number one. *But not for much longer,* he thought. In a few months, he would retire and draw his pension. The thought was daunting. He felt too young to do nothing.

A buzzer sounded. Alas, this morning was not a time to ponder either pristine whiteness or the trepidations of retirement. There was serious business afoot. Turning, he put the mug on a round conference table, walked to the door and through it into the anteroom. There he observed an exceptionally attractive young woman. She was, he thought, almost as attractive as his wife had been at that age. Seeing him, she arose. He offered his hand. She took it.

"*Frau* Bauer?" he asked with a warm smile.

"Mizz," she interjected.

"I'm sorry. Please forgive me. I am Rudi Benzinger. Please call me Rudi. Any friend of Murdock McCabe is a friend of mine."

The abundant woman glanced at him and frowned.

Grace flashed a disarmingly warm smile, shook his hand, and said, "Please call me Grace. But I don't want to travel under false colors. I'm not a friend of Mr. McCabe's. I've never met him."

"That's unfortunate. I think that's only a matter of time. He was quite impressed with your *curriculum vitae.* He's looking forward to meeting you—professionally, of course."

Rudi escorted her into his office. Ingrid closed the double doors behind them and remained outside. Rudi motioned toward the conference table and offered coffee.

"Black, please." He poured the aromatic liquid and placed it before her. "Thank you," she responded. "You're most gracious."

He nodded. "Murdock and you have much in common."

A practiced frown crossed her face. "Really? How is that, Rudi?" She was careful to appear slightly under-impressed.

Rudi ignored the gamesmanship and continued. "I understand that you graduated from the criminal justice program at Michigan State University. So did Murdock's regional supervisor and old friend, Allison Spencer. You both had police experience before joining Veritus. He spent twelve years with the FBI; you spent eight with the Michigan State Police.

Your first assignment for Veritus was Buffalo. Murdock is a native of the Buffalo area. If you wonder why I know so much, that's my business. I presume you have a heads-up on me, too."

She smiled graciously. "I have. In regard to Mr. McCabe, you neglected to mention that he's a powerfully built hunk and a widower. Of course, that's only what I'm told."

Rudi grinned, shook his head, and took a sip of the hot brew. "Anyway, I talked with Murdock yesterday. He told me that Veritus is involved in a criminal investigation on Grand Cayman Island. I understand that it involves Ricardo, the son of José Enrique Perez-Krieger. Have you met Enrique?"

"I think everyone in the world has heard of him. I've not met him and don't know much about him, other than the fact that he's fabulously wealthy. Ernst Müller, my station chief, sent me to inform you that we're involved, but obviously that isn't necessary."

Rudi took another sip and continued. "No doubt you know that Perez-Krieger is Chilean. Enrique, as he prefers to be called, owns more than two dozen highly profitable corporations including two re-insurers based here in Munich. The CEOs of all his businesses report to his *mayor domo*, Linda DiStefano. She runs his business empire from a compound on the North Coast of Grand Cayman Island."

Her eyes met his. "She must be an impressive woman."

"I've met her. She is indeed." Rudi smiled. "I believe that she's also noticed that Murdock is a hunk. In the world of commerce, Linda is one of the most powerful women in the world. She'll write the check that pays Veritus's bill. She's also a lawyer. Enrique has asked her to represent his son."

"I presume she's brought in associate consul."

"I believe she has."

Grace's eyes met his briefly again. She extracted her laptop from her travel bag, flipped it open, brought up the file and briefly studied the first page. Rudi took another sip. Grace said, "I've received an e-mail background briefing from a Susan Ling at our Portland office. I've spoken to her on the phone but I've not met her, either. Have you?"

"No, but I understand that she's Murdock's assistant station chief and a meticulous researcher."

Grace's eyes met his briefly again. "Her voice on the phone sounded young, intelligent, and socially accomplished. She's probably noticed that he's a hunk, too."

Rudi chuckled. "From what Murdock has said, I believe his relationship with Mrs. Ling is purely professional. She *is* married."

Grace returned a contrived chuckle. "Even the marvelous Murdock McCabe can't see everything, Rudi, and I've met several married women who couldn't be fulfilled by only one man; some probably not by a troop of cavalry."

Rudi's eyes met hers. "What did Susan's research tell you?"

"Señor Perez-Krieger's grandfather emigrated from here to Chile in 1899."

"Not from Bavaria," Rudi injected. "He emigrated from the State of Saxony, which was one of the princely states of the German empire just north of what was then the Kingdom of Bavaria."

Grace smiled. "Thank you, Rudi. Ms. Ling did point that out. When Grandpa Krieger arrived in Chile, he went into the nitrate business, and in a short time became prosperous. He diversified into copper and agriculture. His agricultural investments included vineyards and a winery, plus market gardening near Valparaíso."

Rudi learned back in his chair. "The blueberries that you eat in wintertime may have come from Enrique's lands in the Lake District of Chile."

She smiled. "They're too expensive. I can't afford them. When the nitrate market disintegrated after World War I, Grandpa expanded into steel. He bought iron mines and built mills. Between the two world wars he made millions by exporting scrap iron to Japan. He kept a wife and six mistresses—content. Grandpa was a prolific man."

"An authentic Chilean folk hero," Rudi added, smiling. "His son, Enrique's father, was even more successful and became one of the wealthiest men in Chile, if not all of South America."

Without looking up from her laptop, Grace muttered, "Our client is indeed a fortunate fellow. Is this Linda DiStefano one of Enrique's several mistresses?"

"Murdock seems certain she isn't. Enrique is an old friend of her father's. I don't know that he has *any* mistresses."

Without lifting her head, Grace raised her eyes to meet Rudi's. "He's not a chip off the old block, right? How did you put it earlier, 'I believe his relationship with her is purely professional?' When the mind interprets reality, Rudi, it creates within itself whatever illusions are necessary to make it fit into the spin that the mind favors. If Mr. McCabe has invested emotional resources into this woman, I hope he doesn't get mugged by reality."

Rudi was impressed by such an erudite statement. He shifted his weight in his chair, uncomfortably and said, "Murdock's assessments of people are not usually far off, Grace. He trusts his instincts. What else did Mrs. Ling say about Enrique?"

"Ms. Ling reported that he was born in Santiago de Chile in 1946. He graduated from the University of Concepción, where he majored in economics and business administration. He completed post graduate work at the University of Wisconsin where he received a master's degree in finance. He served three years as an officer in the Chilean army before joining the family businesses. After his father's death, Enrique gained control of the family empire. He's a business genius. Recently, he's branched into hotels by acquiring properties on Grand Cayman Island. He lives there now."

"He founded the College of the Caymans."

Her eyes met his. She asked quizzically, "Why?"

"He told me that he wanted to provide an opportunity for deserving young Latin Americans to become entrepreneurs and educated in the ways of capitalism. Many of these countries have only two classes—the very rich and the very pour. Enrique wishes to encourage the growth of a middle class and opportunities for the very poor to raise themselves into it. Many students can't afford the tuition or the cost of living in a foreign country. Enrique provides fully paid scholarships for them."

Grace smiled. "Obviously, he's impressed you."

"I'm most impressed by the fact that he saved my life, but that's another story."

Grace looked up. Her eyes widened. "Was this recently?"

"Two years ago. He saved Murdock's and Allison Spencer's lives, too. Murdock had a client who paid Veritus to assist us in an investigation. A monk had been murdered near Saint Luke's Monastery on the slopes of the Zugspitze Mountain. The inquiry led us to Cyprus. Murdock, Allison Spencer, and I were taken prisoner by operatives of a mysterious organization called Traction. Enrique came upon us almost accidentally and freed us at great risk to himself. Since then, Enrique has been impressed with Murdock's work. He's hired him several times. In fact, he's the only Veritus agent Enrique will deal with. Actually, Miss DiStefano does the dealing. That's why your Portland office is involved in a Cayman case."

Grace looked up from her laptop. "Really? That's interesting. Linda DiStefano, the virgin Crown Princess of World Commerce, writes Enrique's checks. Tell me more."

Rudi grinned. He was beginning to enjoy this woman. *She certainly doesn't mince words,* he thought. He responded, "Perhaps at another time. What else did you learn from Susan's e-mail?"

"She informed me that Perez-Krieger—"

"He prefers everyone to call him Enrique."

Grace smiled. "That Enrique's son, Ricardo, is charged with rape on Grand Cayman Island. The alleged victim is a German tourist, Gretchen Weidner. She hails from your hometown, Landshut. The Cayman crown prosecutor alleges that Ricardo helped hold the girl while two of his buddies took their pleasure. Under Cayman law, an accessory is as guilty as a principal. If convicted, Ricardo could be sentenced to life in prison. He's committed no crime in Bavaria, so you normally wouldn't be involved, but Gretchen was given permission to return home until the trial date. Last week I was assigned do a work-up on her."

Rudi stirred some sugar into his coffee. "I understand that she and her mother disappeared from a train between here and Landshut."

"So it appears. They had flown from Grand Cayman Island to Miami to Munich. They boarded a train to Landshut but never arrived. I interviewed the conductor. He remembered an older and a younger woman who came on board just minutes before the train was about to leave. Ten minutes later, when he entered their compartment to take tickets, they were gone. I went to Landshut and interviewed their neighbors. I've found no one who's seen them since. Or, at least, no one who admits seeing them. It looks like foul play."

Rudi grinned. "It only *looks like* foul play?"

"It could have been staged to keep her out of circulation until the trial. However, because a criminal act may have occurred in this state, Veritus's rules require me to notify the police. My instructions are to deal with you rather than an underling. I'm not sure why. I presume you'll enlighten me."

Rudi slowly raised his coffee mug, took a sip, and leisurely placed the mug on the table. His eyes met hers. "Both Murdock and I suspect that something more sinister than a gang rape is afoot."

Her eyes met his. A wry smile crossed her face. "What *can* be more sinister?"

"At this point, we've merely a hunch with no evidence to support it."

"Without a hunch, many investigations wouldn't go anywhere. I was called the Queen of Hunches back in Michigan. What tickled yours, Rudi?"

Rudi took yet another sip of coffee and considered his answer before he spoke.

"Murdock and I would prefer that what I'm about to share with you would go no farther."

"I would have to share with my station chief."

His eyes met hers. "I think not."

8

"But I must—"

"No, Grace. You mustn't. If our hunch is correct, our suspects must not know that we're on to them. Your life would be in danger."

She pressed the top of her pen to her chin. "My! I agree that *does* sound sinister. I take it that you two don't trust Ernst."

"You may take it that we've decided to trust you. Eventually you'll be able to tell your station chief almost everything."

"Almost? I have a duty of loyalty—"

Rudi interrupted, "To your client, Señor Perez-Krieger."

Grace corrected, "Enrique."

Rudi laughed. "Touché."

Grace glanced at her notebook, placed her elbow on the arm of the chair, and touched the top of her pen to her chin again. "You were saying?"

"Did you interview Gretchen's father?"

"Yes. Herr Weidner fed me a story about how Gretchen and her mother diverted to Torino for a skiing holiday to recover from the trauma. He went on about how much fun they had and how sympathetic his neighbors were to poor Gretchen's tragedy. I checked. Gretchen and Mom weren't registered in any hotel, ski lodge, or hostel there that I can find. Josef Weidner seems bigger than life. I got the impression that he has a charmed ability to accurately describe in infinite detail events that never happened. How could the two women have changed trains? Did they leap from the train moving north to one moving south? He was trying to deceive me, and I think that *he* knew that *I* knew it and he really didn't shiv-a-git."

Her eyes, more narrow now, met his again. "You didn't answer my earlier question, Rudi. What could be more sinister than a gang rape?"

I truly do like this woman, Rudi thought. *She reminds me of me when I was her age.* He responded, "A gang rape staged for the purpose of destroying innocent people and inflicting catastrophic economic and political chaos in the world."

"Catastrophic chaos in the world? That sounds like a stretch, but I guess my job is simply to smoke out the young lady, hopefully uncover a sordid past, and ignore the hyperbole."

"Whether or not it's hyperbole that would be helpful."

She's a perceptive gal, Rudi thought, *but she doesn't discern the extent of the terrifying evil that lies at the heart of this.* "If this rape was staged by Traction, and if it results in a successful prosecution of Enrique's son, then any person possessed of commercial or political power and their families would feel vulnerable to blackmail or worse. It's critically important that Ricardo is exonerated and Traction exposed."

9

For several seconds Grace's eyes locked onto his and she didn't speak. Presently, she asked, "Why me? Why not you cops?"

"Suffice it to say that there are political and security concerns."

She typed a brief note and boldly inquired, "Do you have a mole in your state police headquarters?"

Rudi smiled. *She does indeed remind me of me.* He said, "We consider that possible."

"What difference would it make? Why would this investigation have to be so cloak-and-dagger that you'd have to worry about a mole? One gang rape doesn't exactly sound like international intrigue."

"Did Mrs. Ling give you a heads-up on an organization called Traction?"

"Briefly. She made it sound mysterious. What can you tell me about it, Rudi?"

"It's a shadowy organization. We have no idea of its size. It could have several thousand adherents or only a few. We think it's bent on destabilizing the world economy, undermining national governments, and turning most of civilization upside down."

Grace typed a note to herself. Without looking up she said, "That would seem ambitious for only a few. If they're such bad boys, why don't they get media attention? The pseudo-journalist jackals should be on top of them."

"We can't even prove Traction exists. We think it's ruled by a bad girl."

"Girls can be naughty. Why should these anarchists mean anything to me?"

"Because Enrique is your client. Traction sees Enrique—"

Grace corrected, "If Traction exists—"

"Yes." Rudi grinned, somewhat frustrated. "If Traction exists, it sees Enrique as one of its foremost enemies. He organized a huge nonpublic mutual fund called Plato. Its shareholder list is confidential but Murdock informs me that they are some of the world's wealthiest men. Plato injects venture capital into third world countries to stabilize their economy. Their projects involve making venture capital available to small but promising entrepreneurs who wouldn't qualify for loans from weak, third-world banking systems."

"Like the graduates of his college, I assume. Enrique and his Plato buddies sound bigger than life. What's their endgame?"

Rudi looked puzzled. "I don't understand *endgame*. Is there a German cognate?"

Grace shook her head. "I don't know of one. What's in it for them?"

"I'm not talking about handouts. Plato doesn't invest unless Enrique and Plato's board think the investment will make money for both Plato and the local entrepreneurs. Profits are poured back into the fund. Not only must the entrepreneurs benefit, but the labor force must also benefit by drawing a better wage. As poor people rise into middle class, the phony lure of socialism becomes more obvious to them. I understand that the fund makes a profit most years. Plato is a Cayman corporation. It's also headquartered there. That's another reason why Enrique lives there."

"May anyone invest in this mutual fund?"

"Each investor must be approved and invited by Plato's board of directors. The test is whether or not an investor is personally committed to Plato's moral high ground."

"It sounds like you're a true believer. I find that, if you look too closely at those who occupy the moral high ground, you often find that what passes for morality often shields a shabby reality. A gentle Kansas Sunday school teacher can be a mass murderer during the week. There could be an ugly subscript for Enrique and those Plato folks—something more sinister than Traction. What's their politics?"

Rudi replied patiently, "Wielding great economic power necessarily has a political effect. To my knowledge, Plato never directly supports any party or politician. You can accuse the members of being idealistic, but they're not foolish."

Grace placed her laptop on the conference table, folded her hands on her lap and stared at Rudi quizzically. "This is fascinating, but how does any of it affect our poor, allegedly misused Bavarian, Gretchen?"

"Enrique is the front man for Plato. His is the only name known to the public. Plato works because the investors have confidence in Enrique's honesty and moral intensity. His son's indictment for rape is a dent in his armor. Any dent also tarnishes Plato. Naturally, the indictment has caused a journalistic feeding frenzy. A mere trickle of facts produces oceans of opinions with no line thrown out to delineate which is fact and which is opinion. The media become awash with seas of innuendo and speculation, and truth drowns. Journalists interview other journalists who speculate what the news might be if they could find any. It's seldom flattering to the subject of their feeding frenzy. Meanwhile, Enrique's nose is being rubbed in the dirt. Plato investors get wobbly."

Grace was silent, her eyes focusing on a blank screen on her laptop. She'd had no clue as to the seriousness of the investigation, or how important it must be to Murdock McCabe who had chosen her sight unseen. Susan Ling had told her that Murdock didn't want to talk about the details over an unsecure phone line; nor did he wish to e-mail them. That's the reason she was sent to Rudi.

Grace said, "Of course, Ricardo could *be* guilty, although Ms. Ling reports that he swore he was innocent."

Rudi nodded assent. "It wouldn't surprise me that he's telling the truth. However, he will go before a common law jury, just like you have in most of the United States. Truth is irrelevant. The only thing that matters is what the jury believes to be true."

Neither spoke. Both sipped their barely warm coffee. Rudi waited. Finally, Grace, staring out the window, broke the silence.

"Perhaps the Plato investors suffer from a moral overconfidence. That leaves people open to manipulation by others who may be genuinely evil. Plato sounds egalitarian beyond belief—much too good to be true. I hope you'll forgive me if I take it with a grain of salt. You portray Enrique as some sort of superman. Maybe you're right. If you are, I agree that this case is major league." Her eyes shifted to meet his. "I'm pretty low on the totem pole at Veritus. Why did your friend, Murdock, ask for me? Am I expendable?"

"No, of course not. Forgive me for saying so, but Traction—"

"If it exists—"

"Of course. No offense intended, but Traction will see you as a lightweight. If Veritus suspected Traction, it would use a heavyweight. Play dumb. Never mention the word Traction. Hold your cards close to your chest. Keep Ernst in the dark as best you can. Ernst would be in danger, too. You're both safe as long as Traction thinks you're less competent or misdirected. In regard to my staff, I've passed off our meeting today with the story that our meeting is social, and that you and I are mutual friends of Murdock's."

"I hope it works. Your receptionist heard my false colors remark."

"That was unfortunate. I'm sure you can be relieved of the assignment, if you wish."

"Perish the thought. I don't wish. Scarlet scandal is just what the doctor ordered. Perhaps I'll find that our poor victim, Gretchen, is the whore of the Alps."

"I doubt it. There's one other thing. Ernst told Murdock that you're working part-time on a master's degree in ancient classical literature."

"How is that relevant to anything?"

"Is it true that your thesis deals with ancient mythology, particularly the Greco-Roman gods and goddesses?"

"And the Teutonic gods and goddesses, too. I hope to expand it into a book. My thesis explores theories as to the ancient origins of the myths, and explores the reasons for their insertion into modern religious cults like Wicca."

Grace stared at Rudi, awaiting a response. He leaned closer to her and spoke in a subdued voice, which seemed strange to her. If he thought the place was bugged, why had he already shared confidences?

"As I said earlier, we believe that a woman is at the head of Traction."

"If she exists."

Rudi added impatiently, "She creates an annoying elusiveness and an illusion that she's a goddess with unnatural powers. Murdock thinks she does it to scare her more simple-minded followers, especially the superstitious mules that run narcotics for Traction from Colombia to the United States. That's how they fund their terror. Murdock thinks she's a master of disguise. He believes he's met her as two or three different people."

"The Roman goddess Diana is a *triformis.*"

Rudi cocked his head. "I'm not familiar with that word, either."

"Diana appears in the myths in three forms—sort of like a trinity. In one form, she's Diana, the virgin goddess of the hunt. In another, she's Selene, goddess of the moon. In a third, she's Hecate, a chthonic, or infernal, deity—the mistress of Hades. Her Greek counterpart is Artemis. She's the daughter of Jupiter, the king of the gods, and Latona, his wife."

"When your thesis is finished, I'd like to read it. In your research, have you run into a person named Verbius?"

"One legend has it that Diana tricked her twin brother, Apollo, into impregnating her. They had a son whom she named Verbius. In pre-Roman Italy, another legend paints Verbius as the first priest of the Diana cult. The Romans thought of him as a forest god. His Greek counterpart is Hippolytus. Do you take this goddess stuff seriously?"

Rudi finished the last of his cold coffee. "I take seriously the fact that this woman wants us to. She also wants her followers and us to believe that she has extraordinary powers because she is extraterrestrial."

Grace raised an eyebrow. "Bottom line, what do *you* think?"

"I think that you and Murdock need to meet. But, let's get back to the immediate matter at hand. You were inclined not to believe Gretchen's father. Did you believe the train conductor?"

Grace pushed her chair from the table and arose. "I begin by believing no one. As in any inquiry, one must decide which dog is hiding the bone amongst a pack of liars."

Rudi stood up, nodding in agreement. *She might even be a little sharper than I was.* He said, "That's wise. Before you leave, do you have any questions?"

Grace closed her laptop and replied, "I think not. I can see the obvious. I should coordinate closely with you because you are *numero uno* at the Bavarian State Police; and because you're Murdock McCabe's close friend; and because you're scheduled to retire in a few months and soon I might be working for you at Veritus. Do you have any final thoughts, Rudi?"

Rudi mused, walked over to the window, and stared outside briefly with his hands folded behind his back. Turning toward her, he said, "I shall advise Murdock that he's chosen the right woman."

2

Portland, Oregon
Monday, March 6, 7:30 a.m.

Veritus Investigations International occupies the entire twentieth floor of the Northwest Office Towers Building. Murdock McCabe, its station chief, arrived early. He liked to be in his office at least a half hour before his associates arrived. He seldom succeeded. His assistant station chief, Susan Ling, was consistently there to greet him with her cheerful smile. Today was no exception. He glanced at his watch. It read 7:30. As he passed her desk, he said, "Good morning, Susan." She looked up, smiled, handed him a mug of hot coffee, and responded, "Good morning, Boss."

A cold, bone-chilling drizzle had been falling outside. His office was warm. Susan had turned up the thermostat. Murdock took a sip of the coffee and then placed the mug on his desk. He walked to the window, stood with his hands behind his back, and glanced down upon the fog that hid the street below. *No view of Mount Hood today*, he thought. He was disappointed. He seated himself on his Italian leather high-backed executive chair behind an oversized desk of polished mahogany, its surface mirror bright. Extracting a coaster from a side drawer, he parked the mug on top of the desk. He ran a comb through his thick mop of red hair. The office was enormous. In front of the desk were three over-sized and equally impressive matching leather chairs. An eight-foot diameter matching circular conference table with four chairs was off to the right side. Bottom line—a Veritus station chief had to look important. Clients ushered into *that* office would expect to pay a substantial fee.

Susan's laptop had already been planted on the conference table. With a mug of coffee in one hand, she breezed through the door and into the office. She seated herself next to the laptop, facing the chair Murdock would occupy. He joined her. She had worked for him for over a year but she had never ceased to be astonished at the power of his physical presence. *What woman wouldn't be?* she thought. A handsome face, broad shoulders, full head of red hair and a six-foot-three frame were not lost on her. His rugged good looks teased her fantasies. There was no scintilla of romance between them. Both seemed certain of that. Besides, Susan was married, and she was positive that Murdock was still in love with his late wife, Karen.

Murdock and Karen had met at the State University at Buffalo where they did their undergraduate work. As soon as they received their degrees, they were married. He went on to law school at the University of Michigan and then into the FBI. At the same university, Karen took a master's degree in linguistics. Fascinated by encryption, she developed a freelance business in decoding messages and breaking codes. In the pursuit of that business, the FBI had contracted with her to break a code being used by some group that they claimed to be unfamiliar with. The group used the name *Traction*. When she was close to success, she was kidnapped. During a botched FBI raid to free her, she had been killed in the crossfire.

Susan Ling was in her late twenties, five-two, with coal black hair turned under into a page-boy style. Warm oriental eyes set in a cherubic face masked her solid self-confidence and invited people to underestimate her. A graduate of the University of Oregon, she was in charge of research. If information existed anywhere, she located it and prepared a succinct report that assessed nuances of interpretation and recommended the one she thought most legitimate. Disciplined and intense, she exhibits a phenomenal work ethic.

Murdock's impression of her was clouded by one fact. She was involved in sadomasochism. Her sexual high came from playing the tortured slave to a master. Her personal fetishes normally would be her private business, but Murdock was concerned that she had used sex as a key to open doors that led to desired information.

Although she had been married for seven years, she had no children. Murdock was uneasy with her husband's apparent tolerance, particularly because he was not into SM. She had to get it elsewhere—often from a high official at the FBI lab in Washington who liked to play master to her slave. He fed her information that he shouldn't have been feeding her.

Keeping their relationship strictly professional hadn't been effortless for Murdock. Concentration on business when Susan Ling sat across from him tested complicated emotions. He suspected that it tested some of hers, too.

Susan intuitively knew what Murdock wanted. Although he resisted the thought, he suspected that she understood his sensitivities more precisely than even his wife had. She was judgmental, but always constructively so.

Today, as usual, she wore a short-short miniskirt. As he seated himself at the conference table, she crossed her legs with scientific precision. Red faced, he looked at the ceiling and said, "Honestly, Susan, you must hold a record in the company for wearing the shortest skirts. If you'd been just a little less careful, I'd have seen your panties."

She thought of saying she was sorry to disappoint him, but she suspected that, unfortunately, he was merely embarrassed. She said, "Boss, be assured there was no chance that you could have seen my panties. Even if it were possible, it shouldn't turn your head from the business at hand. We need to prepare for our meeting with a Mr. Proteus."

The flush left his face.

She scrolled down a few pages as Murdock tried to avoid fixating on her crossed legs. She continued, "I spoke with Mr. Proteus briefly when he made the appointment. He's strange."

"Strange in what way?"

"First, he claims he has no first name. Second, he refuses to meet here. He has arranged a table for 11:30 a.m. in a cocktail lounge in Multnomah Village. I've been there. It's dark—candlelit. People who don't want to be seen together often meet there. Third, Mr. Proteus identifies himself as an agent of the U.S. government, but he declines to mention which branch. My contact at FBI Washington told me that he's only recently heard of him. He says that whatever Proteus does, it's obscured in secrecy. He assures me that Proteus is *not* FBI. His actual governmental breed is indefinite. My contact is curious himself. I promised him feedback, if that's okay, Boss."

"Is this FBI contact your SM friend?"

"Yeah, Boss. He's given me a lot of info. I owe him."

"Give him whatever you feel appropriate—by way of information— so long as it doesn't compromise our client. Speaking of clients, Proteus is not one. Why does he want to see us?"

"He avoided giving a reason, but I was left with a gut feeling that it would deal with Señor Perez-Krieger's son. I can't imagine why a U.S. government spy-guy would be interested in an alleged gang rape on Grand Cayman Island."

"Did he specifically ask for you, too?"

"No, Boss, but I think I'll be useful to you. Insist on my being there, and see what he says. My short skirt and perky little boobs bet that he'll agree."

Murdock chuckled. "Are there any men's eyes that you can't turn?"

Her eyes sparkled. "Sure, Boss, but they're all dead."

They both laughed. Murdock folded his hands behind his head and stared out the window. Susan waited. He turned to her and said, "I'm always suspect of secret agents. During my twelve years with the FBI, I never met one that I trusted. Nor did I meet one that ever trusted me. You wouldn't guess that we worked for the same government. I even doubted *that* sometimes. Let's play this cool. We listen. We give him nothing."

"I'm good at that, Boss." Susan scrolled down a few pages. "Let's move on to the report from Grace Bauer. Did you read it, Boss?"

"Yes. It was preliminary, but she was thorough and professional. What was your impression?"

"If we're relying on this Grace in a matter this serious, it's important that we understand her. Since neither of us has met her, I've done some checking. She's a straight arrow. The more I read about her background, the more she reminds me of you. Her head is on straight. She has no known romantic connections, male or female. She doesn't even date. Her station chief says she's a skillful investigator, totally reliable, and loyal to the company. Her assets include a keen mind and a healthy skepticism."

"But?"

"But the lack of *any* sex life worries me. It's unnatural."

"How would *that* interfere with her job?"

"I can't say exactly, but I know it would interfere with mine, Boss."

"That concerns me, Susan. Your job does *not* require you to use sex as a tool. Company policy doesn't condone it. When you do it, it leaves me in an awkward position."

A sporty grin crossed Susan's face. With a lilt in her voice she responded, "Don't worry, Boss. I don't use *it* often—only when *we* desperately need information and it would be inefficient or impossible to get it any other way. Besides, the men never complain about our company policy. Guys think I'm an empty-headed sexpot. They're half right. It's the half wrong that gives me the advantage."

Murdock stared out the window, uneasy that she might uncross her legs. "Okay, Susan, but I haven't authorized it. I don't need to know about it."

"Of course not, Boss."

18

He looked back at her. She *had* uncrossed her legs. She was sitting sedately, her knees tight together, her skirt as useful as possible, and a self-satisfied smile demurely crossing her face.

Murdock glanced over at a document on his desk, and said, "It might be a good idea for Grace to visit St. Luke's Monastery. My friend, the Abbott, Brother Martin, phoned me at home last night and said that a man fitting the description of Herr Weidner, the purported victim's father, worked there before the alleged rape. My instinct tells me that we need to know everything we can about this man."

"My instinct says the same thing, Boss. Grace reached the same conclusion. She's working on him."

"Good. Please keep me informed. We need her to come through for us if Ms. DiStefano is going to have a chance with a jury. On another subject, Brother Martin found an uncompleted manuscript of a book that Professor Klugman and Brother Stephen were apparently writing jointly. He thinks it might have some interest for us."

"Were they the two who were murdered a couple years ago, Boss?"

"Yes. We had a client interested in the death of Brother Stephen, so I assisted the Bavarian State Police in the investigation. He's sending it to us by courier. I'm hopeful that you and I can review it."

"Why couldn't we, Boss?"

"I'm not sure who owns it. Brother Stephen's will bequeathed everything to Saint Luke's Monastery. Professor Klugman left everything to his putative daughter."

"Professor Amy Gallagher. We've met. Shall I phone her or drive out to Cannon Beach and talk to her?"

"Don't use the phone. I hope our office isn't bugged, but one can never be too safe."

"It was clean yesterday afternoon, Boss. I personally ran the check, but I'll play it safe. I've not had occasion to research this Brother Martin, Boss. What order of monks operates this monastery? Why would anyone murder a poor monk?"

"They're not poor. Most aren't Catholic, with the exception of Brother Antonio. They're all former businessmen. Each is wealthy. Each sold his business and pooled his money with the others. Wishing to withdraw from the secular world, they bought an abandoned monastery in the Bavarian Alps. It's located near the Austrian border on the slope of a mountain called the Zugspitze. Brother Martin is their abbot."

"Thanks, Boss. That's all I need to know for now. I can easily find the rest. What's the manuscript about?"

"Brother Martin says that it deals with Brother Stephen and Professor Klugman's interest in the search for extraterrestrial intelligence. The professor created a trust fund for Amy to use in that search. You might recall that she's a professor of astrophysics at Cascadia College. I'd like to make a copy of the manuscript, but not without her permission. The puzzle is why the people who call themselves Traction are so interested in their work. They've killed twice and threatened Amy. I imagine that they're behind this gang rape charge against Perez-Krieger's son."

Susan frowned. "I'm with you, Boss. I wish we had some evidence to prove it."

"Me, too."

* * *

It was near noon when Murdock and Susan entered the cocktail lounge in Multnomah Village. It lived up to Susan's description. There were no outside windows. Candles on the tables produced a dim light that would lend itself to romantic liaisons. The hostess led them toward a booth in the most discrete corner. A man was seated there. As they approached, he arose. Murdock noticed that he was built like an NFL linebacker, a bear of a man, and slightly shorter than himself. Dressed in an expensive black business suit tailored to perfection, he smiled at them with an easy assurance. A green silk tie was meticulously knotted. Around his neck was a thick but plain gold chain. Murdock couldn't see his shoes in the dim light, but he guessed they were spit and polished to a drill sergeant's satisfaction. Under a thick mop of straight sandy hair of medium length, somewhat unruly, disciplined gray eyes peered from a devilishly handsome face accented by bushy eyebrows and balanced by a perfectly proportioned nose. A huge hand with thick fingers reached out to grasp Murdock's. The two men's eyes met and they shook hands. The man introduced himself as Mr. Proteus. Murdock observed that, even though Proteus's eyes were firmly fixed on his, the man didn't miss the slightest twitch of Susan's body. When Murdock's eyes met Susan's, hers told him that every twitch was choreographed. Murdock introduced Susan. Mr. Proteus, making no objection to her being there, bowed, took her hand and kissed it—or at least nearly so. Susan smiled at Murdock. He read the message; her perky little boobs and mini skirt had bought her a ticket.

As they seated themselves, a waitress appeared. Each ordered coffee. Murdock observed his two companions. Proteus's body moved with carefully orchestrated precision; Susan's with the casual confidence of a cat. *They're a pair of matched adversaries,* he thought. Mr. Proteus stared at Susan intently and said, "I'm really very pleased to meet *you*, Miss Ling. I've heard many good things about you."

Susan returned the smile. "Actually I'm married, but I use my maiden name professionally."

"Oh? I mean that's fortunate. Please forgive me for misspeaking, dear lady."

"There's nothing to forgive."

Mr. Proteus folded his huge hands and rested them on top of the table. Murdock broke an awkward silence. "May we have your first name, Mr. Proteus?" His eyes met Murdock's. "I'm just Proteus." Susan grinned. "Was your father named Poseidon?"

Slowly a sincere laugh rumbled up from deep within Proteus. "Very good, Mrs. Ling. I'm impressed with your knowledge of Greek mythology. I've heard that you have been scrupulously educated."

Susan, with a hint of naughtiness in her eyes, responded. "Everyone calls me just plain Susan. I'll call you Proteus, without the mister. Okay?"

"Okay," he replied somewhat uncomfortably.

"Tell me," Murdock injected, "what branch of the government do you represent?"

"I'm afraid that's highly confidential."

Murdock pushed. "If we're dealing with a government agent, we need to be assured that he is what he claims to be. Do you have any ID?"

"Not of the traditional kind, Mr. McCabe. Most people in the government don't believe that I exist, and only an elite few have ever heard of my agency. However, I have access to information in every government computer. I've checked on you. A woman by the name of Allison Spencer fell hopelessly in love with you when she and you were freshmen at the State University of New York at Buffalo."

Murdock's eyes widened. Susan glanced at him. Proteus continued.

"She is presently the regional manager for Veritus at Seattle, and she is your boss. But in college you were in love with her roommate, Karen. You introduced Allison to *your* best friend, Jerrod Blair, who promptly fell in love with Allison. The four of you were inseparable through the remaining three years of college. A double wedding followed graduation. You and Jerrod went to the University of Michigan law school. Karen obtained a master's degree in linguistics at Michigan and became an expert in encryption. Allison obtained a master's in law enforcement administration at Michigan State University.

"After law school you and Jerrod went into the FBI. Jerrod was assigned to Seattle, but Allison had accepted an offer from Veritus Investigations

International in Chicago. After two years of almost total separation, she and Jerrod decided to call it quits. They divorced. He's presently the agent-in-charge of the FBI office at Omaha. Your wife, Karen, free-lanced as a cryptologist. Among her clients were several government entities including the FBI. One of her projects was to break a code used by an organization called Traction. She was killed in a shoot-out. You left the FBI because you felt that either their negligence had precipitated her death or her killing was intentional to protect someone in the Bureau."

Murdock stared at him, rather uncomfortably. Susan resisted fidgeting.

"Allison was made station chief for the Veritus office in Munich. You were hired by Veritus and assigned to her office. While you were there, you investigated the murder of a monk by the name of Brother Stephen. I confess that I don't know who your client was. You cooperated with Rudi Benzinger of the Bavarian State Police, who you had met during your FBI career. In the course of your investigation, you met a professor from Oregon by the name of Klugman. He'd been a friend of the murdered monk. Klugman was murdered shortly after you two met. He and the monk had been working on some unlikely method of contacting extraterrestrials. After that investigation, you were transferred from Munich to Portland as station chief. That was a rather meteoric rise in the company.

"José Enrique Perez-Krieger's son was a participant in a gang rape on Grand Cayman Island. You're involved in an investigation for the purpose of discrediting the unfortunate victim's story. As you can see by the very volume and detail, I *must* have access to unlimited government files. The information itself is my credential."

Murdock's eyes burned into his. "My love life isn't in government files. That suggests, Mr. Proteus, you're being less than candid."

"It's in my files. I'm the government. May I continue?"

A wry smile crossed Murdock's face. He was impressed with Proteus's knowledge and persistency. He hadn't figured out his game. Why would the government obtain such personal information about him? If indeed Proteus was the government. Showing no emotion, he nodded in the affirmative.

"The government is concerned about this organization called Traction. Traction may pose a serious threat to the security of the United States. I need to know everything that you know about it."

Murdock's eyes met his again. "That's not very much."

Susan added, "Practically nothing at all."

A waitress delivered a seafood luncheon including a Mexican beer for Murdock and a gin and tonic for Susan; a meal which Proteus had obviously pre-ordered. Murdock was impressed that Proteus knew what both he and Susan preferred.

Murdock thanked him and added, "What little I've seen of Traction, I'm convinced that it's one of those organizations that, the closer you look, the less you see. It's a wilderness of mirrors. It bewilders and confuses the observer."

Proteus smiled, and ignoring the remark, said, "Last year you two were involved in an investigation of a missing person—an employee of José Enrique Perez-Krieger. The man later turned up dead. We believe Traction was responsible for both his kidnapping and the murder. Incidentally, Perez-Krieger is also a person of interest to us. As part of that investigation, you traveled to a jungle in Honduras. There you witnessed a ceremony designed to horrify and put fear into Traction's mules—the people who transport their drugs. At that ceremony, one of the mules had sex with a bizarre iridescent Green Lady. Appearing to walk on air, she disappeared into a cave. He was ritually murdered. You met her weeks later on a ship off the coast of Oregon. Again she dissolved into the night. We believe she is—or was—the head of Traction. We're led to believe that she perished aboard ship during a storm at sea. We're not so sure. What exactly went on between you and her?"

Murdock smiled. "What little went on between her and me didn't then and doesn't now affect the national security of the United States."

Proteus chuckled. "You're testing me. Be cautious. You have a duty as a citizen to provide the government with information in your possession if that information could pose a threat to the United States. If you fail to do that, you can be prosecuted for a serious crime. You know that she was planning to introduce biologicals into the United States that could inflict disease and death upon millions. We understand that. We don't fully understand her motive. She and her ilk don't appear to be motivated by foolish religious fantasies like radical Islamists. This Green Lady claims to be a goddess of some sort. She doesn't seem to have a definable political agenda. What does she hope to gain? Is Traction a large cadre or a small group of self-radicalizing and self-directing individuals?"

Murdock glanced at Susan. "I don't have any idea. Do you?"

"No, Boss. I've researched those specific questions and I've come up empty."

"Susan's our best researcher. If she comes up empty, the information isn't out there. One of your guys needs to become a mole in their organization. Do you expect Veritus to have more assets than the government of the United States?"

Proteus's face steeled. "May I speak confidentially?"

Murdock and Susan nodded in agreement—Susan barely able to restrain a grin.

"There's a wild theory afloat in our organization that this woman is from an alien civilization—from another world."

"Or another universe?" Susan injected, restraining a grin.

"Whatever," Proteus replied. His eyes met Murdock's. "Have you ever seen another iridescent green woman who can walk on air and dissolve into darkness?"

Murdock didn't respond. Proteus continued.

"The national security may be endangered by this group in ways that you can't imagine."

Murdock feigned a friendly smile. "I might be able to. Try me."

"That's not important now, Mr. McCabe. It is urgent that I know what you know about them, and I need to know it fast."

"Tell me why. I'm a small fish who's had very limited contact with this woman."

"I can't tell you why."

"I'm afraid Ms. Ling and I are wasting your time, Mr. Proteus. I'm confident that we know less about this Traction than you do. I don't mean to be impolite, but if you'll pardon us, we have an office to run and clients to represent. Unless you wish to employ the services of Veritus, we have no useful purpose in being here."

"Okay. That's exactly what I'll do. I want to engage Veritus to investigate Traction. I want you personally to be in charge. Use all of your assets and don't spare the cost. Find out who this green woman is or was, and whether she's still alive. In addition to what Veritus charges, I will pay each of you a reward of $100,000 if you can confirm her death or can turn her over to me."

Murdock chuckled. "You expect Veritus to do what your whole big government can't do?"

"I'm not certain that you're taking me seriously."

Susan injected, "Mr. McCabe is not convinced that you are who you say you are. And even if you are, it might be helpful, Mr. Proteus, if you could give my boss a reason that you've focused on him. Or me."

A prolonged silence followed. Murdock was convinced they'd gotten him off balance. His face read confusion. Both Murdock and Susan enjoyed tipping pompous bastards off balance. When Mr. Proteus settled down, he chose his words carefully and said, "That answer is simple. You're both the best."

Murdock's cell phone rang. Excusing himself, he left the table.

Susan smiled at Mr. Proteus. After another brief but awkward silence, he said, "I can offer you more money, Mrs. Ling. Would you consider working for me and the government?"

Susan countered with her most childlike and disarming smile and asked, "What branch of the government?"

A wry grin crossed Mr. Proteus's face as he said, "Touché."

Murdock returned and re-seated himself. "Sorry for the interruption. Your offer is most generous. Neither Susan nor I can accept it. Taking a reward for doing what Veritus pays us to do would be unethical. As to the company, my problem is that Veritus has never acted as an agent of any government. I need to obtain authority from my superior."

"Do you mean the celebrated Allison Spencer, your regional supervisor in Seattle?"

"Yes. How can we get back to you?"

"You can't. I'll get back to you tomorrow. I need your help. These people are terrorists."

Murdock smiled. "It's been said that terrorism is the strength of the powerless. If you identify the specific powerless involved, you'll have your motive and you won't need us."

Mr. Proteus countered, "We suspect that these folks are *not* the powerless."

He arose and hastily bid them goodbye. They watched as Proteus walked toward the exit, taking care to avoid even slightly more lighted areas. After the outside door closed behind him, Murdock turned to Susan and asked, "What did you make of all that?"

"First, there's only one way he could have gotten that perspective of your love life. It came from a woman. That had to be our boss in Seattle, Allison Spencer. I've met her twice, Boss. You know her better than I. In my opinion, it would have taken more than one date to pump your life story out of her. Proteus must have romanced her. It probably came out of repeated intimacy. She wouldn't just fall into bed with anyone on a first-nighter, would she?"

"No. He would have had to invest for a considerable time. I'd be surprised if they were intimate. Allison wouldn't have sex outside of marriage."

"Boss, this is the twenty-first century. Allison's been divorced for several years. Unless she's doing herself, which can be helpful in a pinch, somebody must be doing her."

Murdock frowned and shook his head. "I suppose you may be right, but I'm convinced that it *would* take time—considerable time."

"Yeah, Boss. You're thinking the same thing I am. He doesn't impress me as a guy who falls in love or develops enduring relationships with women. What attracted him to Allison if it wasn't to get the information about you? I wish I had a gut feeling as to why he bothered."

"Me, too. Did you learn anything while I was away?"

"Of course, Boss. I learned the most practical thing that I needed to know about him. Remember, Boss, I plan ahead. Everything I do is done for a reason. You hadn't gotten five feet from the table before his left hand discovered that I wasn't wearing panties."

What she didn't share with Murdock was the fact that he'd made his brief exploration as painful for her as possible.

3

The meeting with Mr. Proteus had produced more than sufficient puzzlement to have made it interesting. Murdock and Susan Ling were preparing to meet and debrief one another about the man. She was looking forward to the meeting, but then, she always looked forward to meetings with Murdock. In her eight-year career with Veritus, Murdock was her favorite boss. She knew he took pleasure in their relationship—nothing romantic, at least, she thought, not in the traditional sense. Susan doubted that the unfortunate man would ever think to make a move on a married woman; and never on a subordinate. He had Victorian values that red-blooded Victorians would think humorous. He had dated two women, but she didn't think he was *in love* with either. A gush of irritation crossed her mind. He never had paid attention to her as a woman. He was the kind of man that any woman might be tempted to love. Although her temptation was well under control, it did enrich her fertile fantasy life. Besides, bottom line, she almost loved her husband.

She was concerned that Murdock couldn't accept her fetish—sadomasochism. She had tried to explain that she couldn't experience sexual climax unless pain was being inflicted upon her. He had been surprised that the inflictor was never her husband. Her husband was tolerant of her fetish but he couldn't hurt her. Disconnecting her laptop from the power, she closed the cover. She filled her mug with black coffee and breezed into Murdock's office. Depositing both laptop and mug on the conference table, she seated herself across from him. Her skimpy skirt revealed dark blue pantyhose and knees locked together. Her perky little boobs were concealed by a loose-fitting blouse. She noticed that Murdock noticed. Did he show just a tinge of disappointment? Smiling inwardly, she convinced herself that he had. Such fun. Smiling, she asked, "Would you like a third mug of coffee, Boss?"

"No, thanks, Susan. I had one just before you came in. What have you got?"

"We just received this e-mail from Grace Bauer at our Munich office. I haven't read it yet. What's your pleasure?"

"As usual, please read it aloud."

"Okay, Boss."

> *"Mr. McCabe:*
> *After talking to Rudi Benzinger in Munich, I drove to Landshut and interviewed the neighbors of the unfortunate Gretchen Weidner, the alleged Screwee."*

"I like this girl, Boss."

"Go on."

> *"The Weidners moved into the neighborhood a few months ago. They kept to themselves. It's rumored that they came from somewhere in the Alps. I'll check that, of course. All of the neighbors remarked that Frau Weidner has startling green eyes. I found it curious that that is the item the women remembered most. The men noticed that her figure was nifty and her demeanor youthful for a woman having a daughter Gretchen's age. Some of the women suggested that she is trying to look older than she actually is. Based on admittedly meager contact, all agreed that her personality is plain vanilla, except the psychologist who lives next door. She cracked that the plain vanilla is topped with wild red raspberry. She refused to explain.*
> *"Herr Weidner is seen as gracious, but distant—a rather enigmatic person. He's disinterested in his neighbor's lives and gives the impression that he doesn't want them to be interested in his. Weidner did mention to one neighbor that he'd worked overseas. He didn't*

mention a country and the neighbor didn't ask. No one has seen him going to work. The neighbors speculate that he retired early. That's contradicted by several neighbors who don't believe he's reached retirement age. All agree that the Weidners have money. They live comfortably and drive a new BMW.

"No one knows the ill-fated Gretchen much beyond 'good morning' or 'good evening.' They all described her as a shy and reticent girl who goes to mass every day. No young men visit. She wears a Blessed Virgin medallion and mentioned to a woman over the back fence that she was planning to enter a convent. She will make a daunting witness. The shy virgin routine should play well for the Crown. It might even be true. Of course, even error believed in is truth in affect."

Susan paused. Skillfully crossing her legs, she took a sip from her mug and observed, "This Grace *does* impress me. Do you think we could get her transferred to Portland?"

"I'm impressed, too. Getting her transferred to Portland is another matter. Is there more?" Susan nodded in the affirmative and resumed reading.

"None of the neighbors knew that the Weidners had planned to vacation in the Cayman Islands. That's not surprising in view of their obsession with privacy. When the local newspapers reported that Gretchen had been allegedly gang raped, the neighbors were shocked and dismayed. They would all make good character witnesses for the Crown except, perhaps, the psychologist. Somehow, Frau Weidner must have pissed her off. Herr Weidner left home to join his family in the Italian Alps. I still don't know where. I've asked Ernst Müller's permission to travel there. I'm awaiting his decision. He's complaining about cost. I'm complaining about the cold freeken weather here. Perhaps an e-mail from you would help.

> *"One other item. I invitingly befriended the old postman, hinting a passionate promise I won't keep. He said that Frau Weidner and Gretchen moved in almost a month before Herr Weidner. She received several letters from him postmarked in Garmisch-Partenkirchen which is near the Austrian border."*

Murdock interrupted. "That's near St. Luke's Monastery on the Zugspitze Mountain where Brother Stephen and Professor Klugman were murdered. Is there more?"

"No, Boss, but now I'm even more impressed with this girl. She shot the postman with an intimation of sex just like a silver bullet. The girl knows how to use the tools in her arsenal. I like that. Is there a reply?"

"Yes. Send an immediate response thanking her for her good work, and tell her that I'll phone Ernst Müller first thing in the morning, their time. We need her to check out the Garmisch-Partenkirchen connection. She also needs to talk to Brother Martin at St. Luke's."

"I noticed you perked up when I read the part about the green eyes. Green keeps popping up. Do you think it might be that same gal who performed the green woman act in the jungle of Honduras—the one the natives call the Green Lady? She had green eyes, didn't she?"

"Believe me, *everything* she had been green, but she apparently drowned last year in that shipwreck off the Oregon coast."

Susan frowned. "Her body was never found. Proteus isn't so sure she drowned. By the way, did you talk to Allison Spencer?"

Murdock frowned. "Yes. She's quite taken by Proteus. She's dated him a half dozen times. I really don't know what she sees in him."

"What could she possibly see in a big, strong, virile, handsome man with an apparently limitless expense account who pays attention to her? Have they done it?"

"It?"

"Come on, Boss, you know what I mean. For Proteus to get her to open up with all that really personal information, their relationship is more than casual. It sounds to me like pillow talk. I think this big hunk could come across as an earnest lover."

"Would his earnestness be genuine?"

"I don't think so, Boss. Remember, he was exploring my crotch yesterday. By the way, Boss, I wiggled when he touched me. He'd interpret that as an invitation. Most men can't resist that. When he calls, let *me* give him Allison's decision if he doesn't already know. I presume she approved taking him on as a client."

"You assumed wrong. Allison's first loyalty is to the company. She'd never take it upon herself to change such a basic policy. Governments are by nature political. Veritus isn't. She's e-mailed Chicago, but I don't expect them to change it, either. Besides, Proteus will probably want to talk to me."

"He'll settle for me, Boss. I can make my voice wiggle, too."

4

Grand Cayman Island
Thursday, March 9, 6:16 a.m.

The first hint of dawn had shown on the north shore of Grand Cayman Island. A half mile east of Old Man Bay along the Queen's Highway just past Old Robin Point was the compound and villa of José Enrique Perez-Krieger. It's located on the north side of the highway and extends from the road's edge to the waters of the Caribbean Sea. The compound is enclosed by concrete walls ten feet high. His security people had recommended razor wire on top, but Enrique had insisted on crushed glass that wouldn't be an eye-sore from the road. Embedded within the concrete at three-foot intervals are two-foot thick steel cylinders filled with concrete. These are firmly anchored into the earth. It would be difficult for a tank to pierce that wall and the Cayman Islands don't have an army. Security guards constantly patrol its perimeter and guard the arched entrance and its heavy iron electric gate. When one passes through the gate, a curved driveway leads up a knoll to the white stucco three-story villa. Its main entrance is a Spanish arch dominated by thick hand-carved oak double doors.

There are three floors. The first contains the pool and guest facilities. Enrique's apartment plus the bar and dining area, are located on the second floor. The west two-thirds of the third floor contain the offices of Linda DiStefano and her administrative assistants. The east one-third is her private apartment.

Linda is in her late thirties, five-eight, slim, with an eminently pleasant face, and she wears her dark-brown hair in a short wavy bob. She is the chief operating officer of the holding company that controls all of Enrique's corporations worldwide. All through law school she had intended to join a trial practice firm in Calgary, Alberta, her home town. But, shortly after she was admitted to practice, her father had introduced her to his friend, Jose Enrique Perez-Krieger. The rest was history. She had gone to work for him. In the last twelve years, she had become his *mayor domo.*

Linda stepped through the French doors, out of her apartment, onto her balcony and into the soft light of dawn. She searched the eastern sky. Rays of the still hidden sun singed the eastern edges of scattered puffs of stratocumulus clouds floating over the Caribbean Sea. She looked down. Three stories below her lay a lush garden punctuated with coconut palms, royal Poinciana, jasmine, Jamaica red hibiscus, and brilliant flaming red ixora, their petals fused to form a funnel-shaped corolla.

She loved her private apartment. Through the entrance door there was a tiled area and closet that opened to a hallway which led to the kitchen on the left, and a great room on the right. The kitchen window faced the sea. In the great room, on either side of the French doors, were tastefully upholstered love seats facing each other—one offering a view of the water. Along the south wall was a partitioned couch that curved around the corner to her bedroom door. The great room could easily hold a party of forty people. The bedroom and bath were elegantly appointed. All walls were painted coral with white woodwork.

Murdock McCabe had flown in late last night and would shortly be joining her for breakfast.

Linda returned to her bedroom and seated herself in front of the mirror on her dressing table. Painstakingly she brushed her short, dark-brown hair. Her five-foot-four frame was trim and well-proportioned for a woman adventuring past her mid-thirties. It captured men's eyes. She knew it had captured Murdock's.

She had never seriously thought of marriage and a family until she had met him. Electricity charged between them when they were together. They had dated several times, but their relationship had remained—professional. A short time ago she had invited him to room with her at Timberline Lodge while they were skiing on Mount Hood in Oregon. He had declined. Unfortunately, Enrique had offered him the opportunity to leave Veritus to set up a private investigative agency for his empire. Murdock had suggested that Enrique was better off using the facilities of Veritus. But the offer remained open. If he accepted, Linda would be his supervisor. To Murdock, romance with a superior was unwise. Linda couldn't argue with that.

She wondered about her competition. Murdock had fairly frequently dated a woman who owned a restaurant in Cannon Beach, Oregon, but Linda wasn't too concerned. If that were going somewhere, she felt it should have arrived. Murdock often heaped praise on his assistant station chief, Susan Ling, but he also felt that romance with a subordinate was unwise. Besides, Murdock said that Susan was happily married. She felt confident that he hadn't been in bed with either woman. Nor with her, either, unfortunately. She suspected that he might be one of that rare breed who believes that sex is inappropriate outside of marriage. Perhaps he was still grieving for his murdered Karen. After two years, he should be coming out of that. If he hadn't yet, Linda wanted to be there when he did. She wasn't a silly schoolgirl with a penchant for romance, but Murdock was the most attractive man she'd ever met. He was intelligent, loyal, considerate, and had a powerful physical presence.

She did have needs. The toys in the drawer of the end table next to her bed were fast becoming unproductive.

To her delight, they would have breakfast together on this glorious morning on the veranda outside her apartment. The waters of the Caribbean would be colored aquamarine. An easy breeze would drift off the water. Palms would lazily respond. The chef would prepare an exquisite meal. But beyond all this, Linda looked forward to electricity. She was optimistic if not confident that today Murdock was, too. Murdock, she hoped, was close to taking their relationship beyond the professional. It couldn't come too soon.

* * *

Dressed in an ivory colored shell with a scooped neck and light blue shorts, she inspected the breakfast table. It was flawless. At precisely 7:30 Murdock appeared sporting a brown polo shirt and white slacks. He was dressed casually in a khaki short sleeve shirt and khaki shorts which exposed his muscular legs. They shook hands, as they always did, and seated themselves at a circular table. Murdock said, "When I left Portland, it was rainy and cold. This tropical climate agrees with me."

"Then it should tempt you to take Enrique's offer. You could establish your headquarters here on Grand Cayman. You'd be just over an hour from Florida so it wouldn't seem so foreign to you."

Even though it was her duty to promote the offer, she wasn't anxious to change their relationship to employer-employee.

"It's tempting, Linda."

"Good. How is the investigation coming along? Have we learned much about the girl?"

"Not yet. Grace Bauer, who replaced me at the Munich office, is working the case. From what Susan and I have seen so far, we have confidence in her."

Linda smiled. "And you have confidence in Susan?"

"Unqualified confidence. Grace has conferred with Rudi Benzinger of the Bavarian State Police. You remember him from the investigation of the murdered monk. Rudi is a good friend. As you know, Enrique saved his life and mine. He'll keep his ear to the ground. The investigation is still too preliminary to report any results. Miss Bauer will devote whatever time is necessary to track and expose the fraud, if that's what it is. We know that time is of the essence. How much of it can you buy?"

"We'll have our next court appearance in three days. I'll petition for a bond to be set."

"Are you licensed to practice law in the Cayman Islands?"

"I'm licensed to practice in Alberta which is a common law jurisdiction within the Commonwealth. That's all that's required. As you know, I went to work for Enrique shortly after law school so I've had precious little trial experience—none at all in a serious criminal matter. Enrique insists that I lead the case. I've chosen a local attorney, Michael Sudbury, to serve as co-consul. In addition to serving as Crown Prosecutor, he's also defended several serious criminal matters."

"How can he do both?"

"The attorney general chooses a lawyer to represent the Crown on a case-by-case basis. Michael could be crown attorney on one case and defense attorney on the next."

"Who chooses the attorney general?"

"The governor. He's appointed by Queen Elizabeth II, who is their Chief of State. That keeps it out of local politics, unlike your country where prosecutors are elected. Politics can restrain them so that they aren't always free to do justice in unpopular cases."

"Good point. How do you feel about Ricardo's story?"

"Bottom line, I believe him. He was passed out drunk on the lanai when the girl was allegedly assaulted."

"I've never seen him drink. You told me that he doesn't drink. Obviously, he does?"

"Obviously he *did*. Once. Probably those beach bums talked him into it—you know the old macho routine. Because he wasn't a drinker, the booze hit him harder."

"That may be. I'm meeting with the beach bums this afternoon."

Linda stared off into the distance and said, "The sad thing is that he's not accused of having sex with her; just holding her when the others did it. Unfortunately, an accessory is as guilty as a principal. He could go to prison for life. Bottom line, the jury has to choose whether to believe the young woman or the young men."

35

Enrique joined them. Having heard the end of the conversation and after the polite greetings, he said, "We don't have a jury system in Chile. I don't understand the reason for it. You take a driver out of a taxicab and women out of their homes. You ask them to decide whether my son should go to prison for the rest of his life. Well—I guess I don't have to understand. That's where we are. Do we depend on fate?"

Linda smiled. "An American Supreme Court Justice by the name of Oliver Wendell Holmes once said, 'The mode in which the inevitable comes to pass is through effort.' Murdock and I are both making that effort."

"I know that. I deeply appreciate it. You're both good friends."

Murdock turned toward Linda and asked, "If worse comes to worse, is there some chance of a plea bargain?"

Linda replied, "Yes, especially because he isn't charged with having sex with her—only holding her while the others did. A possible lower offense is attempted rape. That carries a maximum penalty of imprisonment for fourteen years. Still another is a charge of indecent assault on a female. That carries a max penalty of seven years. I doubt that the Crown would let us plead to insulting the modesty of a woman which carries a max of one year."

Enrique stood by the railing, looking far off across the faceless sea. He said, "Does that mean my son could go to prison for fourteen years even though he's innocent?"

Linda arose and stood next to him. She said, "If a plea is offered, we must consider it. The jury is always an unknowable factor. If they believe the young woman and convict him of rape—"

"Yes, I know. I guess that's the price of innocence."

Murdock poured a mug of coffee for each and asked, "What will actually happen at the hearing?"

Linda returned to the table, seated herself, took a sip of coffee and said, "Ricardo and the others accused will appear before the Summary Court. The magistrate will inform them of the charge against them and that the proceeding is a preliminary inquiry. In the presence of the accused, the magistrate will take down in writing statements under oath in narrative form from Gretchen Weidner and the medical person who examined her. Those statements are treated as depositions. We have a right to cross-examine the witnesses, and that would form a part of the depositions. If the magistrate is satisfied that a crime has been committed, he will commit Ricardo and the others for trial. At that point, the magistrate will set bail. Under the circumstances, that bail could be very high."

Enrique turned to Murdock. "Have you considered the possibility that Ricardo was set up?"

Murdock looked at Linda. She said, "Even if he were suckered into it, if he held her while the beach boys had sex with her against her will, he'd still be guilty of rape. The accessory is guilty as a principal."

Murdock added, "We're exploring the possibility that the Weidners programmed this thing to extort money from you. It's possible that it wasn't rape at all. We need history on them. We'll get it."

Enrique's eyes met Murdock's. "Will it be in time for trial?"

"Veritus is dedicating all of its resources toward that end."

* * *

All day Linda had been distracted, looking forward to the evening. Now, driving north on Seven Mile Beach Road, she checked her watch. It was nearly five o'clock. She turned her Mercedes CLK 350 convertible V6 into the parking lot of the Britannia Beach Club and found a spot where someone was less likely to park on either side. Exiting the vehicle, she walked into Hemmingway's, seated herself on a bar stool, and ordered a Cosmopolitan. She checked her watch. It was five o'clock. Murdock would be along soon. Hemmingway's at the Beach Club was Murdock's favorite cocktail lounge. Hers, too. She checked her watch again. His interview with the beach bums must have lasted longer than he'd planned.

Normally her entire day was spent in Enrique's compound. She lived there and worked there. It was elegant and comfortable, but it brightened her day when she could entertain a business contact at Hemingway's— especially someone who enjoyed its ambiance as much as Murdock did.

As she made small talk with the bartender, Murdock came up from behind, greeted them both, and seated himself next to her. Dressed in a lightweight white sport coat, light blue open collar shirt, and darker blue summer slacks, he ordered his usual Manhattan-on-the-rocks.

He said, "I met with both co-defendants. They assured me that the girl consented—that the party was her idea."

"Isn't that what you'd expect them to say?"

"Yes, but I'm inclined to believe them. Judging by the enthusiasm that they say the young woman demonstrated, she'd make a rather worldly nun. Our best shot is to play that angle and dig deep into this Weidner family. We only have to create a reasonable doubt."

"Maybe she wanted one good fling before the convent."

"Perhaps she wanted something worthwhile to confess. Grace Bauer paints a different picture. The Weidner's neighbors in Bavaria will testify that she was a sincerely religious woman who avoided contact with men. I also talked to the physician who examined Gretchen. In his opinion, she was a virgin before the alleged attack. It's difficult to reconcile both stories. Nobody said our business would be easy. I've e-mailed Grace with the information I picked up today."

The bartender delivered his drink. Murdock raised it and said, "To Veritus; to truth."

She raised hers. "To truth." She took a sip and added, "It's been said that truth is the daughter of time. We need that daughter delivered in a fairly short time. We're depending a great deal on this woman named Grace. How well do you know her?"

"I've never met her. Susan shared your concern, as do I. Susan is very thorough. She checked her out and is of the opinion that the woman is a competent and dedicated investigator. Her station chief highly recommends her."

"Does Susan recommend him?"

Is Linda jealous of Susan? Murdock wondered. Had he given her reason to be? He said, "It makes little difference now. As of today, the head office has authorized Grace to report directly to me. I'll assess her for myself in a very short time, but Susan's assessments are usually dependable."

Linda sipped her drink. "I've never met this Susan. She sounds like an interesting person. Would you agree?"

"Very much so."

"Is she attractive?"

"She's not difficult to look at."

"Is she difficult to work with?"

"Not at all. She's one of the most congenial and capable people I've known."

"Does she like you?"

Murdock grinned. "She's married."

Linda wondered whether the answer was naïve or coy. She guessed the latter. She said, "Since I saw you this morning, I received a phone call from Boris Romanovsky. I'm sure you remember him."

Murdock shook his head and then took another sip of his Manhattan. He said, "I certainly do. I'd sure like to know whose side he's on. I suspect that answer is his own side. Is he still trying to set up a meeting with Enrique?"

"Yes. Enrique won't consider doing business with him."

"What did old Boris have to say this time?"

"He opened with his usual, wounded little boy routine." Reaching into her travel bag, she extracted a recorder. "This is worth listening to, if only for its entertainment value."

She pushed the start button.

"Lovely lady, Boris must meet with Señor Perez-Krieger. You must arrange. Boris knows you will not take money. Never! Boris would not offer you bribe. Besides, Boris has royal blood. Boris's great, great, etc., etc. grandfather was bastard son of Tsar Alexander II—Tsar of all the Russians—a motley lot but there was an abundance of them. Boris's royal blood does not permit bribe. Especially to you, most honorable lady. You are scrupulous. But so, Boris offers marriage. Boris will give you children with royal blood. Kind lady, who else can offer you children with royal blood? How many women are able to be impregnated with royal babies? You have reached age, kind lady, where woman should create children if she is ever going to. You need husband now. Boris is rich. Boris owns banks on Aruba and in Cyprus which have branches in Saint Petersburg and Moscow, and which own important politicians and businessmen who control big chunks of Russian economy, both legal and illegal. Boris owns shares in leading world corporations. Boris's bank in Aruba is making offer to buy Veritus Investigations International. But so, nice lady, it is not necessary that you marry Boris. Boris will still give you same children with royal blood and huge trust fund for all their lives. But before children are created, Boris must have business meeting with Enrique."

Murdock laughed out loud. "Now there is a truly generous man."

Linda shook her head. "I don't know what to make of him. He's offered us deals which at first blush appear to be attractive. I've told him that I'd discuss them with Enrique, but Enrique won't consider them. His banks seem to be properly capitalized but none of his businesses operate in your country. Thus, regulators in the United States haven't had jurisdiction to take a hard look at them. He's avoided my country, too."

Murdock took a sip of his Manhattan and said, "It's temptingly easy to misjudge him because he made his way up the ranks of Soviet apparatchiks. Although he was trained in the Soviet system, he's now Western oriented. After the fall of communism and the dissolution of the Soviet Union, Boris purchased state assets for a song. He was one of President Yeltsin's back door buddies—probably the smartest because he moved his fortune to Cyprus and got out of Russia before he got arrested or assassinated. He's generous. He offered Professor Amy Gallagher a sizeable grant for her astrophysics program if she'd come live with him on Aruba so that he could *protect* her. I guess he just likes to help women. But you're one up. He never offered marriage to Amy."

Linda ordered another Cosmopolitan and asked, "Do you know whether Boris is involved in any dodgy deals?"

"Rudi Benzinger told me that his banks in Moscow and Saint Petersburg move huge sums of money off shore. Business is a dangerous game in Russia. Banks are infested with crime. I wouldn't invest there on a bet. Billions of U.S. dollars in cash float around, sight unseen. They call it 'black cash.' Their economy couldn't function without it. It's used for bribes and terrorism. Government officials are poorly paid. A business can't get anything approved without paying enormous bribes. If your business has competitors, you can hire terrorists to intimidate them and encourage them to go away while they are still alive. Complex international financial transactions are used to conceal the sources of black money. Boris's claim that he's freed himself from all that is dubious at best. He may still be awash in it."

Linda sipped her drink, and then said, "When I reminded him that you, Enrique, and Rudi Benzinger almost lost your lives on his compound in Cyprus, he insisted that he didn't know that men he trusted were misusing his property."

Murdock thought before he responded, and then said, "That *is* possible." Linda cocked her head. Murdock continued. "It's a big compound. Boris spends more time in Aruba. I'd like to know more about that. Without a client we can't investigate him. If Enrique becomes genuinely interested in doing business with Boris, you might employ us to do a thorough background check."

Linda nodded. "From my experiences with him, believe me, I'd engage you immediately. Is Veritus up for sale?"

"I've heard a rumor that it's going to be if it isn't already."

"I've heard from several sources that the owner wants to get out of the business. We'd be interested. Let me know." Her eyes studied his. She continued, "Have I ever told you that you're the most handsome and nicest man I've ever met?"

Murdock's face flushed. His eyes met hers. "No, but thank you. What brought that on?"

Her eyes fixed on his. "First, it's the truth. Second, I'm slow to give compliments and I've resolved to change. I have the highest regard for you, and I thought it might be caring to let you know."

He lifted his Manhattan as if to pose a toast and said: "At the risk of sounding insincere after that, I have the highest regard for you, too. Regard is too weak a word. Admiration would be more accurate. I don't mean merely as a businesswoman; I mean as a person; as a lovely, most attractive, warm, and most intelligent lady."

Linda raised her glass to meet his and said, "To highest regards, then."

Murdock smiled and said. "That's a good place to begin."

So it is, Linda thought. The Cosmopolitans had relaxed her. She felt comfortable with this man. Being near him put her at ease. Perhaps it was the warmth she saw in his eyes.

Murdock's eyes searched her face. He wondered if it was the drink or frustration that had made her bold? He needed to deal with her more honestly. He rationalized that he could fall in love with her on the spot, but it wouldn't be fair. Karen's murder was still too raw in his mind. He knew that he would love Karen until the day he died. What puzzled him was if he could learn to deal with loving both of them.

Linda interrupted his thoughts and suggested, "Boris was correct, of course. The time is ripe for marriage and children. Honestly, I'm afraid to fall in love with you, Murdock McCabe. I'm afraid that you might love me back. Where could it lead? I recall you telling me about your college friends, Jarrod and Allison, and how their long distance marriage failed. With you in Portland and me here, an airline marriage capsulated into weekends would be maddening. You've a bright future with Veritus. Someday soon, you may become the top administrator. Enrique's confidence has given me control of assets worth billions. That makes me one of the most powerful women in the world. Could I move to Portland and become a housewife? Would you give up your career?" She chuckled good-naturedly and added, "Besides, our kids wouldn't even have royal blood."

Murdock laughed. "Aruba is a lot closer than Portland."

She chuckled. "I can't argue with that. I try to dislike Boris, but there's something about him—perhaps it's his irrepressible ebullience that's appealing."

Murdock took her hand in his and said, "Linda, I haven't had a vacation in over a year. I need to rediscover who I am. When this rape investigation is completed, I'd like to spend a few weeks here on Grand Cayman. Maybe you can wiggle free, too. Would you like that?"

Linda took another sip of her drink. Then, holding her Cosmopolitan up to a candle's light, she studied the flame through it. With him, there would be no love making without commitment. She was up against that rare breed—an old-fashioned man. She loved him for that. Suspecting his thoughts had already locked on a different subject and guessing what it was, she asked, "Are you ready for dinner?"

"Absolutely. Perhaps you can give me an answer tomorrow."

5

Susan had been at her desk for almost two hours when the call came. The voice was unmistakable. It belonged to Mr. Proteus. Susan tingled. Proteus knew that Murdock was on Grand Cayman Island so it was she that he wanted. That pleased her. They agreed to meet for lunch at the same restaurant in Multnomah Village. After he hung up, she opened her center desk drawer. Taking from it a small clear plastic capsule containing white powder, she placed it in her handbag.

Her thoughts turned to Murdock. Right about now he'd be meeting with Linda DiStefano. Tonight they would have cocktails and dine together. Susan was distressed. If he married Linda, Murdock could end up being her lapdog. Taking out her mirror, Susan looked at herself. *Am I looking at a jealous woman?* She wondered. *It's a rather delicious feeling—a feeling I've seldom felt before. I hope they won't fall into bed together tonight. No,* she thought, *not Murdock.*

At precisely 10:00 a.m., her phone rang again. It was Murdock. She reported the call from Mr. Proteus. He agreed that she'd made the right decision to meet with him. He suggested, "Mr. Proteus may have more information about Ricardo's situation than he's shared with us. See what you can pry out of him, but don't sleep with him."

"No, Boss. I promise that I won't sleep with him."

* * *

Susan seated herself in the same booth at the same restaurant in Multnomah Village. She checked her watch. It read 11:40. Mr. Proteus was late. Susan smiled inwardly. *He's probably doing it for effect. The master warns the slave that he's more important than she is.*

Five minutes later he appeared, wearing the same suit as last time. Seating himself next to her, he reached under the table. Satisfied, he motioned for the waitress and asked for a menu. After she complied, he said, "I talked to Allison Spencer this morning. I told her I was disappointed that Veritus would not work for me. She repeated Murdock's line that it was company policy to never take on governments as clients."

Susan's eyes met his. "Perhaps if you admit that you really don't work for the government, she would reconsider."

He chuckled. "Clever, Susan, very clever."

Her facial expression turned serious. She said, "I need some help. I'm working on the Ricardo Perez-Krieger rape case. Our investigator in Germany has found very little about the victim, Gretchen Weidner. We suspect that Traction set this up. I'm confident that your people know more about Traction than we do. It would be helpful if you could tell me where and when she was born. We'd have a point of beginning."

Proteus referred to his notes. "She was born in the German settlement in Paraguay. Her baptism is recorded in the records of a Catholic church outside Asunción named San Martino."

"Didn't some of the Nazis escape to that settlement in Paraguay?"

"I'm sure some did, but Weidner's ancestors weren't one of them."

"Can you give me some insight into Traction?"

"Not really except to say that what we're exploring is pretty weird. That's all I can say for now."

"Is there a government agency that studies weirdness?"

Mr. Proteus laughed as their lunches arrived. They enjoyed their meal with animated conversation. Susan was not able to redirect him to either Traction or Ricardo's case. She felt comfortable with him, but she wasn't comfortable with the vagueness of his answers. As lunch came to a close, Mr. Proteus became less interested in conversation. Reaching under the table, he inflicted pain where he had before and invited her to follow him to his hotel.

* * *

His suite was huge and more elegant than government employees normally enjoy. On top of the desk was a laptop computer. The bar was unusually well-stocked for a hotel room. She walked toward it as he locked and bolted the door. When she turned to face him, he was unbuttoning his shirt. With his eyes hard-fixed on hers and with a gruff voice nearly choking, he commanded, "Take off your clothes, **now**."

Startled at his impatience and rudeness, she froze. He walked over to her and seized the front of her blouse with his powerful right hand. Scowling, he said, "If I have to rip this damn thing off, you'll have to go home without one. You can't stay overnight. I don't permit women around when I'm sleeping. You take your pleasure and you leave."

Take my pleasure? Overnight? It's early afternoon. She fumbled with her buttons so he'd think she wasn't in control of herself. She walked toward a chair and dropped her blouse on it—making it appear accidental. When she bent over to pick it up, her perky little boobs took an assist from gravity and filled her bra more alluringly. She hung the blouse on the chair and walked toward the bar.

As he loosened his belt, he demanded, "Take off the damn bra. I want to see what you got."

Susan's eyes widened and met his. "Why are we in such a hurry? Couldn't we have a drink and enjoy each other's company for—"

He slapped her across the face with such force that she involuntarily spun around and landed on her belly on the floor. Dropping down to join her, he placed one knee on the floor and the other firmly in the small of her back. He clutched her bra strap. She wondered how he would ever unhook it with those thick fingers. He didn't. Severe pain across her chest informed her that he'd ripped it apart. Rolling her over, he removed it and tossed the tattered remnant into her face. Her tiny skirt was no challenge. Having stripped her naked, he arose, grabbed her left arm and jerked her to her feet. Forcing her hard against the bar, he manually examined her. He scowled and said, "You'll do."

She forced a smile. "You must use a prophylactic. My husband and I are trying to make a baby this month."

With his right hand, he vice-gripped her throat. Sharp pain shot into her shoulders. "When I've got a naked woman in my possession, she does what I want. You knew why we came here and what was going to happen. You had to know that a man like me wouldn't hold back. You came here of your own free will to play my slave. Slaves don't make rules. Besides, I guarantee that my sperm are superior to your husband's. If today's your day, woman, you should both thank me."

I've got him, she thought.

Dragging her to the back of the bar, he flung her against it. "Fix drinks while I shower. I'll have a martini." He walked into the bedroom, taking her clothes with him. He locked the door behind him.

Susan wondered how he'd learned that she enjoyed sadomasochism. In the usual slave-master relationship, each partner respects the other. The master needs to inflict pain; the slave needs to receive it. It's consensual and mutually beneficial. No permanent harm must come to the slave. Mr. Proteus was a question mark. Susan wasn't sure he understood the rules, or even if he was really into SM. Maybe he just abused women for the hell of it.

She prepared a martini for him and a gin and tonic for herself. Taking the capsule of white powder from her handbag, she poured its contents into his martini and stirred it.

When he returned, he was wearing a bathrobe. He commanded her to sit next to him on a bar stool. She obeyed. He raised his martini in a toast. She responded. She sipped. He didn't. She smiled coquettishly. Mr. Proteus turned his back to her, arose, and seated himself in a stuffed chair. From there he carefully studied every inch of her diminutive body. He sipped his martini. Susan sipped her gin and tonic, her knees held firmly together, modestly.

Mr. Proteus was amused. He liked what he saw and deliciously recalled a glimpse of what she was now decorously concealing. He resolved to gorge himself on this Chinese dessert sometime soon, but not today. He closed his eyes and consciousness abandoned him.

Susan found her clothes, dressed, sat at the desk, awakened his laptop, connected to the net, and transferred all his files to her computer at the office.

When Proteus awoke, Susan was gone. A note on the end table next to him read,

Mr. Proteus. I'm sorry that I had to drug your drink, but you scared me. I was afraid that you'd actually impregnate me. I really do want the baby to be my husband's. Double sorry. (signed) Susan.

A smile crept across his face. On the same end table within easy reach she'd placed her torn bra. He knew why. Susan had been thoughtful. It wasn't just a trophy. Picking up the bra, he used it as she had intended. He sat there for several minutes. *She's a magnificent woman and a real professional. She's totally in control of herself. No woman whom I've met had the skill to work this charade as flawlessly as this astonishing Susan Ling. I hope it won't become necessary to kill her.* He arose and walked toward the bathroom. The laptop was still on the desk, but it had been moved. Not much. Just enough that he could be certain. *She took the bait,* he thought.

6

Grace returned to her office a few minutes before quitting time. She seated herself behind her desk. Staring at her computer, she speculated whether she should e-mail a report to Murdock or wait until Monday. She had followed up on the mailman's remarks about the letter from Herr Weidner postmarked in Garmicsch- Partenkirchen. She'd spent the day there but found neither records nor anyone who recognized the picture of any of the Weidners. She hurriedly e-mailed that report to Murdock. The weekend beckoned. When she left the office, she would hang out at the Mädchenhaus Café—a popular gathering place for Munich's lesbians. She wasn't really into that, but the clientele interested her. Occasionally she touched souls with someone she needed to know. Several powerful women in the state government and the private sector hung there. Useful intelligence often can be gathered over a few drinks with the right people.

She checked her phone messages. There was one from Rudi Benzinger of the Bavarian State Police. His message said,

> *"Grace, just following up on our meeting.*
> *Our police in Garmisch-Partenkirchen could find*
> *no evidence of Herr Weidner, which only means*
> *he never filed a complaint nor was he arrested. I*
> *know that's not much help. Sorry."*

She sat back and chuckled. Was that a suggestion that *she* invade their privacy?

Ernst Müller, her station chief, knocked at her office door, stepped in, and sat across the desk from her. That was bad news. He liked to talk. Besides, it was awkward. She was temporarily assigned to Murdock McCabe and not authorized to share all information with Ernst. She had the impression that neither Murdock McCabe nor Rudi Benzinger trusted him. She frowned and said, "It *is* Friday, Herr Müller. I'd like to get out on time."

"This won't take long. Have you heard the rumor that Veritus is up for sale?"

She knew that short replies would speed the conversation. She replied, "Yes."

"It's true."

"Who owns it?"

"It's a closely held corporation, so its' shares are not traded on any exchange. I understand that all its' shares are held by one man. No one that I know can tell me who he is."

"Is there a waiting buyer?"

"Shortly after the announcement was made at the headquarters' office in Chicago, an offer was received from a bank in Aruba. The bank is controlled by a man named Boris Romanovsky. I've heard a few rumors about him. He might be connected to the Russian mafia. By the way, you're off my budget now. Your travel expenses will be reimbursed out of the Portland office. However, I'm still your station chief, so keep me informed. Have a nice weekend."

He arose and left.

* * *

As Grace walked into the Mädchenhaus Café, it was filled nearly to capacity. Greta Himmelreich, who owned the place, had saved a bar stool for her next to where she was seated. Greta stood up and greeted her with a hug. A vodka and tea was waiting for Grace. They seated themselves. Greta offered a toast, "To love." Grace lifted her glass and replied, "Okay."

Grace liked this place. Its architecture was old-world Bavarian. This was reflected on the exterior by the low-pitched roof of heavy shakes, designed to hold snow for insulation. Normally there would be expansive overhangs on the front and sides, but the city-setting crowded the sides. Stepping through the arched outer doorway and into the Mädchenhaus Café made Grace feel like she was stepping back in time to an era of an earlier, quieter century. She found the ambiance festive and inviting. Lights were dimmed. Traditional Bavarian religious murals were intermixed with scenic murals on the walls. Women enjoying companionship added a congenial, warm feeling. There were no men. Most of the women had come from downtown office buildings. Some were Grace's casual acquaintances.

After a few minutes of small talk, Greta said, "I promised you last week that I'd network with one of us in the state government. I did. My contact recommended two things. First, you should check with the monks at Saint Luke's Monastery on the Zugspitze Mountain, just west of the village of Garmicsch-Partenkirchen. She heard that Herr Weidner may have worked there as a gardener. A man who calls himself Brother Antonio supervises the employees. He's not the abbot. She says that a man who calls himself Brother Martin is. Second, the absence of deep roots suggests that he, or more likely his father, had a Nazi past. Many of them escaped as American troops poured into Bavaria. Some went to various South American countries and later returned here under different names. There was an organization of former Nazis who produced and sold passports and other documents that are almost impossible to tell from the real thing. Records of the passports found their way into federal records in Berlin, giving them the appearance of legitimacy. Bottom line: Herr Weidner may have some connection to the German colony in Paraguay. She hopes this information is helpful to you."

"Thank you so much, Greta. This is a pleasant surprise. You and I are just casual acquaintances. Idle talk and casual promises made in a crowded cocktail lounge are often forgotten by the next morning, but you kept your promise and came through for me. Is she here tonight? I'd like to thank her, too."

"She wouldn't want you to. It's not necessary to know who furnished it. I have many friends that come in here. We help each other. It's fun— sort of like being in a secret society. If you need access to privileged information, and if it's available in the Bavarian government's data, I can get it for you."

"Might that be illegal?"

"Yes."

"Why would you do that for me?"

Greta grinned. "Obviously, I want to be your friend. Besides, stealing confidential information is naughty and I enjoy being naughty. Of course, it's also naughty for you to use it, so never disclose your source. Keeping little shared secrets amongst us girls is devilishly good fun."

Greta motioned toward the far corner of the bar, and continued, "That blonde superwoman is my roommate. Her name is Lore. She's a medical doctor. If you, or someone you vouch for, should ever require a confidential procedure, I can arrange it. Lore is both highly competent and suitably discrete."

Grace observed the doctor. She was having a serious conversation with a woman seated next to her. Lore's motions were animated and fluid. Grace estimated she was less than five feet tall. Her long blonde hair was braided. She was wearing no makeup that Grace could detect, but her coloring and deep pools of dark eyes set in a cherubic oval face made it unnecessary.

Greta nudged her and said, "She's a rare beauty, isn't she? As you can guess, I'm the butch. We've been together for over a year now. You'll like her. Can I buy you another drink?"

"No, but thank you. I've got to pick up some groceries and I want to turn in early. I've had a frustrating week. Your help tonight lightened the burden. I'm butting up against a dead end in an investigation, plus my station chief wants to be kept informed about things that I'm not at liberty to share with him."

Greta smiled. "One of our customers plays both sides of the fence. She likes Lore, but she also likes your boss. I'll see what she can give me."

"Do you mean what I think you mean?" She studied Greta's face. "You do. Does his wife know?"

Greta took Grace's hand and held it firmly with both of hers and said, "Don't I always mean what you think I mean? I don't think his wife knows. Now that *you* know, that knowledge may someday become useful to you. I've got an idea. Please come to our apartment for lunch tomorrow."

Grace hesitated. "I don't think that would be a good idea. I don't know how to put it. I've never had a gay relationship. I'm looking forward to it, but I'm not ready—if that makes any sense. Perhaps my first time will be with you."

"And Lore."

"Okay. And Lore."

Greta squeezed her hand and said, "Believe me, I do understand. Take your time. You'll need us soon enough, for one reason or another."

7

Portland, Oregon
Friday, March 10, 7:12 a.m.

Dawn was beginning to convert black rain clouds into gray rain clouds. As Murdock's BMW entered downtown Portland, his windshield wipers lent an easy cadence to his thoughts. He'd lived in Portland for a year and had adapted himself to prolonged periods of rain, but every time he returned from Grand Cayman he had to admit that its warm sunshine had more than a modicum of attraction. He wished that he could have stayed a few more days, and he wished it for more than one reason.

Had he led Linda on? He hoped not. She's too fine a woman to toy with her affections. He was convinced that that feeling was mutual. He resolved to take a week's vacation on Grand Cayman Island as soon as he could break away. If they could spend more time together, perhaps their emotions could better define themselves.

How fortunate his parents had been. Both were born in Buffalo, New York, grew up there, and resided there all their lives. His father practiced law there for his entire career and his mother taught at Buff State. He'd never heard them talk about moving elsewhere. They had a sense of place. They knew where *home* was. How times have changed. Couples, if they're to advance their careers, face tough decisions. Today, *place* is wherever opportunity leads.

Did his fondness for Linda amount to love? What is love? He had loved Karen. Of that he was sure. What was there with Karen that wasn't there with Linda? *Or is it,* he wondered, *and I can't see it?*

He entered the parking garage underneath the Northwest Office Tower building, descended to the second level, and parked. A brief trip in an elevator and he'd be in a warm, dry office. He looked forward to Susan's report on her meeting with Mr. Proteus, and he was looking forward to a hot mug of gourmet coffee.

He found Susan already seated at the round conference table near the window. Murdock poured two mugs of coffee, added cream to hers, and placed them on the table. Susan was sitting sideways to the table and close enough that both could read the screen of her laptop. As Murdock seated himself, she crossed her legs with the usual scientific precision. He couldn't help but wonder whether she was or she wasn't. He put it out of his mind.

After taking a sip from her mug, she said, "I suppose the co-defendants claimed that Gretchen was the instigator and then cried rape after she'd had some fun."

Murdock laughed. "Of course. I also spoke to the physician who examined her approximately three hours after she claimed the guys released her. He confirmed that she had injuries consistent with rape. I asked whether the injuries could have been self-inflicted. He believed some could have been but he also believes that her virginity had been taken. Someone apparently pummeled her breasts with a closed fist."

Susan cringed and shook her head. "The medical evidence has a hard edge on it. The doctor's testimony will be difficult to rebut."

"To say the least. How did your meeting go with Mr. Proteus?"

"Boss, the other day when I told you he'd checked me out under the table, I neglected to mention that he made it hurt.

"It?"

"Use your imagination, Boss. Somehow he knew I was into sadomasochism. I'd sure like to know who told him. Does Allison know?"

"Yes. She's my boss. I had to report it because you sometimes use it to benefit the company. She made a note but didn't say anything."

"He must have romanced her pretty good to get that information. Anyway, he took me to his hotel room and beat me up. I begged him to use a prophylactic because my husband and I are trying to get pregnant. He slapped me hard and told me that he'd use me anyway he wanted to. He showered before he did anymore. While he was in the shower, I doped his martini. It put him out long enough for me to copy the files on his laptop to my office computer and disappear. I left a note saying that I had doped his drink because I really did want to have my husband's baby."

Murdock was delighted. Thinking of Susan as a mother softened the hard edge of the relentless researcher and sadomasochist. He said, "I'm pleased that you and your husband are planning a child."

51

"Don't buy a baby gift anytime soon, Boss. It was a flat-out lie, but it wasn't an unfair lie. Men playing his game should take the word of a woman playing the same game with a grain of salt and a dash of pepper. I've met guys like Mr. Proteus. When they get me in their apartment, they knock me around and get my clothes off. *Then* we have cocktails. They're dressed. I'm naked. It's the first domination of the slave by the master. I lied to Mr. Proteus so that I could give him a reason for putting the knock-out powder in his drink."

Murdock experienced an uncomfortable mixture of being both disturbed and pleased. He was disturbed because the game was dangerous; pleased because Susan had controlled the circumstances. He said, "You never cease to amaze me, Susan. You artfully blended astuteness and deception to get what you went after. I can't imagine who else could have pulled it off. I'm relieved that it didn't turn ugly."

Susan uncrossed her legs, again with scientific precision, unobtrusively watching Murdock's eyes. She didn't know why the semi-tease gave her so much pleasure. *Maybe it's because he's so straight,* she thought. She said, "There was nothing in that scene that I couldn't handle, Boss. It was worthwhile. The laptop contained eleven files. I've had a chance to review two of them. One was entitled *Perez-Krieger*; the other *Cosmology.* According to the first, and assuming it's legit, the government spooks reported that the co-defendants in Ricardo's case were lying. The spooks have identified a third young man, a Thomas Bayer, who allegedly had been with Ricardo that evening. When the noble Thomas got back home in Kansas City, he went to the FBI office and reported what he'd allegedly seen. The FBI will notify the RCIP. Thomas will testify that when Gretchen resisted to the utmost, he urged them to stop, and when they persisted, he left."

"RCIP?"

"The Royal Cayman Island Police."

Murdock sat back and digested that information. Susan waited for him to speak. He said, "Good grief, Susan. Have we been totally wrong? Have we ever seriously considered the possibility that Ricardo might be guilty?"

"Yes, Boss, but we didn't give it much credence. I've notified our KC office. They promised to check out this Bayer guy soon."

"How soon?"

"They're up to their ears in alligators, Boss. I couldn't get a commitment."

"I'll break the news to Linda as soon as we're finished. If the RCIP know about Bayer, the Crown hasn't notified Linda as of yesterday. What else have you got?"

"What do you know about parallel universes, Boss?"

"I've heard the term."

"Me, too. We received the manuscript of Brother Stephen's unfinished book that we are to deliver to Professor Amy Gallagher. A note from Brother Martin said that it mentions parallel universes. So does the SETI document that I poached from Mr. Proteus's computer. It was a memo to him from some ambiguous government agency and marked Top Secret. Their experts consider it possible that this woman leads Traction. She may not be a fakir, but an alien from another universe. It proposes that intelligence and consciousness can be deposited in an electrical charge that has no mass, like the transporters on Star Trek. It promises Mr. Proteus that supporting data will follow."

They both sat silent. Murdock had seen this woman—this maven of magical illusions. Her ability to disappear and apparently to walk on air, were strange, to say the least. Coming from the government, this theory goes beyond strange. If she is what they suppose her to be, what is her motive for creating Traction? In his encounters with her, she appeared to be interested in him personally. He was puzzled. Meeting Susan's eyes, he said, "I can't believe that a government agency would take such a theory seriously."

"Maybe they can't afford not to. Tell me about her, Boss."

Murdock didn't respond. He was deep in thought and only half listening.

"Boss?"

"Sorry. I met her in Germany two years ago when I was investigating the murder of the monk. She was a businesswoman—by all appearances, a very successful one. I found her to be clever, comely, knowledgeable, and a fascinating conversationalist. I dated her. I felt our acquaintanceship was on the verge of romance when I learned that she had a second identity—a nefarious one. Rudi arrested her for suspicion of murder but she escaped custody. A year ago, I saw a woman that strongly resembled her presiding over a cult ceremony in the jungle of Honduras. There she appeared as a mysterious green woman who walked on air and dissolved into a cave."

"And a man was ritually murdered."

"Yes. When I met her on that ship off the coast of Oregon, she was trying to get the computer chip that Brother Stephen had invented and Professor Klugman sent to his daughter, Professor Amy Gallagher, after

Stephen's death. At that time, she came on to me sexually and offered me the biblical kingdoms of the world if I'd join her."

"And you still have no idea why she chose you?"

Murdock shook his head. "Not a clue."

"In each of those contacts, Boss, our client was José Enrique Perez-Krieger."

Murdock sat silently. After seconds that seemed to Susan to be minutes, he asked, "What are you intimating?"

Her eyes locked on to his. "Boss, you've often said that we must always take a second hard look at things. It may be that Ricardo is guilty. It may be that your pal Enrique isn't all he's cracked up to be. It may be that his Plato Foundation has a hidden agenda. It may be that your gal Linda is leading us down the primrose path."

Murdock went silent again. Presently he said, "She's not my gal."

"Not yet?"

"Touché. I feel confident that I haven't misjudged her. Nor can I believe that I'm that far wrong on Enrique. Government intelligence is at best shoddy. Let's take a second look at the file from Proteus's computer. It all could have been planted to mislead and destroy our confidence in people we've trusted. What do you think? Were we suckered?"

"I've considered that, Boss. Anytime a charade works as smoothly as mine, I tend to duck. I'm good, but that was almost too smooth. When I handed him the martini, he was sitting on a bar stool. Before he took a sip, he seated himself in a stuffed chair—as if he didn't want to fall off the bar stool. If it's the government he's working for, what's their motive for letting us discover that information? Or for even obtaining information about an alleged rape committed outside the United States?"

"Or misinformation."

"Right, Boss. And if it isn't the feds he's working for, whose agenda is it that focuses on us? Where do I go from here, Boss?"

"Meet with Amy Gallagher and her new associate, Dr. West. See if she's being contacted by anyone about the computer chip. Find out what this parallel universe idea is all about and whether they think it has efficacy."

Susan crossed her legs with somewhat less scientific precision than usual. She smiled inwardly. Murdock's eyes froze on hers, but she was confident that his peripheral vision was directed elsewhere. *Such a tiny tease isn't unfair,* she thought.

As she picked up her laptop, she said, "I've already set up a meeting with Amy and this Dr. West on March 18. I need to see Mr. Proteus again, but I don't know how to contact him. If he's really unhappy with me, I probably wasn't set up, which would lend credence to the info. If he's smug, I probably was."

As she turned to leave the office, Murdock said, "Great work, Susan. Regardless of whether you were set up, it's really great work."

"Thank you, Boss."

She never ceased to amaze him. Before he told her to meet with Amy Gallagher and Dr. West, she'd already made an appointment. She seemed always to know what he wanted to say before he knew that he wanted to say it.

Murdock gathered his thoughts before he phoned Linda. He'd pass on the information and express his and Susan's doubts. The net result wouldn't be helpful. He reassessed mentioning Susan's name. Linda had pointed out that he mentioned it often. He didn't know how to interpret that. Did she mean that he should take full credit for their work, or did Linda think it indicated a romantic interest in Susan? If it's the second, it must trouble her. That was not what he was trying to do, but that was a good sign. No time to dwell on it. The Proteus information could be true or false.

Susan returned to her desk and checked her e-mail. Among those listed was one from Mr. Proteus. With a tingle of excitement, she chose it. It read,

> *"We must meet again after you're firmly pregnant and before you're so far along that I could hurt the baby."*

Firmly? She chuckled. *If he's concerned about the baby, maybe he's not as cold a fish as I thought. Of* course, *it may take a very long time for me to get firmly pregnant unless the pill fails.*

The e-mail continued,

> *"You're an intelligent worldly woman. We worldly people can be blunt. The strongest mainspring of all exploits—especially the art of gathering intelligence—is always a personal passion to find truth. Truth often masquerades. Sex removes more masks than money. We're sadomasochists. If we share our fetish, we can gain the mutual confidence that makes penetrating masks doable. My dear Susan, we are perfect counterpoints. I take pleasure in inflicting pain*

on women; you take pleasure in receiving it from men."

From women, too, but she wouldn't tell him that.
The e-mail continued,

"With my strength I can apply pain more forcefully than most men and still protect you from real harm. I can do what your husband would never dare." (signed) Mr. Proteus.

Grinning with pleasure at having her dog on the leash, Susan typed a reply.

"I was relieved to receive your e-mail. Walking out on you was callous, but I saw no alternative. I want there to be a bond of intimacy between us. It was sensitive of you to be concerned about hurting the baby. Thank you. I'll encourage my husband daily. Hopefully fortune will be kind to all three of us and I'll be firmly pregnant soon." (signed) Susan.

Grinning, she sent it. *If he buys that bullshit,* she thought, *he's delightfully vulnerable.*

8

Saint Luke's Monastery, Bavarian Alps
Tuesday, March 14, 7:00 a.m.

The Zugspitze is the highest mountain in Bavaria. Its peak is over 9,700 feet above sea level and is located on the border between Germany and Austria. At the base of the mountain is a hotel called Zugspitze Hof. Grace, who had arrived there the night before, arose at 6:30. At 7:00 a.m., the dining room was still empty. She had breakfast alone. She had chosen the hotel because it was near St. Luke's Monastery, a mile laterally and up slope at the tree line. The hotel had made arrangements to have a young man transport her there by snowmobile. Precisely at 7:45 a.m., bundled up warmly in woolen slacks, a knee-length coat, insulated boots, and her Casmir scarf, she stepped out the front door. The first hint of dawn silhouetted the southeastern peaks of the Bavarian Alps. The young man was waiting. She mounted the snowmobile and sat behind him. As a dull gray twilight began to catch puffs of stratocumulus clouds, they set off up a serpentine trail walled in on either side by the pitch blackness of the deep woods. The trail widened into a broad clearing. As they reached the tree line, they came upon massive stone walls rising twenty-five feet. The walls surrounded a large enclosure. Piercing the wall that faced down-slope was a twelve-foot high oak doorway standing open. The young man brought the snowmobile to a stop in front of it. Grace dismounted. The young man turned toward her and said, "Please phone the hotel when you are ready to be picked up." She thanked him. He turned about and roared off back down the trail.

Inside the gate a man was standing. She figured him to be in early middle age. He was wearing an ankle-length dark brown hooded cloak secured by a white rope around his mid-section. He smiled and said jovially, "You're delightfully punctual. My name is Brother Antonio. You must be Grace Bauer. May I call you Grace?"

"Of course. May I call you Antonio or is the Brother stuff necessary?"

He chuckled, amused by her straightforward manner. "No *stuff* is necessary. We're very informal here. We sometimes refer to God as the Great Guy in the Sky. However, if you please, I do prefer Antonio to Tony."

She offered her hand and said, "I'm very pleased to meet you, Antonio."

He shook it and motioned for her to follow. "I'm pleased to meet you, too."

Brother Antonio closed the door, and slid a heavy bolt into place. He motioned for her to follow. They entered a large open yard. A businesslike smile crossed his face as he said, "You have a reputation as a clever and a meticulous investigator. Few women visit here so you present a refreshing change. I'm confident that our meeting shall be beneficial for us both. We've not had an investigator here since Murdock McCabe and Rudi Benzinger over a year ago. You must know them, do you not?"

Brother Antonio led at a fast pace. Trying to catch her breath in the thin air, she replied, "I've met Rudi Benzinger but not Murdock McCabe. Veritus is a big company. Our paths haven't crossed."

They passed a stone chapel topped with a traditional Bavarian onion dome.

"That's where we celebrate matins and vespers, our morning and evening prayers," he explained.

Grace marveled at the delicate work of the stone masons who had fashioned the statues of men and women who she presumed to be saints. She didn't believe in saints—God, either, for that matter. There had been a few times when she wished she could, but down and dirty she believed religion was just too illogical. She felt that she handled herself quite nicely without a mystical crutch. *People need a moral conscience,* she thought, *but even if God existed, he wouldn't help. According to tradition, he's the one who gave us freewill.*

Beyond the chapel, an archway invited them into a covered walk. As the first rays of the sun sliced through the cold air, the bare dark brown wood of the cloister starkly contrasted with the whiteness from a late-night snowfall. In the center of an open courtyard quadrangle, she noticed a fountain—silent, and surrounded by snow-covered wooden benches.

"We frequently sit there to contemplate," Brother Antonio explained, "but not so often in the wintertime."

Brother Antonio paused before a formidable single oak door. Pushing it open with some effort, they entered a warm, long, rather narrow room dominated by a thirty-foot heavy oak table surrounded by twenty high-back commodious leather chairs. The walls, constructed with white pine and finished with a clear varnish, were decorated by murals of Alpine scenes of the four seasons. Four corner tables each contained vases filled with fresh cut flowers. *They must have their own greenhouse,* she thought. A high-pitched ceiling peeked at least forty feet above them. Light from the rising sun streamed in through a series of narrow stained glass windows high on the wall. She presumed that important decisions were made around that impressive table if sequestered monks could think of important decisions to make. A three-foot crucifix dominated the far wall. Gray, irregular flat stones, obviously hewn by competent masons, were closely fitted and covered the floor.

Brother Antonio invited her to take a chair at the corner of the table. He took one around the corner from her.

Grace smiled. "I take it that you hold an important position here, Antonio."

"Oh, yes. Every living person has an important position in the eyes of God. My claim to fame is the fact that I was the research assistant to Brother Stephen, the monk who was murdered a year ago. Have you heard about him?"

"I've read a report. He must have been an important man."

"Stephen was a brilliant man. He'd been a scientist and industrialist. He got his business start in the Silicon Valley. From there he moved to Wilsonville, Oregon, where he opened a computer chip fabricating plant. He made a fortune in semiconductors. All of us are or have been scientists or businessmen except our abbot, Brother Martin, and Brother Gustav. Martin is our only theologian. Gustav had been a professor of classical literature and a linguist. As you can see, we're not the usual religious brotherhood."

"What was the impetus for this place?"

Eight years ago Brother Martin wrote a book. He challenged the amorality of scientists who delve into research that pushes the boundaries of what makes us human without sufficiently taking into consideration its moral and spiritual implications. For example, they develop weapons without accepting the responsibility for what the weapons destroy. Martin's book touched on the conscience of many scientists and businessmen. He brought together over one-hundred of us who were Christians. A small number of us formed our brotherhood. We bought this old abandoned monastery and restored it."

"You aren't Catholic?"

Brother Antonio smiled. "I am Roman Catholic. I attend mass every Sunday in the village. Most of us are not. We're an independent order made up of former successful businessmen and scientists who dedicate their lives to both prayer and science, and to making the world cognizant of the moral imperatives that our business practices and our science compel."

Grace smiled. "Wasn't that open area that we passed through called a cloister?"

"Yes."

"I thought that cloisters were closed to lay persons."

"We're not a secret cult. We don't turn our backs on the world. There is no vow of poverty. Most of us are quite wealthy. Nor is there a vow of chastity. Our only vow is one of loyalty to our order—the Order of the Penitents of Saint Luke. We have a few oblates who have not even taken *that* vow as yet. We pray ceaselessly for the world. Ours prayers ask God to grant to scientists, industrialists and other businessmen the power to accept social and moral responsibility for their discoveries and actions. Profit is not a god. Worshipping it is a tragedy because it diminishes the worshiper by diminishing his or her social consciousness. In addition to praying, we write scientific articles with a distinctly Christian flair. We use our reputations to cajole those unfortunates who wrongly believe that religion and science are mutually exclusive. Above all, we spend our days praising God."

"Are you guys constantly praying?"

"We do pray frequently and we praise God constantly. Praising God is a lifestyle."

Her eyes fixated on the crucifix at the far end of the room. It fascinated her that men as intelligent as these could find religious inspiration in a Jew who was killed like a criminal over two-thousand years ago. She wondered what notion gave power to the symbol.

His eyes met hers and he smiled. "End of sermon. I understand that you're here to inquire about Josef Weidner."

"Yes. To whom do I need to speak?

"Me. I don't like to share personal information over the phone or by e-mail. I apologize for inconveniencing you, but it might be important that you get to know us anyway. To the point, our Abbot, Brother Martin, is a friend of Rudi Benzinger of the Bavarian State Police. In a recent conversation, Herr Benzinger mentioned a family whose daughter had been allegedly raped on Grand Cayman Island by a son of one of Herr Benzinger's friends. There seemed to be some mystery about the family. When Brother Martin heard a description of the victim's father, it reminded him of a gardener whom I'd recently hired. The man introduced himself as Max Gephardt and said that he was from Innsbruck, Austria. He also claimed to be a gardener, which he was not. He tried. He appeared to be a man who had fallen upon hard luck and desperately needed work. God might just forgive such a misrepresentation by a man who needed a job to support his family."

"How long did he work here?"

"Almost two months. His work did improve some, but the quality of his work was not why I invited him to leave. He was inquisitive—much too inquisitive. We don't lock doors except the main gate. Brother Martin caught Max in Brother Stephen's former apartment where he had no legitimate reason to be."

"What was in that apartment?"

"Brother Stephen's computer and his storage disks. Are you familiar with integrated circuits?"

Grace smiled kindly. "I know what they are but I have no technical knowledge."

Brother Antonio walked over to a side table where there was a carafe of coffee. He looked toward her and she nodded in the affirmative. "Black, please."

He poured one for both, handed one to her, reseated himself and said, "Brother Stephen and I were interested in the search for extraterrestrial intelligence. Many scientists have been involved in SETI, as we call it, for decades. They have used radio telescopes to search the heavens for a radio signal that could only be transmitted by an intelligent being. They have checked out thousands of frequencies; all to no avail. Either we earthlings are the only intelligent life created in the universe, or such life is so far away that their signals have not reached us yet."

"Or the correct vehicle has not been found that can receive it."

Brother Antonio stared at her. "That is a very astute observation."

Grace's eyes met his. "It seemed a logical conclusion."

"You're very observant, Grace. You live up to your reputation. Without going into details, we developed a chip—"

"A computer chip?"

"Chips are used in many devices that people don't think of as computers. We don't think of an automobile as a computer, but without its computer, it wouldn't work."

Grace smiled patiently. "Would it suffice to say that the particular structure of this chip made it useful in a transceiver dedicated to transmitting and receiving extraterrestrial signals? And that such a chip would be extremely valuable?"

61

Brother Antonio's eyes fixed on hers. "Another logical conclusion? Or has someone briefed you on our project?"

Her eyes fixed on his. "It seemed obvious. Was Brother Stephen murdered because someone wanted to get a hold of it, or to prevent him from using it?"

Brother Antonio twitched uncomfortably. This woman was a little too astute for him.

Grace continued. "Or are there little green people from another solar system who simply want to know how much you guys know about them?"

Brother Antonio's face flushed.

Grace pushed. "Tell me about Professor Otto Klugman and his daughter. From our file, I learned that he was murdered a few weeks after Brother Stephen."

"That's true. Klugman was a retired professor of philosophy from Oregon with an interest in astrophysics. He was a close friend of Brother Stephen."

"And your friend, too?"

"Yes, but we were not as close. He explored the philosophical implications of exchanging knowledge with an alien society."

"I take it that the professor was a religious man, too?"

"Not at all. He did acknowledge, however, that religion had a tremendous impact on the lives of millions of people."

"For better and for worse?"

"For worse, he thought, because it deluded them. He hoped that contact with extraterrestrial civilizations would expose the seductive deceptions of religious belief. Perhaps that's what attracted him and Brother Stephen to each other. They were at opposite poles on that issue."

Grace made a note, and asked, "Why was he killed—I mean, who'd want to kill a philosopher?"

"Who'd want to kill a monk? Perhaps Professor Klugman knew too much about somebody."

"Who?"

"I don't know. That's pure speculation on my part. He wasn't directly involved in our work with the chip. He had little knowledge of electronics, so far as I know."

"Our report mentioned that Professor Klugman had a putative daughter named Amy Gallagher. I understand that she lives in Oregon and that, before he died, he sent the chip and/or the schematics to her. Which is it?"

"Maybe both."

"Why? Why didn't you keep them?"

"I can't say."

"You can't say, or you won't say?"

Brother Antonio frowned. "The distinction is irrelevant."

"Our report also says that one of Amy's friends was kidnapped in Oregon and held hostage on a ship offshore to compel her to turn them over to some woman named Selene."

Antonio volunteered, "This woman, Selene, may have also gone under the name of Diana."

Grace was surprised. She extracted her laptop from her travel bag, fired it up, and made several notes as she considered whether to ask the next logical question. She hesitated, not wanting to digress; then she decided that it might not be a digression. She had to know. "Are you aware of the legendary Roman goddess that has been identified under both names?"

"Yes, and Brother Gustav says this goddess used the name Hecate, too."

"Who used the name Hecate, the woman who wanted the chip and schematics, or the Roman goddess?"

"Both."

Grace raised an eyebrow. Looking down at her laptop, she made several more notes. Without lifting her head, she looked up toward Brother Antonio. "Does it seem to you that they are one in the same—the goddess and the woman in Oregon?"

Antonio grinned. "I don't believe in pagan goddesses. Do you?"

"That's unimportant. Do you believe that this woman—or whatever she is—was responsible for the deaths of Stephen and the professor?"

"Brother Martin does."

Grace eased back in her chair, folded her hands in her lap, and crossed her legs at the ankles. She took a deep breath and exhaled slowly, watching Brother Antonio's reaction. He appeared confused. Grace smiled. "You mentioned that Brother Martin is your Abbott—the top man in your order. May I meet him, please?"

He laughed. "Actually, he is quite interested in meeting you. I didn't think we'd be finished this soon, so—"

"Are we finished?"

Brother Antonio arose, walked over to the side table, and pushed an intercom button. Looking over his shoulder, he said, "I think it's time that you meet Brother Martin."

The door opened and a huge hulk of a man entered. *He could have been an offensive lineman for the Packers,* she thought. He, too, was dressed in an ankle-length dark brown hooded cloak, secured by a white rope around his mid-section. His hair was tonsured in traditional fashion. His jovial smile seemed inconsistent with that of an offensive lineman. He greeted her with a warm "good morning" and seated himself across the table. Brother Antonio prepared a cup of black coffee for him. Brother Martin placed a bag on the table. She smelled the aroma of cinnamon rolls—her favorite. How did he know? Was it coincidence? What difference did it make? Brother Antonio extracted napkins from the drawer of the corner table and Brother Martin placed the rolls on them. They were obviously fresh baked. As she tasted the splendid succulence, Brother Martin asked, "May I call you Grace?"

She smiled. "That's fine, and I'll call you Martin. Or do you prefer Marty?"

"Either will be fine. Are you a religious woman, Grace?"

Her eyes met his. "I don't believe in God."

Brother Martin frowned. "There are many people who don't believe in God who nonetheless fear him. Do you fear him?"

Grace reciprocated the frown. "I'm not afraid of what doesn't exist."

"You must believe in something."

"I believe in Veritus Investigations International because it gives me a paycheck twice a month."

Brother Martin sipped the hot coffee. He hadn't touched his roll. "I presume that Brother Antonio has explained what we do here. What do you think of our order?"

Grace smiled. "I'd say that you fellows have a rather unpromising task. Most scientists have logical minds. They don't tolerate mysterious religions. Surely, most of your pious opinions fall upon deaf ears. Do you guys enjoy frustration?"

Brother Martin's smile brightened. "We rejoice in frustration. Frustration produces endurance. Endurance produces character. Character produces hope. Hope does not disappoint us, because it's a gift of love from the Holy Spirit. That love has been handed down to us over the centuries through the scriptures. We believe that that is most certainly true."

Grace shook her head. "Good grief! Religion is like politics where truth is created by perpetual repetition. Hitler was a master of it. He demonstrated that if you repeat a lie long enough, there will be a growing constituency that'll believe it. The longer and louder you repeat it and exaggerate it with visual symbols, the bigger that constituency will grow. You Christians have been doing it for twenty-one centuries. But perpetuation of foolishness doesn't make it fact. It may give the appearance of fact, but most scientists scoff at the so-called mystery religions. I don't mean to be rude—just practical. I'm not here to discuss theology. The bottom line is that it makes no sense to me that Traction would be concerned with what you're attempting to do. From what I've heard, they're bent on creating chaos and grabbing world power. No offense, but you guys are small potatoes. Your goals aren't earth-shaking, to say the least. What am I missing?"

Brother Martin emptied his cup and toyed with it. No one spoke. Brother Antonio arose and refilled everyone's cup without asking. Finally, Brother Martin broke the silence.

"I can't argue with anything you've said. They're all points well taken. But God's thoughts are not our thoughts. God's ways are not our ways. The rain and the snow come down from the sky and do not return to it without watering the earth and making it bud and flourish. Our work will flourish to the extent that it is watered with God's blessing. I agree that that's not what Traction fears. I'm convinced that they fear that we have futuristic knowledge gained from the use of Brother Stephen's chip. They want to know what it is. Brother Antonio has given you some background."

"He mentioned that you guys are concerned with how extraterrestrial communications might impact religious belief. Is that the main thrust of your interest in his chip?"

"Yes. Would beings from another planet or even a parallel universe have knowledge of God? Did they fall into sin? If yes, did God send a redeemer? Do they know Christ? If these questions were all answered in the negative, the next question would be, 'Why is our world different?' I don't think that's what interests Traction. I'm convinced that they fear that we know some particular thing. I have no idea what that something is."

Grace sipped her coffee. "Do you suppose that *something* was what your gardener was looking for in Stephen's room?"

Brother Martin looked at Brother Antonio. Antonio responded, "I don't think he was that smart."

Grace typed a note. Brother Martin injected, "Both Antonio and I suspect that Perez-Krieger's son has been set up by Traction. That would be reinforced if my guess is correct about the gardener—that either he was masquerading here or he's masquerading as the victim's father. In either event, he'd appear to be smarter than Brother Antonio thinks. Antonio knew him better than I. It's unfortunate that we don't have proof, but then that's your job. We'll do whatever we can to help."

"Do you know whether this gardener took anything?"

Brother Antonio responded, "I inventoried Stephen's possessions immediately after the murder. When the gardener left, all were still there."

"However," Brother Martin added, "the man could've copied a great deal onto CDs. He could have been in there on days that I didn't discover him. Since he departed, the lock on the front gate has been changed. I don't think he'll be back."

Brother Martin sipped his coffee. "Yesterday I talked to Rudi Benzinger at the Bavarian State Police. Murdock and Rudi have been friends going back to when Murdock was with the American FBI. Rudi told me that you're working on a master's thesis on ancient mythology, particularly the Greco-Roman gods and goddesses. Tell me about it, please."

"I'm supposed to be asking the questions."

"It may assist us to assist you. Please trust me."

Grace put down her notepad and laid her pen on the table. "Okay. No big thing. I'm exploring theories about the ancient origins of the myths and about their absorption into modern religious cults."

Brother Martin asked, "Like Wicca?"

"Yes."

"Are you into Wicca?"

"I don't believe in anything supernatural. I'm interested in the theory that postulates that these so-called gods and goddesses were giants who visited us in an ancient time from elsewhere in the universe, and that our ancestors mistook them for deities. By *acknowledge* I mean that it's within the realm of physical possibility. The fact that *we* don't have the ability to travel to other star systems doesn't mean that no other civilization has; or has had. If it were true that we've been visited, it might explain many reasons for events that the ancients mistook for supernatural."

Brother Martin's eyes fixed on Grace's. "During the investigation of Stephen's death, the medical examiner found a datebook in Stephen's cloak. Stephen had written in it, 'It looks like Odin has found the wolf, and its name is Hecate.'"

Grace looked surprised.

Martin noticed. "Does that ring a bell?"

Grace's eyes met his. "It's interesting that an educated man like Stephen would use a puzzling mixture of Germanic and Roman deities. Odin is the king of the Germanic gods. In the Roman myths, there is a goddess who takes three forms. In one, she's Diana, the virgin goddess of the hunt. In another, she's Selene, goddess of the moon. In a third, she's Hecate, a chthonic, or infernal, deity—the mistress of Hades. Her Greek counterpart is Artemis. She is the daughter of Jupiter, the king of the gods, and Latona. She has a servant god who carries out her wishes. His name is Verbius."

Brothers Martin and Antonio exchanged glances. Martin said, "Apparently these Traction people have simply piggybacked onto the ancient myths rather than inventing their own. Their followers—their mules who carry the drugs that finance them—appear to be unsophisticated. They can be easily misled by cult ceremonies."

Grace smiled a crooked smile. "Christians are easily led or misled by ceremonies, too. Ceremonies can be the tail that wags the dog."

Brother Martin injected, "I think that's true to a point. We sometimes become enchanted by ceremony, but God gives us the power to see through that enchantment without becoming disenchanted."

"Bravo. Good line." She turned toward Brother Antonio. "What else can you tell me about this gardener? Did he say whether he had a family?"

"He said that he had a wife and a two-year-old daughter to support. The little girl was sick. Jobs were nonexistent in Innsbruck. I did think it strange that a middle-aged man would have a daughter that young, but he could have been a bachelor until recently. I felt sorry for him. He seemed like an honest man."

"All con men do. Did he give an address in Innsbruck?"

"Yes." He handed her a scrap of paper. "I knew you'd want it."

"That'll be my next stop."

Brother Martin, deep in thought, emptied his coffee cup and slowly returned it to its saucer. Grace waited. His eyes met hers. "I heard today that Señor Perez-Krieger is making an offer to buy Veritus. If he were to succeed, do you think that his son's publicity would cast a shadow over your company?"

Grace hesitated, wondering why he had asked *her*. Presently she answered, "It's not my job to have an opinion on my employer, or to state the obvious."

"I'm sorry," Brother Martin replied. "It was an improper question."

Grace arose and offered her hand to Brother Martin. "Thanks for the interview. You've been very helpful."

"You're most welcome. I hope we'll have an opportunity to meet again. Please visit us again when you have some free time. We could have a pleasant conversation about Christianity. We do have something more to offer than Wicca."

"Thank you. I would very much like that. I shall, sometime soon."

Grace turned to leave, and then hesitated. She turned back toward Brother Martin. "By the way, what exactly is it that you guys know that Traction wants to know?"

Brother Martin's eyes met hers. "I'm afraid that's highly confidential. Suffice to say that if they knew that you knew that, your life would be in danger."

"How would Traction know that I knew? Surely you don't have a mole in your faithful religious fraternity, do you?"

Brother Antonio frowned.

Brother Martin smiled. "Even Christ had his Judas."

* * *

As she rode down the trail on the snowmobile, Grace was troubled by a feeling that Brother Antonio had been less than candid, or had been flat-out deceitful.

9

Grand Cayman Island
Tuesday, March 14, 6:00 p.m.

Enrique entered the cocktail lounge at Hemingway's. He enjoyed tourist season because invariably he'd meet someone at the bar who didn't recognize him and would take him at face value. Being a celebrity wasn't his cup of tea; especially now.

He seated himself next to a stranger—an older man with a gray moustache and beard. The man was wearing a jaunty blue sport coat over an open collar golf shirt, white slacks and a Greek captain's hat. Without waiting for an order, the bartender handed Enrique a Kettle One martini. The other man looked at the bartender and said, "I'll have another Gray Goose." Then, smiling, he turned to Enrique, offered his hand, and said, "Hi. I'm Jarrod Hastings. My friends call me Jack. They're not very imaginative."

Enrique took his hand. "I'm José Enrique. My friends call me Enrique. They're not too imaginative either. I see a yacht club insignia on your sport coat. Do you sail?"

"You guessed it. I've got a fifty-four foot Irwin Cutter Sailer. It cruises at eight; maxes at ten. Right now it's under repair at Sarasota."

"Is it enclosed?"

"Yup. It has a walk-in cockpit, hardtop with full enclosure and custom helm seat. It's normally moored at the Sarasota Yacht Club."

Enrique raised his glass and said, "To sailing. May our sails always catch a fresh wind."

Jack responded, "And may our crews always show up on time."

They sipped their cocktails, and Enrique inquired, "What are you doing down here, Jack?"

"I flew down for some diving on the coral."

"We've got the best diving locations in the world."

Enrique liked the looks of this man. He admired the cool confidence with which he handled himself. It was obvious that he'd had power; maybe still did. *Besides,* Enrique thought, *he has good taste in liquor.* His outfit was expensive but not ostentatious. Enrique's wasn't either. He didn't need to impress anyone. Apparently Jack didn't either.

Jack took another sip of his martini and said, "You haven't mentioned *your* boat."

Enrique brightened. There was little he enjoyed more than talking about sailing. "Mine's a one-hundred-foot Peter Ebbutt Live-Aboard. She cruises at ten; maxes at twelve. She's sailed faster than twenty-six knots."

Jack added jovially, "And she's named Plato. I've seen her from afar. I recognize you. You're Perez-Krieger. Where did you have those new sails made?"

"New Zealand."

"I thought so. Is that mast about 120 above water line?"

"Actually, 130. What business were you in?"

"Avionics. I'm retired now. Have been for a few years. I know that this is a sore subject, but I was sorry to read about your son. Young women dress and act like they're inviting the boys to do exactly what the boys end up doing. They didn't dress like that when I was young, which was a hell of a long time ago. It just seemed like a more wholesome age, or maybe the hanky-panky was hidden better. I can remember two or three girls who were rumored to be generous, but boys liked to make up stories. If any were true, they were the exceptions. Heaven knows how many times *I* struck out." He paused and his eyes met Enrique's. Jack frowned and said, "I'm sorry. It was rude of me, a stranger, to mention your son's problem. I just wanted you to know how I felt about it. From all I've heard, you're one of the good guys in this world. I hope it turns out well."

"Thank you."

Without finishing his drink, Jack got up. "I've got to meet someone in town for dinner. It's been a pleasure. I hope we can meet again soon and get to know each other better."

"Would you like to see my boat up close?"

"Absolutely."

"Can you meet me tomorrow at noon at the Yacht Club Marina restaurant for lunch?"

"I'll be there."

They shook hands and Jack departed. The bartender came over and said, "I'm with him, Mr. Perez-Krieger. You wouldn't believe what I see in here. They've got too much money, too little common sense, and no sense

70

of modesty. If I didn't have a good wife, I could get anything I wanted, and more than I could handle. I hope it turns out okay for your son."

Enrique thanked him.

He stared at his reflection in the mirror behind the bar, just above the bottle of Blue Goose. His fifty-fifth birthday would be next week. His hair, including his chevron mustache, was still dark. His face was not wrinkled. His body was slim and firm. His bodily strength had not diminished. His success in business had been astronomical. He could afford anything he wanted. A few weeks ago the world lay before him. Not now. In a mood bordering on desolation, he recalled a few lines he'd memorized from Shelley's poem, "Oyzmandias," about a traveler who'd found trunkless legs of stone standing alone in the desert with an inscription:

> *"My name is Oyzmandias, king of kings,*
> *Look at my works, ye Mighty, and despair!"*
> *Nothing beside remains. Round the decay*
> *Of that colossal wreck, boundless and bare,*
> *The lone and level sands stretch far away.*
> *With hue like that when some great painter dips*
> *His pencil in the gloom of earthquake and eclipse."*

Enrique's wealth and power were eclipsed by the horror that plagued him. Ricardo had assured him that the young lady had given her favors willingly to the other young men, and that he'd never even touched her. But, unfortunately, sometime soon, twelve ordinary folks would decide whether a rich man's son, who could buy things they could never dream of affording, had held down a poor young woman who wanted to become a nun while two other men raped her. If these people believed the young woman, Ricardo could spend the rest of his life in prison. He wondered if his success and his huge personal fortune would now become the curse that turned an envious jury against his son.

Enrique was pleased that both Linda and Murdock believe that Ricardo was set up. No evidence other than Ricardo's testimony supported that. The medical evidence was devastating. Information gleaned by Veritus in Bavaria supported the virginal innocence claim. His son's life depended on the persistency of a young woman named Grace; a woman that neither he, nor Linda, nor Murdock had ever met. Murdock assured him that she had an exemplary reputation as an investigator. He'd rather, though, that Murdock would personally handle the investigation in Bavaria.

Of one thing Enrique was certain—but it wasn't evidence. Ricardo would *not* lie to him.

10

Susan turned the BMW X3 SAV off the highway and pointed its nostrils onto a serpentine access road climbing uphill to Cascadia College. Her Camry was in the shop. She'd borrowed Murdock's vehicle. She'd rather not return it.

The entrance road cut through woodlands populated by Sitka Spruce, the shortest being at least seventy-five-foot tall. Grouped by nature so closely, the brush below was dark as night. Or so it seemed to Susan. Outside the car a thin drizzle was falling, misting the windshield and fogging it. She turned on the defroster. Large drops of water dripped from the lower branches of trees on either side. Windblown spruce needles carpeted the road intermittently, creating slippery spots. She fought drowsiness induced by insufficient sleep and aided by the lazy cadence of the wipers. She took the last gulp of her coffee. It was cold. Amy would have some hot coffee waiting for her.

The parking lot was nearly empty. She parked within thirty feet of the office of Professor Amy Gallagher. They'd met a year earlier. Susan looked forward to seeing her again. In Susan's travel bag was the late Stephen's unpublished work. As she exited the vehicle, the damp coldness and the promise of Amy's always stimulating conversation honed her senses. Susan enjoyed that. She considered herself a well-read lay person on modern research into physics—well-read enough that she could ask intelligent questions—more or less.

As she entered the door to the outer office, a man walking at a fast pace saw her and stopped. He then hurriedly approached her, and offered his hand. He said, "You must be Susan Ling. You're much more eye-catching than had been described to me. I shouldn't rely on women's descriptions of other women. You're splendid. I'm Dr. Roy West from the University of New South Wales."

Susan had met Australians before, but she was mildly surprised at Dr. West's appearance. He was short and brown but didn't look like an aborigine. His melancholy eyes displayed a quiet intensity, which he focused on her. He smiled kindly and said, "You're surprised to see a man of my race from Australia. You hear me speak and I don't sound Australian. I was brought up in Detroit. I did my undergrad and masters at Indiana University. My PhD in astrophysics is from the University of New South Wales. As part of their post doctoral research program, I'm working with Professor Gallagher for several months—possibly longer. She has a trust fund which provides money for the search of extraterrestrial intelligence."

"I'm pleased to meet you, Dr. West."

"Yes. Me, too. I mean I'm pleased to meet you. No matter how much money a trust provides, it's never sufficient. Your station chief, Mr. McCabe, has suggested we talk to the multi-billionaire, Señor Perez-Krieger. His chief operating officer, Miss Linda DiStefano, may come here to meet with us. Mr. McCabe suggested that Perez-Krieger might be interested in underwriting a chair on SETI at some university; maybe at his College of the Caymans."

Professor Amy Gallagher stepped out of her office, put her arm around Susan's shoulder, and said, "Susan, I'm so glad you could come. We must get together more often. I'm sorry Murdock couldn't come with you. I suppose you are, too. I see you two have met. Let's go into the conference room. It's more comfortable. Has he worn you out with conversation yet?"

Susan smiled warmly. "No. Not at all. He's delightful."

Dr. West walked before them into the room. When they had seated themselves around the round conference table, Dr. West asked, "Are you married, Susan?"

Amy looked at him askance. Susan replied, "Yes, are you?"

With a hint of disappointment, he replied, "Not presently."

Amy injected, "Perhaps we should get directly to business, Susan. There should be time for you and me to lunch together before you head back. I understand that you and Murdock are curious about the concept of parallel universes."

Dr. West chimed in, "It's not easy to explain. For those of us wrapped up tight in the physics, it's difficult to find the sweet spot between our esoteric jargon and sentences which don't mislead the public by oversimplification.

When we translate for the layman, often the elegance of the idea is lost. Do you understand?"

Susan nodded and said, "I understand the two terms *parallel* and *universe*, but when used together, do they simply mean that you've found another universe that runs parallel to ours?"

Dr. West cocked his head. "Why is it that you ask?"

"I managed to get some confidential information from an alleged government source that suggested that an alien may have come to earth from another universe. It seems sort of weird. I need to understand what they're talking about, and if it's likely that my source's information could be accurate."

He asked, "Does the government know that you have the information?"

"If it does, it hasn't told me."

Amy injected, "Does this have anything to do with that eerie woman from Traction that wanted the computer chip that Brother Stephen invented and my father had sent to me?"

"It could."

"What eerie woman?" Dr. West asked.

Amy interjected, "Roy, I'll explain later rather than take up Susan's time." She turned to Susan and said, "Our universe is infinitely complex. There may be marvelously intricate life forms governed by elaborate physical laws. There are people who argue that its complexity couldn't have happened by chance—that it was the result of intelligent creation. Some, not I, call that intelligence God. Einstein was one of them. He believed that his theory of relativity merely offered a clue as to how God did it."

Dr. West injected, "Here's the bottom line. For life to exist, many things had to come together. I'll mention some. The earth had to go into orbit within the Goldilocks Zone—not so close to the sun that it's too hot like Mercury and Venus, and not too far away that it's too cold like Mars and the outer planets. Our moon had to be just the right size to stabilize our orbit. If it were too small, the earth would wobble, creating drastic changes in climate."

Susan looked mystified. Amy offered, "At the beginning of the universe, if gravity had been weaker, stars couldn't have emerged from the primordial soup, and fusion couldn't have occurred. Fusion created the heat that made the stars shine. Our star, the sun, was one of them. Fusion also cooked the basic elements into existence inside them. After the earth came into being, it took hundreds of millions of years of stable climate and stable protons for DNA to evolve. We needed volcanoes to produce carbon dioxide so plants could develop and produce oxygen. Without oxygen, human life couldn't have happened. I could go on and on. The question remains, did our universe evolve and become finely tuned by billions of accidents, or did God command it to be so?"

Dr. West added, "It's incredible to believe that all this could come together by accident unless billions of universes were created so that one of them, ours by chance, turned out to be hospitable to life."

Susan stared at them and exclaimed, "That's fascinating. I've never thought about that."

Dr. West, doodling on a pad, added, "If billions of parallel universes are the answer, it leads to more questions. Were all the universes accidents or were some created by the same god or different gods? If there were multiple creators, do they like each other? Why did he, she or they, bother? What if no gods actually exist? Did all of everything spontaneously pop into existence out of nothing? If so, where did the 'nothing' come from?"

Susan shook her head. "Can we ever be certain that we know the answer?"

Amy smiled and said, "We're able to see much smaller things than ever before and much bigger things than ever before. Our telescopes can look into the past and see the first stars and galaxies forming thirteen billion years ago because that's how long it has taken their light to get to us. But there is serious doubt that we'll ever see beyond the Big Bang from which our universe sprang, or to see things as small as superstrings which may be the most elemental building blocks from which all things are made. Some scientists have semi-seriously suggested we're merely virtual characters in a web game universe that's gone independent of its designer, and that whoever did the mouse clicks is God."

Susan chuckled. Her eyes met Amy's. "But seriously, is it possible that a woman from another universe could have found her way into ours?"

Amy took a deep breath and released it. After a short pause she said, "As one acquires genuine knowledge, one begins to appreciate the enormity of what one doesn't know. I don't know. My limited knowledge embellished by gut feeling tells me it's improbable, even assuming those other universes exist."

Dr. West added, "If they do exist, such a woman might have had a shorter journey if she came from another universe than if she'd come from another planet in our universe. Some theorize that our universe may be a vibrating membrane. A parallel universe could be only one millimeter from ours, perhaps vibrating at a different frequency which we are incapable of sensing. Think about the millions of frequencies of radio waves going through your body right now. Take a radio and tune it to one frequency and its inductance-capacitance circuits will filter out all the others. They're still there. You can't hear them because you're not tuned to them. If a parallel universe were only the thickness of one atom away from us, we wouldn't know it because it's vibrating on its own particular resonant frequency and abiding by its own unique physical laws. Those laws would have created matter and energy that are incomprehensible to us. Could the resonant frequency of another universe intermingle with our universe and create our mysterious dark energy? We don't know. If a being came from another universe, it would take an unimaginable amount of energy to transport it. The trip, however, might be very short, indeed."

Amy added, "One theory suggests that if an advanced civilization could focus enough energy at a single point in empty space, virtual universes would pop into existence."

"From out of where?" Susan asked.

Amy smiled. "As I said before, from out of nowhere."

Susan shook her head in disbelief. Amy added, "That's a little deep. However, we find that the deeper it gets, the stranger it gets. The more we learn, the weirder it seems." Her eyes met Susan's. "Do you have something for us?"

Susan had almost forgotten. She reached into her travel bag, took out a package, and handed it to her. Amy removed the heavy brown paper and examined it briefly. Dr. West asked, "Is that the manuscript from the monastery in Bavaria?"

Susan replied, "Although we didn't break the seal, I believe it is. Brother Martin thought it would raise fewer eyebrows if a courier delivered a package to Murdock rather than here."

"I'm sure he was right," Amy replied.

Susan added, "Murdock would appreciate a copy. Since Traction has an interest in it, it might have a bearing on a case we're investigating."

Amy glanced through it. A look of surprise crossed her face. She said, "It deals with using optical communication in addition to radio waves to discover extraterrestrial intelligence." She looked at Susan. "It's highly technical. When I've had a chance to review it, I'll provide you and Murdock with a summary in layman's terms. In the meantime, Susan, let's go into town for lunch." She turned to Dr. West. "I'd invite you, Roy, but it'll just be a lot of girl talk. We haven't seen each other for awhile."

"That's fine. When I'm in Portland, Susan, perhaps we can find time to have dinner."

"I'll look forward to that."

Amy nudged her arm and they headed outside. As they walked through the drizzle toward Susan's car, Amy leaned toward Susan and warned, "He's a lady's man."

"Is that bad?" Susan asked.

11

Linda DiStefano, having just finished her breakfast, sat on her balcony staring out to sea, while trying to relax. A cool early morning breeze drifted off the water. She hadn't smoked for seven years, but she felt like lighting a cigarette. Time was getting short. Depositions were scheduled be taken before the magistrate on April 10. Her co-counsel, Michael Sudbury, advised her that they should not cross-examine Gretchen. It would only prepare her to better face their cross examination at trial. She agreed. The Crown's case was already convincing. Besides, she didn't want to give the Weidners a clue as to how thoroughly Veritus was investigating them—not that much had yet been learned.

Linda had a vague feeling of insecurity. During the years that she'd worked for Enrique, she'd had no reason to feel that way before. Her comfort level as his administrator was much higher than her comfort level as his son's attorney. Even though her co-counsel was experienced, she was the lead lawyer. The strategic decisions were hers to make. If the Crown's prosecutor should offer Ricardo the opportunity to plead guilty to a reduced charge of attempted rape, should she recommend that he take it? That offer might be made soon. Both she and Michael were convinced of his innocence, but taking a hard look at the evidence, the jury would likely find him guilty. It boiled down to whether the jury chose to believe Gretchen, the doctor, and her neighbors in Bavaria, or the self-serving testimony of the young men. Also, the jury might be determined to prove that Enrique's wealth couldn't buy everything. If he pleaded guilty to attempted rape, he would receive a maximum of fourteen years. That's a steep price when one is innocent, but life in prison would be steeper.

Linda was perplexed by an ethical problem. If Ricardo chose to plead guilty to the lesser offense, he would have to admit holding Gretchen while the others raped her. That would provide the factual basis necessary for the judge to accept the plea. But Ricardo denied it. He insisted that he didn't hold her. Linda believed him. Ricardo would have to lie—he'd have to admit doing something that he didn't do so that he could go to prison for fourteen years instead of life. *As an attorney*, she thought, *I'm an officer of the court. It's unethical for me to advise Ricardo to lie to the court. Michael and I both could be disbarred.* She sighed. None of this would be an issue if Veritus could debunk Gretchen's story. *If.*

She glanced at her watch. Shortly, there would be an hour of—perhaps, comic relief. Enrique had encouraged her, against her better judgment, to meet with Boris Romanovsky. The intercom buzzed. His limousine had just passed the gatekeeper and was rounding the circular driveway inside the compound. She wondered what new scheme he would offer today. She arose and descended the broad circular stairway.

As Boris Romanovsky's six-foot-four frame exited the limousine, Linda marveled that his broad shoulders fit through the door. He extended his massive right hand and took hers. With a grand gesture, he bowed and kissed it. She, responding with measured civility, escorted him into the foyer, into the elevator, and up to her office on the third floor.

"It is a glorious day, is it not, kind lady? You are pleased to know that Boris's flight from Aruba was smooth like silk. Boris is happy you are looking well. You are well, aren't you, kind lady? A strong young woman like you, raised in the Canadian prairies—of course, you are. You are even more comely than Boris remembers. It has been a year that Boris has not seen your exquisiteness—much too long. Fly to Little Cayman Island tomorrow and marry Boris Romanovsky, a prince descended from loins of Alexander II, Tsar of all Russians, unfortunately from wrong side of sheets. But what do sheets matter? A slight irregularity in lineage of a great, great, et cetera, et cetera bastard grandfather should mean nothing to a sturdy, sophisticated woman of world. The lineage is still royalty, is not so? You should make handsome royal children for Boris."

"Is that why you've come here—to propose my having your children out of wedlock? Or are you proposing marriage to me again?"

Boris laughed. "But, of course, among other things. Eventually you must marry Boris. But so, if you wish not to marry Boris, Boris can arrange for you to have royal children anyway."

"You would work with me on that?"

"In a heartbeat, most kind and lovely lady. Boris is a gentleman."

A wry smile crossed Linda's face. She considered for a moment whether his proposal of marriage could possibly be sincere, or was it part of the schmooze? He was one of the more intriguing men she'd met. Pushing the question aside, she said, "Is it true that you're building a hotel on Little Cayman Island?"

"Actually, beautiful lady, my bank in Aruba is financing it. Boris personally has an equity interest. Boris is searching for another investor."

He reached into his briefcase and extracted a prospectus two inches thick. He pushed it across her desk and said, "Perhaps Enrique would like his lawyers and accountants to study this. It presents an opportunity to create many new jobs on Little Cayman Island. Boris and he could take an equal interest. Boris would even consider offering majority interest in return for a proper investment."

Linda's curiosity was piqued. She picked up the prospectus and casually paged through it.

Boris continued, "My bank in Cyprus is also positioned to finance a new tourist hotel in Saint Petersburg, Russia. Enrique could get in on that, too." He reached in his briefcase again, withdrew another prospectus, and slid it across her desk. "Boris has been e-mailing you for over year suggesting that Enrique and Boris could do much business together and make much money."

"Enrique does not want to do business with you in Russia."

"Boris understands, smart lady. He feels that Boris's wealth is tainted. When Soviet government fell, huge international laundering scheme concealed transfer of state assets to individuals. What could Boris do? What future was there for an unemployed communist apparatchik? Should Boris gawk in the face of opportunity and demur? No! Never! When opportunity screams, wise men listen. Boris is wise man. Today is great opportunity to make or steal money in Mother Russia. Same difference. Boris can open doors. Enrique needn't get hands dirty. Boris's organization will get hands dirty for him. In Russia, delightful lady, there is great profit in bottom feeding. Don't worry about conscience. Those who are Russia's true conscience are shot or poisoned."

Linda's eyes met his. She smiled and said, "It sounds dangerous."

"Not for Enrique, exquisite lady. Boris absorbs danger. Many attempts are made on the life of Boris. Those who attempt it taste their own medicine. Boris knows. Bullets are cheaper than doctor bills."

Linda smiled and asked, "Do your banks launder drug money?"

Boris feigned shock. "Why is that question important, intelligent lady? It should be of no concern. So called laundering aggravates American government. But, most exquisite lady, laundering drug money is illegal in America, but it is not dishonest. Economic civil war is being fought in United States. Many millions of Americans spend billions of dollars buying illegal drugs. Many millions of other Americans insist that billions of dollars of tax money be spent to interdict drugs. Interdiction forces up price. So, many more millions of crime victims must be robbed so users can afford higher price. Neither side is honest. That is truth. American politicians pretend otherwise, but you and Boris understand the world. You and Boris know it is truth. When Americans tried to interdict whiskey and beer, they created wealth for Al Capone. *That* economic civil war was won by whiskey and beer."

Linda shrugged. "I can't argue with you. We do live in an age of relativism. The very idea of *truth* is politically incorrect. It's killed by spin doctors. Its instrument of death is the TV sound bite. Tediously repeated rhetoric substitutes for intelligent debate. The bottom line, Boris, is that until drugs are legalized in America and Europe, Enrique is apprehensive of doing business with you."

Boris grinned and said, "Boris should be apprehensive of doing business with Enrique, but Boris is brave. This rape case is first shot. My intelligence people predict that Traction will soon completely trash Enrique's reputation. Investors in his Plato Fund will get goosey just like you are goosey about Boris. American senate will investigate Plato Fund. It will be painted as a scheme to aid the privileged classes against the welfare of workers. Boris knows matter is complicated because politicians cannot afford to see every side of issue. They will believe the worst, because it makes better sound bites. Senators will strut like peacocks as they attack evil Chilean billionaire, and urge government to freeze assets of Plato Fund. Boris is friend. Boris can help. Boris can hide Plato assets among several of Boris's banks. Tell Enrique. The time will come when Enrique and you will need Boris. Be assured, kind lady, Boris will be there."

"Thank you, Mr. Romanovsky. That is very kind of you. Please be assured that I will mention it to Enrique."

"Please to call me Boris."

"Yes. Be assured that I shall discuss all of your offers with Señor Perez-Krieger, except, of course, the one that is personal to me."

"But so, wise lady. Now Boris makes business offer in which you personally might like to invest. One of Boris's many businesses is Hidebound Transport, Ltd., a Bahamian corporation. Hidebound owns small ship that operates from Odessa across Black Sea to Istanbul. Hidebound signs up women from all over Eastern Europe who wish to become domestic servants in Turkey. Hidebound arranges jobs and transports them."

Linda's eyes met his. "And when they get there, they find out they must work as prostitutes to pay for their passage before they can hunt for the nonexistent jobs?"

"Yes, smart lady. If they cannot find job as domestic, they must work again as prostitute to reimburse for passage to Istanbul and passage back to Odessa. Very profitable, nice lady. Boris has good inventory control—Boris has them; Boris sells them; Boris still has them. Turks like light-skinned prostitutes from Eastern Europe. Girls' work is honest. Customer gets service he bargained for; girl gets money she bargained for, less our surcharge. If business were not honest, Boris would not be involved. Boris is a gentleman."

"How young are these women?"

Boris grinned again. "Who can say? As young as Turks want them."

Linda arose as a signal that the discussion had ended. She said, "Thank you for your Hidebound offer. I'm not in a position to invest right now."

"Wise lady, human trafficking in women is more profitable than African slave trade two centuries ago."

"It's not for me. I'll phone you after I've had a chance to discuss your other proposals with Señor Perez-Krieger."

"Thank you, kind lady. Boris cannot stay for lunch, thank you. Boris must fly to Little Cayman Island. Boris has appointment to inspect boat that Boris might buy." He arose, and with another flourish, bowed and kissed her hand again. "Perhaps until tomorrow, lovely lady."

Linda chided playfully, "But tomorrow never comes. It's always today."

"It will come, gorgeous lady. Boris will make it come and you will recognize it when it happens."

* * *

Linda had been amused by Boris's tenacity, but she was glad to see him go. She walked onto the balcony and stood at the railing. Off shore, sea birds soared, lifted by a gentle breeze. Then, suddenly, one would dive into the waves and capture its lunch. She mused: *How carefree their lives seem. Each bird knows what he or she is. It flies and feeds and sleeps and procreates. Its ancestors have done those very same things in the very same way for millions of generations. Their descendents will do them for millions more. Their lives are uncomplicated. Oh, to be a bird.*

Her thoughts turned to Murdock. She yearned to meet him at the Timberline Lodge on Mount Hood for a skiing weekend, but her life *was* complicated. A skiing trip to Oregon was out of the question until

Ricardo's case was resolved. Maybe it was silly, but she wanted to stop at Murdock's office and meet Susan Ling. She searched her own psyche but it didn't tell her why this married woman seemed a threat.

Murdock would return to Grand Cayman soon. They could swim nude in the pool again as they had done several times before. *He's straight*, she thought, *and unfortunately he's superbly disciplined.* He'd never touched her. She was certain he wouldn't again. *How can I demurely tempt him?* Whatever it was, she wasn't sure she wanted to do it. *Maybe there isn't anything I can do. Maybe the psychological scars inflicted by his wife's murder can never heal. No. 'Never' isn't a word in my vocabulary. I can compete with a dead woman. Flesh and blood can whip a mere memory. Maybe I'm fooling myself, but I don't think so. The effort is worth it.*

12

Portland, Oregon
Thursday, March 30, 9:34 a.m.

While Murdock was on a conference call, his private line rang. The caller ID indicated Linda DiStefano. Susan picked it up in her office and said, "Ms. DiStefano, this is Susan Ling. Murdock is on the phone. He should be free shortly. Would you like to wait? I know he wants to talk to you."

"Yes, Mrs. Ling. By the way, I've wanted to meet you. Murdock speaks so highly of you."

And frequently, Susan hoped. "And I look forward to meeting you, Miss DiStefano. Perhaps it will be soon. I'm delighted that the Boss speaks well of me. Murdock and I team-up quite nicely. We seem to instinctively know what the other is thinking. That makes for a comfortable and intimate working relationship." *Am I being catty?* "Murdock speaks highly of you, too, Miss DiStefano. He thinks you're one very capable lady. He's free now. I'll switch you."

"Thank you, Mrs. Ling."

Did I succeed in sending a message that the Boss and I are very close? Why did I try? Has some subconscious warning told me that this Linda woman is after the Boss? Why should that wave a red flag in front of me? I already have a husband and Murdock and I are merely co-professionals. Aren't we? I've seldom thought of going to bed with him and never too seriously. Anyway, maybe I shouldn't have used the word intimate. It may have distressed Linda. Why don't I regret that? Is that what I wanted to do? Why is life such great fun?"

* * *

When Susan noticed that the phone call had been completed, she filled two mugs with coffee and joined Murdock at the conference table in his office. After handing one to him, she asked, "What did Miss DiStefano have to say?"

He took a sip. "The alleged victim, Gretchen, has been ordered to appear in the Magistrate's Court on April 10. Their procedure requires her to give a deposition. Yesterday her father, Josef Weidner, arrived on Grand Cayman Island and demanded to speak to the attorney general. The local newspaper reports that he was denied, but he did manage to talk to the AG's secretary by phone. Weidner screamed at a reporter that he's enraged that the Cayman government has refused to provide security for his daughter. He insinuated that Enrique has so much money he can buy anything. He ignored the reporter's invitation to define 'anything.' When asked about the Bavarian State Police, he admitted that they had refused, too."

"He sounds scripted, Boss. He's playacting for the media. I'm sure they can see that, but if he feeds them quotable lines, they've got to use them. It's the nature of the animal."

"I have an uneasy feeling about this guy, Susan. Whoever is writing the script, knows what he or she is doing. They've injected just the right dose of melodrama. Please pass Linda's information on to Grace. Urge her to do her utmost."

"I don't think that's necessary, but will do, Boss."

"Do we have any further information on Gretchen's birthplace?"

"Our office in Asuncion, Paraguay, reports that there's a paucity of information available. They've come up dry. No public birth records exist. The next best evidence is a baptismal record in the parish church. There was a fire in the church a year back. The records covering baptisms around the alleged date of Gretchen's birth were destroyed. Our office reports that they've had that problem before. They call them expediency fires. They're trying to locate the priest who would have baptized her. I hope that doesn't put the poor man in mortal danger."

"It probably will."

"Shall I call off our dogs?"

"Our duty is to our client. Ask them to be as discrete as possible. Bottom line—we can't be overly concerned about the priest."

"It's a cruel world, Boss. We received an e-mail from Grace. You were stationed in Munich before you came here. Are you familiar with a cocktail lounge called the Mädchenhaus Café?"

"Yes. One of my associates was a regular patron. It's a lesbian gathering place. Is Grace—"

"Apparently Grace is a patron, Boss, but that doesn't necessarily mean that she's gay. Anyway, she's established a rapport with the owner, a Greta Himmelreich. Do you know her, Boss?"

"No. I never knew who owned it."

"This Greta keeps her proverbial ear to the ground. Some of her patrons share a clandestine information network. Several have confidential positions high up in the state government. Greta heard that Josef Weidner has a bank account on Cyprus with a 'significant' balance. Does that ring your bell, Boss?"

Murdock, who had been staring out the window, looked at her, smiled broadly and exclaimed, "Eureka. Brief Grace on everything we know about Boris Romanovsky and ask her to fly down to Cyprus and interview him. Rudi Benzinger tells me she's an attractive woman. She'll catch Boris's attention. Besides, he owes Enrique a favor. If the money isn't in one of his banks, he should be able to find it."

"If he wants to, Boss."

"Right. You set up the appointment. Boris likes you."

"Mostly because I'm a woman, Boss."

"I can't argue with that. Make him want to talk to Grace. Tell him that Grace is coming at the request of Linda DiStefano. Boris is really sweet on her. I'll phone Linda and give her a heads-up."

"We have a delicate problem, Boss."

"I know. We need to know if Grace is on the inside of Greta's loop. We can't have her sharing confidential information on our clients. I know you'll handle it with diplomacy. What else have we got on our platter?"

"One of the files that I copied from Mr. Proteus was encrypted. None of my decoding programs worked. I farmed it out to our code-breaking service and got it back from them an hour ago. I reviewed it and put a copy of the decryption in this file for you. It deals with the purposes of Traction, as Mr. Proteus's people interpret them."

"If the encryption is *that* sophisticated, this info might be straight stuff."

"Everything I copied might be straight stuff. Tricking him was almost too easy, though. It might be all queer, too. Shall I summarize it?"

Murdock nodded in the affirmative.

"The Traction people want to destroy the capitalist West by making a three-pronged attack. First, they want people to lose faith in democratic institutions by discrediting the ruling classes that control the levers of power, both political and economic. José Enrique Perez-Krieger is the first prime target at the economic end. They have started by demonizing his son and causing it to reflect upon him. Against others, they will make corruption so tempting and profitable that few politicians and industrialists will be able to resist. A rumor campaign will be waged in the media against those who *do* resist so that few people will believe that they're clean. At the same time, they'll tempt their targets into exotic sexual deviations beyond commonly accepted norms. Those who resist will be tarred with rumors so shocking that people will believe that they must be true. In other words, their purpose is to paint our leaders as so despicable that their power will dissolve in an ocean of scorn."

Murdock stared out the window and quipped, "That may not take too much effort."

Susan nodded in agreement. "Second, they want to replace capitalism with radical socialism and make it appear so attractive to the poorly informed public that they'll not notice as it subtly devastates productivity. By that they hope to shrink everyone's standard of living and force the world into poverty and a new Dark Age."

Murdock arose, refilled his coffee mug and Susan's. "Susan, I think we've already fallen into a new Dark Age. Feudalism governs the neighborhoods of our inner cities. They've disintegrated into feudal fiefdoms where the actual power is not held by the police but by the gang lords. Their edicts are the laws of the street. Those streets are flooded with drugs. Is there more?"

"Yes, Boss. Third, they want to create a feeling of helplessness throughout the world by spreading uncontrollable fatal diseases, by convincing people that their religions are false, and by convincing everyone that Traction's minions are aliens from another world who have insurmountable powers to destroy every living creature unless everyone submits to their rule. What do you think, Boss?"

Murdock, pensive, sat silently, digesting the enormity of what he'd heard. *If this file is genuine,* he wondered, *why haven't they been more overtly aggressive?* Susan interrupted his thoughts and said, "If this is true, Boss, why are they so secretive about it?"

"You've read my mind again, Susan."

Susan leaned closer to him as if she were going to pass a confidence. Winking, she said, "We're a pair, Boss. We think exactly alike on most things. I guess that's what makes each of us think the other is smart. If this information is correct, Traction is a threat to the security of the United States, Boss. Do we have a duty to notify someone in the United States government? If so, can we assume that Mr. Proteus *is* part of that government and that it already knows? Or is he a Traction agent sent to mislead us into thinking that so the feds will come down on us for not reporting it?"

Murdock fiddled with his pen as he stared out the window. From experience, Susan knew not to interrupt. He'd reached a crunch where he had to place an inordinate amount of trust in Grace. He'd not met her. He couldn't be certain that she wasn't in Greta's loop. He didn't know whether that loop was sinister. Enrique trusted him completely. Neither he nor Linda knew Grace. If Murdock could handle the investigation on both sides of the Atlantic himself, Enrique would be more comfortable. *It's an option,* he thought, *but it's a less practical option and inefficient. Grace must be brought inside the loop. That needs to be arranged quickly.* Murdock put his pen down. Susan's eyes had already met his. He said, "We'll assume for now that Proteus is the government, but we have an internal company problem. I'm sure you're thinking the same thing I am. Shall we all meet at Enrique's?"

"Yes, Boss. I checked earlier. Your schedule and mine are clear for April 6. I'll shine up to Boris and get Grace into his lair on Cyprus before that date. Shall I phone Linda and see if the date is clear for Enrique and her?"

Murdock shook his head in the negative. "She may be offended if I don't do it personally."

Susan grinned.

He picked up his phone, and tapped the autodial. In seconds, Linda answered. She agreed that the idea was sound, that the meeting was necessary, and that the date would work.

After the call, Susan asked, "Will she send a bizjet here for us and another to Munich for Grace?"

Murdock was staring out the window deep in thought. He answered, "Yes. Work a schedule with Grace and with Linda's aircraft dispatcher." When he turned his head to look at Susan, she had already arisen and was on her way out the door. He laughed and shouted after her, "I don't know why I bother telling you things. You've already read my mind."

She looked back over her shoulder and quipped, "Like I always say, Boss, we're like two peas in a pod. No matter what happens, we need to protect our pod."

Murdock couldn't quarrel with that.

13

Linda lay naked on her bed in the darkness, wide awake, covers thrown off, restlessly tossing and turning. The hours had crawled by. Thankfully, dawn was near. The sheet beneath her was soaked from perspiration. She groaned. The heat of unrequited passion had for hours risen and fallen and risen again, relentlessly, incessant as the waves of the sea below. She sat up on the edge of the bed. Nights like this occurred more frequently lately. There were toys in the drawer of the side table, but her discomfort had sped an emotional mile past where they could help. Arising, she reached for her robe, put it on, tied the belt, and walked outside onto the balcony. As she stood at the railing, she savored the subtle, almost nonexistent, predawn breeze barely moving her hair.

Her body shook. She struggled to free her mind from the prison of frustration which held it tautly.

The first mellow hint of dawn dimly silhouetted the dark fringes of the tall palmettos against the eastern sky. Inhaling deeply she smelled the sweet scent of tropical flowers. Her mind floated back to yesterday morning—the beginning of the day that had fed the flames that had tormented her all night.

* * *

Yesterday morning she had awakened with an irrational premonition that something magnificent was about to happen. The morning itself had been disappointingly uneventful. When Enrique invited her to join him for lunch, she had gladly accepted. She had wanted to speak to him about the court proceedings, anyway. But that didn't happen.

She walked down a spiral staircase to the second floor and onto his veranda. She saw Enrique and another man, both already seated at the table. As she approached, both men arose. Enrique introduced Jack Hastings. Jack, who appeared to be in his late sixties or early seventies, sported a gray moustache, thick beard, and a full head of gray hair. Sharp erudite eyes gave her the impression of a man practiced in ways of the world. The quality of his royal blue golf shirt with a Sarasota Yacht Club emblem and light blue slacks with a royal blue webbed belt suggested that he was not cursed by poverty. She estimated that he stood just less than six feet. He was solidly built and in obvious good physical shape. Enrique mentioned that he'd met Jack at Hemingway's at the Beach Resort.

Jack's eyes locked on hers. He flashed a radiant smile and said buoyantly, "I'm indeed pleased to meet you, Miss DiStefano. Enrique was lauding you over cocktails last night."

That was how it had started.

Earlier that week Enrique had received an e-mail from an acquaintance who suggested that they both sail to Little Cayman Island and meet there to join the party circuit. "Jack's a sailor," Enrique pointed out. "His boat is being repaired at Sarasota. He's agreed to sail with me to Little Cayman Island. He has a friend there."

As Enrique was talking, Jack walked to the coffee urn, poured a coffee, brought it to the table, and held a chair for Linda. She nodded in appreciation and seated herself. He moved the cream and sugar close to her and then obtained two more coffees. He and Enrique then reseated themselves.

Jack smiled and said, "I understand that you're from Alberta. I've camped out in the mountains there. It would be a real challenge to find more breath-taking scenery anywhere in the world. Those were my sweet innocent years of youth when I had time for such things."

"I lived in Calgary, but I agree that the mountain scenery is spectacular."

Jack's eyes met hers again. "When Enrique described your efficiency, dedication and business acumen, I didn't picture a woman as young, vivacious and charming as you. I could add more superlatives, but I don't wish to embarrass you. You'll find that I'm slow to compliment and too old to play games, so please be assured that I'm not feeding you a line."

During lunch the three carried on a lively animated conversation. Linda noticed that Enrique was more relaxed than he had been for a long time. The stress of Ricardo's predicament had been taking a heavy toll on him. He obviously enjoyed talking to Jack. She was pleased that Jack would accompany him on the trip. Linda felt that Enrique needed to get away, and that he needed a man-friend whom he could talk to. There was nothing he could do to help Ricardo. Sailing was always a catharsis for him. Tension had prevented him from sleeping, too, but the cause of Enrique's tension was quite unlike hers. Hers could be relieved more simply, but the lack of relief was no less perplexing.

By the end of lunch, Jack's relaxed and pleasant manner had endeared himself to Linda. He was a man comfortable with who he was. She detected no pretensions. She found him charming and handsome for a man his age. She estimated that he was a bit younger than her father but not by much. When lunch had ended and Enrique had excused himself, Jack had taken Linda's hand, held it gently, and asked if she could find it in her heart to have dinner with an old man at the yacht club tonight. He seemed quite the gentleman. Besides, if he's a new friend of Enrique's, she needed to know much more about him. She accepted. He bid her farewell until the evening.

* * *

All afternoon she'd felt ill at ease. Normally she didn't accept dinner invitations from men she'd only just met. Why had she so easily caved in to Jack? *Well,* she thought, *he isn't completely strange. He and Enrique did meet over two weeks ago.* But still, there was something about him; something she couldn't put her finger on; something that stimulated an exhilaration that had started within her slowly but accelerated as the afternoon wore on.

She opened her closet door and stared blankly at her wardrobe. *He's too old to be romantically attractive to me,* she thought. *But I'm not too young to be romantically attractive to him. Too old or too young for what? I can't believe I'm I actually trying to kid myself.* She took out several dresses; held each in front of her before the mirror. *A fine, handsome man like he is probably has a wife somewhere, anyway. Of course, somewhere could be very far away. And of course, I've assumed that he's a fine man. Enrique likes him.* She wasn't a high school girl. She knew that when men of the world like Jack weren't with the woman they loved, they tried to love the woman they're with. *But do I want to be one of them? Oh, why all the fuss? He doesn't seem that type,* she thought. *At least that's what I've decided to believe.* She hung the dresses back in the closet. *He wasn't wearing a wedding ring. Besides, we're only going to dinner at the Yacht Club where everyone knows me and I always feel safe. I'm both well armed with and well experienced in all of the most diplomatic ways to say no.* She searched the closet again. *Why am I taking so much time to decide what to wear? I never do.*

She chose a knee-length black sleeveless linen dress with a deep square neck. Her pretty little black lace bra would tantalize when she leaned forward without appearing brazenly immodest. She accented the dress with a wool shawl of lime green and black paisley print. Black strappy sandals would do. Heels would be overkill—Mike the bartender would smile and raise an eyebrow.

She did her hair, dressed, and then studied herself in the mirror. Something was missing. Earrings! Opening her jewelry box, she pondered its contents. Sterling silver hoops—symbols of infinity—perfect to spice his fantasies. Her petite lime green handbag would be sufficient to contain her cell phone and other essentials. Picking up her car keys from the dresser, she headed for the elevator. The drive would take less than thirty minutes.

* * *

Linda was a member of the Yacht Club so she had arrived a half hour before their scheduled meeting. She took her usual seat at the bar. Without asking, the bartender prepared a Cosmopolitan. As he placed it before her, Jack appeared. Seating himself next to her, he leaned over, kissed her cheek, and said, "You're a woman after my own heart. I admire women who sit at the bar. It demonstrates pluckiness and confident independence. When I was a young man, women seldom did that. A woman who sat at the bar by herself was thought of as a loose woman. Attitudes are more sensible today."

Linda was both taken back and intrigued by his bold kiss. She resisted a sliver of temptation to meet bold with bold. Instead, she said, "Thank you for the peck on the cheek. I'm glad you didn't ask permission. I do enjoy daring men, provided their daring isn't inappropriate."

Jack ordered a Gray Goose martini. "I won't test your tolerance. This isn't an appropriate place. During lunch today I'm sure you noticed my interest in you. That's not a line. I'm not putting a hit on you."

"I didn't think you were. You're too much of a gentleman."

"Within reason."

Jack's drink arrived. Linda raised her glass in a toast. "Here's to an interesting evening with good company."

"By all means."

Their glasses touched and they sipped.

He looked at her intently. Answering the first unspoken question, he said, "Yes, I'm a widower. My wife, Alice, died fourteen years ago. No, I don't have a steady lady friend. Yes, I still prefer women. No, I shall never marry again. Yes, I've had countless brief but satisfying assignations and still do. No, I've never met a woman as competent, stunning, or as lovely as you. No, I'm not a toady. Yes, I know that you're no schoolgirl. You've been around. You've been hit on by lots of guys, most of them much younger and handsomer than I. No, I don't go mushy over a woman. No, I'm not mushy over you. Yes, I'm really a quite serious guy. Yes, I seriously think that you're charming. Yes, it's effortless for old men to be fascinated by the physical beauty of an alluring young woman. No, your allure isn't the only thing that fascinates me about you. What is there about you that *does* fascinate me? Everything."

He raised his glass, sipped a drink, and said, "Your turn."

Linda smiled inwardly. *He's not reticent to tell it like it is,* she thought. *He's one of the most up-front men I've ever met. He handles himself in a gentlemanly manner but at the same time invites me to test its limits—to find that borderline across which lechery begins.*

"Well, Mr. Jack, I don't have much to tell. When I graduated from law school in Alberta, my dad introduced me to his friend, Enrique. He took me on. In a few years, I arrived at where I am now. There's never been any romance between Enrique and myself. I take pleasure in my work. I feel that my duties are important. I travel a lot at my discretion. On any given day I could be in Malaysia, Latvia or anywhere. I see the world and meet influential people in every nation I visit. I live in this compound because I choose to. I'm neither married nor engaged. There's a man I'm interested in, but he works in Portland, Oregon. A jet romance leaves a lot to be desired. I'd like to be married and have children, but I'd like to keep my position here, too. Believe me; the number of available men on this island is limited indeed."

"You do have a dilemma. What's the man's name?"

"Murdock McCabe."

As she mentioned Murdock's name, an eyebrow raised ever so slightly.

"Have you met Murdock?"

He hesitated. Their eyes met. "I can't say that I have."

Linda smiled patiently. "Does that mean you haven't or that you have but can't admit it?"

Jack chuckled good naturedly. "That's a very astute question." He motioned to the bartender for two more drinks. "It means that I've met thousands of people and thousands of names ring a bell. We're not children. You understand the world of decorum."

Linda's eyes wandered to the shelves of bottles behind the bar. *And, she thought, I understand the shadow world of intrigue and concealment.* She replied, "Ah, Mr. Jack, there is more to you than first meets the eye. I shan't push it. A taste of mystery is always a delicious treat. I'll settle for the mere taste, and for the time being, savor its flavor."

The bartender brought the drinks. Linda, with a newfound lilt in her voice, thanked Jack and said, "I need to be careful not to drink too much. I seldom do, but tonight I suspect it could be foolish." She added in a mock serious tone, "Is my virtue safe?"

Jack laughed. "At my age I'm happy that you feel the need to ask. Besides, I can't imagine you doing anything that you didn't want to do. You're a clever woman. Your virtue is always as safe as you wish it to be."

She sipped her drink, studying his face, and thought. *He's a delightful man. He handles himself well with a woman—knows how to engross her.* And she was engrossed. She danced around the risk of giving false expectations, but her desire to plumb the depth of his character required taking some risks. Deciding to begin cautiously, she said, "Enrique told me that you were in the avionics business. We own a corporation that's into celestial navigation equipment, but I've never heard your name mentioned."

"And you won't. I'm retired from the United States Navy. My specialty was avionics—those boxes that tell the pilot where he is and permits him to communicate with the outside world—and more particularly, systems integration. When I was younger, I flew for the navy."

"In Vietnam?"

"And Korea. At the very end of that conflict. Are there men on this island that you date?"

She understood the risk of analyzing herself, but she asked herself why she wasn't offended by the impertinence of the question. Coming from Jack, it didn't seem impertinent. She had no answer to her question, yet. She replied, "No."

Jack placed his elbow on the bar and leaned closer to her. In a confidential tone, he asked, "When you travel the world, do you have a man in every port like we sailors do?"

"No, again. I'm afraid you've found a woman who isn't very exciting. I do enjoy having an interesting man who is good company for drinks and dinner."

"You say you're not exciting. I don't see you that way. I see a woman who is warm and outgoing, adept at conversation, not afraid to get a little buzz on, confident she can handle herself with a man, intelligent so she can keep up with any conversation, and discriminating about the company she keeps—except for tonight."

Linda laughed at the self-effacement. "If you're fishing for a compliment, you can reel it in. Tonight I'm being very discriminating or I wouldn't be here. You're not only an interesting man, but I love that tad of mystery about you. It's a bit disquieting. I like to be disquieted occasionally. Most men that I meet in a cocktail lounge are an open book. Their book has very large print, like a child's. The message doesn't require much more than animal instinct to be understood. Your book is different. Yours is complicated. I suspect it has many chapters and that the footnotes alone would be worth reading. I'll bet it's a real page turner. I'm enjoying chapter one."

"You might not like the last sentence of chapter one."

Linda smiled. "Hmmm. That remains to be seen. I hope it doesn't have the word *sex* in it."

Jack stared down into his martini, and without looking up, he said, "You are genuinely enchanting. More than that—I feel magnetism in your personality. On the surface, you're a skilled, clever business person, but I sense that below the surface is a warm passionate woman. *That* woman is without guile. Hopefully, without the intimacy of men, that woman has *some* way of gratifying herself on those nights when she's laying alone in bed in desperate passion. That's not a question. The answer is none of my business. This is the question. If this man Murdock loved you, would you give up everything to be with him? Would you be more concerned about his needs rather than your own?"

"Is that the test of love?"

"It's one of the biggies."

"Did you love your wife?"

"No, but we made a decent life together. We were patient and tolerant of one another. I had my career in the navy and she followed me where she could. She enjoyed socializing with other wives at the officers' clubs. When I was away for months at sea, I'm confident that she solved the problem of intimacy. We never discussed it, and I never wanted to know who they were. But I'm sorry. I've been intruding and I have no right."

Linda placed her hand on top his. "You're not intruding. I do appreciate the fatherly advice implicit in your questions."

Jack pulled his hand from underneath and placed it on top hers. "I may be old in years, young woman, but I'm deceptively youthful in spirit. I wouldn't want to be your father." He chuckled. "I'd rather be your lover."

She laughed good-naturedly. "Point taken."

Her eyes met his. His glistened. He inquired, "How does this Murdock McCabe feel about you?"

"Lately he greets me with warmth. I think he'd like to hug me but he's afraid to ask because of our business relationship."

"It may be his own emotions that he fears. Otherwise he wouldn't feel the need to ask."

"When we have a few cocktails together, he seems to be charmed by me a little bit. I think it's genuine."

"Charm may have degrees, but it's never false. You are by no means getting old, but you need to make a move before all desire deserts you. I've met bitter women in their forties who felt that life had passed them by. They're angry with all men. They're angry with themselves. They're angry about their anger. I can't argue with them. I can't help them, either. You're a warm, caring woman. You're intelligent and bold in your business relationships. Be reasonably bold in your personal life, too. Do something."

* * *

Dinner passed with small talk. They shared stories about the exotic places they'd visited around the world. Wine warmed the conversation. Presently Linda inquired as to whether he had children. He replied, "I have two daughters close to your age. My older, Victoria, is an architect practicing in San Francisco. My younger, Martha, is an obstetrician practicing in Kansas City. Regrettably, neither is married. I can't predict how many more years God will give me, but I'd like to live long enough to meet one of my grandchildren."

"Are there men on their horizons?"

"No. Nothing serious. They're too busy building careers and investing money. I visit them every chance I have, but I've learned not to bring up the subject of marriage. I'd be content if they had children outside of marriage. That's not too unusual these days. It's lost most of its stigma. Would you like to have children, Linda?"

"Yes. When I was a girl growing up, I dreamt of meeting Mr. Right, marrying young, and having a family. My dad, who still lives in Calgary, has no other children, so he's counting on me to produce a grandchild before he dies."

"Is his desire important to you?"

"Oh, yes. Very much so. He's a dear determined old mossback. Dad says I must have a small fortune invested by now. Besides he owns some tar sands up there in Alberta that look like they're going to pay off big time. He wants his old pal Enrique to replace me so I can come back home."

"Have you thought about that?"

Linda was growing even more comfortable with him. *Any other man I'd think was inappropriately prying, but in hours, Jack's become a trusted old friend. Talking about very personal subjects seems contentedly appropriate with Jack.* She responded, "I've mentioned my father's wishes to Enrique. His response is always the same. He raises my salary. I could retire quite comfortably today. I suggested to my dad that he move down here. He says there are more single men my age in Calgary. I pointed out to him that if the single men were my age, there might be a good reason no woman had married them. I half-seriously pointed out that one doesn't have to marry to have a baby—that there are alternatives both natural and unnatural. He responded with exhilarating language and then took another blood pressure pill. I suspect he wants a son-in-law who can chop wood."

"I think you must try some straight talk with this Murdock McCabe. I wonder if he's the fellow I met who's still in love with his dead wife. If he is, it's time for him to kick that habit. Perhaps a little kick-start from you would point him in the right direction."

* * *

At nearly 1:00 a.m., Linda had decided that the evening must end. They finished their after-dinner drinks and then walked to the parking lot together. Although the lot was lighted, her Mercedes CLK 350 convertible V6 was parked in a far corner where it was safe from parking lot damage. That corner was dark. Jack accompanied her to her car. Linda unlocked the door. It couldn't be opened because Jack was standing too close to it. As they faced each other in the darkness, he said, "You've apparently rejected men's advances all over the world. If this Murdock McCabe is the man I'm thinking of, he's a solid citizen. Is he a man your father would respect?"

"I don't know how much experience he's had chopping wood, but otherwise I'm sure he'd fit the bill."

"It looks to me like you're both dancing around; waiting for the music to stop so that you can have a serious conversation. But the CD just keeps replaying over and over again."

"I can't ask Murdock to give up his career and become a house husband. That would emasculate him and I'd lose respect. Perhaps I should test the waters—suggest that I give up my career and see if he takes the bait. But if I became a *hausfrau*, would he lose respect for me?"

There was enough light for her to see his eyes hard on hers. Whispering, he said, "Stop dancing. You know what you have to do. Veritus is at play. Advise Enrique to buy it. Appoint Murdock to the CEO position and move its headquarters from Chicago to here. Have him report directly to Enrique so you wouldn't be his supervisor."

Linda shook her head. "I couldn't do that."

"You could."

"I couldn't advise Enrique to buy Veritus just to solve a problem in my personal life. That wouldn't be a justifiable reason. Besides, no one reports directly to Enrique except me."

"A justifiable reason?"

He reached for her. She felt his powerful right arm wrap around her and pull her close, locking her into an embrace. She tried to speak an objection but his mouth enclosed hers, his tongue searching hers. Every muscle in her body went taut. Her first instinct was to resist, but her blood unexpectedly boiled with the euphoria of a delight she'd long denied herself. His hardness pressing firmly against her sent shivers throughout her body. Her arms, which had struggled to push him away, wilted. His left hand grabbed her appealing black lace bra, jerked it up to her neck, then keenly and methodically explored her. Beleaguered and bewildered, she went limp. With his right arm tightly wrapped around under her armpits, he lifted her feet off the ground. *This old man certainly hasn't lost his strength,* she thought. He pressed her against him so tightly that she gasped for breath. Deftly lowering his left hand to her knees, it wandered under her skirt and quickly upward, examining that which most explorers find most interesting. She was a big girl. This wasn't new to her. Men had done it before, but not recently. Jack's boldness both shocked and thrilled her. Before she could recover her poise, her dampness had answered his unspoken question. Giddy with surprise and perplexity, she relaxed as his fingers slipped into her, eliciting a most intimate and delicious torment. *Here is a man,* she thought, *who knows how to enjoy a woman's body, and who isn't afraid to seize the moment.* Reflexively, she raised her arms and returned his hug, eagerly pressing her lips hard against his.

Slowly, reluctantly she thought, almost ceremoniously, his left hand withdrew. Tenderly he lowered her to the ground. Relaxing his right arm, he released her and said, "As difficult as it is for me, and regardless of how much I regret it, I think we should stop. I'm truly sorry. Before you sleep tonight, remind yourself that *this* is what life is all about—genuine intimacy and love between a man and a woman. *Not* that desk in your office. *Not* that computer or that telephone. *Not* a big salary and retirement funds. *Not* my new friend, Enrique. You talk about a justifiable reason? Screw justifiable. You know what you have to do. Do it."

He'd turned and disappeared into the darkness.

As she'd turned to enter her car, his voice had come again out of the darkness and said, "If you don't do it, I'd like to see you again; alone."

* * *

As the first rays of the sun were poking over the horizon, Linda was struggling to come to terms with her body—a body that had been brought to the very edge of climax from the mere groping by an old man. Nine years had passed since a man had succeeded; and he awkwardly.

Her mind was a tangle of euphoria and self-disgust. She should have fought back. It would've been unconvincing. Her body was still reminding her how cruel his abrupt retreat had been.

Puffs of stratocumulus clouds began to catch the sun's rays.

He was right, of course, about her life. Except for cocktail hours with friends, it was all work. She could afford anything she wanted. When traveling to cities all over the world, she could afford to pay for handsome escorts, but she didn't. She craved intimacy, but gigolos weren't the answer. She needed to know. *Does Murdock love me? Do I love him? If both answers are affirmative, I must do what Jack suggested. First, I must explore my own heart.*

As she searched the horizon, she decided that Jack had never planned to go all the way. *Obviously, he does know Murdock*, she thought. *Perhaps he wanted to be a true friend to both of us and that was his way of jolting me into understanding. Nevertheless, he was hard. His embrace told me that he did feel something. He certainly wasn't uncaring. Still, it had been cruel of him to bring me almost to climax and let me crash. Did he imagine it was some act of nobility? Was that his idea of fun? Maybe he's having second thoughts now, too. I wonder if he had a sleepless night like I did. I hope so.*

A Cheshire cat smile crossed her face. She seriously doubted that the noble Jack could walk away a second time.

14

Grace stared out the window of the bizjet. Ice crystal clouds swept across the sky close above the aircraft. The morning sun set them afire. Particles of ice sparkled like millions of glittering rubies. She was looking forward to meeting Linda DiStefano, the woman who could arrange a bizjet on short notice. Tomorrow she would get her chance, but today her assignment was a man by the name of Boris Romanovsky. The aircraft began its descent. In a short time it was making an approach to the airport at Limassol. The turquoise sea below was empty except for a few fishing boats, their wakes slicing through the almost calm waters. As the pilot lowered the flaps, Grace observed the shoreline of Cyprus pass beneath, followed quickly by a cluster of white stone houses with painted light blue roofs, many with red bougainvillea climbing the walls. The pilot lowered the landing gears and gradually flared the aircraft into a nose-high attitude to bleed off speed in preparation for touch-down. A squeal of tires announced that they were on the ground. As the pilot applied reverse thrust, the aircraft slowed, turned onto a taxiway, and rolled past the administration building and toward a Range Rover parked at the far end of the general aviation ramp. As she disembarked, its driver met her at the bottom of the stairs. In minutes, they were on their way to Boris's villa.

Grace thought to herself that Greta Himmelreich had been correct. Her network at the Mädchenhaus Café had been more efficient than the Bavarian State Police, and possibly even Veritus. The word was that Weidner had used the name Ernesto Flavio to open a large account with the Eastern Mediterranean Bank on the island of Cyprus. There had been no documentation to confirm it, so Grace treated it as a rumor. Her station chief, Ernest Müller, had pointed out that that bank was part of the banking empire owned by Boris Romanovsky, the Russian émigré based in Cyprus—the same one who had made an offer to purchase Veritus. When they arrived at Boris's compound, she was met by the huge man. His green silk shirt, opened at the collar, revealed a jungle of chest hair. His head was totally bald. His eyes were commanding. His demeanor was bigger than life. She assumed this was Boris. She was correct.

Boris looked stunned. His momentary surprise switched to delight. His eyes methodically explored her well-proportioned anatomy. Obviously pleased by what he saw, a genial smile wordlessly expressed his contented approval. He reached out and enfolded her in a bear hug so tight so that upon being released, she struggled to catch her breath. He said, "Susan Ling has played naughty joke on Boris. She allowed Boris to think G. Bauer was man. Boris must thank her. She gave Boris pleasant surprise. Not only is G. Bauer woman, but most attractive woman. Boris has only known one woman more attractive."

Grace smiled coyly. "A movie star, I assume."

Boris roared with laughter. "That's delightful. Boris likes jokes. Boris likes you, but not so. Most beautiful woman is Linda DiStefano. Has Murdock or Susan introduced you to her?"

"No. In fact, I've never met Murdock or Susan. I'll meet them tomorrow on Grand Cayman Island."

"What wonderful coincidence, beautiful lady."

"What coincidence is that, handsome man?"

Boris laughed again and said, "Boris is flying in bizjet to Aruba tonight. You shall join Boris. Is more comfortable to sleep on bizjet than commercial plane. No planes to change. No airport lines. After plane leaves Boris on Aruba, it will take you to Grand Cayman—just a short hop. You will be there by 7:00 a.m."

"A bizjet is awaiting me at Limassol. Besides, travelling with such a handsome virile man like you, I couldn't trust myself to preserve my virtue. Would you protect it for me?"

Boris's laugh started as a slow roll deep down inside him and rumbled out of him, swelling to a mighty roar. He put his arm around her shoulder and said, "Only if you want me to. But so, is it not silly to waste night? Fly with Boris. But is best you tell Linda DiStefano that Boris and you wasted night; even if we decide not to waste it." He laughed heartily again. "You understand Boris's meaning. Boris knows intelligent lady does. If you have religious scruples, do not be concerned. Boris has Orthodox priests on retainer. They will pray for soul of Boris and you all night if you wish to do it. Other priests, wider awake, will give absolution in morning."

"Let me catch my breath. We've only just met. I'm not the kind of girl who does it on the first date."

As the driver garaged the Range Rover, Boris motioned her toward an opening in the tree line which revealed an asphalt pathway. They descended among thousands of red bougainvillea which met in arches overhead. A garden on both sides extended as far as Grace could see. At a lower terrace the garden changed to long grasses and blazing orange geraniums. They passed an oval reflecting pool. In its center, a fountain pulsated a single column of water, alternating from five to ten feet high. Marble colonnades and benches graced both sides. On the next lower terrace she saw another pool. Three large marble fish spewed fountains of water. The final terrace contained the villa and an Olympic size swimming pool. Beyond it a low cliff dropped off to the Mediterranean. Surrounded by the open space she saw the villa, a magnificent structure of high white stucco walls with bright orange roof tiles. They passed through an entrance governed by heavy oak double doors which were standing open. Inside was a large hall—actually a two-story arcade of white stone. They walked through it into a courtyard. Grace noticed a second-story walkway with a finely crafted wrought iron railing. Perhaps the rooms off the walkway were bedrooms.

On the first floor, beyond the arcade and open to the sky, was a bright circular courtyard. She heard the gentle trickling of water. There, in the center, she discovered a small fountain feeding a cascading stream bounded by tropical flowers. It reminded her of a creek she had seen in a meadow in Bavaria near Saint Luke's Monastery. She had been told that in that meadow and near that creek, the body of the murdered monk had been found.

Upon seating themselves at a shaded circular table, iced tropical drinks were served, quickly followed by pan-fried fish with loaves of fresh-baked breads and *Spanakopita*. Boris kept the conversation lighthearted. After lunch, Grace edged the conversation toward Herr Weidner. Boris motioned toward a door. A man entered. He was short and as bald as Boris. The man was dressed in a tan summer business suit with a bright blue and white tie. His stubby fingers held a locked file case large enough to hold only a few files.

Boris smiled and said, "Boris would like you to meet Mr. Georgiou. He is Boris's vice president in charge of large accounts. Boris gave him the information from your e-mail. He is here to see if he can help you."

Mr. Georgiou seated himself at the table.

Grace offered her hand across the table to Mr. Georgiou and said, "I'm honored to meet a vice president of such an important bank."

Both Boris and Mr. Georgiou ignored her remark.

Drawing on a gold chain that led into his pants pocket, Mr. Georgiou withdrew a key. Then, as if a formal ceremony of some significance were taking place, he unlocked the case with a flourish. Expressionless, he extracted a compact disc, nodded toward her, and somewhat reluctantly pushed the CD across the table toward her. Grace picked it up and inserted it into her laptop. Before she could open the file, Boris commanded, "Summarize what you have learned, Georgiou."

With his face still expressionless, he began, "Last year a man who identified himself as Ernesto Flavio came into my office and opened an account. The initial deposits totaled over ten million United States dollars. These deposits came by electronic transfer from more than five hundred different banks and from more than eighty nations other than the United States, of course. His account has been active. All deposits and withdrawals have been by electronic transfers. Several months after the account was opened, a man who identified himself as Josef Weidner applied for a position with the bank as an account manager. He offered adequate references and he was employed. Weidner looked familiar to me. For several weeks, I was puzzled. Then it struck me. I thought maybe he was Flavio, a man of German descent, masquerading as a Latin. Or the other way around. I asked myself if Weidner is Flavio and if he has so much money, why does he need a job at the bank? Of course, I could be mistaken, but I don't think so. I reported this to the director of the bank because he could be laundering and/or transferring drug money. The American government gets especially upset even though its citizens use most of the drugs. Of course, both Josef and Weidner are common names. I understand that the Weidner you are inquiring about worked as a gardener at a monastery. That would surprise me. I cannot imagine the Weidner that I observed doing that."

Grace said, "They could be two different people."

Mr. Giorgio continued. "But I think they are the same. The file contains confidential personnel and account information. Most of the account information was furnished by Flavio, but you will see that we've done some background checking. We also did some checking on Weidner. I've included a copy of his personnel file. He disclosed that he had a wife and daughter. The daughter's name is Gretchen. She was born in a German émigré settlement in Paraguay. They are Roman Catholic. None of our personnel have met either his wife or Gretchen. That is not unusual. That's all I have for you, Miss Bauer."

Grace said, "Thank you, Mr. Georgiou."

"Finally," he added, "you must understand, young woman, that it is illegal for me to give you these."

He arose, bowed to Boris, then bowed to Grace, and without further comment, he departed.

Grace looked at Boris. "Will he get into trouble?"

Boris sat back. He folded his hands behind his head. "Life is trouble because it's full of people. Boris can make great trouble so not many people wish to make trouble for Boris or for Boris's employees."

"May I take the CD with me?"

"Yes, but you must point out to Enrique and the lovely Linda DiStefano that Boris takes risk. Boris wants to help. They are in great danger. Ms. DiStefano must come to Boris in Aruba. Boris wishes to marry her. She doesn't believe Boris. She thinks Boris just wants to get into her panties."

"Do you?"

A broad grin crossed his face. "Of course. Boris could be more helpful to you if Boris gets in your panties, too. Come with Boris on bizjet tonight. Then Boris and Grace can do it together all night."

She dropped her shoulders as if in frustration and responded, "I'd gladly accept but I wouldn't want the bizjet now waiting for me to go back empty. Besides, I have an important meeting in the morning. I must be wide awake. You wouldn't want me to embarrass myself before Señor Perez-Krieger and Ms. DiStefano. If I looked like I hadn't slept all night, she might think that you had been a naughty boy and I had been a naughty girl. Women like her don't marry naughty boys."

Boris grinned. "Perhaps this afternoon Boris and Grace can do it just once."

"Perhaps I can return to this beautiful villa sometime soon when I don't have any pressing obligations and when Miss DiStefano won't know that you and I are being naughty. We could keep it as our own little secret."

Boris laughed a long and jovial laugh with an undercurrent of frustration. "But so. Boris understands. Boris will arrange better to know G. Bauer someday." He chuckled again. "Boris guarantees that today your virtue will be safe. Boris does not need to rape women. Do you like money?"

That made Grace feel uncomfortable. She asked with a genuine hint of indignation, "Whatever do you mean?"

"Not what kind lady thinks. Boris would never make whore out of nice lady. Boris will pay ten thousand U.S. dollars under table if you convince Miss DiStefano she will be safer with Boris at villa on Aruba, and another one-hundred thousand if you can get Murdock McCabe to marry you.

You are beautiful woman. He is handsome man. That shouldn't be too difficult."

Grace was shocked by the offer, and she asked, "Why would you pay such a large amount of money for that?"

"He must not marry Linda DiStefano."

15

Grand Cayman Island
Thursday, April 6, 5:38 a.m.

Murdock, already wide awake, got out of bed, put on his robe, walked out onto the first floor balcony, seated himself on a lounge chair, and tipped it back. The air was cool. Nothing was stirring. He heard only the sound of waves of a nearly calm sea rippling upon the shore. Not even the night birds were singing. He enjoyed arising early. If he missed the crack of dawn, he felt that he'd missed the best part of the day. It was the time when he recreated himself.

Linda's room was above on the third floor. He wondered if she were awake, too.

A sliver of light appeared on the eastern horizon. As an hour passed, the sky brightened. The bases of a few stratocumulus clouds turned fuchsia; then brightened into a brilliant red. An hour after nature's morning show had begun, the sun appeared. Sunbeams skipped off the sea, giving it a silver sheen. Its intensity hurt Murdock's eyes. He arose and returned inside his room. After he found his sunglasses, he picked up his travel bag and extracted the briefing Susan had prepared for the meeting and laid it and the sunglasses on an end table. He stretched, showered, shaved, brushed his teeth, picked up the brief, returned to the lounge chair on the balcony, and reviewed Susan's notes. He, Susan and Grace were scheduled to join Enrique and Linda for breakfast on the second floor balcony at 7:30 a.m.

Susan had accompanied him on the flight from Portland which had arrived late last night. Linda had met them at the airport and driven them to Enrique's compound. Briefly they had joined Linda in her apartment for a nightcap. The conversation between Linda and Susan had been animated and gracious, but Murdock detected awkwardness. At his suggestion, they had retired early.

Murdock looked at his watch. It was 6:45 a.m. Grace's plane had been scheduled to land at 6:00. The car that had been awaiting her at the airport should be pulling in the drive soon if the flight had been on time. He expected that it would be. Linda's crews were usually punctual.

Murdock estimated the conference should take no more than two hours. Enrique planned to leave before noon to join someone named Jack at the yacht club. Jack, whoever he was, would sail with him to Little Cayman Island. Murdock felt a vague discomfort with that arrangement—probably because Jack seemed to appear out of nowhere. Nevertheless, last night Linda indicated that she felt comfortable with him. Linda was a good judge of character.

The purpose of this morning's meeting was to introduce Enrique to Susan and Grace who are the Veritus staff assigned to Ricardo's case. Although Enrique wasn't critical of Veritus, he was disturbed by the lack of progress. Murdock hoped that his meeting would build his confidence.

Another reason for the meeting was that neither he nor Susan had met Grace. That was important, too. The investigation depended to a large extent on Grace's skills and her trustworthiness. The time that Murdock could devote was limited. He was, after all, Veritus's station manager at Portland. He had administrative duties. Some he could delegate to Susan, but it wasn't fair to overload her plate. She had been devoting so much time to her job that he was concerned about her marriage. She never complained. His gut feeling told him that her husband couldn't be too happy. A few months ago she'd mentioned that they'd casually talked about the possibility of divorce. He wondered what a free Susan would be like, although he couldn't imagine a woman freer than Susan already was.

Starting up the broad circular stairway to the second floor, he looked forward to seeing Linda. The bright side of Ricardo's misfortune was that it had brought them together more frequently. The more contact they had, the more impressed he was. Although he'd talked to her several times by phone, he hadn't seen her for almost a month. He'd missed seeing her. *Am I'm starting to need her? Have I given her enough encouragement so that she isn't dating anyone else? She never mentions a name. Before this investigation is over, I'll talk to her about us. But what woman could tolerate a man who's still in love with his deceased wife? Marrying her wouldn't be fair. I'll love Karen until the day I die. I reminisce about our good times. How can any woman compete with a ghost? Linda would feel like a second class Karen substitute.* Strangely, in spite of the logic and his maturity, he had a boyish fear of rejection. *But I have missed Linda.*

A man couldn't ask for more in a woman. She's incredibly eye-catching, competent, and personable. But I think she wants a family. She should marry someone soon. I'd be a poor investment. I shouldn't lead her on.

Grace had already arrived. As Murdock walked onto the balcony, Susan introduced her to Murdock and to Enrique who had followed him close behind. The impression that Grace made upon Murdock was immediate and striking. He observed a remarkably appealing young woman; as attractive as Karen had been and even more attractive than Rudi had described. Her body language signaled a woman who was controlled and dignified. As Murdock and she shook hands, her smile suggested a subsuming sexuality that said *convince me that I'm interested.* His eyes read Susan's. Susan was a practical woman. Hers said that Grace's smile was a priceless investigative asset. When Grace's eyes met his, hers were speculative and questioning. *What question are they asking?* he wondered. None of this was lost on Linda.

Over breakfast, Linda sized up Grace. Grace subtly and masterfully used make-up to attract men's attention without their being consciously aware of it. She's no eighth grade schoolgirl. She uses her sexuality deftly and there's a strong and unambiguous professionalism in her every move.

Although the small talk at the table was lively, Linda ignored the jungle of voices and turned her focus to Susan Ling. She was petite, physically fragile in appearance, and dressed femininely, but Linda sensed a street-wise toughness about her. *She's her own person*, Linda thought. *She enjoys men but she certainly doesn't need a keeper.*

Linda watched Murdock with the two women. He, Susan and Grace shared a professional jargon and a bond of professional intimacy that blocked out all who were not investigators. Although she could never enter their world, she decided that she definitely wanted Murdock within hers. Seeing him with those women made her realize how much she had come to desire him. She realized that even if Murdock invited her into his bed, she could not be more committed to him than she was now. Of course, she wasn't certain she wanted to be invited without the benefit of marriage— or at least not before they'd set a date. As she half-listened to Murdock's report—a report with which she was already familiar—her mind wandered. Each birthday made it less likely she would ever be a mother. Linda wanted to be a mother. If she couldn't get the right man committed, would a time come when *that* need would overpower everything else? Would she succumb to an impersonal modern solution, the Petri dish and the sperm of a faceless father? And if Traction got its way, what kind of a world would her children grow up into? *And,* she wondered, *why didn't Karen have children? Does Murdock have a problem? Could a week-end marriage ever work? Even a week-end only marriage would be better than none,* she thought. *Would it?* Her emotions were confused. She wished she could talk to Jack.

Murdock focused his attention on Grace. He observed that she was able to remain appealing and thoughtful when she challenged a person's remark. If an answer was not forthcoming or responsive, she good-naturedly rephrased the question. However, she did expect an answer. If she didn't get it, the follow-up question had a sharper edge to it. He was pleased that her emotions were expertly masked.

Grace studied Murdock's face. She found it handsome and authoritative. There was a solid sexuality to it. She admired those qualities. She liked Murdock. Grace missed neither his quick glances at Linda and Susan nor their quick glances at each another. *There's a hell of a lot going on other than the published agenda,* she thought.

Murdock's eyes met Enrique's as he said, "She met with Boris yesterday at his villa on Cyprus. Grace, please share with us what you learned."

"Thank you, Mr. McCabe." Her eyes turned toward Enrique. "His villa on Cyprus is huge. It's surrounded by at least a square mile of property. I believe that you, Señor Perez-Krieger, and Mr. McCabe have been there, so I'll spare detail. I found that the man was warm, hospitable, and diplomatic. With perfectly charming diplomacy he made it clear that his helpfulness might be more forthcoming if I'd take my clothes off. I suggested that, while stripping might be exhilarating, it violated company policy and I would never do that."

Enrique chuckled.

Susan injected, "Did you leave the door open—to a possible violation of company policy?"

Grace smiled with faux coyness. "Naturally. That's the way to manage men like Boris. Never send a man to do a woman's job."

"How did he handle the rejection?" Susan asked.

"He accepts adversity with composure and patience, probably because to him all sexual rejections are temporary. If he struck out six or seven times, he'd still come up to bat. The game's the thing. If he sees me again, he'll put the make on me again, but I'm just a plaything. He ardently wants to marry you, Ms. DiStefano. Until he does, none of the rest of us is safe."

Linda injected, "I doubt that the rest of you would be safe if I *did* marry him."

Grace quipped, "I'm sure. If you couldn't be with him every hour, he'd have to find another woman so that he could stay in shape. Of course, to his credit, he'd pay the priests the next morning to pray for her soul and his."

Everyone chuckled. Enrique laughed out loud. Murdock could see that he enjoyed this woman. Hopefully that would relieve some of his anxiety.

Grace continued, "Boris is like a little boy who likes to play with girls."

Linda wondered whether that would also describe Jack, but she decided definitely not. He wasn't a little boy. He was a real man. In a few hours he'd meet Enrique at the yacht club and they would sail together to Little Cayman. She wondered whether Jack would mention her name. She heard Grace adding, "No matter how many women Boris has, I doubt that he can ever get enough. He definitely wants Miss DiStefano to birth his children."

The others turned to Linda, grinning. She laughed uncomfortably.

Grace continued with a recitation of the information about Ernesto Flavio. She handed a copy of the CD to Murdock who passed it to Susan. Both knew the information normally could not have been obtained legally without a court order but said nothing. With so little evidence of probable cause, a court order would have been impossible. That fact moved Murdock to ask, "How do you bottom-line Boris? Do you think he's friend or foe?"

Grace pondered the question before she answered. "At first, I passed Boris off as a buffoon and a dirty old man who preferred women without their underwear. Nothing convinced me that I was wrong about the second, but the buffoon part, I'm not so sure. I need to look deeper."

"Do you think you can do that without shedding your underwear?" Susan asked with faux naïveté.

Again they all laughed.

"I certainly hope so. I'm afraid he'd steal it for a souvenir and then where would I be? I realize that the buffoonery could be an intentional charade hiding a sinister subplot, but I suspect that's simply Boris being Boris. Make no mistake; the man's no fool. In the former Soviet Union, he started as a tractor repairman on a collective farm. Soon after, he joined the Communist Party, and became a minor official in the Ministry of Agriculture. He worked his way up to become an assistant to a third deputy minister. The third minister was a single woman so Boris screwed her nightly. He brags that that earned him a three-room apartment with private heating and an automobile that usually ran. He studied how people worked the system and then worked it himself. As he put it, that eventually meant screwing the first deputy minister, even though she was very ugly—so ugly her husband only screwed his pretty mistress at the Polish embassy."

Enrique cocked his head to one side and smiled at her candor. Linda watched Murdock who was expressionless. Susan grinned.

"When the Soviet Union disintegrated, he became a capitalist. He, like others, bought government assets for a song. Within a year he was a multi-millionaire. He wisely cleared out of Russia. He runs his banking and business empire from Cyprus and Aruba. Boris boasts that now he can afford to screw only pretty girls. He quickly assured me that I was the prettiest woman he'd ever met with the exception of Ms. DiStefano. He promised to double my salary if I'd come work for his private KGB.

She turned toward Murdock. "So, bottom line, Mr. McCabe, if you look beyond his frenetic optimism, I think you'll find a boyish insecurity paved over by illusions of permanence. He mistrusts private confidences, but it seemed like he wanted to share one with me and then thought better of it. It hadn't been overt enough for me to coax him. Besides, we'd just met. I marvel that he feels the need to share anything confidential with me, a stranger."

Murdock asked, "Do you have a gut feeling as to what it might be?"

"No, sir."

"What's your assessment of the personnel file his man Georgio gave you?"

"The personnel file *looks* legit, but Boris could be playing a game, too. I regret that I still have more questions than answers. Are Flavio and Weidner the same person? If they are, is that person on Boris's side or against him? Or is he using Boris's bank because they won't ask questions? Is Boris on our side? Is this Flavio file reliable or is it peppered with funny facts designed to mislead? Again, Mr. McCabe, my gut reaction is that he's playing us straight. I wouldn't go to the bank with it. That's about all, Mr. McCabe."

Murdock restrained an impulse to clap. Rudi had been right. Grace is one sharp lady. If she made mistakes, hers would be errors of judgment; not of carelessness. She's wary, skeptical, and has few illusions about people. He asked her, "Did you have any indication as to whether Boris is connected to Traction? Do they run money through his banks?"

Grace responded, "Have we decided that Traction exists?"

Murdock replied, "As a defense mechanism, let's assume that for the sake of argument."

"That wasn't part of my assignment, Mr. McCabe, so I wasn't looking for it. I saw no overt evidence of it, however. Perhaps Flavio is a Traction agent and the accounts are theirs."

"You interviewed a neighbor of the Weidners in Landshut, Bavaria. Please share what you learned with Señor Perez-Krieger."

"She turned to him and said, "May I call you Enrique like everyone else?"

A broad smile crossed Enrique's face. "Of course. I shall call you Grace."

"Good. What specifically should I cover, Mr. McCabe?"

"Did this neighbor give a description of the alleged victim's mother?"

A wry smile crossed Grace's face. "I had been talking to him in the doorway. When I asked for a description, he gave a naughty wink, stepped outside, and closed the door so his wife couldn't hear." She checked her notes. "He said and I quote, 'She was blonde, about five-foot-ten, neatly packaged with a pleasant face and a slim figure. Her lips gleamed red without lipstick. Her blue eyes were both shy and erotic like yours.' I asked him whether they were eyes that might even turn a married man's head. 'Ja,' he replied with enthusiasm. 'Like yours.'"

Murdock shook his head. "That's a perfect description of Diana."

"Who is Diana?" Grace asked.

"She's a woman I'd met at the Zugspitze over a year ago. I suspect she's wrapped up in Traction. She could be the head of Traction."

Grace's eyes studied his. "This is an interesting coincidence. Brother Martin mentioned that you'd met a woman in Oregon who called herself Selene. Do you suspect they're one and the same?"

"Selene *did* remind me of Diana. She wasn't blonde and her eyes were green, but it's not difficult to change those things. If I imagined the eyes as blue, they were a dead ringer for Diana. They could have been twin sisters, I suppose. If we could determine whether they're one and the same, I think we'd be a long way down the road to getting to the bottom of our investigation."

Grace smiled toward Enrique. "Be assured that I'll work on that assiduously."

Murdock turned toward Enrique. "Grace is working part-time on a graduate degree. As part of that, she's preparing a thesis about the classical Greek and Roman gods and goddesses. Some people believe that super aliens came to earth thousands of years ago and were mistaken for gods and goddesses. They also believe that the Greek and Roman myths were based upon them. Susan has explored the idea that Traction—"

"If it exists," Grace injected, grinning.

Murdock, somewhat irritated but having to admit she was correct, replied, "Yes. Traction may have borrowed concepts from Greek and

Roman mythology in their attempt to project an otherworldly image. Susan has done some research on the subject. What do you have, Susan?"

Susan nodded and turned toward Enrique. "First, let me reiterate that the idea came from Grace. I've used her uncompleted thesis as a jumping-off point. I've found something called the Gospel of the Witches. According to its mythology, the goddess Diana was created before the universe came into being. She existed in chaos. Within her were the seeds of everything else that was to come. She is the mother goddess who is still worshipped today by women who follow a religion known as Dianic Wicca. In Roman mythology she was the virgin goddess of the hunt and a symbol of chastity. Slaves and people of the lower classes held her in great reverence. Her temples were a place of refuge for slaves. I'm told that in Freemasonry today, Diana symbolizes sensibility and imagination. I don't have that confirmed as yet. She's a trinity who has two other names, Selene, who replaced Luna as goddess of the moon, and Hecate, a goddess of the underworld. Diana's temple at Ephesus was one of the seven wonders of the ancient world."

Murdock turned to Enrique and said, "You may recall that a year ago we were investigating the disappearance of one of your managers, Paul Harmon. At that time, I ran into that rather mysterious woman who used the name Selene. She had an assistant named Verbius."

Susan said, "In pre-Roman Italy, Diana was associated with Dianus, the god of nature who had power over herds, woodlands, and fertility. Dianus is also called Verbius. At that time, Diana was worshipped at a sacred grove in the woods around Lake Nemi, Italy. Dianus, or Verbius, was the king who guarded the woods. To her modern worshipers, it doesn't seem to matter whether she actually exists. She's embedded in a belief system. If you believe she exists, and if your decisions and actions are based on that belief, then she *does* exist. You've created her.

"To bottom line this, Traction, if it exists, is playing on these ancient mythologies. They project the idea that the classical gods and goddesses were real; that they visited earth thousands of years ago, and that they've returned to claim the planet. Back around 1937, an actor by the name of Orson Wells did a radio show in which he played a newscaster. Broadcasting live, he vividly described an invasion of earth by Martians. It was so real that some people in fear took their own lives. If one radio show can have that impact, imagine what impact Traction could have if they convinced governments and their citizens that they are deities with extraordinary powers. That's about it, Boss."

"Thank you, Susan." Murdock turned toward Enrique and added, "Susan and I recently met a man who claims to be an agent of the U.S.

government. He calls himself Mr. Proteus. In the classical mythology, Proteus was a minor god of the sea; an assistant to Poseidon. Proteus was indecisive. He often changed his mind. This man appears to know more about Traction than we do. He suggests that our government is considering the possibility that this woman, Diana, et cetera, is actually from another world. We're cautious about taking him too seriously, but we're not ignoring him either. If Traction is a significant organization and its goal is to upset the social and economic order, why does it keep such a low profile? Troublemakers feed on publicity. The answer may be that they want to frighten the politicians without giving them an excuse to use force against them. If the public never hears of Traction, the politicos won't want to look foolish attacking shadows."

Enrique's eyes met Murdock's. He asked, "*Does* Traction exist other than as a small group of drug traffickers who scare their mules into obedience?"

"I suspect that they do."

No one spoke. Murdock eventually broke the silence and gave Enrique guarded assurance that Veritus would unmask the Weidners.

Enrique arose, and said, "If that's all, I'm going to head for the yacht club. I need to get away for a few days. Linda can reach me on the satellite phone, and in an emergency she can have a chopper pick me up. It sounds like you folks are doing a magnificent job. I'm confident that you'll expose the Weidner's sham soon. I thank you all. I'm especially pleased to meet you, Susan, and you, Grace. Murdock has chosen a first-rate team, as always. Now, if you'll excuse me, I'll be off."

* * *

Susan and Grace remained on the balcony after the others had left. They stood by the railing looking out to sea. The shadow of the building sheltered them from the noonday sun. Off shore, near the horizon, a catamaran was sailing eastward over the aquamarine waters of the Caribbean. A breeze rustled the palms of the short palmettos in the planters on either side of them.

Susan had watched Murdock's warm reaction to Grace. She'd also noticed Linda's noticing the same thing. Susan felt comforted by Murdock's attachment to Karen's memory. It protected him from imprudent liaisons with women. That mattered to her. Her husband understood her need for sexual freedom, but sometimes she wished he didn't. Murdock didn't. She thought her husband's tolerance might be wearing thin. Sex was such a useful tool. She'd hate to lose it.

After several minutes of silence, Susan turned to Grace and said, "For what it's worth, I like you, Grace. You strike me as someone I'd enjoy as a personal friend. I'm confident that we'll work well together. Maybe this summer I can weasel my way over to Munich and we can hit the bars."

"That sounds great, Susan. I know all the best. I feel like I've known you for some time. I mentioned in my last e-mail to you that my source for the Flavio lead was a woman by the name of Greta Himmelreich. She owns a lesbian bar in downtown Munich. You may wonder whether I'm one of them. I'm not. At least not yet. I may never be. Is that important to you?"

Susan shook her head. "Not as a friend. As an investigator, if you can at least fake it, it's important because it sounds like Greta can open doors. You come across as straight, so you can open that door, too. You opened it a crack with Boris. That was smart. You were right about never sending a man to do a woman's job. I'm working on Mr. Proteus."

"He sounds dangerous, Susan. I think you should only meet him if you have Murdock or another male agent along."

Susan was pleased that Grace cared. "Thank you for your concern, Grace. By the way, I've downloaded several files to your computer in Munich that you need to digest. They include some weird stuff I got from Mr. Proteus and some even more weird stuff that I got from a couple astrophysicists. From now on, whatever intelligence any of us gets, we must immediately share with each other."

Linda came up behind them. As they turned toward her, Linda's eyes fixed on Susan. She said, "Ladies, lunch is ready."

* * *

That evening Linda sat alone in her apartment. Murdock and Susan had flown off to Portland; Grace to Munich. Enrique and Jack had sailed off to Little Cayman Island.

She felt empty. Maybe everyone was just too busy. Maybe time was just too short. Maybe Susan had insisted on too much of Murdock's time. Maybe he'd devoted too much time getting acquainted with Grace. Maybe Murdock was too preoccupied with everything but her. *I'm being selfish,* she thought. *He'll phone me in the morning. We'll debrief each other on today's meeting. He'll apologize for not spending more time with me. It'll be sincere, polite, and businesslike. He seems shy only when he talks to me as a woman. I manage Enrique's businesses skillfully. I only wish I could manage my personal life with equal skill.*

She wished Jack were still in room 624 at Hemingway's Hotel rather than at sea. She needed to talk to him. He would listen. She also knew that if she had been able to reach him, he would not have misinterpreted what she really wanted.

16

Portland, Oregon
Friday, April 7, 4:34 p.m.

Late afternoon on a rainy day in Portland can be depressing. Susan, however, was seldom depressed. She usually set her mind on something that she could look forward to. Today was no exception. She and Murdock were meeting Dr. West for dinner at one of her favorite restaurants. Not only did she enjoy the food, she also enjoyed its picture window. On a clear day, it had a glorious view of Mount Hood. The rain was forecasted to stop soon, followed by sunshine before nightfall. Maybe they'd get lucky.

She was looking forward to seeing Dr. West again, too. Her discussion at Cascadia College with him and Dr. Amy Gallagher had been both stimulating and helpful. He had phoned and asked her out for dinner. When she checked with Murdock, he wanted to meet Dr. West. It became a business dinner. Dr. West had regretfully acquiesced. She had mixed emotions.

Murdock was looking forward to the dinner, too. He needed to slow down and relax after their whirlwind one day trip to Grand Cayman. Susan had amazingly adjusted. He had particularly enjoyed meeting Grace. He had found her to be an intriguing woman. She had presented herself to the client confidently. He felt comfortable that her investigative skills were finely honed. She understood the real world and had few illusions about people. In that regard, she was another Linda; or Susan. He would be pleased to have Grace working for him permanently.

Susan's phone rang. She immediately recognized the voice. It was Mr. Proteus. She needed to get the measure of the man; convinced as she was that he was important to the outcome of Ricardo's case. His tone was edged with brashness as he said, "Ah, Susan, my dear, we must meet again soon. You would like that, wouldn't you?"

She liked brashness in a man. It gave her an opportunity to exploit his macho fantasies. "Of course, Mr. Proteus. You are a man of mystery. Mysterious men are exhilarating. I like daring men who don't hesitate to reach for and take what they want from a woman."

"It pleases me that I excite you, my dear Susan. How am I mysterious? I investigate in much the same way that you do. I'm sure we both have sources of information that the other doesn't have. When we know one another better, if you take my meaning, I'm sure we can share some of them. Your husband need never know. There's nothing mysterious about that. I am a simple public servant who appreciates lovely women."

"I doubt that there's anything simple about you, Mr. Proteus. How may I help you today?"

"I am on Little Cayman Island. I wish to meet with Mr. McCabe. I heard that he might be on Grand Cayman tomorrow. I will fly over there if he is."

"He is not. What are you doing on Little Cayman?"

"I'm meeting with a man by the name of Boris Romanovsky. He claims to know you. I've learned that he is a connoisseur of lovely women, too. Do you know him well?"

"Not *that* well, if I take your meaning. Why are you meeting with him?"

"I met Romanovsky at a bankers' conference in London a few weeks ago. We had cocktails and spent a few hours together. He mentioned that he was interested in buying a boat. I have some expertise. He asked me to advise him. We met here to examine a Johnson with a raised pilot house. It's a fiberglass with twin diesels. The seller was asking 4.5 mil. I thought the seller was hungry. I advised him to offer 3.8 mil. He took it. Now Boris really likes me. We're about to celebrate the purchase and discuss the hotel he's proposing to build. Perhaps he owes me a favor and will permit a small investor like me to participate. Anyway, I'm sorry McCabe is not in the Caymans."

Susan pushed, "What drew you to a conference of bankers in London?"

"I was an observer for the controller of the currency in D.C."

"Was that for real?"

"An intelligent worldly woman like yourself must realize that there are some questions that worldly men are not permitted to answer."

"I do, and an intelligent worldly man like you must realize that worldly women whose craving for answers goes unfulfilled become parsimonious with their worldly womanly assets. Murdock's in his office. Would you like to speak to him?"

There was a long silence, and then Proteus said, "No, thank you. I have documents that I'd like his reaction to. I can't go into them with you. We'll find another time. I'll be in Portland again soon. I took your meaning. Perhaps by then I can be more open because I'll want to see you, too, of course, and your worldly womanly assets. I must go now. Boris wants to buy me a drink and I want to let him."

After he signed off, Susan sat back and tried to cut through the bullshit. She thought, *I need to know if that London conference actually took place and who the registrants were. How did he acquire expertise in such expensive boats? What really interests Mr. Proteus on Little Cayman Island? What documents does he possess that would interest Murdock? Why would he value Murdock's opinion?* She had no answers. She might have to play her ace of trump.

Arising, she walked into Murdock's office. Seating herself next to his desk, she said, "Mr. Proteus phoned. He said he was on Little Cayman. He hoped you were on the big island because he wanted to meet with you to review some papers. It sounded like bird dodo. I suspect the purpose of his call was to make sure you weren't anywhere in the Cayman Islands. I don't know why, and I could be wrong."

"That's strange."

"Yes, Boss, and when it comes to him, I don't like strange one bit."

* * *

The restaurant was crowded. Murdock and Susan checked their raincoats. The maitre d' recognized Susan and motioned for them to follow. Murdock asked her, "Is there any restaurant in town where the maitre d' doesn't know you?"

"Only the second rate ones, Boss. I *do* entertain our best customers."

They stopped at the table Susan thought was the best in the house, situated next to the large picture window. The weather had cleared. Mount Hood caught the setting sun; its snowcapped top was resplendent in all its glory. Susan nodded approval and slipped the guy a twenty.

As they were about to seat themselves, Dr. West appeared. Susan introduced him to Murdock. After the common pleasantries, they seated themselves as the cocktail waitress appeared. They ordered drinks.

Dr. West turned to Murdock. "Professor Gallagher—I believe you know her on a first name basis—Amy told me that you were acquainted with her putative father, Professor Klugman. Did you know him well?"

"I had contact with him for only a few weeks before he was murdered. We met at the bar in the Zugspitze Hof in the Bavarian Alps. You might say we became bar buddies. I was investigating the murder of the monk, Brother Stephen. Professor Klugman and I met for cocktail hour almost every day. I got to know the man fairly well. I'd never met a philosopher before. He was especially intriguing because he also had a degree in astrophysics. He shared with me his thoughts on superstring theory. I was fascinated."

"What fascinated you?"

"The Professor, as I called him, described the universe as an enchanting melody written by an anonymous composer and played on an instrument of vibrating superstrings. That metaphor stuck with me. As a man, he was amiable, humble, and good company. He appeared to be scrupulously knowledgeable in his fields. In that short time, I developed a great admiration for him. His death was a tragedy. The world can use more men like him."

Dr. West nodded in agreement. "From what Amy's told me, his was a rich intellectual life ardently lived. His writings disclosed a keen insight into the implications of making contact with extraterrestrial intelligence. He was, as you said, a philosopher. His work with Brother Stephen was unique. As you two know, Stephen had owned a computer chip manufacturing lab in Wilsonville, Oregon. When he joined this unusual monastery, he dedicated his efforts to developing a chip that would, as he put it, cut between the chaotic radio frequency signals that pellet us from outer space, and within what we call the *white noise* he hoped to discern intelligence. Stephen's monograph, the one that Susan delivered to us a couple weeks ago, suggests that he succeeded. He detected a message from somewhere."

Susan injected, "What did it say?"

"I can't say. We're in a dilemma. If it *is* intelligent, its language seems to be illogical—so much so that we can't be certain that it's intelligent. Stephen and the Professor thought it was. We need to identify a linguist who can be trusted. We don't want this information to become public or even available to other scientists until we're sure of what we have. Professor Gallagher trusts you two. I understand it was you, Murdock, who found her father's killer."

The waitress delivered the cocktails.

Murdock sipped his and said, "The Veritus *team*, working with the Bavarian State Police, found the killer. I wonder if Stephen shared the problem with Brother Gustav. It would seem strange if he didn't. He's a linguist. I'd be even more surprised if Brother Martin didn't show the monograph to him before he sent it to us to deliver to Amy. It's the middle of the night there. I'll phone Brother Martin in the morning and get back to you. Perhaps Gustav didn't feel qualified to do the job. You could have him farm it out to a colleague without disclosing its source."

Dr. West nodded in agreement. "When you talk to him, ask him if he knew a linguist by the name of Claude Mitchell. Claude was an archeologist by profession with post graduate training in linguistics. He discovered some writings on a high plateau in Peru. He published a paper in which he reported that the symbols and their arrangements were totally illogical. He speculated that they could have been made by visitors from outer space thousands of years ago. His paper was taken with a grain of salt in the archeological community. He disappeared five or six years ago. To my knowledge, no one has seen or heard from him since. Brother Gustav might want to review his paper. I can fax it to him."

Murdock asked, "Have you or Amy compared the writings on the Peruvian plateau with the unsolvable language from Brother Stephen's monograph?"

"No."

"We need someone to do that. I wonder if that idea occurred to Brother Gustav."

"If he ever saw it," Susan added. "Do you or Amy have an opinion as to whether the communication, if that's what it was, came from somewhere within or without our universe?"

"No."

Murdock said, "Susan tells me that some cosmologists believe there may be innumerable universes. Ours, by chance, permits life."

"Yes. That's the multiverse theory."

Murdock pressed. "During one of my discussions with Professor Klugman, he mentioned the anthropic principle. He explained that this principle suggests that the constants in our universe were fine tuned to permit life and intelligence to exist. That would suggest that a greater intelligence existed that did the fine tuning."

Dr. West nodded. "That's called the Strong Anthropic Principle."

Murdock studied his eyes. "Is there a Weak Anthropic Principle?"

"Yes. It agrees that the constants must have been fine tuned, but it leaves open the question of whom or what tuned them. To bottom line it, some scientists believe the fine tuning is evidence of a cosmic creator; others believe it is evidence of the multiverse in which ours, by the law of averages, turned out to support life. All this reminds me of Einstein's famous question, 'When God created the universe, did he have a choice?'"

Susan asked, "Do you think we'll learn the answer during our lifetime?"

"Maybe in the next decade. Maybe never. If God exists, he may not want us to know how he did it. He might fear that in our hands that knowledge might be too dangerous."

Murdock said, "You also mentioned to Susan that it might be easier for someone to come to earth from another universe than from another solar system in our own universe. Why is that?"

"Are you familiar with the term black holes?"

"Yes. I've heard it."

Susan added, "That's the limit of my knowledge, too."

"Perhaps this Green Lady, if she's genuine, could add to our knowledge. She certainly does seem to have unnatural powers."

Amy smiled. "Perhaps."

The waitress interrupted to take their food order. When she had finished, Dr. West said, "For a rocket to escape earth's gravity, it must achieve 25,000 miles per hour. That's called its 'escape velocity.' Out in space there are objects with gravity so strong that their escape velocity is equal to the speed of light. In theory, nothing can move faster than light, so even light can't get out of them. We call them black holes. The point at which its gravity becomes that strong is called the 'event horizon.' Some cosmologists speculate that if one could pass through a black hole, it would open the door to another universe. As Carl Sagan put it, 'Black holes may be entrances to wonderlands, but are there Alices or white rabbits?'"

"So it *is* possible?" Murdock and Susan asked in unison.

"Not without difficulty. If our Green Lady succeeded, she is indeed a great wonderment. If you or I approached a black hole, we believe the event horizon would rip apart all the atoms in our body. Admittedly, there's some evidence that our belief is wrong. There are many more questions than answers, and the theories become stranger and stranger—some bordering on absolute weirdness."

Murdock's eyes met his. "Our Green Lady is bordering on weird. What if there was technology that could reconstitute those ripped atoms on the other side?"

Dr. West chuckled. "Like a Mr. Scott to beam you up?"

"Yes."

"Then you'd meet the Alices and the white rabbits if they exist. But there might be a better way. Some astrophysicists believe there are wormholes inside the black holes. A wormhole might be a gateway to another universe or another dimension, whichever way you choose to phrase it. Their theories disagree as to whether a person could pass through a wormhole without destabilizing it. If it were destabilized, the person would die in the attempt. If not, the person might be sucked into the wormhole and spit out in another universe or dimension."

"So," Murdock added, "the opposite would also be true. A traveler from another universe could have been spit into ours."

"Yes, and if you find him, I'd sure like to meet him."

"Or her," Murdock added. "If a woman came from another universe, could she have skin that could become iridescent or change color at will?"

"Anything is possible. Of course, the physical laws of her universe would need to be very close to ours or she would be destroyed upon arrival."

Susan asked, "Might such a person possess powers that would seem bizarre to us, like the ability to walk on air?"

Dr. West shook his head. "I'm afraid that we've strayed from the discipline of science into the undisciplined area of mere speculation. I'd rather leave that to the science fiction writers."

Susan said, "Some of the science fiction I read as a girl is no longer fiction."

Murdock's cell phone rang indicating a call-back message. He excused himself.

Dr. West's eyes feasted on Susan. She felt his hand move up her leg—a maneuver not unfamiliar. He said, "Would you like to join me in my hotel room for a little private after-dinner drink?"

Susan smiled. "You'd be disappointed. It's a bad time of month."

His hand stopped. "That's disingenuous. Surely you could have given me a truthful reason. Is it race?"

She took his hand and moved it to where the proof was. A look of humiliation crossed his face. He said, "I'm sorry for questioning your veracity. That was unforgivable."

Susan smiled warmly and said, "You're forgiven. Maybe another time." She thought, *a girl has to be prepared with the necessary props. That ruse never fails.*

* * *

Boris's phone call was taken by Jeannie, the night agent at the office. She had recorded it, got through to Murdock, and now played it as Murdock listened.

"*Mr. McCabe, Boris has tried to reach Linda DiStefano but she has not returned Boris's calls. Pay attention to what Boris says. Boris is on Little Cayman Island. Gretchen Weidner has arrived. She stays in cottage near shore. On Monday she flies to Grand Cayman for deposition, but Boris fears ace of trump will be played tonight. Linda must warn Perez-Krieger. You are warned. Boris is friend. Goodbye.*"

When he returned to the table, Dr. West was in the men's room. He set the phone to replay and handed it to Susan. She listened. Murdock's eyes met Susan's questioning eyes. There was a momentary bewildered silence. Boris wasn't a man prone to practical jokes. He had sources of information which had proven amazingly accurate.

When Dr. West returned, Murdock said, "Something urgent has come up. I've enjoyed your company and your stimulating conversation, but I must regretfully excuse myself. Susan will remain and take care of the check. I hope we can meet again, soon."

Murdock's eyes met Susan's, and he said, "I must reach Linda immediately. There's nothing you need to do before morning. Relax. Enjoy the evening. I'll see you then."

As Murdock stepped out the door, he stopped. A flash of sheer focus struck him. His heart sank. He raised his eyes to the stars and thought, *Oh, my god; we've been blindsided and suckered. Why couldn't we see it coming?*

He pushed the speed dial for Linda.

17

A gentle offshore evening breeze drifted over the marina as Enrique, Jack and the crew secured the boat. The crew headed ashore to do whatever sailors can find to do when they come into a port saturated with female tourists from everywhere.

Enrique was uneasy. Linda hadn't checked with him. It wasn't like her. Normally she would have phoned before she left her office. Maybe there was nothing of importance that needed his attention. If that were true, she would have phoned to tell him that. He hesitated to phone her. It was after work hours. He didn't want to disturb her, but that had never seemed to bother her. He took out the satellite phone and speed dialed her number. Nothing happened. He tried again. Still nothing. He turned to Jack and said, "I think this thing's gone bad on me."

Jack took the phone. From a miniature tool kit in his sport coat pocket, he extracted a tiny Phillips screwdriver. Removing the back panel, he examined it. His eyes raised to meet Enrique's. He said, "It hasn't gone bad. It's been sabotaged by someone who knew what he was doing. Someone didn't want Linda to get through to you. Take mine."

Enrique accepted it gratefully and punched in Linda's numbers. She answered almost immediately and said, "I'm glad you called. I've been trying to reach you."

"Someone sabotaged my phone. Why were you trying to reach me?"

"I missed a call from Boris Romanovsky, probably while I was in the shower. I didn't immediately check my messages. Boris contacted Murdock's office after hours. His night clerk recorded it. I'm going to give you the recording and then we'll talk."

125

Enrique listened intently. Jack excused himself and walked onto the dock. When the message was complete, Enrique asked, "What do you think Boris has up his sleeve?"

"Maybe nothing. Remember that Grace Bower had the impression that he's playing us straight. I still don't know what to make of him. It might not hurt to move on immediately."

"I've lost my crew."

There was a long silence. Linda finally broke it.

"Be very cautious, Enrique."

"I'm in the marina. Every dock is full. There'll be people partying all evening. I'll join them, of course. When I turn in, I'll double lock the cabin. No one's likely to try something with this many people around. Besides, I've got a Smith and Wesson 38 hidden away. There's security at the gate. Enjoy your evening, Linda. I'll be all right."

After the call was terminated, Jack came back on board. Seeing the look of consternation on Enrique's face, he asked, "Bad news?"

"Someone's sent me a threatening message. It may be a prank."

Jack shook his head. "Was the sabotage of your phone a prank, too? Don't stay here alone. Stick with me tonight. I have a girlfriend who is the night manager of an inexpensive hotel. If anyone were looking for you, they'd never think to look there. You need to relax. Denise will register you under a fake name. She could find company for you too, if that's what you want. You'd be safer there."

Enrique hesitated. He really didn't know Jack that well. He wanted to trust him, but dare he? Had it been too much of a coincidence that Jack happened to appear at the yacht club when he did? Jack was waiting for him to speak. He said, "Why don't you stay with me on the boat? I've got anything you want to drink. You know boaters. I'm sure that everyone tied up here has worked themselves into a party mode."

Jack ran his hand over his beard and smiled. "I'm sure your friends are good folks, but I need to see Denise, and I suspect that Denise needs to see me."

Enrique winked knowingly. "I understand."

"I'm not sure you do. You'd enjoy meeting her. Denise has a PhD in forensic psychology. She retired from teaching at Iowa State eighteen months ago, and as she puts it, moved to paradise. She's working as a night clerk at the Lost Flamingo Hotel to learn the business. The hotel is on the market. She and I are attempting to negotiate a leveraged buy-out. I think we'll succeed."

Enrique's face reddened. "That was clumsy of me. I'm sorry that I put it in a sexual context."

"Oh, it *does* have a sexual context. I'm a great believer in sexual contexts."

Enrique smiled. "Is she your *numero uno*?"

"No. I have relationships—liaisons—whatever you want to call them, with a number of women. Like Denise, each is cultured and has an intriguing personality. We share sex with mutual respect and esteem because we're genuine friends. In some cases, the husband is my friend, too."

Enrique's eyes widened. "Some have husbands? I mean—do the husbands know?"

"One does. I had to consult him first because he's my best friend."

"Does his wife know that her husband knows?"

"*I* didn't tell her."

Enrique shook his head. "Is her husband still your best friend?"

Jack grinned. "Oh, yes. In fact, he admits that I'm a connoisseur of fine women."

After a period of silence, during which Enrique decided to try to hold Jack in close tonight, he said, "Please give Denise my best regards. I *would* like to meet her. You're good company, Jack. I'd miss you. Please come back and party with us. Bring Denise if she can get away."

"Can't do. Thanks for the lift."

Jack picked up his backpack and headed ashore.

* * *

There were two other boats tied to the same pier as his. One was out of Galveston; the other out of Sarasota. They'd both arrived earlier that day—two couples on the first; three on the other. Between them there was an oversupply of food and booze. Enrique contributed a couple bottles of good malt Scotch. He put his wounded satellite phone out of his mind. He'd use a shore phone in the morning and reassure Linda that everything was okay. Tonight he needed to relax and enjoy himself.

The partying for the others had started at mid-afternoon. By midnight, everyone was spent. Enrique wasn't disappointed. He was ready to be alone. Seating himself in a lounge chair on deck, he poured a nightcap of Grand Marnier. It was a moonless night. Not one cloud was in sight. The sky was alive with innumerable stars. He lay back and allowed himself to be captivated by the wonder of it. But something that Jack had said troubled him. He knew that Jack and Linda had had dinner together a few nights ago. He sensed that Jack had been fascinated by her. That puzzled him. *A good part of my success has relied on my being a good judge of men. Jack's no romantic. I imagine his relationships with women are shallow, uncomplicated, and noncommittal. I wonder how many copies of Denise there are. Jack probably has a woman in every port. The age difference between him and Linda has to be* thirty *years or more.*

One thing about Jack disturbed Enrique. He thought, *if Jack's taken an interest in her personal life, that very well might be to my disadvantage. I really didn't appreciate his telling me that my expectations of Linda prevent her from having a personal life. That's none of his business. That's strictly between Linda and me. I encourage her to take time off. She's never discussed marriage and children. It would be presumptuous of me to inquire about such personal things.* He knew that his old friend, her father, certainly wanted her to find a husband and produce grandchildren. *But she's a strong woman. She knows her mind. If she felt her career was interfering with her personal desires, she would've said something. But would she? For the last several years, she's taken on so much responsibility and been so completely dedicated to my interests that maybe she didn't have time to think about herself. Maybe Jack's right. I've ignored her needs and taken her for granted. Eligible men on Grand Cayman Island who might be attractive to a woman of Linda's caliber are as scarce as hen's teeth.*

He hardly knew Jack but the man had become his conscience. Perhaps he should turn back to Grand Cayman and have a heart to heart with Linda. With e-mail and cell phones, she could work from any remote location—someplace where she could have a more rewarding social life. He knew they would both miss the personal contact—the decisions made over a casual lunch or relaxing over an evening cocktail. *But, if I have Jack sized up correctly, he sees women as convenient sex objects. Why is he so interested in the happiness of Linda DiStefano whom he has known for so short a time?* When he finished his nightcap, he descended the stairway into the cabin, locking the door behind him. That was unusual. *Maybe tonight I just need to feel more secure.*

* * *

The Lost Flamingo Hotel was one of the smaller and older properties on Little Cayman Island. Its seventy-six rooms on two levels had been refurbished last year. Laid out in a U-shape, they surrounded three sides of a courtyard festooned with palms and myriads of brightly colored tropical flowers. In the center was a forty-foot diameter decorative pool stocked with multicolored tropical fish. Planters intelligently placed added lush tropical vegetation and created an image of a tropical rain forest. The clerk's desk was open-air and faced the courtyard. Denise Perkins was on duty.

Denise looked at her watch. It was nearly 1:30 a.m. Jack had dropped his backpack behind the desk at 10:30. He had business to attend to and said he'd be back shortly after midnight. She had to work until 6:00 a.m. so that wasn't critical, but she worried. She knew in general what he wanted from her professionally, but she didn't understand why he always had to be so mysterious as to the specifics. What was his real interest in her, personally? Younger women are often the target of single men his age. She assumed he was single. Every time he arrived, he had some purpose in addition to her. It was always secret. The idea of cloak and dagger adventure made Jack more interesting. But why would a man almost seventy be chasing around the world on secret business? Last week she'd put the question to him directly, "What business could you possibly have on Little Cayman Island at nighttime?"

Jack had run his hand over his beard, grinned, and said, "If I gave you a true answer, it would just sound like a mixture of abstraction and fantasy."

More verbal diarrhea, she'd thought. But she loved him, and she knew that was the best answer she was going to get. He'd get back soon. They'd sneak a drink at the counter, as usual. He'd flop into bed, as usual, and sleep until she flopped in with him after 6:00 a.m., as usual. They'd do it, and then they'd lay there and talk for hours about meaningless things. But tonight he'd looked solemn; his body language stiff. She hoped he didn't have another woman on the island. It's a small community. It would embarrass her. She was sure of that.

A man had shown up around 5:00 p.m. looking for him. The guy was over six-foot tall, broad shoulders, and had a full head of sandy hair. He'd driven up in a rented van. She'd noticed that he wore a tool belt. She'd seen tools like his recently—the man who'd installed their new telephone system. But this guy didn't look like a telephone installer. He spoke grammatically flawless Midwestern American English. Denise knew. She'd taught psychology at Iowa State before she'd retired and found this job in paradise. She'd first met Jack in Iowa two years ago.

Denise felt sure he had other women, although he'd never said so. She didn't need to feel special. He'd never told her that she was. She knew that Jack lived in a netherworld that she could never share. However, whenever he was near, he came to her—as far as she knew, that is. She felt free. In between his visits, she'd have dalliances from time to time with men who were nothing. Jack would never marry her, but she hoped that he would never stop coming, either.

At 4:47 a.m., Jack exited a van and ran up to the desk. His clothes were soiled with wet beach sand; his eyes hard; his body language tense. "Christ," he exclaimed, "Murphy's goddamn law." He threw his arm around her and gave her an extra tight hug. "I'm truly sorry, Denise, honey, but I can't stay. I'll be back in a few days."

Without another word he retrieved his backpack from behind the desk, ran back to the van and climbed in. It was driven by a man with broad shoulders and sandy hair. Without headlights they disappeared into the night.

"Christ," she said out loud to herself. "Jack's the most thrilling man I've ever known."

18

After Murdock left Susan and Dr. West, and after he had relayed Boris's message to Linda, he drove to the Veritus office. It was dark except for one cubical. That was Jeannie's. She handled after-hours communications. Murdock made his presence known, went into his office, and turned on the desk lamp. The Perez-Krieger CD was on his desk. He inserted it into his laptop and carefully reviewed Susan's research, Grace's daily reports, and his own notes. What had he missed? Finally, weary from lack of sleep, he put the file aside, laid on the couch, and slept fitfully for nearly two hours. When he awoke, he sat silently in the dark. He had an uncomfortable feeling of foreboding. During his twelve years in the FBI, he'd been involved in several investigations where false leads had been explored—where erroneous assumptions had wasted precious time by leading him down wrong-way streets. *Misdirection,* he thought, *is a curse that comes with the territory.* He felt cursed.

His three years at the University of Michigan Law School had taught him to think outside the envelope. He'd learned that lawyers weren't trained to memorize law. They were trained to advocate positions—whichever position served their client. If they hoped to do that astutely, they must be prepared to argue the opponent's side equally well; in other words, they must anticipate. He prided himself in his ability to anticipate. It made him a better investigator. Failure to anticipate is the cardinal sin. Its punishment is being blindsided. Had he committed the cardinal sin?

His college years had been filled with the comfortable certainties of youth. He was certain that he knew right from wrong; that gray scales of doubt were for lesser beings. He was sure of Karen's love and his undying

131

love for her; that they would have happy children, spend the rest of their contented lives together, gently fade into old age, and be separated only by death. Those certainties died a cruel death. He had been robbed of Karen, and robbed of the children they would have had. She had been murdered because of her skill in cryptology; because she was on the verge of breaking a code which Murdock now attributes to Traction. He was convinced that, unwittingly, she had been about to expose how Traction's tentacles had reached into the United States Government—even into the FBI. Yes, he believed that Traction existed, and he was its embittered and frustrated enemy.

He arose from the couch, turned on the overhead lights, went into his private washroom, and splashed cold water on his face. Upon reseating himself at his desk and opening the Perez-Krieger file again, Jeannie entered his office. She said, "Mr. McCabe, we've received an e-mail from the Veritus office in Asunción, Paraguay. This one is from the station chief and addressed directly to you."

He thanked her and read the message.

> *"Greetings, Murdock. We're closing our file in the matter of Gretchen Weidner. As we mentioned to you previously, there is no public record of her birth in the small village where she is supposed to have been born. That's not unusual. Births there are seldom recorded in public records here. Normally a baptismal record would be found at the parish church. Unfortunately or conveniently as I mentioned before, the records of the parish church for the two-year window in which she would have been born have been destroyed by fire. That's not unusual, especially among German émigrés who wish to cover their tracks. We have tracked the parish priest who would have performed the baptism, if there had been one. He has retired. He has also come into good fortune. Someone has paid his airfare for a pilgrimage to Rome. He, or someone using his name, flew to Rome three days ago. The pilgrimage appears to be of indefinite length. There is no return ticket. Perhaps you should have the Veritus office in Rome take over. However, from our experience in Paraguay, it would be well for you to consider*

*the potential impact of such a choice. If the man
who flew to Rome is in fact the priest, and if the
supposed birth and baptism are nefarious, then
your inquiry in Rome might become the priest's
death warrant. Of course, if you do find him, you
may win our client's appreciation. How important
is winning?"*

He glanced at his watch. It indicted 3:30 a.m. Oregon was on Pacific Daylight Time. The Cayman Islands were on Eastern Standard Time, so Linda was four hours later. He debated whether to phone her. He had nothing to report other than the feeling of foreboding he'd expressed to her last night.

His phone rang. It was Linda. He felt calmed at the sound of her voice. Without small talk she said, "The 7:00 a.m. radio news reported that Gretchen has been murdered in a cabin Josef Weidner had rented on Little Cayman Island. The commentator said that a next door neighbor reported hearing a gun shot. The neighbor opened his door and saw a man running from the cabin. The cabin door was open. He ran into it and discovered her body. A police officer reported that the cabin was located among the tall pines close to the marina. I have Enrique on the ship-to-shore. Do you have a recommendation?"

"Yes. I suggest that Enrique remain at the marina until noon so it doesn't appear that he's running away. After noon, he should set sail back to Grand Cayman."

There was a silence, followed by Linda saying, "He's agreed to do that."

"Ask him whether the friend he was supposed to meet there has shown up."

Pause. "Not yet," she replied.

"Please immediately send us a copy of his friend's e-mail that set up the meeting. Ask Enrique if he's ever had reason to distrust this friend."

Pause. "He says no. They've met at Little Cayman several times before. Enrique says he's just opened the panel in the cabin of the boat where he hides his Smith & Wesson .38. It's missing."

"Is it registered with the Cayman government?"

Pause. "Yes."

"That changes things. I recommend that Enrique report the theft to the police immediately, as well as the sabotage of the phone. He should tell the police that I suggested that they check his hands for black powder residue. Its absence would suggest that he hadn't fired a gun. I suspect that

Enrique is about to be trashed by media. You may wish to contact your publicity agency and have it put a professional spokesman on the scene as soon as possible. Decline interviews. What happened to Enrique's new friend, Jack?"

"He went ashore shortly after they arrived. He has a girlfriend who is the night manager at a small hotel."

"Do you know the name of the hotel or the girlfriend?"

Pause. "Enrique doesn't remember the name of the hotel; only the girlfriend. Her name is Denise."

"Okay, Linda. Thank you. We have a whole new ballgame. Where does that leave Ricardo?"

"Without the complaining witness and without any deposition, the matter of Her Majesty the Queen versus Ricardo Perez-Krieger will be dismissed. He'll go free."

* * *

Susan arrived shortly after 6:00 with a bag of Egg Mc Muffins; two for each of them. Murdock hadn't had dinner last night. His appetite was ravenous. As they polished off the breakfast, he brought her up to speed and then said, "We need three things quickly, Susan. First, we need to know whether the e-mail that brought Enrique to Little Cayman actually came from his friend; and if not, from whom did it come? Second, we need to identify and locate a woman named Denise who is the night manager of some hotel on Little Cayman. Third, we need to know everything we can find on Jack Hastings who claims he was in the avionics business."

"And who just happened to show up at Hemmingway's at just the right time. Okay, Boss. The e-mail shouldn't take long. My good ole spy program will run it down. I'll obtain the phone numbers of all the hotels on Little Cayman. Tonight I'll start phoning, beginning with the cheapest, and ask for the night manager. Yesterday I anticipated that we might need to know more about Jack Hastings so I went after it. So far I've come up dry. I'll contact my man at FBI Washington who does little favors for me."

"I don't want you to—"

"Boss, I never do anything that I don't need to or don't want to do. We need info on this Jack guy. I can't find it through customary channels. Our client may be charged with murder. I'll pull out the stops. Please don't give me a second thought."

Susan arose and headed for her office.

Murdock sat back in his chair and closed his eyes, fighting back sleep. Collecting his thoughts, he admired Linda's cool-headed handling of the situation. *A lesser person might have become unhinged. Her plate was full. Her level-headedness is one of the best things Enrique has going for him.* The Veritus team was a close second. Murdock's admiration of her went beyond her professionalism. *I feel like I felt when I first met Karen. Am I falling in love?*

He didn't answer the question. Instead he fell into a deep sleep.

* * *

It was nearly 10:00 a.m. when Susan awakened him and reported that the e-mail had originated from a hotel Internet connection in Bismarck, North Dakota. Enrique's friend lives in Grosse Pointe, Michigan. If he doesn't show up on Little Cayman, Veritus's Detroit office will track him down.

* * *

The cafeteria on the main floor of their office building was closed on Saturday, so Murdock and Susan drove to Multnomah Village for lunch. Susan had read the Internet edition of the Cayman newspaper. During the drive of less than ten minutes, Susan brought Murdock up to speed.

"Josef Weidner had been interviewed by a columnist. He claimed that Gretchen and her mother had been hiding in a secluded villa in Tuscany. While there, Gretchen had been threatened several times by phone. She had told her father that the caller's voice was always the same—a man who spoke English with a Spanish accent. Weidner volunteered that the neighbor's description of the man running from the cottage could fit Enrique. Enrique's boat was less than a half mile away at the marina. The police estimated the time of Gretchen's death to be approximately 4:00 a.m. The columnist reported that Josef Weidner, that morning, had flown into the Little Cayman airport by charter aircraft from Jamaica and had arrived at 6:30 a.m. He thought that his wife was staying with Gretchen at the cabin, but he hasn't been able to find her. The neighbor indicated that no one was in the cabin when he discovered the body, and that he hadn't seen another woman there earlier. Weidner was demanding that the Justice of the Peace issue a warrant for Enrique's arrest.

Murdock and Susan stopped at a Mexican restaurant. Both ordered Margaritas. Trying to relax but not succeeding, they both wondered why they hadn't seen it coming. Neither believed that Enrique did it; nor did they believe that he'd contracted to have it done.

Susan said, "It looks like Jack is our prime suspect."

"Yes, it does, but I'm leery of jumping to that assumption."

She agreed.

"Well, Susan, you always anticipate my thoughts. What have you already done?"

"I have you booked on tomorrow's 7:20 Southwest flight to Tampa. Make sure you have your passport. There you'll catch a Cayman Airways flight to Grand Cayman and change to another Cayman Airways flight to Little Cayman. You'll show up as a tourist. Make certain you dress like one—sort of casual; maybe a little sloppy. Sometime ago you mentioned that you and Karen were into scuba diving. The Cayman Islands are one of the prime scuba diving centers of the world. I recommend that you take your equipment with you. I've made reservations for you at the Lost Flamingo Hotel. Denise Perkins is the night manager. I told the woman at reservations that you're a freelance writer of romantic short stories. She feigned a sultry voice and wondered if you'd like to do some research. I asked her if Denise still worked there. She does, of course. Wednesday is her day off. Single mature women are often flattered by the attention of younger men. Now it's your turn to give your all for the cause, Boss."

19

Grand Cayman Island
Wednesday, April 12, 1:12 p.m.

Linda DiStefano, seated behind her desk, felt decidedly uncomfortable. The police had executed a search warrant on Enrique's boat and found a pistol. It wasn't Enrique's missing pistol, but it was the same caliber as the murder weapon. More than uncomfortable, she felt irritated. Enrique was a suspect in the investigation of Gretchen's murder. At that very moment the news media were trashing him worldwide with all the ugly sensationalism they're capable of spinning. Regardless of the final outcome, Enrique would be convicted in the minds of a large segment of the public. She was powerless to prevent it. He'd had the opportunity, weapon, and motive. She might even be powerless to prevent a jury from convicting him.

She was uneasy about her position, too. If Enrique went to prison, his sister Estrelita would most likely take over the business. *She was appropriately named,* Linda thought. *She's a small star compared to Enrique who's a superstar. Working for her would be difficult. She's been jealous of me for years. She thinks that she deserved my position. She's told Enrique so. Estrelita is a procrastinator. She doesn't have the cerebral fiber to make the really hard-ass decisions when they're necessary. Indecisiveness or just wrong-headed choices can cost billions. Estrelita is as poor a listener as Enrique is a good listener. With Estrelita in charge, Enrique's carefully crafted financial empire would tumble down like a house of cards. I don't want to be at the bottom of the pile when the dust settles.*

I need a plan, she thought. *First, I must prepare a defense for Enrique in the court proceedings and push Veritus to put some weapons in my arsenal. Second, I must convince Enrique that even though blood is thicker than water, he must hold off Estrelita as long as possible.* She paused, staring blankly out the window. *Maybe things will look better tomorrow. Of course, tomorrow never comes. It's always today.* She smiled, remembering that Boris Romanovsky had said, "Tomorrow will come, gorgeous lady. Boris will make it come and you will recognize it when it happens."

Today she didn't think of herself as a gorgeous lady, but she was tempted to give Boris Romanovsky a call. Grace had thought him sincere. But what could he do? Could he bring Gretchen back to life? Could he make the gun go away? He had made an attractive job offer, but she didn't need the money. For the present she tried to put him out of her mind. *Why did I think of him in the first place?*

She composed an e-mail to all the investors in the Plato Fund, assuring them that Enrique was framed, and that the truth would come out. She knew it was of dubious value. Boris was right when he'd said, "Investors in his Plato Fund will get goosey just like you are goosey about Boris." She didn't think "goosey" best described her sentiment about him. "Bewildered" might be more appropriate.

What would she do with her life if she left here? She could practice law here in the Cayman Islands or in Alberta. She'd be starting at the bottom. She could write the bar exam in Florida and maybe find a position with a top firm in Miami specializing in international law. There were a lot of CEOs out there who would give their eye-teeth for her, to use her in the same capacity that Enrique did. Did she really want that, again? She really could marry Boris. *Good grief,* she thought. *Am I losing my mind? Maybe it is time to think about marriage, though. Boris would set me up in the reinsurance business. I know the drill. When Enrique's case is finished, maybe I should just have some fun.* She stared blankly at a historical sea chart, artfully framed, and hanging on the wall. *Producing children for Boris isn't my idea of fun, but my father is aging. He's looking forward to grandchildren. He mentions it diplomatically almost every time we talk. If I could find time in my schedule for children, Murdock McCabe is the only man I'd consider. I definitely wouldn't mind producing children for him. That's one thing Karen never did.* She was convinced that Murdock would make a devoted father.

Linda pushed back from her desk, stepped out onto the balcony, and glanced down at the disturbed waters of the Caribbean Sea. A storm moving in from the east was producing whitecaps. Down the beach children were building a sand castle. She could hear their laughter. She shook her head. *If you take away this well-equipped office; the luxurious apartment for which I pay no rent; the luxury car I can easily afford; the professional respect I receive from many of the wealthiest entrepreneurs in the world; the CEOs of subsidiary corporations who report directly to me; the bizjets at my command to fly me anywhere in the world that I deem expedient; and if you take all that away, who am I?* She wasn't at all certain that she knew.

The phone rang, jolting her out of her reverie. She turned away from the outside world, returned to her desk, and answered it. It was Murdock. He was calling from Little Cayman Island.

"I'm glad you called," she said. "About an hour ago I talked to the detective chief inspector. The police executed a search warrant on Enrique's boat and found a pistol. It's the same caliber as the murder weapon. It's not Enrique's missing pistol."

"Where did they find it?"

"It was concealed in the engine compartment of his boat. I talked to the attorney general this morning."

"Who is the attorney general?"

"His name is Robert Grayson. He's new. He hasn't met Enrique. The man is from Yorkshire so he's not wrapped up in local politics. He was chosen to handle the case personally, which I think is good. He's not difficult to talk to."

"Is he sharp enough to consider that the pistol was probably planted? If it's the murder weapon, a man as intelligent as Enrique, if he were guilty, would have tossed the pistol in the sea somewhere between Little Cayman and Grand Cayman."

"I discussed that with him. He acknowledged that the naïve location of the hiding place is some evidence to suggest that it was planted. He questions who might have had the motive to do that. He also suggested that it's some evidence that Enrique is shrewd enough that he set it up to look like a plant. He also admits that a man in Enrique's position would be more likely to hire a hit man rather than do it himself, although anger can motivate even wise men to do foolish things."

"He has an open mind. That's a break."

"Yes. We appeared before the Summary Court. He and I stipulated that Enrique will be under house arrest while the investigation is pending. We posted a million dollar bond to guarantee that he won't leave the island. The Court is holding his passport. Grayson admits that his evidence thus far is circumstantial, but it's rather strong circumstantial. When it comes to discovering who might have planted the pistol, the police may be out of their depth. Grayson will give us some time to find the answer. How much time? He didn't say."

"What will happen to the weapon?"

"The government has a contract with the FBI lab in Washington. A police officer will personally deliver it there so as not to break the chain of evidence. Their forensic lab will determine whether it's the murder weapon. It probably is. How is the investigation going?"

"Those Traction people do a masterful job of covering their tracks. The most positive thing I can say is we've been taught one more thing about Traction. Menace is their formula for power. They're willing to perform acts of outrageous moral irresponsibility, like murdering Gretchen, to boost this menace."

"What can be done to stop them?"

"There are few effective deterrents to real evil or to real evildoers. They need to be crushed. I've mentioned Mr. Proteus. He claims to be investigating them. Hopefully, he and the U.S. government are up to the task. That assumes, of course, that he is who he says he is. Susan hasn't been able to confirm that, yet. In the meantime, unfortunately, Enrique makes a perfect target. He's respected worldwide as a wealthy businessman and as a philanthropist. Traction will manage the media, which isn't difficult. I suspect that they'll paint Enrique's philanthropy as a masquerade designed to hide sinister undercurrents. The public will question the motives of all philanthropists. Every philanthropist will fear Traction's menacing presence because it has the power to put an evil spin on all philanthropy. Every gift will carry a shadow. That ubiquitous shadow will have a chilling effect on all giving and create ambivalence to charity. If they dry up charity, they choke the life from the institutions that benefit. Chaos will result. Enrique is their opening gambit."

After a long pause, Linda said, "I know you're doing your best, Murdock, but time is short."

"Be assured, Linda, that I'm using every resource available. Is there anything else?"

"Yes. One thing more. I'm going to say it and hang up because I don't want an awkward impetuous answer. I've fallen in love with you, Murdock McCabe. You'd better make up your mind whether you love me."

Click.

20

Murdock was glad to hear the click. His feelings were too complicated. Making a choice would involve a mixture of reasoning and emotion. His logic told him to work out some arrangement with Linda so their careers wouldn't conflict and marriage would make sense. But his emotions carried too much baggage. Admitting to himself that he loved her seemed disloyal to the memory of Karen. During their entire marriage he had never given a single thought to being married to anyone else. He had his perfect wife. His love had been reciprocated. Before his mother's death, she and his father had discussed the idea of his remarriage after her death. She didn't expect him to live alone. But Karen had died so unexpectedly that they had never discussed it. Not only had she died unexpectedly, but the dreadful circumstances of her death still disturbed him. In the confused crossfire of a botched raid to free her, Karen was struck in the head by a bullet and died. Ballistics showed that the fatal shot had been fired by an FBI agent. Months later, Murdock learned that that agent was a traitor. Traction had ordered her execution. Shortly afterward, he resigned from the FBI and took the position at Veritus.

He imagined that Karen wouldn't want him to live alone, either, but he knew that that wasn't really the problem. He was saddened for Linda's sake that he couldn't come to terms with Karen's death. *I've handled every other emotional shock in my life. I've been decisive and resilient. Why is this memory so consuming and so devastating? Why did Linda choose to face the issue now? How can she possibly compete with Karen until I shake off this gloom?* There were no obvious answers—at least none that he could see.

Three days ago he had checked in at the Lost Flamingo Hotel. Since his arrival, he'd spent each day scuba diving. He was good at it, so he fit in with a group from Indianapolis who were staying at the Grand Turtle Inn, an upscale venue. Yesterday morning he had taken a cab to the cabin where the murder had taken place. Upon exiting the cab he saw a man sitting on a lawn chair in the side yard of the house next door. Murdock waved to him. The guy waved back so Murdock walked over to him. Murdock said, "Good morning. My name is Murdock. I hope I'm not interrupting anything."

The man looked up at him, mildly curious, and replied, "I'm Bud O'Hara. There's not much to interrupt. What can I do for you?"

"This morning I was diving off shore with a group. You probably saw us."

"Yeah. I saw a bunch on a boat that was flying one of those scuba divers' flags."

"Well, one of the people on the boat pointed to that cabin and said that that's where the woman was murdered. Is that the cabin?"

"It sure is. I own it."

Murdock smiled and said, "Let me shake your hand. I remember seeing your picture in the newspaper. I bet it's been flashed all over the world. That gunshot made you famous. The paper said it awoke you at 4:00 a.m. and that you saw someone running from the cabin."

The man offered his hand, shook, and said, "I sure as hell did. I got up quick. You never hear gunshots around here. We don't have much excitement. Once in awhile some diver drowns, but that's not too exciting. I used to work as a cabbie. Sometimes I got some interesting customers, but I'm too old and cranky to drive now. That damn gunshot has made my life interesting again. You're the eighth person who's stopped here today already. My wife ran off with a guy from the big island so I get a little lonely. Grab that chair. Sit down. Want a beer?"

"Yeah, thanks. Let me pay you. You can't afford to give a beer to everyone who stops."

"I sure can. I make those bastards from the newspapers and TV pay me both interview and photo fees. I can afford lots of beers, but this is the first I've handed out today. I like you."

He went into the house to get the beer. Murdock observed that the cabin was set far back from the road, behind a wooded area of tall pines, and not far from the shore of the Caribbean. The bottom branches of the tall pines were high off the ground, but the numerous huge trunks limited the view. If he had planned the murder, he would come by boat and approach the cabin from the water without being detected. If he used a silencer on the gun, he could have retreated safely by the same route. Someone wanted the shot to be heard and wanted to be seen leaving. And this someone who ran from the scene approximated Enrique's height and build.

Bud came out with a cold one, popped the cap, and handed it to Murdock. He didn't offer a glass. Murdock thanked him, took a swig from the bottle, and said, "I bet you must have known her pretty well—the young woman who was murdered."

"No. I rented that cabin for a year to a guy from Clearwater, Florida. He paid in advance in cash, which is unusual as hell, so I didn't overcharge him too much. He wasn't much good at bargaining. He probably has more money than he knows what to do with."

"He must really like the place. Does he spend much time here?"

"No. He lets friends stay there. I've only seen him twice. It's vacant most of the time."

"What's his name?"

"You wouldn't know him. I never saw the girl until the day before she was killed. I talked to her a few times. She seemed real nice. She was educated—seemed like one of those artistic people I'd met in my cab. Her mother came with her from Italy, but they sounded like Germans. The mother was a real looker—the most beautiful blue eyes I've ever seen and perfect knockers, if you take my meaning."

"I know what you mean. Did you give the mother a beer or two?"

"No. She was a looker, but a cold fish. You know—the kind of broad who acts like she's too good for you. I waved to her but she sort of looked the other way. I'd liked to take her over my knee, pulled down her panties, and give her a few good whacks on the ass. That might've taught her a little humility. It might have landed me in jail for a few days, but it'd been worth it."

"Yeah, but if you'd been in jail you wouldn't be world famous now. The newspaper said that after you saw the guy running, you ran into the cabin and found the dead girl. Was her mother still sleeping?"

"Naw. She wasn't there. I don't think I saw her at all after one o'clock that afternoon. I was sitting out here most of the day reading. If she was there, I'd a seen her."

"When you walked in, could she have been hiding in another room?"

After a long pause he said, "That's possible, I suppose."

"What do you like to read?"

"I like American Western novels and travel magazines. Maybe one or two down-and-dirty girlie magazines, if you take my meaning."

"I sure do. You certainly know your beer. This is my favorite. It must be expensive, coming all the way from Canada."

"Yeah, it is."

"Well, I sure appreciate it. Could I take a few pictures of the room where you found her? I could try to sell them to the media and split with you."

"Naw. Them yellow ribbons says that the RCIP don't want no one to go in there. We could get arrested. Them damn cops make it rough for anyone who gets out of line. The Magistrate on this island ain't too friendly, either. He remembers my name. He told me last week not to suck on any beer bottles again unless I'm in my own yard."

"It sounds like you're a mighty important witness for the RCIP. Can you identify the guy who ran out of there?"

"Hell, no. I'd spent the evening next door with the Widow Thomas. We sucked too many beers. Didn't get in bed until nearly 2:00 a.m. At least not in *my* bed, if you take my meaning. Besides, it's dark at 4:00 a.m. Them cops keep bugging me. I keep telling them that if the damn government had put a lamppost by my curb like they should've, I could've seen his face. After two six-packs and two hours sleep, all I could tell them was that he wasn't awfully tall—maybe average build. I couldn't even make out hair color, but the cops just keep coming at me. From the way they ask questions, I think the bastards are trying to plant answers in my head. I learned at lot about cops when I was a cabbie. They're trying to tell me what to say."

"I wouldn't let them, if I were you."

"I won't."

"Good for you. I've got to meet my diving friends. It was great talking to you, Bud. You're an interesting man. Thanks again for the beer."

"You're okay, Murdock. Nice meeting you. Come back again."

Murdock offered his hand and said, "Thanks. I may just do that."

* * *

The last two nights he'd joined the Indianapolis crowd for cocktails and dinner at the Grand Turtle Inn. Afterward, both nights, he'd spent having a late coffee with Denise Perkins, the night manager of the Lost Flamingo Hotel. Murdock calculated that she was at least twenty years older than he, but they hit it off. The first night he had wondered why such an attractive woman, obviously well educated and with such an intriguing personality, would be assigned to a night job. She should be meeting people and checking them in during the afternoon. She could easily be the general manager.

Denise had enjoyed both the flirtation and the flattery. She assured him that she was pleased with the night clerk assignment. She wanted to learn all the facets of the business. The hotel was on the market. She and her boyfriend, Jack Hastings, were putting in an offer for a leveraged buy-out. Murdock had decided not to pick up on Jack's name. Today was Denise's day off. Murdock had invited her to be his guest for cocktails and dinner tonight at the Grand Turtle Inn.

Murdock was convinced that Denise was a woman with few illusions. She was comfortable with herself. They had agreed to meet at 5:00 p.m. in the cocktail lounge. He had arrived at the Grand Turtle at 4:30 and had taken a seat on the pool side of the U-shaped bar. His new friends wouldn't be there until after 6:00. That was fine. He'd told them he couldn't join them. This evening would be devoted to Denise. He ordered his usual Manhattan-on-the-rocks. While the bartender was mixing it, Murdock glanced across the U and recognized a familiar face. It was Mr. Proteus. Proteus recognized him, smiled warmly, paid for Murdock's drink, moved around the bar, and seated himself on the bar stool next to him. They shook hands. "Good to see you, Murdock. I'm alone. If you are too, shall we get together for dinner? It's my turn to pick up the tab."

"Thanks for the drink and the dinner offer. I'd enjoy that, but a lady friend will be joining me."

"You're not so generous that you'd share your good fortune?"

"Not when it comes to women. What brings you here?"

"Two things. First, a new friend by the name of Boris Romanovsky may build a hotel here, and I'd like to invest in the project. Second, Mr. Romanovsky is interested in buying a boat and he asked my advice."

"Did you give it and did Boris take it?"

"Why, yes. Do you know him?"

Murdock took a sip of his drink and said, "I've met Boris. Are you good friends?"

Mr. Proteus's eyes met his. "No. Not really. It would be more accurate to say that we're casual acquaintances. We met at a cocktail party in London a few months ago. I found him fascinating. I think he found me rather dull. He was talking about buying a boat then, but he just now got around to it. I saw one just like he was looking for. It was foreclosed by the Cayman branch of the Royal Bank of Canada. I heard about it and phoned him. He flew over from Aruba, bid, and got it for a good price. It has an elegant stateroom with all the comforts of an expensive hotel. It's perfect for a womanizer like Boris. I don't think he'd mind my saying that. He's proud of it. How is Mrs. Ling?"

Takes one to know one, Murdock thought. "She's fine. Busy as ever."

"Please tell her that I asked about her. Is she still married?"

"Yes, last time I heard."

Mr. Proteus took out a thin cigar, lit it, and asked, "Are you into scuba diving?"

Murdock nodded in the affirmative. "Yes, but I haven't since my wife died. We used to dive together. It's been great fun the last few days. I've been diving every day with a group from Indiana. They're staying here. Have you met them?"

Proteus blew a smoke ring. "No. I've met a number of folks, but I don't remember a group from Indiana. I assume your investigation of Ricardo Perez-Krieger's rape case is finished now that the young woman is dead."

"Yes. That freed me up so I could take this vacation. It was a piece of good fortune for us. We weren't getting anywhere."

Murdock wondered if this were an accidental meeting. *Surely Proteus would guess that Veritus was working for Enrique now. He's playing it cool and coy.* He said, "Veritus is investigating the possibility that Perez-Krieger was set up. Susan Ling is in charge. As you know, she's extremely competent. How long have you been here?"

"Six days. That means I was here when the murder was perpetrated. Am I one of your suspects?"

"Should you be?"

"Of course not. Our government doesn't pay me to go around murdering innocent young women. I thought this hotel was full. How did Susan get you in?"

"She didn't. I'm staying at the Lost Flamingo."

"I haven't heard of that one."

He sounded sincere. Murdock hoped he hadn't. If Proteus would recognize Denise, that would expose the lie. But maybe he doesn't know about Jack. Maybe Jack and he are associates. Maybe anything is possible when you have no leads. Murdock said, "You probably haven't heard of it because I'm rooming on the cheap."

Mr. Proteus laughed. "Nothing is cheap in the Caymans." He nodded over his left shoulder. "A lady just came in. I think she's looking for you. I'll excuse myself. I need to go to my room and change."

Denise seated herself next to Murdock. She'd had her hair and nails done. She was dressed in an expensive print blouse with a white skirt. She leaned over and kissed Murdock on his cheek.

The bartender arrived and asked, "A Belvedere martini straight up, Denise?"

She flashed him a generous smile and said, "Naturally. Thank you, Sam." Turning to Murdock she asked, "Was that man a friend of yours?"

"No, merely an acquaintance. My Veritus office does investigations throughout the state of Oregon. I met him once in Portland. Do you know him?"

"I saw a guy that looked like him the other day when I stopped at the Lost Flamingo for lunch. He walked around the exterior of the hotel. I thought he might be a competing bidder. He didn't stop and talk to anyone."

Murdock's eyes met hers. "That's interesting. He told me he'd never heard of the Little Flamingo Hotel."

Denise shrugged. "I could be mistaken."

The bartender delivered her martini. Denise took an enthusiastic sip. "I know gulping a martini isn't lady-like," she said. "I hope it didn't embarrass you."

"Of course not."

Murdock raised his glass, took another sip and said, "I'm with you, kid."

"That sounds like a Bogart line. I like it. You're a nice man, Mr. Murdock McCabe. I understand that you're checking out tomorrow. I'm going to miss you."

"Or the next day."

"That would be nicer. Last night you said your wife died. Do you have a steady girlfriend?"

"No. If I did, she'd be here."

"So you pick up older women like me?"

"No. I don't pick up women at all. I like you, Denise. You've been great company and you make good coffee. I thought we might enjoy conversation over dinner. Last night you mentioned a boyfriend named Jack. I forgot his last name. Is he your steady boyfriend?"

"Jack Hastings. He's about as steady as I've got. He shows up when he's in the neighborhood, which isn't too often. I love him but I'm not a seventh grade girl. I know he doesn't love me. He *does* like and respect me. He flatters me like you do. Most women like a little flattery. It's sort of *gosh, gee* stuff. We don't put much faith in it, but it does make a good opening gambit for a guy. By the way, you need to know before you spend your money, I never do it on the first date."

"Nor do I."

Denise looked genuinely surprised. "Really?"

"Really. Now that we have sex out of the way, we can relax and enjoy ourselves. Tell me more about Jack. Does he come here on vacation or does business bring him here?"

"Business, but don't ask me what it is. He doesn't talk much about it. Sometimes I think he's a spy, but why would any country want to spy on Little Cayman Island? He's a mysterious man. I like that. I bet it charms a lot of ladies besides me."

"Is he about due? I mean, what if he caught you out with me tonight?"

"Don't worry. He has no claim on me. He doesn't expect to have. Besides, he was just here four days ago. He said he'd be back in a few days, but he hasn't shown up. The last time he was here it was only for a few hours. He blew in late in the afternoon and blew out by 5:00 a.m. I hardly had a chance to talk to him, not to mention hanky panky."

"That must have been the day that the girl was murdered. Maybe he's afraid he'd be a suspect. It's none of my business, but I've noticed that policeman hanging around the Lost Flamingo the last two nights."

"He's sort of a friend. He's not looking for Jack."

Murdock winked. "By the expression on his face, he looked like he wants to be your lover."

"He does, but his wife is nosey and jealous. I don't wish to speak ill, but she's sort of dense and homely. He thinks I'm sort of pretty."

"I do, too."

"Gosh, gee. Thank you."

Murdock smiled. "Please. I'm sincere."

"Double thank you. He just stops in for coffee and we talk, just like you and I. That's how I keep up to date with what's happening on this island."

"What's new on the murder? Do they have a suspect?"

"Haven't you heard?"

"I've been under the water most of the day."

"They've arrested that rich guy, Perez-Krieger—the one whose son they say raped the murdered girl. I don't think they're looking for anyone else. They think that a gun found on his boat is the murder weapon."

Murdock was silent, contemplating her remark. He knew that when police focus on one suspect early in the investigation, it often blinds them to evidence pointing to the real perpetrator. He said, "You know, as a detective, I have to say that your boyfriend's behavior was strange. The *Oregonian* newspaper reported that the girl was murdered about 4:00 a.m. You said that Jack came back to the hotel about 5:00 a.m. That's a hell of a coincidence."

"Maybe he witnessed something. I don't know. Jack is a gentle and kind man, like you, Mr. McCabe. He knows how to treat a woman right, like you do. Oh, I think Jack killed during the Vietnam War. Now he's involved in secret stuff. I don't know whether he has to kill. I hope not. What could his motive possibly be for murdering that girl? To frame Señor Perez-Krieger? No. He sailed to the island with him. He genuinely likes him. I know Jack well enough to tell when he's genuine. If that gun were planted on that boat, it must have been done in the morning when Perez-Krieger went ashore. My friend the cop said he came ashore to report that his gun was stolen. I suppose that was to throw the cops off. Jack didn't have a gun. When he came back from wherever he was, he gave me a big hug when he said goodbye. I would have felt a gun. Besides, he's not the type who'd have enough anger to murder an innocent young woman in cold blood."

"Is there a type?"

"Well, Murdock, I have a PhD in forensic psychology. May I call you Murdock?"

"By all means, Denise. Please go on."

"I taught and did research at Iowa State. I recently read a case study done in the Netherlands a few years ago. It discussed a family of violent criminals. Each member had a faulty gene—an enzyme by the name of monoamine oxidase A. People without the gene have a very short fuse. They're easily angered and likely to perpetrate impulsive violent acts. All the family members had been seriously abused during childhood. The combination produces extremely violent antisocial behavior. There can be other causes, too. But Jack isn't antisocial. He doesn't anger easily, nor does he have any other symptoms. When a man makes love to me, I can tell what kind of a man he is."

"I'm sure you're right." He wasn't sure at all, of course. "You impress me as a keen judge of people."

"Jack did phone me last week. He asked a strange question—at least strange for him. He wanted to know in what part of the brain consciousness exists, and whether consciousness can exist outside the physical realm that we can understand."

"That's interesting. I've never thought about that. What did you tell him?"

"I told him that many experts have thought about it but there are no clear answers, yet. He said he'd get back to me, which sounded like a strange response. I barely talked to him while he was here four days ago. He didn't mention it. Jack has never been curious about things like that. He's an interesting man. You are, too, Murdock McCabe. Believe me, Jack didn't do it."

"That settles it, then." It didn't, of course. "Besides, the murdered woman's cabin was near where we anchored our boat today. It would have been a long walk from the Lost Flamingo."

"Jack wasn't walking. A guy in a rented van picked him up and delivered him. Say, you're not working undercover for the cops, are you?"

"No. Not hardly. Murder is sort of depressing. Let's change the subject and talk about something more cheerful. The Pacific Northwest is beautiful in the summertime. If you like to get away from the tropics, come to Portland. I can show you around. Oregon is a state with many climates. It has a marine west coast climate, high grass steppe, desert, and tundra in the high mountains. We have the Cascade Mountains with Crater Lake, Mount Hood, Mount Washington, and the Three Sisters. The Pacific Coast range has cliffs that drop precipitously into the sea. In the spring you can see whales off shore and sea lions on rocks near the shore. I know the best restaurants. You and I could do the cocktail and dinner scene. And, it wouldn't be a first date."

"No, it wouldn't, would it? Thank you, Murdock. I know you're sincere. That's touching. I just might do that."

"I'd like that. If you need another investor to make your hotel deal work, give me a call. I'm sure you don't want to spread the ownership too thin so I'd be a minority investor. Keep me informed."

"Thank you. I shall. I've saved a tidy little nest egg while I was working at Iowa State. I think Jack has enough money to handle it himself, if he wants to. Jack says he wants to set me up—to take care of me; not that I need taking care of."

"You impress me as a woman who can take good care of herself. If I understood Jack's other question, he asked whether consciousness can be free of the body. That intrigues me. Is that possible?"

Denise cocked her head. "That leads to the speculation on whether non-corporal intelligence is possible. For example, could there be intelligence in differing frequencies of the superstrings which appear to be the essence of all existence, and which may or may not have mass? Or can it exist in the pure electrical charges that exist within all matter? I don't have a clue, but I suspect that I have lots of company. I don't know anyone who does. If such intelligence exists, I can't even give it a name."

"Maybe spirits? Could there be intelligent spirits that we can't detect with our limited senses?"

"I'm afraid that those answers are far beyond my expertise. That realm is inhabited by philosophers and theologians. There was an extensive paper published on the subject a few years ago by a Professor Otto Klugman from Oregon. If you're really interested, you might want to get a copy."

"I know his daughter, Professor Amy Gallagher."

Her eyes met his. "Is she one of those old-fashioned professional women who use their married name?"

"No. Amy's never been married."

"But she's Klugman's daughter?"

There followed an uncomfortable silence. Denise broke it and said, "My, my. Did naughty old Professor Otto do someone's wife?"

There was another silence. Denise broke it again. "Okay, Murdock McCabe. You're a gracious man. Denise has the picture. What does Amy do?"

"She has a PhD in astrophysics and, I think, cosmology, too. She's teaching at Cascadia Collage in Washington State and doing research in cosmology."

"That's no surprise. Her daddy had a PhD in philosophy with a minor in astrophysics. I hear that he was murdered in Germany. Is that true?"

"Yes."

There was another long silence.

"Okay. I suppose you had something to do with investigating it and you can't breach client confidentiality. You'll find Klugman's paper interesting. He points out that many questions which were subjects for philosophers thirty years ago have moved into the realm of science. Even the theologians have scored. In the Book of Exodus it says that when God created the universe, it was dark. After some time he said, 'Let there be light,' and there was light. Cosmologists have proved that after the Big Bang the entire universe was dark for about 300 million years. Then gravity was able to bring together billions of hydrogen atoms which exploded into the first stars. Then there was light. Did you meet Klugman?"

"Yes. We briefly discussed some of the things you've mentioned over cocktails, but I've never read his paper."

"I have a copy somewhere. I'll photocopy it for you."

"I would greatly appreciate that. You mentioned that not much is known about human consciousness. Is it located somewhere in the brain? What *is* known?"

"Are you familiar with the word *qualia*?

"No. It sounds scientific."

"It's just inside the outer rough edge of science. *Qualia* mean the things that people feel they are experiencing. For example, the world is colorless. The retina of our eyes has cells that react to three different frequencies of light. Our brain combines them and interprets them together as a phenomenon we call color. The colors aren't real, but they're useful, so we're hardwired that way. We're conscious of something that really isn't there. Some people equate consciousness to soul. René Descartes, the French philosopher and mathematician, thought that the soul is located in the pineal glad of the brain. I think that's highly unlikely, but who can say?"

Murdock shook his head. "Certainly not I. You're a fascinating woman, Denise Perkins. I feel fortunate that I've run into you. Would you be interested in serving as a consultant for psychological profiles?"

"No, but thank you. I've done my time. I came here to start a fresh new life without all the grief. It would be interesting, though, to discuss some cases with you as a friend. Maybe you could justify your expense account flying me up to Oregon if I consulted for free."

"I just might be able to do that. You would enjoy meeting Professor Klugman's daughter. I'm confident that she's very familiar with her father's works. She'd be interested in the psychological issues that would confront us if humans communicated with or met conscious extraterrestrial beings. I'd like to be a fly-on-the-wall when the two of you compare notes. You are two gifted people."

"I really like you, Murdock McCabe. Maybe it wouldn't be such a bad idea to break the first date rule tonight."

"Maybe we should wait until you come to Oregon. It'd give us both something which we could look forward. "

She smiled warmly, leaned over toward him, planted another gentle kiss on his cheek and whispered in his ear, "Jack would *never* have said that."

21

As before, Brother Antonio met Grace at the entrance. He escorted her across the cloister to the heavy oak door. Together they entered the long, narrow room dominated by a thirty-foot long heavy oak table that was surrounded by twenty, high-back commodious leather chairs. Seated in one was Murdock McCabe. Brother Antonio excused himself.

Murdock arose and shook hands with Grace. After inviting her to be seated, he said, "First, Susan asked me to say 'hello' for her. You've really impressed her. She wants some temporary duty in Munich so she can get to know you better. I'll see if I can arrange that. I would have sent her on this mission, but Brother Martin asked for you and me specifically."

"Does Marty get everything he wants?"

"Yes. Brother Gustav will be joining us shortly; and then Brother Martin when Gustav is finished. In the meantime, I'd like you to give me a briefing on your progress."

"Susan said that you don't mind being called Boss, Boss. Okay?"

"Okay. It'll make me feel at home."

"Well, Boss, nine months ago, Josef Weidner checked into the Hotel Kaiserin Elisabeth in Vienna. With him was a wife but no daughter. That's three months after the man calling himself Ernesto Flavio opened the account at Boris Romanovsky's bank and about two months before a man calling himself Max Gephardt arrived here at the monastery from Innsbruck. Brother Antonio hired him to garden. The Kaiserin Elisabeth Hotel is located near the city center and is moderately priced. The Herr and the Frau stayed there for eight days. I checked the hotel records. When they checked in, they presented passports issued by the government of

Paraguay. That, you'll recall, is where Gretchen allegedly was born. If you come here by rail from Vienna, you'd change trains at Innsbruck. That's where Max told Brother Antonio he was from—according to Brother Antonio. I understand that you hesitate to trace the priest in Rome, but I have some sources that may be able to clandestinely obtain the information without endangering him. It's still a risk. I just need your go-ahead to contact the sources and to follow up and confirm any results."

"Go ahead if you can get it done surreptitiously without getting the priest killed. It's unlikely that we can use him as a witness, but he may confirm that we're on the right trail. With the thousands of hotels in Europe, how did you learn that the Weidner's used that hotel in Vienna?"

"From my clandestine sources."

Murdock's eyes locked onto hers. "I need to know who these sources are."

"Okay, Boss. I recommend that you keep this information off the record except for Susan. When you were stationed in Munich, did you hear of the Mädchenhaus Café?"

"Yes. One of my colleagues spent considerable time there."

"A woman by the name of Greta Himmelreich owns it. She befriended me. I think she wants me to be her lover."

Murdock sighed. "I regret that I must ask you a very personal question, but it's professionally necessary. Do you want to be?"

"I don't think so. In either event, I'm playing her along. Some of the women who frequent the place obtain classified information from Bavarian government files; probably easier than Rudi Benzinger can. I wonder sometimes whether these girls aren't more efficient than Veritus."

"How did you get to know this Greta so well that she's wired you into their network?"

"I walked in the Mädchenhaus Café alone a couple months ago and sat down at the bar. She was aware that I was new and alone. She joined me and bought the first drink. Whenever I go in there, she sits with me for a few minutes. She's a caring and helpful person."

As soon as she said it, she knew it was a feeble answer, but she didn't have a better one. She noticed Murdock staring at her. She admitted, "You've raised a point that I've missed, Boss. It doesn't make a lot of sense that she should be *that* good to me. Perhaps I need to look deeper. But why would she have heard of me in advance? Who would have told her and why? I guess we need to know those answers. All her information so far has been accurate. It would have been costly and time consuming for me to dig out the hotel information, even assuming that I could figure out where to start looking. Bribing hotel clerks alone would have taken a pretty penny. I assumed that her motive was to entice me to bed. If I'm correct, she's been serenely patient. Do you want me to check her out?"

"Definitely. When I was stationed in Munich a little over a year ago, the colleague that I mentioned, Moira Zawadska, was active in the lesbian community and frequented the Mädchenhaus Café. She never mentioned Greta Himmelreich. Where did Greta come from? Where did she get her money to buy the place? Munich is the state capital so it's easy to believe that the Bavarian government information may come from a lesbian spy network. The Vienna hotel information is a whole other story. How did these women know to check with that hotel in that city for that date? Some organization with more assts than these women have is feeding you. I suspect Greta is their front. She may have bought the place as an agent for an undisclosed principal. There's more here than meets the eye. We need to know who they are, how they get the information, and why they want you to have it."

"Should I give priority to the investigation of Greta or Joseph Weidner?"

Murdock flashed an affable grin. "I suspect they're connected, don't you?"

Grace smiled and shook her head knowingly. "I see that now, Boss. I guess that's why you're a station manager and I'm a lowly peon."

Murdock laughed. "Not for too long, I suspect. You're not the peon type."

Grace felt uncomfortable with the praise. She moved on and said, "Most of these monks had some business or profession before they joined the monastery. I know that Brother Martin is a theologian, but did he or does he have a business, too?"

Murdock smiled. "You can ask that question directly of him a little later."

There was a knock on the door followed by the door opening. They both arose. A man in a monk's robe entered. He was a short man with balding gray hair and a gray beard. His lively eyes fixed on Grace. He walked directly to her and offered his hand, saying, "I'm Brother Gustav. You must be Grace Bauer. I've heard so many good things about you, including a few from this guy here."

He shook her hand, then offered his to Murdock, and said, "It's good to see you again, my friend." He seated himself and they did likewise. Brother Gustav continued, "I won't waste time. I understand that Dr. West mentioned Professor Claude Mitchell. Mitchell is indeed a foremost expert on linguistics and encryption. He had a fascination with the ancient Etruscan language and had translated recently discovered documents dealing with their mythological gods and goddesses. I've read two of his books and met him once at a conference in New Orleans. A month before the conference, he'd published a paper on inscriptions he'd discovered on a high plateau in Peru where those famous lines were discovered. He postulated that the lines and the inscriptions were made a thousand years before humankind developed a written language—possibly before human language itself developed. He speculated, based on the length of the lines and the size of the inscriptions that they were made by giants who had landed on the plateau from another world. He also postulated that these giants were mistaken for gods by the ancients. In his lecture at New Orleans, he suggested that many of the god-myths of the ancient world might have originated from legends that proliferated from their visit. He suggested that they could've actually been gods, perhaps using the word loosely. The inscriptions reminded him of the ancient Inca; or rather that the Inca language could have come from their linguistic stem. He admitted that the inscriptions could have been faked, but he asked who would do it and for what reason."

Grace injected, "How long did he suppose that these giants stayed and why did they leave?"

"He didn't pretend to know."

Murdock asked, "Where is he now?"

Brother Gustav shook his head. "I don't know of anyone who's heard from him for six years or more. He just disappeared."

Murdock continued, "Was there a known motive for his disappearance?"

"I can't say. He was unhappy that his lecture was not well received. Some scientists rudely laughed at his god proposition."

Murdock asked, "What kind of man was he?"

Brother Gustav frowned. "Let me caution you that I didn't care for him, so what I say may be biased. He's a tall, burly man. I found him arrogant, impatient and conceited. His eyes suggested a man at peace, but I thought they were masterfully hiding a turbulent personality. He would make a good con man. I can't say that he's dangerous, but I didn't feel comfortable around him. He manipulated people. Frankly, I'm surprised that no one has heard from him. He enjoyed media attention and manipulated journalists masterfully."

Grace asked, "Did you get the impression that he believed the god theory?"

There was a long silence. "I didn't trust him. He impressed me as one of those scientists who, if the evidence were slim, would fill in the missing links with reckless conjecture and masquerade it as fact."

Murdock suggested, "Let's move on to the message on Brother Stephen's CD. My researcher, Susan Ling, could find no computer program or cryptologist that could decode it. Have you had time to review it?"

Brother Gustav sighed. "Brother Stephen gave me a copy two years ago, just before he was murdered. He speculated that it was an extraterrestrial message that he had received from his experiments. I never thought it was an encryption. At first, I interpreted it to be what we call noise, completely nonsensical random radio frequency disparity. He encouraged me to look at it again, perhaps more closely. The second time I wasn't as sure. One has to guard against pure mental suggestion. The third time I was even less sure than I had been right the first time, to the point of feeling uncomfortable with giving any opinion at all. I'm a man of words. Words, their etymology and delineation, have been my area of expertise for most of my life. I confess that I don't know quite what words to use to tell you this. Let me simply say that the markings appeared to be an attempt to construct a human language. I must admit that they aren't dissimilar to the language of the markings that Mitchell discovered in Peru."

Murdock injected, "An attempt by humans or nonhumans?"

Brother Gustav shook his head. "I know this is going to sound silly, but it looks to me like an attempt by someone ignorant of any of the languages of the world. So much so, that it could all be nonsense."

Grace speculated, "Could it have been an attempt by a computer?"

Brother Gustav shrugged.

There was another knock on the door. Brother Martin stuck his head in. Brother Gustav said, "Please come in. I have nothing more to offer." He shook hands with Murdock and Grace again, and excused himself. Brother Martin seated himself.

Murdock turned to Brother Martin and said, "Before you begin your agenda, I believe Grace has a question for you."

Brother Martin smiled kindly and asked, "What is your question, Grace?"

"I understand that most of you monks have or did have businesses before you organized this monastery. Did you or do you have a business?"

"Yes, I have one now."

"May I ask what yours is?"

Brother Martin grinned. "It came to me rather involuntarily. While I was a missionary in Honduras, my father died. He left all the cash and securities to my sister and the business to me. That was a complete surprise because I'd had no part in it. I've never felt quite comfortable with it, but as a result, I'm the one you people call Top Dog."

Grace's eyes met his. "What?"

"I own Veritus Investigations International. You work for me."

Grace's eyes widened. She couldn't think of anything to say. She looked at Murdock. He shrugged, and then nodded in agreement.

Brother Martin smiled warmly and said, "That brings us to the main reason that I wished to speak to both of you. As you know, Veritus is on the market. My agent has received several offers. Two are outstanding, and far above the others. That Russian émigré banker, Boris Romanovsky, put in the first and still the highest offer. We just received another offer with a purchase price close to his. My agent said that it came from a woman by the name of Linda DiStefano who represents one of our clients, Jose Enrique Perez-Krieger. Other offers are so low they aren't worth considering. However, my late father and I have always been proud of Veritus's sterling reputation for integrity. I have a problem with the two high bidders. I've heard rumors that Romanovsky is connected with the vicious Russian mafia. Perez-Krieger seems about to be indicted for murder. I need some advice."

Murdock replied, "First, let me advise you that I know Linda DiStefano quite well. We have a budding personal relationship. I'm sure she doesn't know that you're the owner or that we're meeting with you today. Veritus is conducting an investigation on behalf of Perez-Krieger. I believe he's been set up."

Brother Martin's eyes fixed on Murdock's. "By whom?"

"By Traction. We have evidence that suggests that the murdered woman may have been an actress hired from Frankfort. Grace is working on that angle. The bad guys have succeeded in pulling a dark veil over their activities. We feel that we know what they're up to, but we have no concrete proof. Grace has a contact which we believe gives us a foot in the door. Someone else is investigating the matter. We don't know who. But whoever it is, they have fed us with verifiable information."

"Where does that leave me?"

"Are you in some financial situation where you must sell now?"

"No."

"Then don't. Be patient. Grace thinks that Boris Romanovsky is playing straight and tying to help us. He has the hots—excuse me; he's interested in marrying Linda DiStefano, so I may be biased. I don't trust him. I'd feel uncomfortable recommending him as a purchaser. However, Grace has met with him at his villa on Cyprus. She's prepared a report on him which may shed a different light. She'll see that you receive a copy." Grace nodded in agreement. Murdock continued, "Linda and I are meeting with the attorney general next Thursday to convince him to give us more time. I'm optimistic that we'll get Enrique exonerated. In my opinion, he'd be the better buyer."

"Grace, when can I expect a copy of your work-up on Romanovsky?"

"I'll fax it as soon as I get back to the office this afternoon."

"Good. Murdock, I'm very much concerned about these Traction people. I understand that they claim to be ruled by a woman from another world with magical powers. That sounds rather improbable, but after Brother Stephen's work searching for extraterrestrial intelligence and the fact that it apparently motivated his murderers, and the murder of Professor Otto Klugman, I have to wonder. Is Traction's claim all smoke and mirrors?"

"I've witnessed the magic show twice. I suspect it's trickery, but if it is, they're very good at it. Whether it's real or not, if they convince the ruling classes that it's real, they will achieve great power."

Brother Martin frowned. "I'm concerned that this supposed space-time traveling woman could claim that her civilization is superior to ours, and that they know that God and Christianity are frauds. There's a powerful constituency that would like to hear that."

Grace injected, "No offense, sir, but that could be true. In fact, most Europeans are secular and don't believe in that stuff anymore. Only Islam is growing here."

Brother Martin nodded in agreement. "Is this Diana or Selene, or whatever, seeking to disprove Islam, too."

Murdock answered, "Yes. We believe she is. Susan told me that yesterday she received an e-mail from Mr. Proteus, who claims to be a U.S. government agent. He told her that even Al Qaeda fears this Diana-Selene person. She could contradict the Bible and the Koran and weaken the faith of all believers. Al Qaeda's most effective weapon is suicide bombers. These people need to believe that when they die killing infidels, they'll immediately go to heaven and receive seventy-seven dark-eyed virgins, among other wonders. If they stop believing that, blowing themselves up will seem less attractive."

Grace's eyes fixed on Brother Martin's. "May I play the devil's advocate?"

He smiled kindly. "Yes. By all means."

"Other than dissolving the motivation for suicide bombing, what difference would it really make? No offense, Marty, but perhaps the net effect would be good because less time and energy would be wasted on superstition."

"In addition to the story of Christ opening the door to heaven for all who simply believe in him, the gospels are a powerful motivation for moral and ethical behavior. They motivate us to train our emotions so that our responses to situations are appropriate."

Grace replied, "Marty, I'm not convinced that we need the Christian or any other religion for that purpose. We have generally accepted ethical philosophies handed down from the Babylonians, Greeks, Romans, American Indians, and even the Australian aborigines. We have freewill to choose to obey these ethics."

"Oh, yes," Brother Martin exclaimed. "But when you look at all the crimes committed by people against people on city streets and on countless battlefields, and at all the untimely, cruel death and destruction, one must question how effective these off-the-shelf moralities are. Jesus didn't offer a new ethic. He offered a new way of obeying older traditional ethics. Our freewill does indeed give us the right to inflict hell upon ourselves."

Grace responded, "I don't meet too many people who expect go to heaven. When they die, they expect to be dead."

"What's important is that heaven should exist. It's less important that any of us should attain it. I believe that what *is* important is that we praise God."

"Why bother?"

"Why not?" Brother Martin leaned forward in his chair. "If the universe has no purpose, why does it and we exist?"

Grace leaned forward in her chair. "Each person must deduce that answer for him or herself. I don't think anyone can answer with any degree of certainty. At least this Diana of Traction is real."

"If we can't explain why the universe came into existence, it must be a miracle. This may be circular reasoning, but I think the universe and we were created and given intelligence and freewill so that we could choose to praise God for our creation."

"Or choose not to."

"Exactly. If we had no choice, praising God would be meaningless."

"Why does God need to be praised? Why not praise and fear Diana? At least she is a real presence who seems to be affecting us all. There is a modern belief system built around this Dianic Wicca which we discussed last time. Maybe the Traction woman is she."

"God has no need to be praised. On this planet the ability to choose and the ability to praise are joys given only to humankind. The cross reminds us that God deserves our praise. I can't imagine Diana being willing to die to save anyone."

Grace injected, "To me, a cross is a symbol of barbarism and cruelty. It offers me no comfort. I've met so many disagreeable people who were certain they were going to heaven. As Mark Twain wrote, 'Heaven for climate; hell for society.'"

Brother Martin chuckled. "I know what you mean. What concerns me most is the fact that scientists shortly will be able to create human life crafted to their liking—to design people as they please. If all scientists were noble and followed those ethical philosophies that you alluded to, that might not be so bad. But you know better. You understand human nature. Some will be too proud to believe that anyone other than themselves can judge morality. That's freewill; and that's bad. God didn't create bad things. He created only good things, some of which are perverted by human pride. You've heard of the perverted ceremony that Murdock witnessed in the jungle of Honduras. It was perpetrated by intelligent people. This Diana-Selene used fear and perversion of religion to control simple people and she made them do her bidding."

Grace smiled and said, "If these people who call themselves Traction want to pervert religious faith so as to corrupt the world, they have a huge constituency that's ripe for it."

Brother Martin responded, "I can't agree with you more. In ancient times people feared God as a judge. Today people judge God. So if this green woman who walks on air is from hell, or whatever you call her place of origin, we need to know exactly what her science is that creates her illusions. Our effort to free Señor Perez-Krieger and to free the world of the contagion of Traction seems like one and the same project."

Murdock injected, "I hope that you won't sell Veritus until we've resolved both questions. I don't think you can afford to."

A long silence followed. Presently Brother Martin arose and said, "I suspect you're right, Murdock. In any event, I think this concludes our business."

He shook hands with Murdock and Grace; then departed.

Grace's eyes met Murdock's. She said, "I hope I didn't overplay the devil's advocate. I didn't mean to be rude."

"Not at all. Brother Martin enjoys a good debate. Since you're playing a vital part in the investigation, I'm sure he's pleased that you understand the issues. You defined them clearly. He respects your opinion. You represent the opinions of many people."

"I suppose he'll pray for my soul, now?"

"I suppose he will. He's prayed for mine. It isn't painful, Grace."

"I wasn't concerned about the pain. By the way, Boss, I could use a photo of Gretchen. I talked to theatre people in Frankfort. Three young actresses fit the general description of Gretchen. None of the three is still in Frankfort. Those folks were not too anxious to talk to me. They're afraid the women are wanted on drug charges. With a photo I'd go back and try again. I could talk to restaurateurs in the theatre district. Susan tells me there were no photos of Gretchen in the newspapers. That must be by design. It's some evidence that suggests a plot to set up Señor Perez-Krieger. It wouldn't convince a jury."

"Contact Rudi Benzinger. Maybe he can get a search warrant to enter Weidner's house in Landshut. If there are no family photos, that would be some evidence that the Weidner family is a sham."

"Okay, Boss, but Rudi Benzinger is going to say it's thin ice. We don't have probable cause. I doubt that a judge would issue a warrant. Shall I pay somebody to break in or do it myself?"

"I didn't hear that."

22

Grand Cayman Island
Thursday, April 27, 9:30 a.m.

Robert Grayson, the attorney general, is a descendent of Scandinavians who settled in Yorkshire in the ninth century. He thinks of himself as a Yorkshire man more than an Englishman. His warm and friendly demeanor masks the Yorkshire trait of sometimes being a bit stubborn. His pinstripe dark gray business suit had been tailored for his well-built body. A full head of gray hair was combed back. Horned rimmed oval glasses and full moustache combined to give him a distinguished appearance.

At precisely 9:30 a.m., he opened his office door. Murdock and Linda arose to meet him. After courteous pleasantries he escorted them into his office. An oversized mahogany desk would have dominated the room if it weren't for the more impressive 5x5-foot Royal Coat of Arms on the wall behind it. He offered comfortable chairs and coffee. They accepted both.

Once they all were seated, he observed, "I see that you're impressed with our Coat of Arms. That's not the same one the queen uses. This is a stripped down version that the government uses. The one you see in the courtroom is the queen's own. Only the queen and her judges can use it. Judges directly exercise the power of the Crown in the administration of justice. That brings us to the reason we're here today. We all know that we have a high profile case. Journalists from all over the world are already pouring in and making a bloody nuisance of themselves. I am not looking for personal publicity and I shall make no statements to them. I presume that it will be in the best interests of your client for you to do the same. Are we agreed thus far?"

Linda nodded and said, "Yes. We can't keep them out of the hearing before the Summary Court. I'll waive the reading of the charge. I propose that we both waive the hearing, and that under the provisions of Section 87 of the Cayman Criminal Procedure Code, we both submit written statements to the Summary Court along with the exhibits we propose to offer. That is, of course, without prejudice to either of us to change our mind and hold a hearing if the Magistrate should find the writings insufficient. Will you stipulate to that, and to the present bond remaining in force?"

"I'll stipulate to the bond. For the purpose of preserving testimony and protecting them, I need to take the testimony of Frau Weidner, and William Robert Banter, the witness from Indiana. I understand that you, Mr. McCabe, believe that you will find evidence indicating that Señor Perez-Krieger has been 'framed' as you Americans say. I'll give you a reasonable amount of time to pursue that line of inquiry. I'm inclined not to believe it. I understand that you had twelve years under your belt with the American FBI before you took your present job. You've moved up quickly from a mere investigator to station chief, by-passing assistant station chief. I understand that you are a very competent man. It appears that you are an ambitious man, too. I fear that your judgment may be colored by the fact—which will not be missed by the media—that Señor Perez-Krieger has made an offer to purchase Veritus. You have had a reputation for veracity. I would not want to see that reputation tarnished by your developing evidence of dubious value just to look good in the eyes of Veritus's possible future owner. I'm confident that you won't do that, so I regret having mentioned it."

Linda injected, "Yesterday afternoon we withdrew that offer. Señor Perez-Krieger is not buying Veritus."

Murdock said, "I won't represent that we're close to proving that he's been set up. The people who want to hurt him have gone to great expense and planning to succeed."

"Do we know who these people are? And what their motive is?"

"Have you heard of an organization called Traction, sir?"

"Oh, please. I'm not a 'sir' yet. Neither queen nor government has seen fit to reward me with that honor. But, no, I've never heard of Traction. Pray tell, what is it?"

"It's a shadowy organization dedicated to create havoc economically and politically. They appear to be anarchists. Destroying respected people like Perez-Krieger is a means to that end."

The attorney general smiled. "My, my. How could an organization with such grand ambitions have escaped me? And even more so, how could they have escaped the media?"

"I'm not sure why they're lying low. I believe the American government is concerned enough about them to have placed secret agents on their tail."

"If these agents are so secret, how do you know about them?"

"I've been involved in two investigations where I've come in contact with people who represent themselves to be agents of Traction."

"You've had contact with this enigmatic organization?"

"Yes. I believe so."

"They're so secret that you aren't certain? No need to answer. I'm beginning to sound sarcastic. I apologize. I just find it hard to believe. The police have found no evidence that Señor Perez-Krieger is being framed. As I explained in my e-mail to Ms. DiStefano, the FBI lab in Washington has confirmed that the pistol discovered in the engine compartment of his boat is the murder weapon. A handkerchief with Señor Perez-Krieger's monogram has been found on the beach near the scene. A hair found under the fingernail of the deceased bears his DNA."

Murdock's eyes met his. "It's not difficult to have initials embroidered on a handkerchief. Señor Perez-Krieger told me that one day he found his hairbrush on the sink in his boat; he always keeps it in a drawer. It would have been easy to obtain a hair from it. No killer is likely to leave a monogrammed handkerchief behind on the beach."

The attorney general turned to Linda. "A jury might agree that your client is an inept killer, but with all evidence pointing to him, they will still convict. I presume you will want to talk about plea bargaining to a reduced charge. You and Mr. McCabe need to show me some reason to believe that there is a weakness in my case. If there isn't, my duty is to prosecute him to the fullest. I regret that. I've not met him, but I've heard many good things about him. However, in fits of anger and frustration, some good people do kill. That very well may be the case here. I do look forward to hearing from you."

Murdock replied, "They've prepared a rather elaborate scheme and wound it up tightly, but I'm confident that we'll unwind it."

Linda added, "I hope that you'll drag your feet as long as you can without giving the appearance of impropriety. Even if we expose the plot after Señor Perez-Krieger is convicted, his subsequent retrial and acquittal would be too late. People remember the initial conviction. The acquittal receives less publicity. His reputation would be tanked."

The attorney general smiled. "I do believe it's tanked, as you put it, already. Now I need to move on to other matters and you folks need to get out here and find the scoundrels. Thank you for coming to the office, Miss

DiStefano. It was indeed a pleasure to meet you, Mr. McCabe. I'm confident we'll meet again, hopefully under less strenuous circumstances."

* * *

Upon leaving the attorney general's office, they drove in Linda's car to Hemmingway's for lunch. It was too early for cocktails so they went directly to the buffet. When they were seated at a table, Murdock asked, "Could this man Jack be involved? Enrique thinks he's a friend, but actually, he's just a guy he'd met at the bar here. What do we really know about him?"

"I met him. I consider myself a good judge of character. It would be hard for me to believe that he'd harm Enrique."

"He sailed with him to Little Cayman. He could have taken a handkerchief. Enrique wouldn't have missed it. He also could have obtained hairs from the brush. I know that he was on Little Cayman when the murder occurred. He left suddenly in an agitated state. The really interesting fact, though, is that Boris Romanovsky knew something was going down."

Linda agreed. "The really amazing thing is that he tried to warn me. That suggests that Grace's assessment of the man might be accurate."

"I'd like to fly to Aruba and check it out."

"No, Murdock. I'll go. I've already arranged a bizjet for tomorrow morning. As Grace said, 'Never send a man to do a woman's job.'"

Murdock laughed. "She did say that, didn't she? She's a very alert gal. I'm impressed."

Linda smiled and met his eyes. "Don't get too impressed."

"I promise. Besides, it's strictly professional. We need to look at where we are in terms of our understanding of Romanovsky."

Linda shook her head. "I agree. He's offered us deals which at first blush appear to be attractive. I've told him we'd consider them, but we haven't. Enrique wants nothing to do with him or with any business in Russia. Boris's banks seem to be properly capitalized. He gets little or no bad press. It's interesting that none of his businesses operate in your country. I presume that's because he doesn't want regulators in the United States to take a hard look at them. He's avoided my country, too."

Murdock nodded in agreement. "Grace feels that we misjudged him. That's easy to do. He did make his way up the ranks of Soviet apparatchiks. Although he was trained in the Soviet system, he is Western oriented. Boris Romanovsky was one of Boris Yeltsin's back door buddies—one of the smartest because he moved his fortune to Cyprus and got out of

Russia before he got arrested or assassinated. He's a generous man. He offered Amy Gallagher a sizeable grant for her search for extraterrestrial intelligence program. Of course, he wants her to come live with him on Aruba so he can *protect* her. Maybe he wants to marry you so that you can chaperone. I guess he just likes to do nice things for attractive women."

Linda laughed and asked, "Do you know whether Boris is involved in any dodgy deals now?"

"Susan's research shows that his banks have branches in Moscow and Saint Petersburg. They move huge sums of money off shore. The banking business is a dangerous experience in Russia. Banks are infested with crime. I think Enrique is wise. I wouldn't invest there on a bet. Susan says that billions of U.S. dollars in cash float around the country sight unseen. They call it 'black cash.' Their economy couldn't function without it. She says it's used for bribes and terrorism. Government officials are poorly paid so businesses can't get anything approved without paying enormous bribes. Terrorism is routinely used to intimidate competitors. Complex international financial transactions conceal the sources of black money. Boris claims that he's shaken himself loose from all the sleaze. That claim is dubious at best. Susan had our investment expert in Chicago review his companies outside Russia. They seem to be straightforward. You heard Grace's assessment. Susan concludes that Boris plays by the rules both in Russia and in the West. They're just different rules." Murdock lifted his coffee cup and added, "But you apparently know him better than we do. He wants to marry you."

"I'm so thrilled."

With a look of sincere concern, Murdock said, "Linda, he's a billionaire. His offer of marriage carries tremendous economic weight. If he had you not only as his wife, but also as the *mayor domo* of his business empire, his success might surpass even Enrique. The contacts you've made and the influence you have with CEOs worldwide, would be priceless to him. You could write your own ticket. He's got to be close to twenty years your senior. His entire business empire could eventually be yours."

There followed a long silence. It was broken by Linda. "I don't seem to have a serious alternative. If Enrique is convicted, and he very well could be, whether he's innocent or not, I would be out of a job. Is that what you think I should do?"

"I think you must consider it. I have so pathetically little to offer. Karen and I had a small investment plan. I still have most of the money from her million-dollar life policy. You can guess the size of my salary as a station chief for Veritus. Your salary is far greater than mine."

Linda's eyes locked on Murdock's. She spoke in a soft tone. "Well, then, we both need to talk about what's really important. Boris has never mentioned love. When you married Karen, I'm sure the two of you were in love. If another woman had offered you a million dollars to marry her instead, would you have become her stud, or would you have chosen Karen?"

Murdock's eyes met hers. "Karen, of course."

There followed another long, uncomfortable silence. Linda again broke it and said, "May I ask a very personal question that I have no right to ask?"

"Linda, you have every right to ask whatever you wish."

"Was Karen pregnant when she was murdered?"

Murdock's eyes lowered. "Four months."

Linda's eyes, still fixed on his, softened. "So you're grieving the death of your unborn child, too. I hadn't guessed that. I'm profoundly sorry."

There followed another awkward silence. Their eyes avoided each other. Linda raised her cup and sipped her coffee. Murdock followed suit. Finally, Linda asked, "Do you want children?"

As Murdock picked up the coffee carafe and filled both cups, he replied, "Yes, I definitely do."

Linda's eyes searched his as she said, "So do I. We both know it's a harsh world, Murdock McCabe. Please hold this hard thought firmly in your mind—Karen can never give them to you."

23

Aruba
Friday, April 28, 10:17 a.m.

Linda peered out the window of her bizjet. She could make out whitecaps on the aquamarine waters of the southern Caribbean. Minutes ago the pilot had begun his descent to an approach for Queen Beatrix International Airport just outside Orangestad, the capital of Aruba. The small island north of Venezuela is a constituent country within the Kingdom of the Netherlands. Within minutes, its arid, cactus-strewn landscape was racing past beneath them. The aircraft touched down and then taxied to the general aviation terminal. When the door was opened and the steps lowered, Linda descended and stepped onto the tarmac. It was a hot, sunny day—the kind of day that attracts tourists to Aruba in April. Linda was not a tourist.

Boris's chauffeur was awaiting her. She had no luggage; just a travel bag. They drove in a southeasterly direction along the coast road and through the village of Sabeneta. Presently their destination came into view. Situated within a compound atop a hill, the villa commanded a spectacular view of a desert landscape set against the bright blue water of the Caribbean. Other than its arid climate, Linda thought that the three-story stucco mansion bore a remarkable similarity to Enrique's. As she exited the vehicle, she felt awkward. She didn't want to be there. She didn't trust the man who would be her host. A servant met her, guided her through the main entrance, and into a great room. Another followed with a silver platter piled high with tropical fruits. A third offered her a tall glass containing what he described as a fruity nonalcoholic drink. Thirsty, she accepted it gratefully. The first servant assured her that Boris would be with her shortly. At his invitation, she seated herself before a picture window with a panoramic view. She wondered whether she had been too callus with Murdock. She didn't regret thrusting reality upon him. She was confident that he knew her remark about Karen hadn't been meant to hurt. Before she could think it through, Boris swept into the room sporting an enormous grin.

"Good morning, stunning lady. Boris is pleased you have come to Boris's villa. This room has become more beautiful because you entered it. Yesterday Boris could hardly believe when servant gave message you would come today. Boris has invited you so many times. You are welcome here, always. Is too much to hope that, perhaps, you have come to stay?"

"I've come to personally thank you for warning me that Enrique was sailing into trouble. Unfortunately, I couldn't contact him in time."

"But, gracious lady, you have already thanked Boris by e-mail."

"I know. It troubled me that I hadn't come here personally. It was so kind of you."

"But so. Beautiful lady wishes to know why Boris tried to save Enrique. Answer is simple. Boris wants business ventures with Enrique when Enrique is no longer damaged goods. But you, kind lady, are not damaged yet. You have not been painted with scandal brush. You are still above all that. But, smart lady, you must be both wary and prudent. You cannot be free of paint forever."

With some feeling of trepidation, Linda sipped her drink. Was it drugged? It tasted natural. Attempting to conceal her unease, she said, "I know that you have your own KGB, as you've put it, but the information you gave me would have been vigilantly guarded. How did you know Enrique was in danger? And how did you know the nature of it?"

"Lady, wise in world's ways, you know Boris cannot name source. Boris can say source is double agent who has expensive tastes in food, drink, and sex and so needs money from both sides. Yesterday source told Boris that Enrique's enemies are about to leak rumor to journalists. Rumor will say that managers of Enrique's drilling companies in Nigeria and Angola bribe African politicians who murder people that disagree with them. Last part is true. First part you will have to refute. Journalists are uninhibited by question of accuracy. Source of rumor will be unidentified. Huge story will repeat for weeks. What remains of Enrique's good reputation will be destroyed and potential jurors will be tainted. By time journalists bother to discover untruth, public will have lost interest. Journalists will not advertise that they were irresponsible. Is time for you, most illustrious lady, to, as Americans say, bail out."

Linda folded her hands on the table and glanced past him to the shining waters of the sea. She asked, "What would it take for me to learn what you know about this plot, Boris? To know the source of what you know?" Her eyes fixed on his.

"Answer is easy—partnership—you and Boris."

"Business or personal?"

Boris chuckled. "Why does smart lady ask silly question? You play game? Is better for Boris now if Enrique falls. You could never work for sister, Estrelita. You know that. Boris knows that. That might bring you to Boris. That is possible, is not?"

"It's not impossible. I won't abandon Enrique when he's down. I'll make no decision until Enrique is exonerated. If you could help me obtain his freedom, I would certainly be in your debt. I won't mislead you, Boris. That doesn't mean that I'd marry you; or even that I'd become your partner. It means that I need to take a hard look at your offer. What precisely is your offer?"

"Boris is a blunt straight-talking man. Boris is fifty-two years old or so. Boris has no children so far as Boris knows. Boris cannot know everything. Boris has *known*, in Biblical sense of word, over one-hundred women or so. Boris has never found woman that Boris would choose to have his legitimate children—until you."

Linda's eyes searched his. His were unreadable. She asked, "Does that mean that you love me?"

Her question was met with a bewildered look. Shaking his head slowly, he asked, "What means this word love? You are only woman in world that Boris chooses to bare legitimate children; children who will be descendents of Tsars of all Russians; children of royal blood whose ancestors ruled half world—albeit wilder and bad-mannered half. Royalty will come out of your womb because Boris Romanovsky, great, great, great, et cetera, et cetera grandson of Tsar Alexander II from wrong side of sheets, will plant seeds there."

"So it would be from the right side of the sheets, this time? I'd be your wife and your broodmare?"

"Please to listen, lovely lady. Hear facts of life. Recent natural disasters enormously increased need for catastrophe reinsurance. You know big insurance companies shop for reinsurance every day. According to Bermuda Monetary Authority, nearly 40 percent of reinsurance for natural disasters that occur in United States is sold by Bermuda-based firms. Demand is high, premiums are high, and profits are high. Government of Bermuda is politically stable. Is subject to British crown but has had independent parliament since 1620. Its laws and taxes are constant and favorable."

"The point is…?"

"The point is this, most attractive lady. Boris wishes to start new Bermudan reinsurance company. You have supervised the CEOs of Perez-Krieger's reinsurance companies. You know business. Right now you control big chunk of Boris's potential competition. Boris will pay double salary Enrique gives you. You set up company and hire best executives to operate it. When you marry Boris, you will receive 10 percent of common voting shares. If you fulfill wifely duties for Boris, you will receive another 25 percent when each child is born and DNA confirms Boris's bloodline."

"You wouldn't trust me?"

"Nice lady, Boris knows dozens of married women who take lovers, because Boris *is* their lover."

"If you wouldn't trust me, how could I be sure you would transfer the shares to me?"

"Boris will place shares in trust so you will be guaranteed that Boris cannot go back on promise. Soon you will be most successful broodmare in world and own 100 percent of largest reinsurance company in world. You will no longer need Boris."

"And Boris will no longer need me?"

"You know ways of world and how men of power behave. Boris has all women that Boris can handle. Only you will be mother of legitimate children. After four children are born, you own company. You are free to do whatever you wish and Boris can do whatever he wishes. Upon the death of Boris, all billions of Boris's estate will go to our children. Who else can make generous offer of both royal children and wealth? Boris asks you. But so. Boris cannot expect answer today. You must think. Boris is straight arrow, as Americans say. While you are pregnant, you are free to live here, or on Bermuda, or wherever. When you are not pregnant, you must come to Boris's bed when required."

Neither spoke. Restraining a smile, Linda stared out the window. Boris, a satisfied look on his face, lit a crooked malodorous Italian cigar. She suspected that it might be a gratuitous goof for her to slam the door closed too soon, so she decided to push it open a crack. Breaking the silence she proclaimed, "I'll consider your offer."

As his eyes scanned her body, a lewd boyish grin crossed his face. He arose and said, "Good. Boris looks forward to an answer very soon. Now Boris must fly to Little Cayman Island to take delivery of boat."

"And I must get back to Grand Cayman Island. I still have a job there."

* * *

172

Boris's chauffer drove them to the airport where they said their farewells and entered their separate bizjets. On the flight back to Grand Cayman Island, Linda pondered what had happened. She still didn't know the source of Boris's information, and she still wasn't certain whether Boris's warning had been to save Enrique or to impress her. The details of his offer of marriage were certainly unconventional. The financial arrangements were more than generous; they were outstanding. They were more than outstanding. They were astounding. Murdock was right. They *had* to be considered. *Maybe,* the girl in her thought, *showering me with wealth is the only way a man like Boris knows how to say that he loves me.* However, she wasn't a silly girl. *Murdock was right about something else, too. He'd have to hit the jackpot on four or five state lotteries to come close to matching the offer.* Besides, it was the only marriage offer she had. And she *did* want children.

24

Murdock was in Chicago for a meeting of Veritus station chiefs. Tomorrow he would fly directly to Little Cayman Island on a bizjet furnished by Linda. Susan was in charge of the office.

Seated at her desk before the computer with a mug of hot coffee at her side, she was searching theatrical web sites in Germany; particularly in Frankfort. If Gretchen had been an actress, Susan needed to identify German-speaking actresses who appeared to fit the bill. She downloaded photographs from the publicity files of the shows in which each candidate had appeared. A few coincided with the verbal description she had picked up from Linda DiStefano. One young woman particularly interested her. At twenty years old, she had played a nun in a stage production last year. Her name was Hilde Müller. She could find no current address for her in Frankfort. She hadn't been caste in a show for the last ten months. Susan phoned the offices of several theaters, but those who knew her hadn't seen her for some time and had no idea where she was.

She needed to watch the clock. Mr. Proteus had called on Friday. He wanted to meet Murdock and her at the usual restaurant in Multnomah Village at 11:30. With Murdock in Chicago, Mr. Proteus had agreed to meet her alone. Feeling mildly exhilarated in anticipation, she passed the morning with her research and fielded the numerous routine management decisions that employees required from their supervisor. Shortly after ten o'clock, her phone rang. She answered. A vaguely familiar male voice that she couldn't place said, "Be there at 11:00. It's critical that I speak to you in person before your Mr. Proteus arrives. You *will* remember me."

The caller hung up. She searched her memory. Nothing clicked.

* * *

Promptly at 11:00 a.m., Susan seated herself at the usual booth. A solitary man with a heavy gray beard, a moustache, and large horn-rimmed glasses was seated at the bar. He was staring at her. Apparently satisfied that she was who he thought she was, he arose, walked quickly over to her booth, and sat across from her. She searched his eyes. They looked vaguely familiar. She tried to imagine his face without a beard. Her memory didn't click again. Reaching into the pocket of his loose-fitting blue sports jacket, he extracted a pair of women's panties. He laid them on the table. She stared at them. He pushed them toward her.

"Do you recognize them?" he asked.

She did. They were hers. She hadn't seen them for some time. A year ago, when she and Murdock had investigated the disappearance of one of Enrique's key employees, she had checked out a person of interest—a barfly who hung out at a coast bar and called himself Smokey. She had teasingly allowed him to lure her into his car in a restaurant parking lot. One thing had led to another. She had removed her panties and placed them in his glove box. However, before another thing had led to still another and had reached the outcome that they'd anticipated, the Boss had interrupted them. She had been so embarrassed by Murdock's appearance that when she exited his vehicle, she'd forgotten her panties. Now she stared at them. Raising her eyes to meet his, she deposited them into her leather sling bag.

He smiled kindly and said, "You know who I am. Don't speak. There isn't time. I'm using a different code name—Jack Hastings. That name is for your ears alone, Susan. I trust you. I'm authorized to tell you a few things. As you've probably assumed, the name Weidner is a fake. We don't know their real ID yet. We suspect the girl was an actress. I don't have her name. She may be difficult to trace."

"I've learned that—"

"Just listen. I don't have time. We believe Traction offered her big money to play the part, but neglected to tell her that she had to die. In case you had any doubt, Enrique is innocent. Use extreme caution. You could be in great danger. These Traction people are shrewd and exceedingly cunning. We believe that they're committed to total destruction of the moral imperatives of our civilization, and of all religions, they can pick up the pieces. Be careful with Proteus. He's too perfect. If he works for our government, his agency is so secret that even the president may not know about it. That can happen. If he *is* our guy, we don't have a handle on him."

He nodded toward the entrance door. "There he is. I just tried to put the make on you."

As Proteus approached the table, the man calling himself Jack arose, and walked back toward the bar. As he passed Proteus, he said, "Good luck, buddy. She's one tough broad. I think her fucking legs are glued together."

Proteus turned and watched the man seat himself on a bar stool. Then, seating himself on Susan's right, he asked, "Who was that?"

"Just a trolling barroom hopeful. Guys like him are just part of the scenery for a young woman. He had so little subtlety that I found him amusing."

"What did he say?"

"You're a big boy. Use your imagination."

Mr. Proteus studied Jack who had turned his back to them. Susan wondered whether he'd bought the story. As Jack engaged the bartender in conversation, Mr. Proteus turned his attention to Susan. Susan studied his face. Its expression suggested an inner amusement which had not quite turned itself into a smile. He asked, "What's Murdock up to in Chicago?"

A waitress brought coffee and menus.

Susan replied, "He's attending a meeting of Veritus management personnel. Nothing too exciting. By the way, have you ever heard the name Hilde Müller?"

Proteus's eyes hardened. "Why do you ask? Who is she?"

Susan detected a slightly hard edge in his voice. She replied, "Just a name I came across this morning. Nothing important. If you'd heard it, you might have been able to help."

"Possibly I can. Has Murdock heard of her?"

"I haven't had the chance to mention her name to him yet. I just ran into it this morning. Why do you ask?"

For a split second, she thought he seemed confused. Recollecting himself, he said, "No reason. Dumb question. My dear, you ask many favors but you give none in return. You know that I want us to be closer. Lovers learn to trust each other and confide in each other. We can quickly elevate the level of our relationship. We'd both feel secure sharing our sexual favors and the most valuable secrets of our clients. Power is a tool of sex. Or are you just a tease?" His eyes narrowed. "Is that what you are, my dear? Are you just a prick teaser?"

Susan smiled her brightest. "Of course, not. You've seen me naked. Did my body look like the body of a mere teaser? It's just that I'm trying to get pregnant by my husband, so we must be mindful of that."

A grin crossed his face as he reached under the table with his left hand. She felt it touch her leg, and then, as the grin broadened, he moved upward, under her skirt, onto the object of his desire, exploring. His grin broadened into a smile. After withdrawing his hand, his eyes met hers and he said, "I shall give you that information about Hilde, but first I get laid. That Tampax tells me we don't need to worry about getting pregnant this time. Periods never slow me down. The sooner we head for my suite, the sooner you'll have intelligence on that girl. We can have lunch there, if food is important to you at a time like this. You're a strong woman. I'm going to work you over until you can't stand the pleasure anymore. You can be back to the office by three, if that's what you want. How does that sound?"

Susan winked. "I need to know what you know, and you need what I'm perfectly willing to give. It sounds like our trains are on parallel tracks arriving at the same station at the same time."

Susan was cautiously optimistic that she'd identified Gretchen and now she was going to confirm it. Murdock would be pleased. She always enjoyed seeing the astonished look on his face when she came up with startling information that he didn't expect her to find. She'd phone him as soon as she left Mr. Proteus's hotel room.

Mr. Proteus tossed a five-dollar bill on the table, grabbed her arm, practically dragged her from the booth, and spirited her out the front door.

Jack Hastings watched through the mirror behind the bar.

25

When Murdock's bizjet touched down on the runway on Little Cayman Island, the cab he had engaged for the day was waiting on the tarmac. As he stepped out of the plane, Robert, his cabbie, tipped his hat, flashed a broad toothy smile, and loaded the meager luggage into the cab. Just off the airport grounds, Robert pulled into the parking lot of a convenience store. Murdock picked up a case of Bud O'Hara's favorite brand of Canadian beer. The next stop was a bank to exchange money. After stuffing 400 Cayman dollars into his wallet and another 600 into his money belt, he checked in at the Lost Flamingo Hotel. Denise would be working that evening starting at 10:00 p.m. The next stop was Bud's. Bud was sitting on his reclining lawn chair reading a newspaper in the shade of the huge pines. Murdock walked up to him, put down the case of beer next to him, and said, "How are you doing, Bud? Do you remember me?"

Bud looked over his newspaper, first at the beer, second at Murdock. "Yeah. I sure do. You're Burdock."

"Murdock."

"Yeah. Right. If that beer's for me, I thank you. A few weeks ago you claimed you were diving off shore. Are you on another vacation?"

"No, Bud. I'm not. I'm working. I'm a private investigator for Veritus Investigations International." He handed him a business card.

Bud took the card, studied it, then smiled and said, "I'll bet you're working for that Chilean guy that the cops are trying to frame. Is that why you're here? You want to get into that cabin and nose around, don't you? I see you got a camera kit there. Well, like I always say, I thank you for the beer, but we really aren't old drinking buddies, are we? Old Bud has to make hay while the sun shines. Getting in there is going to cost you five-hundred bucks plus the beer."

"Five-hundred American or five-hundred Cayman?"

"Cayman, of course."

Murdock took out his billfold and extracted the currency from it. He fumbled with it, then counted it, and said, "I've only got a little over 400. I don't have a big expense account. I can see whether the company will wire me some more, but I have to go to the big island tomorrow morning. I might be gone before it gets here, but I'll try. If it comes before I leave, I'll be back."

As Murdock turned to leave, Bud said, "No. Don't go. I feel like you're an old friend. I'll settle for the 400 and the beer." Murdock handed him the money. Bud went inside the house to get the key. When he returned, he said, "I'm going in with you."

"When did the RCIP remove the tape?"

"Last week."

"Has anyone been in there since?"

"Nope. It's been locked up tight. No one goes in unless they pay 500 bucks, except you, of course. Like I said, you're my friend."

A four-hundred dollar friend, Murdock thought.

They walked over to the front door of the cabin. Bud unlocked it and they entered. It had one large room with a tiny kitchenette, an equally tiny bathroom, and two bedrooms. Murdock took several photos. He pointed to what appeared to be a smoke alarm on the ceiling in the far corner. "That smoke alarm looks new. Is it?"

"Yeah. The tenant wanted one. A guy came over to install it about a month ago. My tenant paid for it, so it didn't bother me none."

"Did the guy wear a tool belt that looked like the ones that telephone repairmen use?"

Bud thought for a minute. "Yeah. Now that you mention it, I think he did."

"This smoke alarm looks interesting. I need one at home. Do you mind if I take it down and examine it?"

"Not if you put the sucker back up."

Murdock stood on a chair, pressed the device upward, and then turned it to release it. He lowered the device and examined it. "It's quite unusual," he remarked.

Bud said, "You're right, Mr. Murdock. I never seen one with all that funny stuff in it. It don't look right. What's all that stuff, anyway?"

Murdock said, pointing, "This little part is a miniature television camera with a pinhole lens. It's a DC 12-volt low power consumption model so this little rectifier is the power source. This tiny thing is a built-in microphone for audio. Because the installation is in a corner, this camera covers the whole room and records what it sees digitally."

"What's that other thing?"

"That's a wireless transmitter. It'll transmit very clear video images and mono-sound for at least 1,500 feet."

Murdock studied the installation carefully. Judging by the awkward connection of the transmitter to the power supply, he concluded that it hadn't been installed by the same technician who installed the camera. The camera had been installed first—the transmitter later. He wondered whether the first party knew that their video stream was being transmitted.

"Do you remember seeing a van parked near here the night of the murder?"

He thought. "Yeah. I think that was the night that there was one parked across the street from the Widow Thomas's place. I'm not sure it was that night. I can't be too sure. I didn't pay much attention. My mind was fixed on the Widow Thomas. Man, her husband must've died from over-screwing. I can't satisfy that woman no how. By the way, the cops told me they'd used a debugging device, but they didn't pick up anything."

"A lot of police departments don't have the latest technology. Their equipment is tuned for frequencies between 1 GHz and 3 GHz. This transmitter is state-of-the-art. It's transmitting on 5.4 GHz. The RCIP could easily have missed it."

"Isn't that stuff expensive? I mean, wouldn't they come back for it?"

"It's not too expensive. Someone came back for the DVD on which the video stream was recorded." Murdock would have bet it wasn't a technician. A techie would have ripped out the transmitter so that he could study it in a lab and try to figure out who installed it.

"Do you think the damn killer wanted to record the killing?"

"It doesn't make sense."

"Who do you think wanted that thing up there?"

"I could make a guess." Even if he was right, he had no idea why they did it.

* * *

Murdock left Bud thinking about buying a receiver. Spying on some of his female tenants might be better than his girlie magazines.

Murdock phoned Susan's number at the office. After several rings, the receptionist answered. "I'm sorry; Mr. McCabe, but we haven't seen her since yesterday morning. When she left she told me she planned on meeting someone in a restaurant in Multnomah Village at 11:00. She never returned. I phoned her house a half hour ago. I got her answering machine. This isn't like her, Mr. McCabe. What should I do?"

"Does her desk calendar indicate whom she was supposed to meet?"

"Yes, sir, a Mr. Proteus, but it says 11:30."

That seemed strange to Murdock. Susan wasn't likely to confuse the times. Was she meeting two different people? If so, who was the first? Why was he or she scheduled so tightly before her meeting with Mr. Proteus?

Murdock said, "We need to look into this immediately. Is Margaret there?"

"No, sir. She's been trying to locate Susan, so she's taken a late lunch."

"Have her call me as soon as she returns."

* * *

When the cab pulled under the canopy at the Grand Turtle Inn, Murdock slipped the driver a Cayman hundred dollar bill and told him to grab some supper and get back in two hours.

As Murdock walked into the cocktail lounge, he recognized a familiar face—the face of a man he very much wanted to see. Mr. Proteus was seated on the same bar stool he had been a few weeks earlier. The bar stool on his left was vacant. Murdock seated himself. Proteus flashed a big smile and offered his hand. They shook. Murdock ordered a drink. After small talk, Murdock said, "I understand that you had lunch with Susan yesterday."

Mr. Proteus took a sip from his drink, smiled, and replied, "Almost. We were just sitting down to eat when I received an urgent phone call from Washington. I had to leave her high and dry. As I was leaving, I noticed that she went over to the bar and talked amiably to an older man with a bushy gray beard. Apparently she knew him. I guess she wasn't too disappointed." He studied his drink, and then asked, "What are you up to?"

"I'm working this time. How about you?"

"Boris picked up his boat yesterday. He was supposed to close the deal a few days earlier, but there were some issues over a lien that hadn't been properly discharged. I made a few phone calls and straightened it out. We're celebrating tonight. Maybe you'd like to join us. I'm sure he wouldn't mind."

"I'd like that. Where and what time?"

"I've reserved that small private room over there past the fountain. We'll meet here at the bar at about 5:00 p.m. Dress is casual. There'll just be a few of us. I've arranged for a hot smorgasbord. It'll give you a chance to get to know Boris better. I understand that he wants to marry Perez-Krieger's administrative assistant, Linda DiStefano. You surely must know her."

"Yes, I surely do. Veritus has handled a number of cases for them. Does Ms. DiStefano wish to marry him?"

"She should. From what he tells me, he's offered her the kingdoms of the earth, to borrow a Biblical quote. Whenever I've been with Boris, he's never taken any woman seriously. He uses them. He never keeps them. This Ms. DiStefano must be quite a gal. What's your impression of her?"

"She's quite a gal. How is your investigation of Traction going?"

"I'm not sure my bosses in the government are up to speed with me yet, but personally I'm beginning to believe this green woman is a fake; and that Traction is a paper tiger. They're making a fortune running drugs, but I think their supposed threat to world stability is overrated."

"Have you guys heard about some writings on a high plateau in Peru?"

"And those lines? Yeah. That's been around for awhile. I read about them in National Geographic a few years ago. Why? What's going on?"

"Apparently there's more to the story than was reported in the magazine. Have you guys heard the name Claude Mitchell?"

Mr. Proteus slowly lifted his cocktail, took a sip, held the glass up to the light of a candle on the bar, studied its color, and answered, "No. Who's he?"

"He's just a guy who's an expert in linguistics. I have a friend who's looking for him. Nothing important. My question is just a shot in the dark."

"Well, this is important. This is confidential, so you didn't get it from me. Okay?"

Murdock winked. "Okay."

Mr. Proteus stared at Murdock, cocked his head, and then said, "The government has plans to seize all the U.S. assets of Perez-Krieger's Plato Fund if he's convicted. I hear that the U.S. attorney's office in New York plans to obtain a federal court order to freeze all of its assets while the trial is pending, so they can't be moved into another jurisdiction."

Murdock slowly lifted his cocktail, took a sip, held the glass up to the light of the same candle, studied its color, and answered, "Thank you. I appreciate the tip."

Mr. Proteus arose and said, "Please excuse me. I need to check a few details. I'll be back in a half hour."

Murdock pushed away his cocktail and ordered coffee. He looked forward to seeing Boris again. It had been over a year. Boris had been in his office in Portland once and Murdock had found him to be an enigma. He'd taken a liking to Susan. *Every man,* Murdock thought, *takes a liking to Susan.* Her absence was worrisome. Murdock needed to know who the old man at the bar was. He might be the key to Susan's disappearance. Not showing up for work was atypical. His curiosity was elevated by Proteus's invented leaking alleged confidential government information. Linda had mentioned that the Plato mutual fund maintains no assets in the United States. Proteus should have known that. Of course, maybe the U.S. government doesn't know that. He'd discuss it with Linda. The 'kingdoms of the earth' remark disturbed him. Was Proteus's remark embroidery? Linda had shared only bare-bones information about her meeting with Boris in Aruba. Maybe she hadn't taken his offer seriously. Or maybe she had, and didn't want to mention it.

A man sat down next to him. It was a jovial Boris with an ebullient smile.

"Good evening, Mr. McCabe. Mr. Proteus told Boris you are here. Is good to see you. How have you been?"

Without waiting for a reply, Boris turned toward the bartender, ordered drinks for both of them, and then returned his attention to Murdock.

"I'm fine. I understand that you bought a boat. What did you buy?"

"Boris bought eighty-seven-foot Johnson with raised pilot house, galley, master stateroom, VIP stateroom, dining room, and separate crew quarters. It will do twenty knots. Boris is happy man. Soon Boris will have new wife to share boat with. Boris intends no offense, Mr. McCabe, but Boris made offer to Ms. DiStefano that no woman can refuse. Please do not be discouraged. There are many women for you to choose." He chuckled and added, "If you choose to choose at all. Sometimes is better to play field. Share love with many women. Make many women happy." He chucked again, obviously pleased with himself. "How is my friend, Susan Ling?"

His question sounded sincere to Murdock, suggesting that Boris had not been involved in her disappearance, but Murdock was cognizant of the fact that sounding and being are two different things. He decided to test. "I don't know. Yesterday she left the office for a luncheon engagement with your friend, Mr. Proteus, and she hasn't returned. Proteus assured me that he knows nothing about it. He mentioned that he made a phone call for you to clear up a title problem about the boat. Do you know where he called from?"

Boris frowned. "Boris reached him yesterday morning on his cell phone. He told Boris that he was in Portland, Oregon. Boris cannot believe that Boris's friend could have anything to do with disappearance. Boris is not happy to hear this. Boris has intelligence assets. They will help find her. Is Susan still married?"

"Yes."

"That's too bad. And how is Grace Bauer?"

"She's fine."

"Now there is woman you should marry. She is strong, attractive and intelligent. You two have many things in common. Grace is not shameful woman. Many women become shameful when they meet Boris." He laughed; again pleased with himself. "Boris made hit on Grace. She put Boris off. Not many women put Boris off. Grace left door open, but that is polite tactic; not promise. Boris made hit on Susan too, but Susan left same door open. Boris likes to close doors. My people will search for Susan. Is Susan's husband a rich man?"

"I don't believe so."

"Whatever," Boris chuckled again. "Boris can make him richer."

Murdock decided not to touch that remark. He still doubted that Boris had kidnapped Susan, but he was convinced that somebody had. He concluded that Boris had a smorgasbord of women. He couldn't imagine Boris giving them up for Linda. But stranger things have happened. Then again, he wouldn't have to. Murdock knew several powerful men whose wives tolerated numerous mistresses. He couldn't imagine Linda doing that. Regardless, Murdock did not want *that* to happen.

At Boris's invitation they retired to the private room. The party was restricted to six friends in addition to Mr. Proteus and Murdock. The six were all Russians with names he either didn't catch or couldn't hang on to. Murdock noticed that each was packing a firearm in a shoulder holster. He wondered if the RCIP were aware of that. Murdock was pleased that the smorgasbord did not include women; at least it hadn't by the time he left at ten o'clock. Robert was still waiting.

* * *

Denise was pleased to see him. She poured two coffees and they seated themselves at a table under the palms, next to a reflecting pool, and not far from the front desk. She smiled warmly and said, "I take it that you're here on business this time. The lack of diving equipment was my first clue. I assume you've visited the cabin where the crime was perpetrated."

"You've guessed correctly."

"From listening to my frustrated puppy, the policeman, they checked for bugging devices but didn't find any. I presume that you did."

"You presume correctly. I expect that someone has a video of the whole event. It isn't my client. Would you have any idea who that someone is?"

After a long silence during which Denise stared at the tops of the palms, Denise asked, "Do you suspect my friend, Jack? He did make a quick exit, but I can't imagine what motive Jack would have for planting a camera. He couldn't have known a murder was going to be committed unless he had planned to commit it. I don't think he did. His actions after 4:00 a.m. suggest that he was genuinely surprised and confused. He did have the skill to install the camera, though. He's into electronics. Would bugging that cabin be a criminal offense here if he did do it?"

"I don't know Cayman law. It's possible that the tenant planted the camera, in which case it wouldn't be an offense. The tenant might have had a better reason than Jack. The owner said that the tenant seldom used the cabin. He loaned it to friends. Maybe he wanted to spy on friends. Maybe he's a voyeur. Whoever it was would've needed the cooperation of somebody locally. I estimate that the transmitter had about a 1,500-foot range. A receiver would have had to be planted in someone's house or a van nearby and automatically activated by a sensing device which I didn't find. It's possible that one was there and I didn't recognize it. The remote could have been connected to a more powerful transmitter so that whatever went on in the cabin could have been monitored anywhere in the world. If it was, I didn't find that either. It could have been removed that next day. I doubt that the police searched private homes for a receiver. They would not have had probable cause for a search warrant."

He observed Denise carefully as he speculated. She sipped her coffee. When he finished, she asked, "Are you're telling Denise all this because you know that the facts are so juicy that she can't resist dipping into her former profession. You're right, Murdock McCabe. What are you looking for?"

"I'm not sure. We at Veritus usually don't get involved in criminal cases. Insurance fraud is more our line. When I was with the FBI, my expertise was in white collar crime. I've heard of profiling, but I've never gathered evidence for a profiler."

"Okay. I like you, Murdock McCabe, and I think they've arrested the wrong man, so I'm going to wing it for you. A murder that happened so close, Jack's unusual behavior, and an accused so famous intrigued me. My puppy cop likes to show off. He got me copies of the police photographs of the scene, the detective's investigative notes, and also a copy of the autopsy report. Naturally you can't repeat a word of this. If he got caught and fired, his wife would probably kill him. What I'm going to say is not based on any in-depth study. I'd never testify to it. Having said all that, my expert guess is as follows. There was no misogyny involved. The killer was composed and daring. You should expect him to be dignified and harmless in appearance. He attracted the attention of no one that he didn't want to. He's probably middle-aged and tidy in appearance. He is not hypersexual."

"Which means?"

"People who are hypersexual have an overwhelming, manic desire for sex and often engage in sexual acts with the victim before they kill her. This guy is organized. He planned the crime carefully and left precious little forensic evidence. Sometimes false forensic evidence is planted like the gun on Perez-Krieger's boat. He wore a face mask that looked like Señor Perez-Krieger to mislead witnesses. He's psychopathic—short on empathy and nearly devoid of conscience. He feels no remorse. I think you'll find—and this is a really wild guess—that sometime in his life he had been humiliated by ridicule."

"Like by kids in school?"

"That, too, but I think this guy has suffered as an adult. What you're faced with is the fact that the police have arrested an early suspect. Unfortunately, he happens to be your client. Early arrests often foreclose investigating other leads."

"I've suggested to the attorney general that that's the case. He doesn't deny it, but he feels that he's got enough evidence to take it to a jury. Unfortunately, he does."

Denise's eyes met his. "The killer has made sure of that. You'll find that this guy has power and he's accustomed to exercising power. He does not use it for good. He's not a traditional hit-man. It's not Perez-Krieger. It's not my Jack either. If you feel you can share information with me as you progress, I'll be glad to help. Old Denise would like to see justice done."

Murdock filled both cups. "You've been very helpful. In addition to your practice of forensic psychology, did you ever do counseling? Like, is that a prerequisite to specializing in forensic psychology?"

"Yes, I did practice as a counselor for awhile. That's where you really get to know people."

"Did you enjoy that?"

"Very much so, but I needed a greater challenge, and I perceived the forensic field to be that challenge. I was right." She took another sip of her coffee, and then asked, "How long will you be staying here?"

"That's uncertain. I know tomorrow is your day off, but I don't think I can stay until tomorrow night for our second date."

Denise's eyes met his. "Don't worry about that second date promise. You don't want to bed me. There's something else you need to talk about and you think I'm the person you can talk to. What is it?"

Murdock put down his mug of coffee. Their eyes met. "My wife Karen was murdered two years ago. We were deeply in love. I see her in my mind's eye every day. For nearly a year after her death, every night I ached to have her in bed next to me. I felt robbed. Something precious had been torn from the fabric of my being and I couldn't mend it. I think I've mended it now—pretty much. But when I get close to a woman Karen's memory creeps back. I feel like I'm cheating on her. I'm starting to get control of that, too. Karen was four months pregnant when she was killed. Just recently a woman that I'm close to made me realize how much I've been subconsciously grieving for the loss of that unborn child, too."

"May I know this woman's first name?"

"Linda."

"Are you in love with Linda?"

"Yes, but I'm still grieving for Karen and the unborn child. That's two strikes and I haven't stepped up to the plate yet."

Denise put her hand on top his. "It's most frustrating to grieve for a baby you never knew. You desperately want to know him or her, but you never can in this world. If there's a heaven, and I believe that there is, that little angel is awaiting for you there with its mother. Because they love you, I believe they want you to love someone, and be loved here on earth. That someone will become a part of their heaven, too. I believe there's endless room for love there. It's so sad when we don't let it happen here. I love Jack. I don't need his love in return, so that's all right. Does this woman crave your love?"

"Yes, I think so."

"And you feel it would be unfair for her because you can't give it completely?"

"Yes. Exactly."

"Oh, Murdock. I wish I were she. She's so fortunate to have a sincere, honest man. Marry her, if she will marry you. When your first baby is born, believe me, there will be two joyful spirits celebrating in heaven because there are two more spirits on earth they can love—your new wife and your

187

new baby. And, for heaven's sake, please invite me to the wedding and the baby shower. Maybe I'll be able to bring my Jack."

Murdock frowned. "So you do believe that there is a heaven?"

Denise took another sip of coffee. "It's not impossible. I do believe it when I really need to. It's never hurt. Please tell me more about this fortunate woman that this one-woman man feels close to?"

"She has a career. In fact, she's been much more successful than I."

"Do either of you see that as an insurmountable problem?"

"No. I don't think so. Our careers keep us several thousand miles apart. I can't ask her to change careers and become my *hausfrau*. I'm making the best money I've ever made in my life right now. By next year I think I'll be doing even better. Somehow all of that could be worked out. We have so much in common. We think alike. We both enjoy winter sports. We trust each other. We both enjoy cocktail hours laced with absorbing conversation. I can talk to her as confidently as I talked to Karen. My problem is one of the heart. As I said, I can't give myself completely to her. That total love and commitment that she deserves would be missing. That's unfair."

"Don't dwell on what's missing. Dwell on those things you like. Don't dwell on the past. Anticipate joy in the future. You're a strong, intelligent, and thoughtful man. The future is your chestnut. Crack it open."

A warm smile crossed Murdock's face. "I hope you're right, Denise."

For what seemed like several minutes, they both stared into their coffee. Denise asked, "Is there something else?"

"Yes. I'm concerned that we're too similar in our likes and dislikes, and in our personalities. I've heard that opposites attract."

"A couple can thrive on similarities or on differences, provided that both people know themselves well enough to determine which works best."

There followed a thoughtful silence. Both sipped their coffee. Finally, Murdock arose and said, "Thanks for the profile on the killer and the personal advice, too. You're a warm and caring woman, Denise. Thanks for the coffee, too. It's getting late. I think I'll turn in."

"Before you do, let me give you a caveat on the profile. Profiles are often based on information gathered from more than one crime scene. Mine is based on this one event. It wouldn't surprise me if this man has killed before but we don't know. The RCIP are so certain they have the right man, that they're not bothering with a profile. You may encounter several men who fit it. That's why some question the scientific validity of profiling. The bottom line is don't rely on old Denise, but keep her in the back of your mind. Sweet dreams."

"Could it be a woman?"

"I doubt it."

Murdock walked back to his room deep in thought. He was somewhat awed by Denise. She had a talent for clear thinking and wisdom beyond what he'd judged on their dinner date. *Special* is the word that popped into his mind. *She's special,* he thought, *because she so easily became my friend when I needed one. Jack is special to her because of his aura of mystery and his supposed adventurous lifestyle. She feels that she is special because Jack includes her among his lovers.* He shook his head and smiled. *It is indeed an especially interesting world that we live in.*

26

Cascadia College, Washington State
Wednesday, May 3, 9:45 a.m.

Murdock seated himself in Dr. Amy Gallagher's office. It was good to be inside where it was warm and out of the cold interminable rain. The aroma of fresh hot coffee added to the pleasure. He happily accepted a mug-full and a Danish. It was even a greater pleasure to see Amy again. Her personality—her confident assurance blended with a genuine interest in the opinions of others—reminded him of her late father. Murdock had learned to enjoy his company and his opinions. He had learned to respect him during the few brief weeks before his untimely death.

"I'm surprised but pleased to see you, Murdock. I expected Susan Ling. Is she not coming?"

"I wish that I could say that she is, but she's disappeared. That's not like her. She's a very dependable person. We're concerned. Susan left the office Monday morning for a luncheon meeting. She hasn't been seen since. Her husband says she hasn't been home. No clothing is missing that he can tell, so it doesn't appear that she intended to travel when she left the house. He's made a missing person's report to the police. No one at the office saw a luggage bag. No airline tickets were charged to her company credit card."

"Did she leave a note?"

"I'm told that she didn't. Last night I slept on a bizjet en route from Little Cayman Island to Astoria. I rented a car there and drove here without stopping at the office." He paused, thoughtfully. "When Susan and I talked last Friday, she expected that Dr. West would be here. Will he join us?"

190

Amy poured coffee for herself. "He left on Monday for a conference in Columbia, South Carolina. It came up suddenly. I can't question him. He's not under my supervision. He's an independent researcher responsible only to his university." She smiled impishly. "You'll have to settle for me."

Murdock, feigning a serious look, said, "Oh, well, if I must."

They laughed, sipped their coffee, and tackled their Danish. Amy said, "Yesterday I received a communication from Brother Gustav. It was copied to your office. I'll summarize it. Brother Gustav gave a copy of the inscriptions that Claude Mitchell had allegedly discovered in Peru to a friend whose encryption skills Gustav greatly admires. Gustav also found a copy of a thesis written six years ago by Mitchell. He sent his friend a copy of that, too. The thesis is a stretch—by that, I mean, unscientific. His thesis goes a step beyond the position that he took at a conference in New Orleans six years ago; the last time he was seen. He claimed that the inscriptions were written by men and women who had powers foreign to the laws of physics obeyed by our universe. Mitchell claims that the ancients believed them to be gods and goddesses. Brother Gustav's friend described both the inscriptions and Mitchell's thesis as poppycock." She grinned. "That must be a technical term among linguists."

Both laughed. She continued, "The long and short of it is that Brother Gustav's friend believes that either someone concocted the inscriptions to mystify and misdirect anthropologists; or, to use unscientific terms, some really dumb kid was screwing around. Of course, Mitchell could have fabricated them himself, but if he did, he somehow made them appear ancient. We need to be cautious. It appears that Brother Gustav's friend doesn't like Claude Mitchell, so his opinions may be tainted. Brother Gustav remembers Claude Mitchell as a tall man, six-foot-three or four, with huge hands. His impression of Mitchell was that he was a sincere man who did not reach conclusions lightly. Mitchell walked out of that conference in New Orleans because his research had been received dismissively."

"Do you think it's possible that this woman who turns green could be a goddess from another world in this universe or another?"

"You met this woman last year. Tell me again what she said to you about her existence as precisely as you can remember."

"At one point she said, 'There is more intelligent power in the universe than you can imagine.' Later, she added, 'I come from the dark energy beyond creation—from quintessential dimensions that have no need to comprehend light, from where the stars are silent, from before the polluted energy of the Big Bang.' She concluded by saying, 'Life exists in dimensions you don't understand.' So, what do you think? Is she for real?"

Amy puzzled over the question, and then said, "As a scientist, I can't confirm or deny that. I'm inclined to disbelieve her in the absence of verifiable evidence—something beyond just her words and special lighting effects. I must say, however, her response was astute. "

"So, you think it *is* possible that there are multiple universes and that she's from an unknown space and time?"

"Personally, I think there may be as many universes as there are possible realities. Technology is being developed that may help us find the answer. We may be able to use the gravitational wave created by the Big Bang to see back into time as far as the Big Bang itself. I doubt that we'll be able to look beyond it and see whether there have been other big bangs that created other universes. Maybe our descendents thousands of centuries from now may develop the technology by which they'll find the place where her *quintessential dimensions* have no need to comprehend light and the stars are silent. But, it could be sooner. We're making countless discoveries by using technologies that scientists thirty years ago said were impossible. We're discovering realities they said were implausible." Amy smiled. "Arthur C. Clark said, 'Any sufficiently advanced technology is indistinguishable from magic.'"

Murdock pondered that thought, and then asked, "If we were able to see beyond the Big Bang, do you think we'd see the face of God?"

"I don't believe in God. My father believed in the Big Bang. He did admit, however, that, if God existed and was the creator of all things, then, at the point that he first made *some* thing out of *no* thing, there must have been one hell of an explosion."

Murdock chuckled. "Yes. I can just hear the old Professor saying that. Over a few drinks one night he told me that something called *negative matter* might be harnessed to pry open wormholes and stabilize them. What's that all about?"

"A wormhole theoretically is a passageway from one universe into another. In some future eon, our descendents may be able to transmit our intelligence from this universe into another universe. They might be driven to that because our universe is freezing down and dying. Their purpose would be to inject our existence to a universe that's not dying on the other side of the wormhole."

Murdock, looking puzzled, asked, "Perhaps some civilization more advanced than ours has sent this Green Lady through a wormhole into our universe? Could she be an advance party? Could there be more than just her?"

"Like I said, I can't deny it. She might have been transported as a conglomeration of mere particles or superstrings that reassembled when they arrived."

"Like 'Beam me down, Mr. Scott?'"

Amy sighed. "I believe that's how Susan put it, too. When you get into particle physics and into the realm of the very small, there is strangeness beyond belief. Some competent physicists suggest that there may be some form of life after death—that the human intellect—"

"The spirit?"

"I wouldn't choose that word. I'd say that the human intellect in some waveform may continue resonating throughout the universe, endlessly. That doesn't necessarily mean that there is a god and a heaven where spirits live and bodies are resurrected. If there *is* a god who created all this, why would he bother to build a heaven, too?"

Murdock smiled. "I recall reading that Einstein said, 'I want to know God's thoughts. The rest are details.'"

"Yes. He also said that science without religion is lame, but religion without science is blind. An English biologist by the name of Richard Dawkins put it best. He said that the universe we observe has precisely the proportions that we would expect to find if the universe had no design, no purpose, no evil, no good, and nothing but blind, pitiless indifference."

Murdock responded, "I'm not a religious man, but I would feel uncomfortable believing that. I'd like to think there's some purpose to our existence. Look at human consciousness. Where does it come from? It seems like you and your fellow scientists have placed faith in what I'd call accidentalism. You guys seem to believe in an accidental universe that contains accidental galaxies, one of which contains an accidental star called the sun, around which circles an accidental planet called earth. Then it is accidentally stabilized in its orbit by an accidental single moon, and populated accidentally by human beings that accidentally have consciousness, which they have accidentally worshiped a god they have by chance created in their inadvertent minds. Does science prove the nonexistence of God? Is there some fundamental law that says this Green Lady can't be a goddess?"

Amy smiled thoughtfully and responded, "No. To be fair, there are many scientists who advocate the superstring theory. That theory simply suggests that the smallest subatomic particles, if that's a proper term, are strings vibrating at various frequencies. They pop in and out of existence. These scientists believe that all material things that exist are made from them. We wonder whether the Green Lady popped out of existence in one universe and then popped back into existence in ours. Some of these scientists argue that the laws of physics match the laws of harmonics; and that harmonics may be music composed in the mind of God."

"But you don't think so?"

"It's poetic. I'll give it that. The term *mind of God* is beautiful imagery but it's not scientific. The beauty of science is that opinions are tested against reality by experiment and observation. At one time, the Christian religion taught that the sun circles the earth. We know that the earth circles the sun because astronomers made observations and proved it. There's one more thing that's for certain. I'd like to meet this woman you're talking about. Do you think you can arrange it?"

"Brother Martin wants to meet her, too. I'll try. Are you willing to share with her all of Brother Stephen's secrets about the chip? That's what she wants."

"I'd have to think about that. Stephen's discovery is useful. It may take us a giant step in our search for extraterrestrial intelligence. However, if she has the knowledge that her terminology implies, then Brother Stephen's work would be kids' stuff in comparison."

"If that's true, then her purpose might simply be finding out how much you know. If that's the case, it suggests that she feels threatened. If she discovers that it truly is kids' stuff, she'll lose interest in you. Brother Martin is concerned about her. He'd like to meet her, too. I'll try to arrange a meeting for both of you together, if you have no objection."

"Not at all. That would be fascinating." Amy chuckled. "He and I would be like the sacred and the profane. Why does he wish to meet her?"

Murdock suggested, "If she's from another element, she'd have knowledge that could affect the dialog between science and religion."

Amy shook her head in agreement. "It could be a threat to all religious doctrines."

"Perhaps. What if, in her former existence, she believed in a god similar to the triune Christian god; or if she followed the teachings of a Buddha?"

Amy frowned. "That accidental coincidence would be unsettling."

Murdock nodded in agreement. "So, to bottom line it, she might be a woman from another, more advanced accidental universe, who had the accidental technical ability to pass through an accidental wormhole into our accidental universe and accidentally assume a human form."

Amy shrugged. "If you play with *that* idea, she could just as well be a messenger sent by God; or by the devil. Superstition would logically permit either conclusion."

Murdock arose. "Yes. I guess there's no end to the debate. But I *do* enjoy the repartee. I can imagine the debates that you had with your dad. Do you know whether Brother Gustav gave a copy of the message that Brother Stephen believes he received from an extraterrestrial source to his friend?"

"Yes. His friend thinks there's a communication there. It's piqued his curiosity. He's working on it. In the meantime, please see if you can arrange that meeting with this Diana, Selene, Hecate, Green Lady, whoever, on neutral ground."

"It may take time. I have to wait for a man to contact me."

"I understand. I'm alarmed about Susan. Please let me know the moment you hear from her."

"I'm alarmed, too. I shall."

* * *

Murdock's drive from the college to the office took over two hours. The rain hadn't let up. He cruised down US 26 as it curled through the tall Sitka spruce on the slopes of the Cascade Range; the road hugging the banks of the Columbia River. He mused over their discussion. He couldn't refute her arguments. They were logical, but so were his, as he'd played the devil's advocate. Brother Martin once said to him that belief in the supernatural is *the* universal default. Maybe Denise had said about the same thing. He'd agreed with her. Like she, he believed in heaven whenever it was convenient for him.

Arranging the meeting would be problematical. The only person who he could imagine might have insight in how to do it was Mr. Proteus. Proteus had adamantly refused to give a phone number. Susan did have an e-mail address. She had searched to find the physical address attached to it, but that was shrouded in government secrecy.

Susan's computer was another problem. When he arrived at his office, Margaret informed him that on the afternoon of the day that Susan disappeared, a purported representative of their computer maintenance company had appeared to perform a routine check. Apparently, he'd used a forged ID. Every file that Susan had originated over the last week had been, not just erased, but utterly destroyed. Murdock was convinced that she had gotten hold of something devastating; something that Traction feared. But how did they know? She hadn't told anyone what she was working on. I hope that her computer still contained Mr. Proteus's e-mail address. He was convinced that it didn't. He was correct. That gave him an uneasy feeling.

His meeting with Professor Amy Gallagher had left him with an uneasy feeling, too. If it were true that the Green Lady came from another world or a parallel universe, what made her an enemy of our civilization? Are there more of her here, or still to come?

27

Munich, Bavaria, Germany
Wednesday, May 10, 10:51 a.m.

It had been a much more pleasant walk. The last time Grace had visited the headquarters of the Bavarian State Police on March 2, she had walked through a blizzard. Today the sun was warm. Flowers were in bloom. She hadn't needed a coat. Grace looked forward to meeting Murdock's friend, Rudi Benzinger, again. The last meeting had been at her request; this time it was at his.

The Amazon was still at the same desk. Today her synthetic smile seemed almost sincere. Grace imagined that a cat playing with a mouse might duplicate such a smile. The woman invited Grace to be seated. No sooner had she complied then Rudi Benzinger's office door opened. He came out to greet her with a gentlemanly bow. He escorted her into his office. As they passed the Amazon, Grace noticed her frown. It was time for Rudi's morning hot chocolate. She joined him.

After the pleasantries, Rudi said, "As I'm sure you're aware, a few weeks ago Herr Weidner reported his wife missing. He alleged that she accompanied Gretchen to Little Cayman Island; then departed on the afternoon of April 7 and returned to their home in Landshut. It was that evening that her daughter was killed. Neighbors had seen her in and around the house in Landshut."

Grace injected, "Or someone masquerading as her."

"That's possible. She hasn't been seen since. Have you uncovered any information that might help us?"

"If I had, I would have notified you. Is that why you asked me to come here?"

"One of the reasons."

Grace took her laptop from her travel bag, fired it up, and scrolled through her notes. She looked up at Rudi and smiled. "I received an e-mail from Murdock on April 13. He'd talked to a Bud O'Hara. Bud owns the cabin in which Gretchen was killed and lives next door. Bud reported that her mother told him that she and Gretchen had come from Italy. Murdock believes they came from Florida, where they had been for several days. It's possible that they came to Florida from Italy. Bud claimed that the mother was an attractive woman with the most beautiful blue eyes he'd ever seen. He reported that she had perfect knockers." Grace smiled. "Whatever that means. Bud also reported that she was a cold woman and unfriendly. When he waved to her, she was evasive. Obviously, she wasn't interested in making conversation. It appears that Frau Weidner told him only what she intended for him to hear. That's all I've got. I talked to neighbors on the phone, but they told me the same thing they told your people. I'm afraid that I'm not much help."

His eyes met hers. "Are you familiar with the Mädchenhaus Café?"

"Yes."

"Are you a regular patron?"

"I go there on occasion."

"Do you know the owner, Greta Himmelreich?"

"Yes."

"Is she your lover?"

"Do you have a mistress?"

Rudi fidgeted, turned his chair, stared out the window, and with his back to Grace, said, "We have come into possession of some information—"

Grace interrupted, "Does that translate as *rumor*, Rudi?"

Rudi turned to face her. "Possibly. This information suggests that the Mädchenhaus Café is the meeting place for a network of women who are employees of the State of Bavaria, and who may be stealing information from confidential government files. If that were true, it would be unwise for you to be associated with them."

"I agree."

"There may be more going on there than meets the eye."

Grace quipped, "I've never paid much mind to it, but I wouldn't be astonished if some things were going on there that some people in some places, even some officials within the Bavarian government, might consider naughty. I wouldn't even scoff at the idea that some members of the government itself enjoy some naughtiness."

Rudi tried to maintain a dower facade, but he couldn't. He laughed. "Well put. But seriously, has Greta Himmelreich ever mentioned to you where she got her seed money to buy the café and start the business?"

"No. Why would she? I've had no occasion to ask."

"When I say that there's more going on there than meets the eye, I'm suggesting that you find out who her financier is. I suspect that the answer might be useful to you, too."

"How is that?"

"I can't say."

"Because you'd be revealing state secrets?"

Rudi reflected. His hands were folded on his desk. It looked to her like he was in prayer. Then he said tolerantly, "Let's just say that I've been in this business a long time, and I've learned that when you've got nothing better, play your hunch. Let's just say, it's a hunch. There's something going on in this city that's connected to Traction. I believe that a woman who is, or pretends to be, the head of Traction has been in Munich several times, using different aliases and disguises. I believe she's been a patron the café."

"Could one of the disguises be Frau Weidner?"

"Of course, that's possible. I suspect that if you can find out who Greta's financier is, it would profit both our investigations."

"Assuming that she has a financier. Do you suspect that it's Traction?"

"No."

Grace mused. She studied his face. He had an expression of quiet confidence. She asked, "Possibly a foreign government?"

Rudi looked pleased but gave no direct reply. Instead, he said, "For the sake of an old cop's hunch, assume that she has a financier."

Grace grinned. "Okay."

"If we may move to another subject—you must be acquainted with Greta's friend, Dr. Lore Fritz."

Grace stared out the window.

"Well?" Rudi queried.

"I didn't realize that was a question. I've had a few drinks at the bar with both Greta and Dr. Fritz. That's the extent of our acquaintanceship. I guess that answers your earlier question, too."

"Yes. Thank you. Does that mean that you've never consulted Dr. Fritz professionally?"

"Yes. It means I haven't."

Rudi's eyes locked on hers. "You do realize I presume, that both stealing state secrets and abortion are crimes in this state."

"I'm aware of that, but I do appreciate your reminding me. I wouldn't think that abortion would be a major problem at a lesbian bar."

Rudi smiled kindly. "A ridiculous thought. By the way, Herr Weidner reported that his house was broken into two nights ago."

With a deadpan expression that amused Rudi, Grace remarked, "That's interesting. Was anything taken?"

"Nothing appears to have been, which suggests that it wasn't a burglar."

Grace shook her head in disbelief. "Why would anyone break into a house if they weren't going to burgle?"

"A curious person, no doubt—maybe one who likes to take photographs. Even if nothing was taken, we consider breaking and entering a serious crime."

"I agree. We did in Michigan, too. I'll see what I can learn about Greta. Maybe there's someone who hangs there who doesn't like her and will spill the beans. I'll work the crowd. If I come up with something, I guarantee that I'll let you know. I hope that promise can be reciprocated."

"It can be."

* * *

The walk back to the Veritus office was equally pleasant. It had warmed to the point where she actually worked up a sweat. The only thing of any value that her man had photographed in the Weidner house was a German passport in Frau Weidner's name. It had been issued two years ago. Frau Weidner had checked into the hotel in Vienna ten months ago with a Paraguayan passport. Or more accurately, what appeared to be a Paraguayan passport. *Most interesting,* Grace thought.

28

Portland, Oregon
Friday, May 19, 9:35 a.m.

Shortly after 8:00 a.m., Murdock had picked up both Linda and Grace at the airport. Linda had flown in from Vancouver, British Columbia; Grace from Munich. Now they were enjoying coffee and Danish in Murdock's office.

Linda said, "The last three days have been frustrating. I've been visiting CEOs of several of Enrique's companies trying to put out fires. For example, the last is a forest products company. Orders for pulp from newsprint manufacturers have slowed since Enrique's arrest. My purpose was to assure top management of my confidence that Enrique would be exonerated. Senior managers were embarrassed by the negative publicity. The situation was combustible. Putting out fires isn't my favorite occupation, but it's become my major time-burner. Our bottom lines are taking a hit. Two days ago, I received notice from the Plato Board of Directors that a special meeting has been called for next week. These were men and women slow to panic. They realized that even when Enrique eventually is exonerated; rebuilding public confidence would be a major headache."

She sipped her coffee, took a bite of her Danish, and asked, "Have you learned anything about Susan?"

Murdock replied, "We've heard nothing from her in eighteen days. The police and FBI don't have a clue. They presume she's been kidnapped. Neither her husband nor we have received a ransom note. There are no teams searching for a body because no one knows where to begin. Top Dog has authorized a major expenditure of our assets to aid the police."

Linda asked, "Do you feel the police are doing an adequate job?"

"It's difficult to criticize when we can't find a clue ourselves. The last report by anyone who saw her indicated that she was seen talking to an older man with a gray moustache and beard at a bar in Multnomah Village. That's the end of the trail. We've checked all the airlines to no avail. Her credit card hasn't been used. A few days ago we checked all of the bizjet departures on the day of her disappearance and the following three days. It was futile. There were more than a hundred. Their destinations were all over the world. Nothing significant appeared. We've checked the ownership of each aircraft, but nothing rang a bell. The true ownership of some foreign aircrafts is often subtly concealed. Our offices in the country of their registration are calling in favors at government agencies, attempting to pierce the veil on those. These shots in the dark have been off target, so far."

Linda realized that the vague description of the bearded man fit Jack. But she also realized that it would fit millions of other men, too. *It's insignificant,* she thought. *Could Jack be one of them? Could he be a Traction agent?* She couldn't believe that. He'd been forward with her in the parking lot, to say the least, but she felt he'd been sincerely concerned for her. *I'm a good judge of character. Jack would never kidnap Susan; nor would he hurt Enrique.* She asked, "Why would anyone wish to kidnap Susan?"

Grace responded. "We suspect that she learned too much about someone."

"That's most likely the case," Murdock said. "That would explain the purging of her computer records."

Murdock reported on his recent meeting with Professor Amy Gallagher. Linda was fascinated by the science, but failed to see its relevance to the investigation. Murdock sometimes wondered himself, but Susan had been convinced it was important. Grace agreed. She turned to Murdock and was about to say *Boss*, but that was Susan's phrase and she thought better of it.

"Mr. McCabe, I understand that you met this mystical green woman last year on a ship called the SS Selene. This may be a shot in the dark, but do you remember whether it was the night of the full moon?"

"It was stormy. I don't have a clue. Why?"

"The Traction people play on the idea of the mythical gods and goddesses. I've mentioned before that in the ancient mythology, Diana is a triformis—a triple goddess. She is Diana, goddess of the hunt; Luna, goddess of the moon; and Hecate, goddess of the underworld. She's sometimes called Selene. This concept of a triple goddess also appears in Irish mythology in the form of Morrígan, the phantom queen. She is the goddess of battle, strife, and fertility. She also appears as Badb, the crow who designates which men will die in battle, and Nemain, goddess of frenzy and battle ecstasy. The Irish myth reminds me of the valkyries of German and Norse legend. For each of them, the full moon was believed to enhance their powers. If Selene tempted you on the night of the full moon, it could be a coincidence, or these people may actually put faith in the myth. They may claim that they're descendants of the extraterrestrials that visited the Peruvian plateau in ancient times; that their ancestors staked a claim to this world—a claim that the green woman has been sent to perfect. Myth is a weapon. If people come to believe it, the myth gains currency."

Murdock said, "It's bunk that needs to be debunked. I doubt that they can succeed in their end game, but that doesn't prevent them from destroying Enrique along the way." Murdock's eyes met Grace's. "What did you learn at the Mädchenhaus Café in Munich?"

"I checked out both Greta Himmelreich and the Mädchenhaus Café. I spent several evenings there. There's an outdoor courtyard. On the night of the full moon, I noticed a table in one corner. On it were three candles—one red, one white, and one black. Behind them was a small statue of a woman. She carried a quiver of arrows and had a wolf at her feet. Wolves have been symbolically associated with the moon. In front of the candles, jasmine incense was burning. It appeared to be an altar to the goddess Diana. There are covens dedicated to a branch of Wicca known as Feminist Dianic Witchcraft. I understand that this branch has a strong lesbian presence. Many covens are politically active. I asked Greta about the altar. She said that some of the patrons were into Dianic witchcraft. They'd asked if they could set up the altar on the nights of the full moon. They were big spenders, so she consented. Greta claimed that she wasn't personally involved in it."

Murdock asked, "Do you think she was telling the truth?"

"I stayed until the place closed. I didn't see her go into the courtyard, although several others did. I talked to two of them. I gave the impression that I was interested in their worship, but they weren't interested in me. They obviously didn't trust me. They knew who my employer was, and none of them liked Ernst for some reason."

"Is it likely," Murdock asked, "that feminist covens financed Greta?"

"I'm not there yet, Mr. McCabe. I need to cozy up a little closer to her. That means walking a thin line. I don't want to go to bed with her; especially while the Bavarian State Police have her under surveillance. If she's involved in suspicious activities, I wouldn't want to be found under the same sheets; literally. Besides, her roommate, Dr. Fritz, might be there. Rudi Benzinger intimated that she may be involved in illegal abortions."

Murdock pondered her report, and then asked, "Is there evidence that the Traction people are trying to co-opt the Dianic covens?"

"I haven't proof of that, but it wouldn't surprise me. If they could demonstrate that their jaded Diana has unworldly powers, bingo. It's a connection waiting to be connected. It would give them a large cadre of dedicated women; some of them in high places."

Next, Grace briefed them on her meeting with Rudi Benzinger. At the conclusion, Linda asked, "It wasn't you who broke into Herr Weidner's home, was it?"

Grace gasped, faux offended. "Of course, not. It had to have been someone more skilled than I; perhaps a professional cat burglar."

Linda smiled knowingly.

Grace continued. "There's one other feature of this gods and goddess thing that I find interesting. Mr. McCabe, you mentioned that at your meeting with Professor Gallagher, she suggested that many scientists now believe that the smallest subatomic particles may be vibrating superstrings, and that since the beginning, all of existence may consist of their vibrating energy phasing in and out of existence. She told you that that's a rather recent scientific concept. In the ancient myth, the Mother Goddess Diana used sound, which is a vibration—a movement of energy—to set the universe into motion. The *new* idea is more than 2,500 years old."

Murdock asked, "Do you have a plan, other than cozying up close to Greta?"

"Yes, sir. I'm doing a background check on her. I presume the state police are, too. She's not secretive. She told me that she was born and brought up in Garmisch-Partenkirchen. That's in southern Bavaria, but of course, you know that. It checks. People there recognize her from a photo that I've shown. School records confirm it. Her father was in the upper civil service; her mother a *hausfrau*. Her father had modest savings, but I don't know yet whether he lent her money to buy the café. If he did, I doubt that it was sufficient to cover the entire purchase price. It may have been a leveraged buyout. Bottom line, so far she seems legit."

Murdock said, "I'm working on Jack Hastings. I suspect that he was the bearded man who Susan talked to just before she disappeared. I also suspect that both the first and last name is contrived. Enrique says that Jack was in the avionics business. No one that I spoke to in that business has heard of him."

Linda injected, "He told me he was involved in avionics while he was in the United States Navy."

Murdock's eyes searched hers. "Really?"

"Yes. Why?"

"Did he mention the Naval Avionics Center at Indianapolis?"

"I don't recall having heard that."

"No. Of course you wouldn't have. Dead men don't talk."

"Pardon?"

"Sorry. It was nothing. Just a thought." He mused, *but a thought worth thinking about, indeed.* Murdock had known a man who had commanded the Naval Avionics Center, but he thought that man had drowned during a wild storm off the mouth of the Columbia River a year ago. His body had never been found. Murdock needed to talk to Jack. He phoned Denise and asked her to give Jack that message.

29

Munich, Bavaria, Germany
Monday, May 29, 8:46 a.m.

Rudi Benzinger sat back and sighed. He wished that he had a good Bavarian beer in front of him rather than the mug of cold coffee.

Last night the police in Landshut had been called by a neighbor of the Weidner's. He had noticed a dim light in the house that he had not seen there before. Neither of the Weidner's had been there for several weeks and he feared a break-in. When the police responded, they discovered Frau Weidner—the woman whose disappearance they had been investigating. Wisely, they brought her to the police station for questioning. A computer check indicated that the British counsel, on behalf of the Cayman attorney general, had requested that she post a bond to guarantee her appearance as a witness in court on Grand Cayman Island. Earlier, she had ignored a summons to appear for a deposition in Ricardo's case. Now they wanted her for Enrique's case.

Frau Weidner had two passports in her possession. One was German. The other was Paraguayan. The documents indicated different places and dates of birth. Rudi had directed that she be brought to Munich so he could question her. Before they could transport her, her lawyer had posted the bond and had a court order to release her.

There was more. Rudi had ordered her photographed. She refused. Her lawyer insisted that she'd committed no crime and didn't have to submit to such an intrusion on her privacy. As she was being discharged last night, she told the officer-in-charge that she was in a hurry to catch a plane to Florida to meet a connecting flight to Aruba. Rudi had just checked with the airport police. They found no ticket in her name from any departure point in Germany. No private planes had departed for Florida. No one was home at the Weidner residence today.

Rudi shrugged it off. He didn't have the luxury of spending too much time on the problem. He had received evidence of terrorist activity focused on Munich. The intelligence didn't indicate whether the would-be terrorists were Islamic radicals or some Traction-type organization. Neither did he know whether the information was reliable. He did know that implementing a terrorist act usually involves a variety of activities organized according to a time sequence. They're conducted in such a way as to minimize attention. Each step in the process, if viewed by itself, is designed not to appear suspicious. Reliable intelligence gathering is critical.

Rudi was distressed. Their current intelligence gathering was designed more for fighting crime rather than interdicting terrorists. He was well aware that terrorism, to be interdicted, required analysis of data covering activities that began while the act was being conceptualized and continuing to the point of execution. His funding didn't provide adequate tools, training, or systems. He sighed. *The forces of chaos have the advantage*, he thought. *Terror on the streets is their stock and trade. Their sinister leadership finds people who, with almost surreal intensity, are willing to blow themselves up in order to kill innocent people. Those odious characters who convince the suicide bombers are themselves cowards. They melt into the population.*

He remembered how the Israeli athletes at the Olympic Games in Munich had been killed by terrorists over thirty years ago. How much had the police interdicting capability improved since then? Quite a bit, but he still thought it was a lose-lose game.

Since no single organization is responsible for all facets of the process when such outrages are planned, it's necessary to have a large web of undercover officers. That takes budget. Much of Rudi's time was devoted to battling the justice ministry for sufficient funding to adequately address the problem. Crime fighting organizations tended to be reactive. His department's natural instinct was to build a legal case for presentation to a court. He was well aware that was under responsive. Battling terrorism requires prediction, anticipation, and prevention.

Obtaining data was not his problem. His people were deluged by raw data. His discomfort rose from the fact that his people became obsessed with it. They uncovered numerous plots. Some were silly intrigues by bungling fools. Others were planted by fanatics to confuse. His unease was piqued by the likelihood that the big one may be buried in an avalanche of trivia. The dimension of each uncovered plot was speculative. Which data was significant? The one report that's discarded may come back to bite. A dark angel lurks behind every choice. He constantly struggled to resist hypersensitivity. That one out of thousands that his people misjudged as innocuous may cause the colossal slaughterer that would convince the public that he was incompetent. The rhetoric of the politicians protecting their own ass would finish him off. He was indeed looking forward to retirement—but voluntary retirement.

He remembered with some degree of fondness a time when police work had the luxury of dealing with mere crime.

He had read Grace's unfinished thesis along with her accompanying memo on the potential connection between Traction and some of the Dianic covens. He was impressed with both her thoroughness and at the resilience that an antique idea could have. He agreed with her conclusion that some otherwise innocent organizations could be co-opted if their membership put faith in the supposed supernatural powers of Traction's green woman. For every weird idea that one could imagine, a constituency would believe it.

He was in possession of evidence indicating that one or more covens gathered at the Mädchenhaus Café. If they had a political agenda, his people hadn't uncovered it. He wasn't certain that he could trust Grace. He didn't believe she would lie, but she might not be totally candid. After all, Greta was her friend.

His information indicated that a great deal of data was being exchanged at the café. That could be normal networking. That's not illegal. Unless, of course, it's classified government information. He had suggested to the Minister of Justice that there may be inadequate safeguarding of critical information within the state government. He hadn't heard what action, if any, she proposed to take. She informed him that she had discussed it with the minister-president, who is the highest official of the Bavarian state government. The subsequent silence did not inspire his confidence.

He hoped that Grace would come through—both for Enrique and for him.

30

Grand Cayman Island
Tuesday, June 6, 10:10 a.m.

The morning had begun uneventfully for Linda DiStefano except for the flowers. It was her birthday. Two floral arrangements had been delivered. The more modest one was from Murdock McCabe. The enormously extravagant one was from Boris Romanovsky.

Yesterday she had received an e-mail from Boris. He and his boat would be moored at the Grand Cayman Yacht Club today. He invited her to lunch on board. As an added lure, he claimed that his intelligence people had come across information that might be useful to Enrique's defense. The e-mail also reminded her that his proposal of marriage was sincere. The invitation was too interesting to decline. She hoped for Enrique's sake that Boris's information would help to exonerate him.

* * *

At 11:30 a.m., she parked her car close to the moorings. She expected him to meet her at the gangplank with his usual exuberance. Instead, she was met by a crew member who was sloppily dressed. This was the first time she had ever seen an employee of Boris's whose attire wasn't impeccable. He escorted her on board and downstairs into the dining room in the main cabin. There, sitting next to a ten-foot-long solid oak table, she saw Boris and a tall, stylishly dressed man, replete in a red blazer and white slacks. Boris arose and welcomed her, but not with his usual flourish. He seemed awkward and uncomfortable with her presence. The other man arose. Boris introduced him simply as Igor. Igor bowed and kissed her hand. They seated themselves. Boris offered iced tea and Linda accepted. Linda decided that something was amiss. Boris was ill at ease.

After small talk, Linda decided to take control of the situation and asked, "Tell me, Igor, where are you from?"

"I am resident of Saint Petersburg in Russia."

There followed an awkward silence. Linda noticed that the boat was moving. She glanced at Boris. He was staring out a porthole. Igor's eyes were fastened on her. Igor was carrying a pistol in a shoulder holster under the bright red blazer. It was big; probably a forty-five caliber. Boris avoided eye contact. Linda said, "I understood that we would have lunch while moored. I need to be back at the office in two hours."

Igor said, "That will not happen."

Boris blurted out, "Boris is sorry, nice lady. These men are Russian Mafia. This morning they take over Boris's boat. They hold Boris prisoner. They want you. If you think Boris is willing party, you are wrong."

Linda turned to Igor and smiled. "You impress me as a gentleman. Taking me against my will is kidnapping. That's a serious crime. Surely a man of your caliber would not be a party to such a thing."

Igor's steely eyes locked on hers. A diabolical grin crossed his face. With a sneer, he said, "Do not patronize Igor. Igor is proud he is part of forces of darkness and brutality. It is profitable. I and my men hire to highest bidder—even to Russian government. Government and business in Russia are like Godfather movie. They both like to eliminate troublemakers. You, woman, are now Igor's stock-in-trade. I make more money just for capturing and delivering you than I'd make working in factory for lifetime." He laughed. "You my ripe little plumb are special order. I have good contract to sell you."

Linda's voice faltered. "Who are they?"

Igor replied impatiently, "I said, they are people who contract with me."

"Why do they want me?"

Igor laughed. "You are not ignorant, woman, but Igor will paint picture. By evening, they leak to media and bloggers information that you have disappeared. Because of who you are, over million bloggers will publish news on web sites. Some web sites are ours. We have more readers than leading magazines. Our sites are popular because we are undisciplined, freewheeling, outspoken and irreverent. Overnight most people in world will know your name and that you worked for murderer of innocent young woman who wanted to become nun. Do you follow so far?"

"I follow."

"In a few more days, they leak rumor that Señor Perez-Krieger had you put away because you knew too much. That's hot stuff. All journalists and bloggers will jump on it. They will spread rumor at speed of light, claiming information came from unidentified authoritative source." He laughed. "Most unidentified authoritative sources are bullshit. Millions who want to believe worst about idle rich man will convert rumor into truth. Do you still follow?"

"Yes."

"Okay. In another week, Honduran police will discover your mutilated body. Medical examiner will determine that you were tortured and gang raped. It will become obvious that evil men were hired by evil man Perez-Krieger whose son also raped. That will ignite imagination of public to run wild. Everyone will hate Perez-Krieger. Who else had a motive and treachery to have you slaughtered? Public will assume that you must know bad stuff for him to go so far."

"You won't get me off this boat without a fight."

"Okay. You decide whether mutilation begins on board or on shore. It doesn't matter to Igor. Boris's crew must clean gory mess."

Boris pleaded, "You must not do this, Igor, or whatever your real name is. She is the woman I intend to marry."

Igor smiled benignly. "Silence, Boris, you fool. We don't want to hurt you. We use your banks. That marriage will not happen. Tomorrow I deliver her to middlemen. Then you may have boat back. But Igor shows Boris appreciation for use of boat—do you wish to screw her before I make delivery?"

Without hesitation, Boris said, "No."

* * *

Linda awoke, groggy. Boris was sitting close to her. She glanced out a porthole, became confused, and asked, "Is the sun setting already?"

"Actually it's dawn, kind lady."

"What's happening?"

"Your tea was drugged, kind lady. Boris did not do it. You have slept long time. Boris has sat by you. No man has touched you. They have disabled Boris's radio so Boris cannot ask for help when they leave. Boris doesn't know what they have done with captain. Boris cannot operate boat. Right now boat is anchored off shore."

"What is that noise?"

"Boris thinks that is smaller river boat come to take kind lady. Boris has deep regret. Boris cannot stop them."

Linda stared out a porthole. They were about a half mile off shore. Mangrove covered the land down to the beach. Yesterday Igor had mentioned Honduras. She presumed that's where they were. She turned to Boris and asked, "Why do I feel so funny?"

"You have awakened from first drug. Igor gave you another a few minutes ago to put you under again. They tell Boris that they have sold you to Traction."

Linda didn't respond. She had passed out again.

* * *

When she awakened, hours had passed. She found herself below deck on a small, rickety vessel, lying on her stomach on a filthy mattress. She rolled over onto her back and raised herself up. Looking out a porthole, she could see that it was headed up a river with jungle on both banks. She sat upright. A narrow stairway led above deck. She arose and ascended it. On deck, she saw two unsavory boatmen who apparently were her keepers. Boatman Number One was a tall, hairy, muscular brute of a man who had a shaved head. He carried a weapon that she recognized as an AK-47. Boatman Number Two was a smaller weasel of a man with squinty eyes and a narrow craggy pockmarked face. Upon seeing her, Number One pointed the AK-47 at her. He nodded to Number Two. He flashed a smile of rotten teeth, and then handcuffed her hands behind her back. Number One nervously said, "We need to keep you below. You'll be safer there. Please go below."

Faced with little choice, Linda complied. Number Two followed her. When she reentered the cabin, she noticed a galley piled high with dirty dishes. Next to it was a narrow table and two chairs with spilled beans stuck to one of them; something less describable stuck to the other. The only other feature was the cot and its filthy mattress. Number Two came up close behind her. His body odor was revolting. Not only did his breath stink but she guessed his clothing hadn't been washed for months—if ever. She guessed that they didn't have toilet paper on board.

The weasel shoved her down onto the cot and roughly turned her over onto her back. Grabbing her left leg, he cuffed it at the ankle. It was too tight. Linda groaned in pain. The steel handcuffs behind her pressed hard against her back. He proceeded to unbutton her blouse and then loosened the belt on her slacks. She felt like vomiting. Number One shouted down to him, "Hurry up. I need you to hold the AK-47. We're getting near the fucking dock." The weasel yanked her blouse open, felt her breasts through her bra, spit on the floor, swore, fastened the second cuff to her right leg, and went on deck. She felt relief. As long as her ankles were cuffed, she sensed that she was a bit more secure.

A strong rotten river smell drifted into the untidy cabin and merged with the stench of the mattress and the odor of diesel oil. She mustered all her willpower to resist hysteria. She told herself that in a world overburdened with terrorists who killed thousands, that her death would be insignificant. It would break her father's heart. Enrique would be devastated for both business and personal reasons. How would Murdock feel? He was so busy trying to smoke out the Weidner's and trying to find Susan Ling that he wouldn't have time to grieve, even if grief would be his response. A second thought convinced her it would be.

She heard their voices on deck. Number Two asked, "Are we going to stop at the village and rent her out like we did the last woman?"

"Of course. Those natives pay good money for white women."

"When the men are finished, why do their wives torture the white woman?"

"Don't ask me. I don't understand women, especially those ugly Indian crazy ones. They smoke something."

"Can I go down and play with her?"

"No. She's going to have a bad enough time without you."

"Do you feel sorry for her?"

"Yeah, sorta, but I know my business. The village is just around the bend. You stay right here on the deck with the AK-47 or those son-of-a-bitches will rush us and rape her for free."

Linda shuddered. For the first time in her life, she felt frail. She hadn't been to church since she had left Alberta, but it looked like prayer might be the only thing going for her. "Please, God," she said, "If it be your will, spare me this horror. If it's not your will, give me strength to endure it with dignity and have mercy on my soul." After a moment of remembering an old habit in Calgary, she added, "For Jesus' sake." She hoped that there was a god, that he was listening, and that he'd do something about her predicament.

Number Two said, "Please let me go down and give her a quick one. It's been a long time."

"No, you son of a female jackass. You heard me. I'll get an Indian woman for you when we get upriver."

"Why not? Why can't I use her before the damn Indians do? They won't notice any difference. Even if they do, they won't give a shit."

"Don't ask questions. Just do what I tell you."

Linda sensed that the boat was slowing. The engine RPMs wound down to silence. It bumped up against a pier. She heard one man walk onto the pier and speak to someone. She couldn't make out what they were saying. Then, for fifteen or twenty minutes, she heard no talk. A couple times Number Two looked into the cabin, undressing her with his eyes. Then Number One came back on board. She heard Number Two ask, "How did you do?"

"Great. I couldn't believe it. There was a white guy in the village. I'd never seen him before. He had a bankroll and two forty-five automatics to protect it. He paid me $500 to go first. That's him coming now. Give me the gun. You help him."

"Help him?"

"Yes, you son of a female jackass. You have to unlock the cuffs on her ankles so he can get at what he wants."

31

Somewhere on a river in Honduras
Wednesday, June 7, early afternoon

Number Two descended below deck. He unlocked and removed the ankle cuffs and took another quick feel. Linda heard a third voice. She assumed it was the white customer who had paid the $500. Oddly, his voice sounded familiar. She couldn't place it. As Number Two finished fondling her and started to ascend the stairs, the white customer squeezed past him. When their eyes met, he froze. It was Jack. Instantly, he put his finger up to his lips. He was dressed in military style camouflage with two side arms in hip holsters. He lifted his right pant leg. Hidden under it was a knife holster strapped to his leg. He extracted the knife. Leaning over Linda, he grabbed her panties and pulled them down to her knees. Turning toward the ladder, he shouted, "You son-of-a-bitch. You sold me a woman who's having her damn period. Look at this goddamn mess. I want by goddamn money back."

In seconds, Number One sprinted down the stairs, with his AK-47 slung over his shoulder. He leaned over Linda but saw no mess. As he reached to examine her, Jack wrapped his strong right arm in a vice around his neck. With his left hand, he stabbed him through his heart. Number One and the AK-47 fell to the floor. A key to the handcuffs was hanging from his belt. Jack freed Linda. They heard the voices of several men on shore but close to the boat. He grabbed the weapon and crept up the stairway. Number Two was at the gangplank holding off the other customers with a pistol. Jack riddled Number Two. As he fell into the river, dead, the other customers stared in disbelief. Jack fired into the air over their heads. They scattered. He released the line. The key was in the ignition. Jack turned it. The engine fired up. He pushed the throttle forward as he sprayed bullets over the heads of the returning crowd. As he spun the wheel to turn up river, he saw Linda in the stairwell.

"Keep your head below. Those bastards have guns."

She stuck her head far enough above the stairway to see men screaming and running along the river bank, some firing wildly in their general direction. Bullets made splashes in the water near the boat. One struck the foredeck. Some men were pushing out canoes. She read absolute hatred in their eyes. She'd never seen men behave that viciously. She asked, "Why are they so intent on killing us? You didn't shoot to kill them."

"They paid for a gang rape. They think that I shot the boatman to steal both their money and the victim they've paid for."

To Linda, that thought had a powerful resonance. She asked, "But why would they want to *rape* a woman—a complete stranger? Don't they have wives? Aren't they fathers of daughters?"

Jack, who was maneuvering desperately to get and stay out of the range of their weapons, struggled to be patient with her naiveté. Hugging the opposite bank of the river, he said, "Some of their wives bid on you, too. Women can be more vicious than men. Use your imagination. The most horrible torture you can think of is probably less than they're capable of. It turns on their husbands' to know what's coming after they finish."

To Linda that very idea defied analysis. She had no frame of reference. What horrors would she have experienced if Jack hadn't miraculously been there? What horrors could she still experience? Judging from the sound of the weapons being fired, she and Jack obviously weren't home free. Her mind was working overtime. *If we're recaptured, will I bravely endure, or will I grovel, cry, and plead for mercy? That would probably add to their pleasure. But it might buy a few more minutes of life. But what kind of life? Is it worth it? What horrible things can men do to women?" Or women to women?* Her mind conjured up a few. *How will I behave in those last few minutes after I realize that I've been damaged beyond repair? How much pain can I endure on those last few steps on the road to oblivion?* In the heat of the tropical rain forest, she felt cold. She asked, "What would those women have done to me?"

"I've never watched."

The gunshots were starting to fade into the distance. Jack moved further out into the main stream. The river was becoming narrower. He was concerned about becoming stuck in mud that might be difficult to walk through. What seemed to Linda to be an endless hour, passed.

"Listen," Jack said. "There's a motor launch approaching from behind. It's probably still a mile away. Can you swim?"

"Yes."

"In those clothes?"

"I think so. I'll take my shoes off."

"You're going to need the shoes. I'm tying the wheel so the boat will continue up river after we pass a shallow bend up ahead. You won't need to swim far—maybe twenty feet. It gets shallow on the inside of the bend. We need to disappear into the forest. I have friends who live in a village up a tributary. We need to reach them."

"Are we safe on shore?"

"We're not safe anywhere until we get to my friends' village."

After they turned the bend, Jack secured the wheel, pointed to the left bank and ordered her to jump. She did. He was close behind. Swimming was difficult with clothing and shoes on, but both made it. Jack grabbed her hand. Quickly they scurried into the tentative security of the thick, tropical undergrowth. Hidden from the river traffic, he whispered to her, "Never talk out loud. Stay very close behind me. It's easy to get separated in this intense undergrowth, and it'd be unlikely we could find each other without making noise. If I give you a thumbs down, fall on your belly immediately, keep your head down, and don't move a muscle. Don't even think about doing something else. I'd like both of us to live through this."

They struggled to make their way through the gnarled undergrowth, hanging vines, and the immense tree trunks of the tropical rain forest, with Jack leading. She followed a few feet behind. Being so close to Jack gave her an irrational sense of security. The tops of the trees formed a broken canopy, shutting out most of the sunlight, and resulting in their having to move in semi-darkness. The heat was oppressive. Their clothing was soaked with foul river water. She was tempted to remove her blouse but thought better of it. She didn't want to make it any easier for the swarms of biting bugs.

Two hours passed that seemed like five. Welts covered her body. She was near total exhaustion when Jack gave the thumbs down. She hit the ground. It was wet, hot, ant-infested and miserable, but it felt good not to be walking. Suddenly, Jack rolled over on top of her. Bullets whizzed over them. Jack put his mouth very close to her ear and whispered, "We've stumbled on a small unfriendly Indian village. The men are drunk. I think they're firing wildly just to make noise and impress their women. They may not know we're here."

When the men stopped firing, Jack rolled off the top of her. They lay motionless. A half hour must have passed before Jack got on his hands and knees. He motioned for Linda to follow. They crawled for at least a half mile. Linda had been tired of walking. Now she was looking forward to it. When it was finally safe to stand, Jack picked up the pace to make up for lost time. She felt that her first prayer had been answered so she decided to try again. She prayed they'd make the friendly village before nightfall.

Toward nightfall, Linda felt lightheaded from fatigue. How many hours had it been since she'd had a normal life? She'd read countless adventure and suspense novels. Why was she so surprised at the cruelty in the world? Why were so many people so fascinated by sex? Sex wasn't something she'd thought much about until lately. She was too busy being the professional globetrotting top executive of one of the world's foremost financial empires.

In that former world, which had existed before yesterday, she often called on major clients. Innumerable opportunities for sex were presented to her. Not only did their top executives find her striking, but it was standard business procedure to provide handsome escorts or party girls for visiting executives. She was often propositioned right under the noses of wives. Even when it might have been good for business, she'd refused. She didn't want to. Besides, she was afraid she wouldn't be very good at it. And *that* wouldn't be good for business. She was, as a result, held in the highest respect and wonderment.

She'd fallen behind so she ran to catch up to Jack. They came to a foul smelling stream and waded across. She was desperately thirsty. She hadn't had anything to drink for over twenty-four hours. As she stared blankly at the muddy ochre color of the water, Jack noticed and shook his head, no.

If they're caught, she wondered how gross the instruments of her destruction would be. The answer was all too obvious. They'd be any nasty thing available. It didn't require a vivid imagination. Still walking, she'd reached the point of almost total exhaustion. She asked herself, *If I die today, what have I really accomplished? I've lived in style, but I haven't loved. Other than my parents, I've never been loved. Not really.* Years ago a man had feigned love and suckered her into an awkward and unsatisfying one-night stand. The viciousness of the woman amazed her. *Why do women who brought life into the world have such a passion for destroying it?* She was struck by the enormity of her own naïveté.

Jack stopped. He turned to her and whispered, "If you see something that frightens you, don't scream. The tribe following us is especially angry with me because they thought they could trust me. It took nearly a year, undercover, to build up their trust. My contractor will be angry with me, too. It's best we don't talk now. Stay very close."

Linda didn't need to be convinced. She wondered why Jack had risked his life for her. He could have walked much faster without her to slow him down. He'd mentioned a contract. What kind of contractor was he? Why did his helping her hurt the contract? Why did he have a friend in that awful village? She hardly knew this man. Why had he dared to feel her up in the yacht club parking lot? Actually, she supposed, she'd granted him the privilege by not resisting. Why had no one seen him since Enrique was arrested? How can he have so much more energy than she? He's at least thirty years older. Her legs were becoming leaden. She desperately wanted to ask him to stop, but she doubted that he would.

It seemed to Linda that they'd walked ten miles when they came to the edge of a clearing. Jack gave the thumbs down. She fell to the soggy ground under a hammock of palmetto. She heard the sound of raised voices. In the clearing were three almost naked Indians talking in a language she didn't understand. They had made a fire and were roasting a small wild boar. The odor of the meat drifted over to them. Linda hadn't eaten for over twenty-four hours. All were drunk. One started walking toward them. She held her breath. Cold fear absorbed what remained of her life's energy. He stopped ten feet from them, urinated, and returned to the fire.

They lay motionless. Jack's body close to hers gave her some comfort. *What if we are discovered?* She tried not to think of the consequences, but her mind was fixed on horror. *They'd kill Jack,* she thought. *They'll drag me into the clearing and use me right there next to the fire pit.*

The drunken men started firing their guns wildly. Jack rolled over on top of her again. Bullets scorched the air above them. He whispered, "They're drunk. They don't know we're here."

His whispered voice was a comforting reassurance that life was not yet lost. For a moment, it overcame her weariness of spirit. She thought again about the parking lot. She felt a need to come to terms with it before she died. He hadn't been just a man feeling up a woman. There was something more. During cocktails and dinner, she'd sensed that he had been a bit smitten by her. *How is he feeling about me right now?* She didn't dare turn to look at his face. *His body is hard pressed on top of me. He must be feeling something. When he found me on the boat, he could've just raped me. He'd paid for it. He wouldn't be in this predicament now. He didn't owe me anything. But if it had been another white woman, would he have raped her?*

She and Jack didn't move until the men had finished their meal, picked up their weapons and left. Parts of the pig had been left in the dirt. Linda and Jack both ran out of the darkness of the canopy and into the sunlight. Grabbing scraps of meat, they both ran back into the darkness.

They ate as they stealthily circumvented the clearing and began following a small creek upstream. After another mile, they stopped and rested. Sitting against a tree, Jack said, "We're in reasonably safe territory now. We can speak softly. A friend in the village where the boatmen sold you told me that your captors stopped there a few weeks ago with another kidnapped white woman. Traction didn't care whether they delivered her alive or dead. Before they delivered her, they sold her for rape just like they sold you. The same three women bid and—"

"Oh, my God."

Jack starred at her. "What?"

"Could she have been part Oriental, and mistaken for white?"

"The man said 'white' but why do you ask?"

"My friend, Murdock's assistant station chief, Susan Ling, has been missing for a few weeks." Linda sensed that Jack was shaken by that news, but tried not to let on. Instead, he arose and motioned for her to follow. It was nearly dark. He took her hand. She yearned for the creature comforts of her apartment, a casual cocktail, and a good book to read. Her endurance was spent. The sun was low in the west. Under the canopy, the shadows were growing deeper. She didn't look forward to wandering in the jungle at nighttime.

Jack put his finger up to his lips. "Shhhh." He pushed her face down onto the ground. She heard movement. Several men were near. She held her breath. Despairing of what she might see, she turned her head up. Her heart sank. They were surrounded. Two almost naked men were standing over her. She shuddered as she pictured them abusing and tearing at her most private places. Maintaining her dignity until her last breath was important to her, but deep down she knew that pain can become unbearable. If she lost it, who would know that mattered? Both men reached down, grabbed her firmly by her arms, and lifted her to her feet.

Jack came over. "We're safe," he said. "These are my friends."

* * *

His friends laid out a table of succulent roast boar, fruits, and a delicious wine like she'd never tasted before. Their hosts, both men and the women, were jovial. They spoke in a language she didn't understand, but Jack seemed to know when to laugh. Judging by his animated expressions, she guessed that he might have been the butt of some of the jokes.

As the evening wore on, their hosts disappeared into their huts. She and Jack had one last glass of wine. She asked, "How did you happen to be in that awful village?"

"My being in the village was the result of an assignment that I can't discuss. I can tell you that it had nothing to do with you. I heard the boatman auctioning a white woman. I knew why. Of course, I didn't know it was you. Remembering what my friend had said about the other white woman, I couldn't let that happen. On an impulse, I decided to try to rescue you. Besides, if the boatmen were selling her body to Traction, I needed to know who she was and why she was important to them."

"How did I affect your contract?"

"My contract required me to stay under cover. I was supposed to let them kill you rather than express any hostility toward them. It's late. We can talk tomorrow."

"I have a question that won't wait until tomorrow. Did either you or your people kill Gretchen?"

"No."

"Do you know who did?"

"Linda, I'm sorry. I'm not at liberty to say."

A torrential rain started suddenly. He took her hand. They ran to an unoccupied hut just outside the light of the fire. Inside it was pitch dark.

"Sorry, Linda. No electricity here. At least we're out of the rain. Take your wet clothes off and give them to me. I'll hang them where they will have some chance of drying."

"Is there something I can wear?"

"Is there some part of your body I didn't explore in the yacht club parking lot? Here's a dry towel. That's the best I can do."

He found her hand and placed the towel into it. She disrobed, toweled, and wrapped the towel around her. She handed her clothing to Jack and heard him walk—she presumed—into another room. When he returned, he found her hand. "Come with me. There's a place where we can sit."

That was welcome news. She eagerly followed. After taking several steps, he helped her sit herself next to him. His closeness was welcomed. She sensed that he'd taken off his wet clothes, too. With her hands, she explored what they were sitting on. It was a bed.

"Are there two beds, Jack?"

"Linda, we became rather familiar in the parking lot. I didn't think we needed two. These people don't have extra beds. We've been through a lot together today. We faced almost certain death more than once. I'd rather not sleep on the floor. I imagine you would rather not, too."

There followed an awkward silence. All that had happened that day crowded into her mind and piled up on top of all that she imagined could have happened. She turned to Jack in the darkness and whispered, "Thank you."

Jack stood up, reached for her, firmly lifted her into his arms, and then gently laid her in the middle of the bed. Softly, he whispered, "Do you really think that we need two?" He awaited a reply. After what seemed like endless minutes, hearing none, he resolved to expand the liberties he'd already taken, but hesitated. He whispered, "Linda?"

Dreamily, she asked, "What?"

"I'm sixty-nine years old."

After a brief silence, she replied, "Then please don't act your age."

His hands, exploring in the darkness, told him she was offering the traditional position. He wondered if it was the only one familiar to her. He assertively positioned her knees further apart. Again he hesitated. Twenty-four hours ago if anyone had told him that he'd *ever* get between the legs of the renowned Linda DiStefano, he would've laughed. Now, as he positioned himself between them, fearful of offending her, he felt the need of reassurance. He whispered, "Are you sure, young lady?"

Dreamily again, she replied, "Please forgive me if I don't make a pretense of resisting. I'm too tired to play the lady."

"I have a deep regard for you, Linda. Don't submit because I saved your life. I don't want a payback."

"I'll never submit, Jack, but I won't be uncooperative either. So let's not talk it to death."

She felt his hand gently exploring and patiently discovering her body. She shivered. She had forgotten how wonderful a man's mouth could feel in the right places. Already in the traditional position, he lowered himself and she received him. He paused and nearly withdrew. She instinctively raised up to recapture him. Like a beach cannot hold back the power of relentless waves crashing against its shore, she could not hold back waves of pure ecstasy. Her entire body was one with his. She fought to control herself, but it was a fool's fight that she couldn't win. She sensed from his breathing that he was close behind her—maybe a little ahead of her. Then, for an inconvenient moment, common sense reared its ugly head. She froze and begged, "Please stop. I'm not on the pill."

He was beyond stopping. He'd reached the point of no return. In sudden desperation he commanded, "Don't move." But she did. Jack groaned. Time froze. Linda released a long deep sigh of resignation. After seconds that seemed like minutes, he said, "Linda, I'm sorry."

There were no sounds. Not even the night birds of the jungle made a noise. No one stirred in the village. One lone dog barked. For several minutes, they lay next to each other, neither speaking, listening to one another's breathing. Then he asked, "Why aren't you on the pill?"

"I've not been sexually active." After another long silence, Linda added, "Jack, this is the worst time of my month. Please, I need you to be in love with me now, even if it *is* just for one night."

He leaned over, found her forehead, kissed it and said, "Believe me, Linda, I have no problem with that. I feel the same need."

If she were going to become pregnant, she knew it was happening now.

* * *

Near dawn, both drifted into a deep sleep, lying in each other's arms. Near noon, Linda awakened. She was lying on her side, facing a wall decorated with a blend of green mildew and peeling paint. She took a deep breath and let it out. She was alone. Rolling over on her back, she became conscious of her nakedness. Also conscious of it was a young boy, about ten, she guessed, who had brought a pot of coffee. He stared at her, politely wished her a good morning, and placed the pot on an end table. He promised to return with cups. He looked over his shoulder twice as he left. Frantically, she searched for her clothes. Jack stood in the doorway, laughing.

"Why are you searching? He's already seen everything."

"I wouldn't want him to get used to it."

"All I've got to say is *Wow.* You look like you were designed by an expert and built according to specs. Linda, you're a very beautiful and a passionate woman. You're wasting the best part of your life. You need to explore your depths. When you get back in your office, take time to be a woman." He tossed her clothes to her. "Get dressed. In the meantime, I'll get the coffee cups so the kid won't get too used to it." He turned and departed.

Her clothes were as dry as they were going to get in that rainforest climate. She dressed. In minutes, Jack returned. They seated themselves next to a small end table and savored the hot brew. Jack broke the silence. "If you're fortunate enough to get pregnant, you can tell Murdock and your dad that you were raped in the dark by perpetrators unknown; or abort."

Linda didn't respond.

Jack pushed. "So what do you think?"

"I think I need to get married. I'm going to propose to Murdock and see if I can make him forget Karen. Will that be okay with you?"

"Absolutely. But we both know that what happened during last night hasn't been erased by the morning sun. In spite of your wanting to get married, *we* can't end here."

He studied her face. Her eyes were soft. They were *not* the eyes of a career woman. Not this morning. They were eyes that had lost their makeup but were even more exquisite without it. They were young eyes as young as his daughters' eyes. During the long night, they'd had intercourse four times. Regardless of the damage, if any, having already been done, she hadn't wanted to stop—making up for lost time, he guessed. Never before had he had sex that many times in the same night with the same woman. He was noticing his age.

She broke the silence. "Jack."

"What?"

"My period is due in eight days. I thought you had a right to know."

"You'll let me know the moment it starts, won't you?"

"If it starts, yes."

"Are you worried?"

"Yes."

"Regardless of whether you're pregnant, we're going to crave each other's company from time to time."

"I know. Will we always have sex?"

"Yes. So you need to do two things. First, go on the pill. Second, keep me up to date on your itinerary by e-mail. As you hop around the world, I'll make sure that I hop into some of the same locations from time to time. Will you do that?"

"Yes. Will we tire of each other?"

"Not in my lifetime. And you need to consider that if you marry."

"Do you think I need to warn him, or make you a condition?"

"In my experience in this crazy world, one thing is for certain—married women seldom tell their husbands about their lovers."

"I wish it were that simple, Jack. Certainly I'd want to spare my husband the pain of my infidelity, but what about me? What about how I feel about myself? I couldn't be a faithful wife in my heart from the moment I married. I need to come to terms with that word faithful."

Jack went silent—deep in thought; his puzzlement sincere. She waited—her distress sincere. Presently he reached over, folded her hands, covered them confidently with both of his, and drew her closer to him. He said, "We can't set back the clock. Our little world changed. We need to face our new world. You used the word *faithful*. Word meanings are relative. Words have the meanings that we bestow upon them. Last night we made love. Love is a four letter word. I could have said fuck."

Linda's eyes met his as she said, "That's a natural part of making love. I don't find the word offensive." Jack smiled and held her hands more firmly. "I couldn't agree more eagerly, but let me propose this solution." He gripped her hands more firmly. "You and I will define *faithful* in our vocabulary as your being faithful to a pledge. You make a solemn pledge to me right now that when you marry, you will never have intercourse outside of marriage without my permission. If you make that pledge, you must vow always to be faithful to that pledge."

Linda sat silently, grinning coquettishly, her head held high. He waited, holding her hands. She asked, "Wouldn't that give you a sort of proprietary interest?"

"A benevolent one. The benevolence will make it work."

She sat there smiling contentedly, staring out the window into the mysterious darkness of the jungle undergrowth. She turned to Jack and said, "I solemnly pledge that after I marry, I'll never have intercourse outside of the marriage without your permission."

He was obviously pleased; actually relieved, she thought.

"Good. I'm not a young man. When I die, there will be no one who can give permission. Do you understand?"

"Yes. I understood it from the get go. I need to know one more thing, Jack. Do you have other—"

He interrupted. "Yes, of course I do."

"Are they as young as I?"

"Most are a little older. One is much younger. Their number has nothing to do with us. I don't have a bond with any of them like the one you and I formed yesterday and last night. I don't love any of them in the way that I love you. You needn't be faithful to me. I won't be faithful to you. But you *must* be faithful to your pledge. I know you will, so I'll be able to greet your future husband with poise and in a clear conscience. We'll keep our little secret and refresh our bond as often as practical."

"Two more questions. The first one you hedged the last time. Have you met Murdock McCabe?"

"Yes. We know one another quite well. It's important that you don't tell him that you've met me. The time will come in the near future when you can. That's all I can say. What's the second one?"

"Have you met Susan Ling?"

"Yes."

"Now a third question. Is she one of the women that—"

"Once."

I'd bet that he'd like to make it twice.

The little boy returned to retrieve the cups. He smiled at Linda and said, "You look very nice in clothes, too, Señora."

32

Grand Cayman Island
Monday, June 12, 9:17 a.m.

The magistrate's courtroom was hot. Jammed with media people, it was beyond what the air conditioner reasonably could be expected to handle. Fortunately, the magistrate had proscribed the use of cameras or recording devices. They would have produced even more heat plus a carnival atmosphere. Linda and Enrique had entered through a back door. The visiting reporters hadn't discovered that door, yet.

Not only was it hot, it was noisy. A cacophony of merging voices made it nearly impossible for anyone to be heard. She had warned Enrique to speak to no one. They seated themselves behind the defense table. Her co-consul, Michael Sudbury, was already seated there.

At the appointed hour, the courtroom hushed as the magistrate dressed in a business suit appeared and took his seat on an elevated bench. Only the High Court judge wore a robe. Robert Grayson, the attorney general, arose and spoke. "If it pleases the court, the matter before you is that of Her Majesty the Queen versus Jose Enrique Perez-Krieger. The Crown asserts that on the night of April 7 of this year, or in the early morning of April 8, on Little Cayman Island, the defendant did murder one Gretchen Weidner, with malice aforethought, and against the peace and dignity of our sovereign, Her Majesty the Queen. We are here this morning to take the depositions of two persons whom the Crown shall call as witnesses at trial. The first will be Mrs. Hilde Weidner, the mother of the deceased. The second will be William Robert Banter, an American tourist from Carmel, Indiana. The defendant is represented by Ms. Linda DiStefano and Mr. Michael Sudbury. I understand that the defense will offer no witnesses for deposition at this time. Is that accurate, Ms. DiStefano?"

"It is, your Worship."

"The Crown calls Mrs. Hilde Weidner."

The woman, who had been seated next to Grayson, promptly stepped forward and took the witness stand. She was sworn. After preliminary questions, the attorney general asked, "Please tell the Court where you were on the evening of April 7 last and the morning of April 8."

"I was in a cottage on Little Cayman Island owned by Mr. Bud O'Hara."

"Was anyone else in the cottage that night?"

"Yes. My daughter, Gretchen."

"Please tell the Court why the two of you were there."

"My daughter was scheduled to give a deposition in this Court. We hid her there because my husband and I feared for her life."

"As it turned out, justly so. Where had you come from?"

"Costa Rica."

"I had been informed by the Bavarian State Police that you were departing for Aruba. Did you give them false information and if so, why?"

"This man who murdered her has money and influence. He's a friend of Rudi Benzinger who is the head of the state police. I lied to mislead them and protect my daughter. After we'd been in Costa Rica for a few days, their police came nosing around. A friend was renting a cabin on Little Cayman Island so we moved her there."

"That's understandable. Please describe the interior of that cabin."

"It had one large room with a kitchenette, and two bedrooms. One was mine. The other was Gretchen's."

"Please tell the Magistrate what happened in that cabin on the dates in question."

Mrs. Weidner frowned. "I didn't feel well that afternoon. I went to bed and fell asleep. I slept through the supper hour. About four o'clock, I heard a commotion and awoke."

"What sort of commotion?"

"A scream."

"Please tell the court what if anything you did."

"I was afraid. I cracked the bedroom door open and peeked out. I saw a man with a gun. I don't think that he noticed me. He had his mind on shooting my daughter and that's what he did. As my daughter turned toward my room, he shot her in the back of the head. She fell forward onto the floor and didn't move. I saw blood gushing out of the wound."

"What did you do?"

"I was scared to death. The way he put the gun to her head, and the way the blood was gushing out, I knew there was nothing I could do for her. I thought he was going to kill me, too. I ran outside through the sliding glass doors and down the beach. I stumbled over some short palmetto and lantana. I decided to stay right there and hide in them until morning."

"Did you get a good look at the man?"

"Yes, sir."

"Had you ever seen him before?"

"No, sir."

"Have you seen him since?"

"Not before today."

"Is he present in the courtroom?"

"Yes. He's sitting over there between those two lawyers—the man with the chevron moustache. I'll never forget his face. You don't forget the face of a man you've watched kill your daughter."

"Let the record show that the witness has pointed to the defendant, Jose Enrique Perez-Krieger. Your witness."

Linda arose and said, "Thank you, Mr. Grayson. Witness, do you understand that we are taking a deposition and that you have given an oath to tell the truth?"

"Yes, I do understand."

"Is it true that you claim to be the mother of the deceased?"

"I *am* her mother."

"Yes. Of course. That's what you said, isn't it? Please tell the Magistrate, are you her birth mother?"

"Yes."

"Witness, would you consent to have your DNA compared to Gretchen's, your supposed natural daughter?"

After a brief silence, Mrs. Weidner answered, "I am her adoptive mother."

"Were you telling the truth when you said you were her natural mother or are you telling the truth now?"

"I'm her adoptive mother. We kept that from her."

"There's no need to lie about it anymore, is there? Did you adopt her in Germany, and if so, in what state?"

After another brief silence, she said, "My husband and I adopted her in Paraguay."

"That's somewhere in South America, isn't it?"

"Yes."

"Where exactly?"

The woman appeared confused. After a somewhat longer silence, she replied, "I'm not very good at geography."

"Was your adopted daughter born in Paraguay?"

"Yes."

"Please tell the Magistrate where exactly she was born in Paraguay?"

"In a village called Río Rojo."

"Were her parents Paraguayan?"

"They were German immigrants who died in a car accident."

"Were you born and brought up in Paraguay?"

"No. I was born and brought up in Austria."

Linda smiled. Mrs. Weidner had made a mistake. If she's a fraud, records in Austria would be kept with precision; unlike Paraguay. "Please tell us the date of your birth and precisely where in Austria this occurred?"

"I was born on August 25, 1959 in Dornbirn."

"Is that nearer the border with Lichtenstein or Hungary?"

"Lichtenstein, I think."

"You grew up there and you aren't sure?"

Grayson arose. "Your Honor, I realize that this is merely a deposition, but I must warn consul that the Crown will object to this line of questioning at trial. Where the mother was born is entirely immaterial and irrelevant. It is not admissible as evidence. The Crown sincerely hopes opposing consul will move on to another subject."

Linda responded, "The distinguished advocate for the Crown ignores the fact that the veracity of a witness is always relevant and material. We have a right to know the background of Mr. and Mrs. Weidner. Our investigators have found no trace of them before the last ten months. If there is no record of her birth in Dornbirn, Austria, the defense would like to further depose her. A man's life is at stake. Will he spend it improving the conditions for the poor of this world, or will he spend the remainder of it in a prison cell? We need to know more about these mysterious Weidner's, but mystery is all we find." She turned to the witness and said, "What was your maiden name—the name that will appear in your birth and baptismal records in Dornbirn, Austria?"

For a moment, Mrs. Weidner again appeared confused. Linda asked, "Witness, do you understand the question?"

A sour expression crossed Mrs. Weidner's face. After a pause, she responded, "Yes." "Then answer it, please."

She stared out the window and said, "Meier."

"Thank you. I take it that you were born a citizen of Austria. When did you become a citizen of Paraguay?"

Mrs. Weidner smiled slyly. "I don't know. My parents and I moved to Paraguay when I was a child."

"Why did they move there?"

Grayson arose again. "Really, your Worship, she's on a fishing expedition. These questions obviously have no relevancy to the issue of the guilt or innocence of the accused."

Linda said, "I'll withdraw the question, your Worship. Is it true that you came into these islands on a German passport?"

Mrs. Weidner hesitated, and then said, "Yes."

"Witness, do you possess a passport from any other country?"

"No. I don't believe so. My husband handles things like that."

"So it's possible that you could have a passport from France, Italy, or some other country and you might not know it. Is that what you're saying?"

She side-glanced at the magistrate, and then answered, "Yes."

"Witness, I assume that you know whether or not you married Mr. Weidner. Tell me please when and where that marriage took place."

Grayson objected. "It's the same fishing expedition, your Worship."

"It appears to be just that," the Magistrate said. "Your client has been positively identified as the killer by the victim's adoptive mother. Information about the vital statistics of the victim's family hardly seems appropriate. Pursuing them at trial might be seen to aggravate the jury to the detriment of your client."

Linda responded, "I agree, your Worship. I would not use such questions before the jury. I would not ask them now if it were not for the fact that I believe that the Weidner's are and never have been husband and wife. I further believe that the victim was not their daughter, either natural or adopted."

The magistrate appeared confused. He inquired, "Who do you believe she is?"

"I believe she *was* an actress employed to pretend she was their daughter, although these evil people neglected to mention to her that she would be murdered in order to frame my client."

The magistrate's eyes fixed on hers. "If *I* were to believe that this was a cheap stunt playing to the media to influence potential jurors, I would treat this as contempt of court, Ms. DiStefano."

Linda's eyes locked onto his. "I would not be a party to a cheap stunt, your Worship. Because of all the adverse publicity in local media, I doubt that an impartial jury can be found on these islands now. Upon conclusion of the depositions before your Worship, I shall file a motion in the High Court to have the trial removed to England or some other common law jurisdiction where the Queen's justice may be found—perhaps Alberta, where I am admitted to the bar."

The magistrate frowned. "In the bizarre scenario that you suggest, would these people have some motive that might reasonably justify their going to such astonishing lengths to imprison your client?"

"I suspect they want to do more than imprison him. They wish to destroy his reputation and weaken peoples' faith in our economic and political systems, and especially weaken peoples' faith in those whose efforts make it succeed. If we're given enough time before trial to complete our investigation, I'm confident that their motive will become clear. It may also become clear that the Weidner's are not who or what they claim to be. Moreover, they may not be the principal actors. I *am* fishing, but not for small fry. I'm fishing for much bigger sea life—sea life with tentacles that reach out of a deep dark shadow land of evil; tentacles that may threaten our very civilization. At the risk of sounding melodramatic, I say that my client is merely the first lamb to be slaughtered."

Mrs. Weidner rose, turned to the Magistrate, and loudly protested, "Must I listen to this ridiculous diatribe by this wicked, unbalanced woman? I find this deeply offending. She cruelly demeans the memory of our dear daughter—an innocent child who hoped to become a nun." She pointed to Enrique. "First, his son held Gretchen down while two other men raped her and sodomized her. Then this horrible man killed her so she couldn't testify against his son. These cheap courtroom theatrics that play to the media are disgusting beyond words."

The Magistrate's eyes turned toward the attorney general.

Grayson arose and said, "Your Worship, the police have found no evidence of any conspiracy by the victim's parents. All the evidence at our disposal points to the guilt of the accused. However, from the opinions of others whom I respect who know Ms. DiStefano, and from my own limited contacts with her, I doubt that Ms. DiStefano would make such allegations unless she genuinely believed that they were true. I personally believe her efforts will prove futile. However, she has employed the services of Veritus Investigations, an international agency which has an excellent reputation for probity and veracity. If they can find nothing, there probably is nothing to find. The Crown is patient. My distinguished opposing consul knows that that patience has a limit. The Crown feels certain that she will respect it."

The Magistrate turned to Mrs. Weidner and said, "You will please seat yourself and answer the question."

Mrs. Weidner retook her seat, looked directly at Linda, smiled slyly again, and said, "We were married in a rural parish church in Paraguay twenty-two years ago this month."

Linda returned the smile. "Would the church be the same one in which the victim's alleged baptism records were kept—the church in which all records covering the period in question were recently and conveniently destroyed by fire?"

Her answer snapped back, "I don't know about any fire."

"You're under oath. Lying under oath is called perjury. Perjury is a serious crime in these islands and conviction carries a prison sentence. Would you like to change your answer?"

The smile persisted. "No. The truth is the truth."

"Do you have any passports in a name other than Weidner?"

Mrs. Weidner's persistent smile faded somewhat. "No, I do not."

Linda suspected that she'd touched a nerve. Rather than push it, she would pass her hunch on to Murdock. Perhaps the Weidner's would feel compelled to cover some tracks, suspecting that Linda knew more than she did. The activity of covering might lend itself to exposing an inconvenient truth—a truth that could be a door-opener. Linda added, "I think I've heard quite enough, Mrs. Weidner. You're excused for now."

Turning to the Magistrate, she said, "I ask the court to continue this woman, whatever her true name is, under subpoena. The defense may have further questions as our investigation exposes the truth of the matter before the court."

Grayson arose. "The Crown has no objection, your Worship."

The Magistrate said, "Then it's so ordered. Mrs. Weidner, you are still under subpoena. Your bond is continued to guarantee your further appearance at the date to be set by the court. Keep the clerk of the court informed of where you can be reached at all times."

Mrs. Weidner arose, turned to the Magistrate, and said, "This is outrageous."

The Magistrate's eyes met hers. He said, "The murder of the victim was outrageous. This is merely court procedure designed to help us discover the truth and punish the perpetrator or perpetrators."

Grayson arose and said, "For purpose of a deposition to preserve testimony, the Crown calls William Banter."

A short, stocky man with a reddish complexion and a dense mop of receding dark hair, arose in the back of the courtroom and made his way to the witness box. He raised his hand and took the oath. Grayson, standing behind the consul table, began.

"Witness, state your name, please."

"William Robert Banter."

"Where do you reside?"

"Carmel, Indiana."

"Why are you here today?"

"Our local sheriff served me with your subpoena and you paid for my roundtrip flight."

"Where were you on the night of April 7 and 8?"

"On Little Cayman Island."

"What were you doing there?"

"I was on vacation. Two buddies and I were diving off the south shore."

"Did anything unusual happen to you on the night in question?"

"I was looking to join my buddies in the cottage we had rented. A cabbie had dropped me off at the wrong place, so I had to walk about a quarter mile. As I was walking, a man came running down the sidewalk. He was looking over his shoulder and ran into me, knocking me onto the ground."

"Did he stop to assist you?"

"He did not."

"Did you get a good look at him?"

"Yes, I did."

"Do you see that man in the courtroom today?"

"I do."

"Please point him out for the Magistrate.

Without hesitation the witness pointed to Enrique.

Turning to the Magistrate he said, "Let the record show that the witness has pointed to the defendant, Jose Enrique Perez-Krieger." Then turning again to the witness, he asked, "Did you subsequently learn of the murder of Gretchen Weidner?"

"Yes. When I saw it in the newspaper, I realized that it had occurred only five cottages down from ours and that the man running away could have been the killer."

"Did you see where the runner had come from?"

"No. But the cottage in which the poor girl was murdered was behind him."

"Have you seen him again after that night and before today?"

"No."

"Have you ever met any of the Weidner's or talked to them by phone?"

"No, I have not."

"I discussed with you the testimony that you would give today, but did I or anyone else tell you what to say?"

"No."

"So, these were all your answers freely given and based only upon what you saw that night. Is that true?"

"Yes."

"Your witness, Ms. DiStefano."

"Mr. Banter, tell us please what time of day or night this alleged collision occurred."

"I'm not positive. I didn't look at my watch, but I think it was getting near morning."

"But it could have been earlier?"

"It could have, but I don't think so. I left my buddy's party at the Grand Turtle and caught a cab a little after 3:30 a.m."

"Did you make any stops along the way?"

"No."

"When this runner ran into you, it was dark. How well could you see him?"

"Pretty good, ma'am. There was a street light about a hundred feet behind us. It lit his face. I saw him clearly."

"How long did you have a glimpse of him? One second? Two?"

"Yes, ma'am. Maybe two."

"But certainly not more than three?"

"Not more than three. Before the third one, I was falling down on my ass...I mean my butt."

"Did you see where he ran to?"

"No, ma'am. I was on my butt with my back toward him."

"Did you pay any particular attention to his neck?"

Banter exhibited a puzzled look. "No, ma'am. I didn't pay particular attention to anything other than his face. I was too busy hitting the ground."

"Were you injured?"

"Mostly my dignity, ma'am."

"Tell us, Mr. Banter, have you ever seen those masks that a person can pull over his head that would make him look almost exactly like Winston Churchill or some other famous person?"

"Yes, ma'am."

"Are you aware of the fact that you can have a pull-over mask made that could make Mr. Grayson look remarkably like you?"

"Yes, ma'am I'm aware of that."

"You testified that you didn't pay particular attention to the neck of the man who ran into you on the night in question. Could he have been wearing such a mask?"

"Yes. I suppose he could have, ma'am."

"Than you, Mr. Banter. I have no further questions."

Grayson arose and said, "Your Worship, that concludes the depositions scheduled for today."

The Magistrate arose, thanked the attorneys, and departed into his chambers. Linda walked over to the attorney general and said, "Thank you for the testimonial."

"You deserved it. I'm sure it bought you some friendlier reporting. Maybe it will make it easier to pick an impartial jury from these islands."

Linda grinned and said, "Perhaps it will." She turned to her co-consul, Michael Sudbury, and asked, "How did we do?"

"*You* did fine. You didn't need me. You'd make one hell of a fine trial lawyer with a little more experience under your belt. Grayson is right about the publicity. Congratulations. The prospective jurors have a little more to think about before they're called into the High Court where they'll assure us that they haven't formed an opinion, and that they can judge the case fairly based only upon the evidence presented in the courtroom."

Linda sighed. "Let's hope so."

The courtroom emptied except for Linda, Mike Sudbury, and Enrique. Mike turned to Enrique and said, "We need to settle upon a strategy in the event that Veritus can't come through before your trial date. I expect the attorney general will offer a plea to some reduced charge and agree to limit the sentence to twenty years. If we go to trial and the jury convicts, the High Court Judge will likely sentence you to life in prison."

Enrique's eyes locked on his. "You said twenty years. Is that the price of innocence? We will be telling the jury the truth."

Mike nodded in agreement. "That could very well be the price. Actual truth is irrelevant. All that's important is what the jury believes to be true."

"Linda already mentioned that to me. What happens to justice when an innocent man is compelled to plead guilty to avoid a jury convicting him of something more serious?"

Mike arose from his chair, sat on the edge of the consul table, looked down on Enrique, and said, "There's no legal system devised by man that can guarantee justice, Señor Perez-Krieger. All that any legal system can ever guarantee is the opportunity for justice. That opportunity is fraught with hazards. You test them at your peril. Often it's better to settle for a sure thing, even when that sure thing appears unjust. You don't need to make up your mind today. Our candle of hope is still burning, but in a short while, it's going to flicker. Grayson is a gentleman, but as he said, his patience is limited. We need Veritus to come through for us with something substantial in the near future—at least something that will buy us more time. I'm sure Ms. DiStefano has told you that, too."

Enrique nodded in agreement. Then, taking a deep breath, he let it out gradually, and shook his head slowly from side to side. His eyes again locked on Mike's as he said, "My mother didn't promise me that the world would never be cruel. She promised me that God would always give me the strength to endure it. I won't lie and say I did something that I didn't do. I'll never plead guilty, even if I go to prison for life."

33

Cascadia College, Washington
Wednesday, June 14, 8:55 a.m.

It was one of those bright, sunlit glorious mornings which are appreciated more in the Pacific Northwest because of their rarity. As Murdock drove up the approach to Amy's office at the college, the lofty Sitka spruce glistened from the sun striking their massive branches, wet with early morning dew. Paul and Amy were standing outside enjoying the sun. As he parked, they came over to greet him. Paul informed Murdock that he was especially looking forward to this meeting. Once inside, they seated themselves at the conference table in Amy's office. After pouring coffee for everyone, she opened the discussion.

"Two days ago I was visited by a Mr. Proteus. I had heard Susan Ling mention his name. I believe you've met him, Murdock. Dr. West hasn't. He represented or misrepresented himself as a government agent employed by some cloak and dagger branch which he was forbidden to discuss. My suspicion was aroused. I was guarded with him."

Murdock said, "I think that's wise. What did he want? Or better, what did he *say* that he wanted?"

"He demanded that I show him the schematics of the chip that Brother Stephen developed. I inquired into whether he could read schematics. He said he would make a copy and have a government expert review them. I told him they were private property and suggested that it was unlikely that they would be of any interest to the government. He insisted. I reminded him that no government funds went into their development. They were not even developed in the United States. He acted as if he hadn't listened. Instead, he insisted rather vigorously that I surrender them to him immediately or face unspecified dire consequences. I insisted even more forcefully that I would not, and told him that both of his demands and

237

threats were inappropriate. When I demanded his credentials as proof that he was an agent of the government, he danced around the issue with the secrecy routine. I asked him whether he allegedly represented the U.S. government. He stared at me with a look something akin to repugnance. He mumbled something about scientists having no patriotic loyalty. When our dialog began, he had seemed confident, but at this point, he appeared to feel insecure. I told him that I'd discuss the matter more thoroughly when he proved that he represented *our* government. After reiterating that I was making a serious mistake, and that the consequences would become evident in the near future, he promised to phone next week to see if I wished to avoid those unnamed consequences. He threatened that I'd be in serious trouble if the chip and its schematics fell into the wrong hands. I assured him that I had experience handling trouble. The man was extremely agitated when he left. Sometime ago, Boris Romanovsky appeared in my office and made the same suggestion, only he promised to protect me from those wrong hands. Traction, Boris, and Proteus all want the schematics. Are they all connected?"

Murdock shrugged. "Boris works hard at giving the impression that he's not one of them."

Amy shook her head. "I'm convinced that Señor Perez-Krieger's issues and the disappearance of Susan Ling are all a part of the same loop and that I and Brother Stephen's schematics are at the center of it. He and my father have lost their lives over it. I'm tempted to say that we are caught in an *evil loop* but as a scientist I don't believe that evil exists." Her eyes met Murdock's. "How far have you gotten in the investigation of Susan's disappearance?"

Murdock shook his head in the negative. "Not far. We know that Susan was last seen in a restaurant in Multnomah Village. The waitress who was on duty that day remembers her leaving with an elderly man with a beard. The man had been sitting at the bar when Susan came in and watched her as she lunched with Mr. Proteus. After Proteus left, the waitress says that Susan remained behind to pay the check. On her way out, the man with the beard allegedly stopped her and talked to her. They departed together. The bartender claimed that he didn't remember seeing her. Fifty bucks didn't improve his memory but he did indicate that the waitress lies a lot, especially if she's been paid enough. When I asked who was likely to have paid her, he shrugged."

Amy said, "If Susan lunched with this Proteus guy, she probably left with him."

Murdock agreed.

Dr. West said, "The last time we met, you described in general your face-to-face meeting with the Green Lady. I believed you were a prisoner on her boat. Please do it again and be more specific, if you can."

"A man who called himself Verbius took me into a room where the only light came from a candle in a green glass holder. It hung from the ceiling on five golden chains. A woman was seated bolt upright in an antique high-backed baroque chair, her feet flat on the floor. Her arms rested on the chair's arms. Long thin fingers grasped its hand-carved crockets. She was slim; very slim. She was wearing an ankle-length ruby red evening gown that was cut provocatively low. Little was left to the imagination. Her flesh caught the green hue from the candle holder, creating a jarring contrast to the dress."

"Did you have the impression that she herself was not green; that the green hue came from the flame shining through the candle holder?"

"I can't be sure."

"Is it possible that she could have been naturally green and the light from within the candle holder merely enhanced it?"

"Yes."

"What else impressed you?"

"Her eyes were startling—a brighter green than I've seen before."

"Were they different from the eyes of the woman you saw in the jungle of Honduras?"

"They appeared to be the same, but I was much farther away. I couldn't see their color."

"Could it have been two different women who, by coincidence, had very similar eyes?"

"I suppose they could have been twin sisters."

"Did you feel that you were *her* prisoner?"

"Yes."

"What was her attitude toward you?"

"She spoke to me in an unexpectedly tender tone. She told me that she'd looked forward to speaking to me again. When I told her that I didn't remember ever having talked to her, she went silent.

She asked if I remembered her from Honduras when our eyes met. I asked how our eyes could meet when I was hidden in underbrush in pitch darkness 300 or more yards from her. She went silent again. When eventually she did speak, her smile had altered ever so subtly, and she had changed the subject."

"What did she say?"

"She imagined that I was wondering how she created that green iridescence and how she had walked without touching the ground."

"Obviously, you were. How did she explain it?"

"She said that I don't have the knowledge to comprehend; that human understanding is chained to the four dimensions of time and space. She explained that there are many dimensions and more intelligent power than I could imagine. She was right. I couldn't imagine."

Dr. West stared out the window. "I'm not sure that I can either, and I *am* educated on that topic."

Amy asked, "Are you certain that she used the phrase intelligent *power*?

"I'm positive."

Dr. West turned to Amy and said, "She seems to understand the polemics. We need to understand what she means." Turning to Murdock he asked, "What happened next?"

"I asked her name. She answered that I may call her Selene. I asked why my friends and I were being held. She ignored the question. When she spoke again, the timbre of her voice had subtly shifted to a lower harmonic. She demanded that I obtain the chip and schematics. At that point, her facial expression changed to one of profound sadness. She told me that if I didn't or couldn't do that, my friends would be tortured to death."

"Interestingly, she threatened your friends, but not you. How did you respond?"

"I didn't. Neither of us spoke for awhile. I took particular notice of her body. It was flawless to the point of being disconcerting. Her smile seemed childlike. When she wasn't smiling, she had a vacant expression that seemed— unnatural."

Dr. West interrupted. "Unnatural? In what way?"

"It looked like the face of Roman goddesses chiseled in stone."

Dr. West inquired, "Did this unnaturalness seem contrived or real?"

"It seemed surreal."

Dr. West smiled. "You're a handsome fellow. Did she ever react to you as a man?"

"She studied me with the curiosity that I'd expect from an explorer observing a strange animal. Her hands and feet were motionless as if they too had been chiseled in stone. After a prolonged silence, she remarked that Amy Gallagher is interested in life elsewhere in the universe. She asked me whether either her father or Brother Stephen believed in extraterrestrial life. I told her that I didn't know. Not a muscle in her body moved. Then, her eyes subtly mellowed. She leaned forward—close to me. Speaking softly she said, 'Sapient life is always a conflict between two powerful forces. You're on the wrong side. You believe that morality must determine lifestyle. It is easier when lifestyle determines morality.'"

"Did you interpret that as a religious statement?"

"I didn't interpret it. What happened next was bizarre. She held out her right hand, inviting me to take it. I decided to play her game for the sake of my friends. Speaking gently but firmly she said, 'Join me, Murdock McCabe. I will make you unimaginably powerful, and rich beyond comprehension, my prime minister over all.'"

Dr. West pulled his chair closer to Murdock. "That's most interesting. Please tell me exactly how you responded."

"I told her about a Sunday school lesson I'd learned as a child. A fellow named Satan tempted a fellow named Jesus. Satan offered him the kingdoms of the world."

"Good retort. How did she respond?"

"Gripping my hand, she leaned further forward and whispered, 'If Jesus had had the simple sense to accept the offer, he wouldn't have been killed.' An easy smile crossed her face as she added, 'He was an absurd itinerant preacher; a tragic troublemaker who roamed dusty alleyways in the junkyard of the world. History might have awarded him the dubious status of a two-bit philosopher if he hadn't claimed to be God. Who believes that junk anymore?'"

Dr. West smiled. "My, my. How impetuous. How did you respond to that?"

"I didn't. Speaking a little louder, she asked if I thought of myself as another Jesus. I declined again to reply. I sensed that my silence had made a chink in her self-assurance. The subtle softness in her eyes transmuted momentarily into a threatening glare. Then, inexplicably, her expression swung to a sad, subdued admonishment. She confessed that she was disappointed and suggested that she and I could create a syllogism beyond belief."

Amy turned to Dr. West and said, "Before he was taken prisoner aboard the ship, I'd told Murdock that if he ever met this green woman again, he should ask her where she had come from. Her answer was remarkable." She nodded toward Murdock. He said, "The question created another radical mood swing. Her eyes literally sparkled as she replied, 'I come from the dark energy beyond creation—from quintessential dimensions that have no need to comprehend light, from where the stars are silent, from before the polluted energy of what humans call the Big Bang.'"

Dr. West's astonished eyes met Amy's. Murdock continued, "At that point, she released my hand and provocatively lowered the straps of her evening gown. They floated down her arms, exposing tantalizingly full-rounded, firm breasts, their hard nipples the color of fresh-picked red raspberries. Her body changed from rigid to liquid. I became sexually aroused. A coquettish smile crossed her face. She held out both arms again, and the motion produced a delightful ripple in her breasts. My head swam. I felt as if her soul possessed mine. I was obsessed by a sudden all-consuming barbarity—a desire to brutally rape her. I gripped her hands and jerked her toward me. I stared into her eyes, searching for an ardor equal to mine. But in her eyes, I thought for a moment that I saw a devil-woman—the woman who took part in the scene where they tortured and killed. I froze. We exchanged confused stares. I felt that nothing I could say would save me or my friends. Sickened, I stepped back and reminded her that that two-bit philosopher had responded to his temptation with the imperative; *Get thee behind me, Satan.* So I told her to go to hell, whoever or whatever she was."

"Did that anger her?"

"No. In fact, I was astonished. Instead of anger, she stared at me musingly. Raising her arms straight upward, she moved the gown to conceal her breasts. Then, to my astonishment, she began quietly laughing as if she were pleased with herself. Then, falling silent again, her eyes became melancholy as if she were remembering the wound of some enduring sadness. Then she seemed to stare upon something behind me in the dark shadows—something that, when I looked over my shoulder, I couldn't see."

"Did you feel that was a psychological ploy, or did you feel that she actually saw something that you couldn't see?"

"I felt that it was an act. At that point, I suggested that she'd become the prisoner of her own illusions; that her friends are cutthroats; and that she couldn't tell the difference between things human or inhuman. A sardonic grin crossed her face. She exclaimed, 'Human?' Then she repeated that life exists in dimensions I didn't understand. Lazily, she waved her right hand. From behind, Verbius wrapped his powerful left hand around my left arm and said firmly, 'Come now. It's over.'"

"As if some unfelt wind had entered the room, the candle flickered and went out. In total darkness, Verbius dragged me toward the door. As he opened it, a crack of light entered the room. I glanced over my shoulder again toward where she had been sitting. The woman who had called herself Selene was gone."

Dr. West seemed puzzled. He said, "That was a fascinating story about a most interesting woman."

Dr. West stared out the window, with his hands folded behind his neck. "Does she need the schematics or does she merely want to know how much we know? That's still the critical question."

Murdock's eyes met his. "Do you think that you know the answer?"

"I have a suspicion. That's the beginning of science. We dignify suspicion by calling it a hypothesis or a theory. It sounds better. There follows a lengthy process of trying to prove the hypothesis. That often means indulging in educated guesses that aren't always too educated. That's where I am. I have another question. When Selene called Jesus a two-bit philosopher, how did you feel about that?"

"I was annoyed."

"Why?"

"I'm not sure. Besides, the conversation moved on and I didn't have time to think about it."

Amy turned to Paul and remarked, "She's educated. I know most of the people in our field. Could she be one of our people masquerading as an alien?" She turned to Murdock and asked, "Has that been investigated?"

Murdock nodded. "Six months ago all of our offices worldwide were requested to make inquiries at all educational and scientific institutions. No scientist had turned up missing other than Claude Mitchell. Someone could be feeding her the lines."

Amy shook her head in the negative. "I don't think so. Her remark is teasingly evocative. She suggests that our universe was not created by a Big Bang."

Murdock, bewildered, said, "I thought that almost all cosmologists agree that our universe is expanding from a big bang."

"There are some new theories," Amy said. "The Christian myth suggests that God created the universe out of a void—out of empty space—essentially out of nothing. Many theorists today go even farther. They suggest that not even the void existed—not even space itself. Everyone's heard of Einstein's equation $E=MC^2$, which essentially says that mass and energy are interchangeable. They're different aspects of the same thing. Gravity affects them both—it attracts every *thing* to every other *thing*, so in effect gravity is negative energy. If, as we believe, mass and gravity are equal, they cancel each other out so that nothing really exists."

Murdock's eyes locked onto hers. "That sounds silly."

"It's very strange. I'll give you that. If the universe is made of nothing at all, its existence is easier to explain. Have you heard of quantum mechanics?"

"I've heard that it's being used commercially in the electronics industry."

"That's true. The idea of separating *nothing* into energy and gravity created the *uncertainty principle*. The exact position of any object can never be determined. An object can find itself on either side of a barrier, because in effect, it tunnels its way through—back and forth, even if that barrier is high energy. That principle predicts what we call *quantum tunneling.* Some believe that there was no Big Bang—that the universe just quantum-tunneled its way through into existence."

"I don't understand that, but do they have proof?"

Amy smiled. "Neither the Big Bang, nor quantum tunneling, nor any other theory of the beginning has been proven yet. That's why Selene's cynical remark is fascinating. Was she tunneled, so to speak?"

Murdock returned the smile. "It all sounds rather muddled to me. It seems that these theories are mere myths, competing in the marketplace of ideas with the Christian myth."

Dr. West injected, "We have some scientific evidence in support of our myths. We have no extrinsic evidence that God ever existed."

Amy said, "My father was basically a philosopher who was interested in cosmology. He felt that our human learning had reached the point where science and theology meet. That's why he and Brother Stephen meshed so well. Stephen was the scientist. My father felt his writings in philosophy bordered on a secular theology."

Murdock added, "All you've said leads me to a rather curious conclusion. It suggests that those who believe in any of these myths, whether they're scientists or theologians, believe it as a matter of faith. Who said we don't live in an age of faith?"

Amy replied, "I assume your rhetorical question requires no answer. Selene's remark also raises the question as to whether there can be intelligent consciousness in the form of pure energy. *Form* may be a poor choice of word. Can it exist without mass—that is without body as we know it? Could it be present here, now, without our being able to sense it?"

Murdock added, "If so, Brother Martin might call them spirits or angels."

Dr. West frowned. "I still want to meet this Selene, or Diana, or Hecate—whatever she wants to call herself. Please see if you can arrange it."

Amy shuddered. "She'd hold you captive to get at me."

"I'll stay close to Murdock." He turned and faced him. "I suspect there's a deep-seated conflict disturbing her mind. You're the cause of it. In her own strange way, I think our Green Lady is in love with you."

"Women," Amy suggested, "have killed because they were frustrated in love, and I'm not sure this gal is too tightly wrapped."

34

Portland, Oregon
Monday, June 19, 9:40 a.m.

Frustrating investigations were nothing new to Murdock, but this one was a pacesetter. Starting as an investigation of an alleged rape victim, it redirected itself into an investigation of murder. And, tragically, Susan had gone missing. The police had other fish to fry. He had stretched out his staff in an effort to identify the gray-bearded man who had allegedly accompanied Susan out of the restaurant. The effort failed. He had assigned a woman to track down the waitress who had claimed that Susan left with the bearded man. She didn't work there anymore and no one knew where she worked. Murdock was convinced that her evidence had been bought and paid for. He hoped that *she* hadn't paid the final price, too—and not only her. Murdock had to admit to himself that Susan, if she were still alive, most likely would have found a way to communicate with him.

Another check on the Weidner's by the Veritus office in Paraguay came up dry.

Murdock turned to his computer and clicked on e-mail. There was one from Grace. It read:

> "As you instructed, I flew to Rome in search of Father Juan Robles, the Paraguayan parish priest who had been the custodian of the baptismal records that might have established Gretchen's birth date and her parentage. I had phoned him numerous times from Munich, left messages, but he'd never returned my calls. I found his third floor apartment in a rooming

245

house on a shady tree-lined street within three blocks of the Vatican. I knocked several times without success. When I descended the stairs and stepped outside, neighbors had gathered. Although my Italian is shabby, the neighbors were eager to communicate. They liked their "little priest." They were concerned. He hadn't been seen for two weeks. His landlady, who was among the crowd, told me that someone sent cash by messenger to pay his rent. Soon after his arrival from Paraguay, several older priests had visited him. She had written down their first names and she shared them with me. She'd never heard their last names and knew no addresses. After a fruitless check with authorities at the Vatican and with city officials, I became concerned that the closer I got to answers, the more other people became endangered. These Traction people cover their tracks with death.

"Boris Romanovsky's banks in Cyprus have strong ties with a correspondent bank in Rome—the Banco d'Alma. As you and I decided, I explored the financial dealings of a man who Boris's bank manager identified as Ernesto Flavio. Thank you for wiring the money for the indispensable bribes. I learned that Flavio is an investor, possibly the principal investor, in an ocean freight hauling company called Pleiades Transshipments. I traced the history of the company and attempted to identify its other shareholders, if any. The company operates five cargo ships on the high seas.

"That's all I have for now, Grace."

Murdock was pleased. Grace was indeed an efficient asset.

Rudi had phoned Murdock earlier that morning. He suggested that Grace have another serious talk with Greta Himmelreich. He impressed upon Murdock that Grace should never mention his name. His state police inquiries, the results of which he couldn't share with Murdock, had fortified his suspicion that the café operations were a subterfuge, and that Greta and her friend, Doctor Lore Fritz, had a hidden agenda. He was able to tell Murdock that they'd been unable to trace the funds with which Greta had bought the café. The trail ended at a blind trust in Bermuda. He needed assurance that Grace could handle herself. Uncovering the secrets of the Mädchenhaus Café could be dangerous. Murdock reminded him that she'd served several years with the Michigan State Police. Rudi reminded Murdoch that it was unlawful for her to carry a gun in the State of Bavaria. Murdock assured him that she probably didn't. Rudi mentioned that he was thinking of retiring and looking for employment in the private sector. Murdock expressed confidence that he could get Rudi a management position at Veritus. In the meantime, Murdock urged Rudi to buttress Grace if she became over exposed to hazard. Rudi indicated that buttressing was a definite probability.

Murdock was aware that jury selection for Enrique's trial would begin soon. He and Linda were both convinced that the attorney general would like to give Enrique a break. He needed something to hang his hat on. Murdock had suggested that she explore the legal doctrine called *diminished responsibility* or *diminished capacity.* Her co-counsel, Michael Sudbury, had mentioned it, too. It would necessitate obtaining a physiatrist. Upon examining Enrique, he would have to find that the allegations of rape against his son, which he passionately believed to be untrue, so frustrated him and unsettled his mind that his mental state was disturbed to the point that it impaired his ability to make rational choices at the time he killed Gretchen. The attorney general could hang his hat on that. It's a defense that hopefully would diminish the punishment. At their last meeting he had admitted that a rational man in Enrique's position would logically have hired a professional hit man. Michael was phoning psychiatrists, trying to find one who would fly down to Grand Cayman Island and examine him.

The media coverage had reached a frenzied peak. Murdock was disgusted. Linda had best described it as "misleading information buttressed by vivid speculation." All of Enrique's business ventures were hit and colored gray. Financial success was demonized. Even if he were acquitted, Murdock knew his friend's character had been enduringly soiled. People remember the dreadful and forget the worthy. In the last week, Veritus started taking slashes. Ridicule is a sharp sword. Inept is a hard word. The media alleged that this prominent international investigating company was billing for enormous time and charges in a vain attempt to discover exculpatory evidence where there was none. Murdock regretted that this diminished Brother Martin's ability to obtain a fair price. Even Boris Romanovsky had tentatively withdrawn his offer.

The Veritus office in Indianapolis had completed its investigation of the eyewitness, William Banter. Murdock reviewed their report. Banter was a genuine article. He was a well known and well liked owner of a printing shop in downtown Indianapolis. Among other jobs, he printed all the legislative acts for the state legislature. Banter assured the Veritus agent that he had clearly seen the man running from the cottage under a light, and that his identification of Enrique was unequivocal. The agent's opinion was that Banter would be cool and confident—an outstanding witness for the prosecution.

Murdock assigned four agents in his Portland office to research, identify, and contact all sculptors of theater masks worldwide. Susan's incomparable research skills were sorely missed.

Murdock had been careful to request that the Veritus agent in Indianapolis not question Banter about the possibility that the man he saw was wearing a mask. He, Mike, and Linda had all agreed that it shouldn't come up again until her cross-examination at the trial.

Taking a pipe out of his right top desk drawer, he put it in his mouth. He hadn't bought tobacco for years. Chewing on the stem tended to relax him. He reviewed the notes he'd made at the cottage where Gretchen was killed. Too many questions were still unanswered. Who had placed the hidden camera and recorder in the ceiling? Did the Weidner's have a reason to plant it? He couldn't imagine one. Were Denise's Jack and his technician accomplices? Why would *they* do it? Who controls them and what's their game? Did they place the transmitter there anticipating the murder? Did they perpetrate the murder? Was the transmission of the TV images recorded to a DVD? Did the recording prove that Enrique wasn't the murderer? If so, Jack and his accomplice must know that they possessed exculpatory evidence. Why hadn't they come forward? What had they done with the recording? Why didn't they want to see Enrique set free?

The phone rang. It was Linda. Sounding stressed she said, "The AG just phoned. He's offered a deal—take it or leave it. I think he's taking heat for not moving the case."

"Heat from where?"

"He didn't come out and say it, but I assume it's from the government in London even though they hold the Cayman Islands at a very long arm's length."

"What's he offered?"

"Enrique's charged with murder under the Cayman Criminal Code Section 180. The AG admits that our allegation of diminished capacity could have some buoyancy with a jury. He will agree to accept a plea of guilty to manslaughter under Section 181. He's given us three weeks to respond."

Murdock groaned. "I've read 180 and 181. Both carry a maximum penalty of life in prison. Where's the *quid pro quo*?"

"If Enrique doesn't accept the offer, the AG will go for the whole shot and request the court to sentence him to life in prison. If he accepts the offer, the AG will urge upon the court the fact that the plea has been entered with the expectation that the court not sentence him to more than fifteen years; and that the AG's justification is the potential weight of the diminished capacity argument."

"Does Mike think the judge will buy that?"

"Yes. In spite of journalistic ridicule, those in the know are aware that Veritus wouldn't be so intensely pursuing the investigation unless they expected to find something that could hurt the Crown's case. The AG insists that it will fly."

"Can't we do better? Linda, I can't believe that that's really a final offer."

"My problem is that Enrique has changed his mind. He wants to do it."

"My god, that's a catastrophe. Why?"

"Murdock, I wish you could have seen him today. He's emotionally shattered. His son's being threatened with life in prison and now him—his reputation destroyed—he's about to lose control of the family empire to his sister Estrelita—it's too much for him. From a squeaky clean image he's been distorted into a scoundrel and a killer. I've never seen him like this. If there ever was a case of diminished capacity, he has it now. He wants to get it over. I've suggested therapy. He won't hear of it. Estrelita phoned him. She wants him to take the plea while he can get it. She says the media-inflicted wounds are the bleeding the family businesses. She wants control now. First, she'd get rid of me. After me, the deluge."

Murdock, speaking with determined firmness, insisted, "Ethically, you can't do it."

"I know. He's innocent. The judge can't accept the plea unless Enrique admits killing Gretchen, which I know he didn't. I've explained to him that he'd have to lie to the court and that I, as an attorney and an officer of the court, can't advise him to do that."

"Even more than that, Linda. You can't knowingly present false evidence to the court. You could be disbarred in both the Caymans and Alberta. The judge could find you in contempt of court and punish *you* with imprisonment."

"Yes, and because my job's on the line with Estrelita reaching for control, I have a conflict of interest, too. I'm between the proverbial rock and a hard place. The whole world in which I've functioned successfully for over twelve years is evaporating. For Enrique's sake and my own, I'm trying to remain composed and professional. I know I should withdraw as his attorney. If Enrique felt that I was abandoning him that would crush him. I desperately need you to come through for us. We need hard evidence before the conflict of interest compels me to withdraw as his attorney."

"It already does, Linda."

"Help me, my love."

She hung up.

35

After an irksome day, Linda was looking forward to the evening. She and her two girlfriends were meeting for cocktails and dinner at the outside garden at Hemingway's. Opening her closet door, she studied her wardrobe. She chose a white silk ankle length slim pant and a matching white top with spaghetti straps. To go over it, she chose a Chinese red flowing silk long sleeve shirt with a print of white dogwood. She studied her collection of shoes. She couldn't compete with Imelda Marcos, but she liked to buy shoes and her collection filled two sizeable shoe racks. But there was no doubt. The red patent leather pumps with open toe, sling back slight platforms and high heels would do nicely. Her collection of purses nearly equaled her shoe collection. She chose a red patent leather envelope handbag with a silver shoulder chain.

Her dark hair was short casual. She brushed it, combed it, applied makeup, and in minutes she was in her car and on her way.

* * *

The evening was magnificent. Most evenings on Grand Cayman Island were magnificent. A late afternoon thunderstorm had brought relief from the heat. Above them a moonless canopy of night sky offered countless stars for their viewing pleasure. A cool sea breeze drifted off the Caribbean, gently rustling the fronds atop the tall royal palms. The night was alive with the humor and the camaraderie of three women who thoroughly enjoyed each other's company. Stir in a few pomegranate martinis and supercharge them with the gusto of youth, and the problems of the nasty world vanished until morning. They'd never experienced a dull evening when they were together.

But this night, one thing was different. Linda wasn't into the pomegranate martini routine. She chose non-alcoholic drinks. Her friends chided her. Had she gone soft? Non-alcoholic drinks violated the oath of the sisterhood. What oath? They were sure they'd remember it sometime; maybe, Linda suggested, if they had one more martini. But Linda indicated that she'd had an exasperating day and little sleep for the last two nights. As tired as she was, she certainly didn't want to drink and drive. That was a half truth. Disappointed, they had accepted it and called it an early evening. Shortly after 10:00 p.m., they separated in the parking lot. As Linda walked to her car, her friends noticed there was a certain lilt missing from her step. Something was troubling her—something other than the legal situation; something she didn't want to share.

Driving southward along the Seven Mile Beach Road, the nasty world hounded her. She was fearful that Enrique was slipping into depression. *Am I becoming a tad high-strung myself? Is my representing him as his chief criminal defense counsel distracting me too much from my normal activities—administering the family financial empire? Any blunder will be duly noted by Estrelita. She isn't a bad person; just jealous, ambitious, cunning, and unpredictable.*

The drive took twenty-five minutes. As she turned into the driveway of the compound, an armed security guard opened the gates. She parked on the circular drive. Upon exiting the car, she proceeded directly to the elevator, and selected the third floor. Within minutes, she entered her apartment and locked the door behind her. She stopped. *I never do that. Why did I just now?* She didn't have an answer, but it remained locked.

As she opened the French doors leading to the balcony, the sea breeze wafted in and enticed her outside. Too exhausted even to undress, she kicked off her shoes and dropped herself onto a reclining chair. She sighed. The day had seemed endless.

While at the restaurant, a text message had come from Murdock. She picked up her cell phone and retrieved it. It was brief. It said, "I'll come through for you, my love." She chose to believe him, but cautiously. His last two words resonated. They hung in her mind and sang in her heart. They were her keys to paradise tonight; albeit a fool's paradise. Would he be likely to marry her if he knew she was carrying another man's baby?

Exhaustion and the fog of sleep played with her consciousness; half dreams; half rekindled memories. Shadows of ancient memories drifted into and out of her mind—a memory of lust igniting relentless passion; a memory of all but forgotten bliss; and a bitter memory of the sublime ecstasies of sex being hollowed and cheapened by the cruel discovery that her body had merely been used. *Crudely screwed and dumped,* she thought, disgusted. The shadows passed. Murdock, she knew, was a man who could never just use her. Her lips curved into a sleepy smile, but she wished he would do something, soon.

The almost imperceptible sound of gentle waves from a tranquil sea below soothed her. Placing a pillow under her head, she focused on the stars. They blurred. She drifted off to the soft edge of a dream. A noise. Startled, she awakened. Another almost imperceptible noise. A sound that didn't belong. It came from behind her. She looked over her shoulder. No lights were turned on in her apartment. She had locked the door. Maybe it was an ice cube dropping in the ice maker. Maybe she just imagined it.

Murdock would be high over the Atlantic Ocean now. When they'd talked earlier, he had mentioned that an abbot of a Bavarian Monastery named Brother Martin had requested that he and Grace meet with him. She knew it was the monastery where a monk had been murdered by Traction.

A more perceptible noise behind her. Linda sat upright. She turned and starred into the darkness of her apartment. She had dropped her travel bag next to her chair. Reaching into it she extracted her penlight. She was too late. From behind a strong arm reached around her chest and immobilized her; a hand firmly covered her mouth. Her body went rigid. She felt hot breath on the back of her neck. A man's voice whispered into her ear, "Relax. It's me. Jack. I'm going to release you now. Don't scream. Okay?"

"Okay."

In the darkness, she could make out that he was wearing only wet swimming trunks. He dropped a coil of rope, took her hand, and said, "Let's go inside."

"Let's stay right here. How did you get into the compound?"

"I swam from that ship out there and scaled the wall. My wet suit is in your bathroom."

"Are you talking about that large boat a half mile out with a helicopter pad?"

"Yes. Now let's go inside. We're being watched."

"Watched? By whom?

He pointed to the ship. "I'm sure those bastards have got us on the infrared scope. They spy on so many people that they've become professional voyeurs. They especially like to take dirty pictures. Let's go inside."

"Are we going to get dirty?"

"Yes."

"How could you scale the wall?"

"That's not important. Let's just say that a simple thing like that is part of my job. Let's go inside."

"Who are those people?"

"Let's just say they're my friends for now. They brought me here. I don't want those bastards seeing you naked."

"But I'm not—"

Before she could finish the sentence, Jack swept her off her feet and carried her into the bedroom. Seating himself on a chair, he lowered Linda onto his lap. It was wet. She felt his left hand grasp her hip so she wouldn't slide off. His right arm was wrapped around her. She pressed her head against his shoulder. He kissed her hard on the lips. She whispered, "I'm afraid that I won't be very good, Jack. I've had a perfectly awful day."

He removed her shirt—the one with the print of dogwood, as he said, "It can't be more perfectly awful than the day a couple weeks ago when we had sex in the jungle of Honduras." With some sense of urgency, he lifted off the white top with the spaghetti straps. "Just close your eyes and tell me about your day."

"I can't. Attorney-client stuff. You know."

He unfastened her bra, removed it, and cupped both hands over her beasts, pinching the nipples hard between his fingers. She made no attempt to help or hinder. Obviously, none of this was a challenge to his expert hands. Linda couldn't believe it was happening. She closed her eyes. The harder he pinched and the firmer he held them, the more she groaned in sheer ecstasy. He reached down to remove her slacks; and then paused. With an edge of irritation in his voice, he said, "You didn't keep a promise."

She opened her eyes, stared at him in the half-light, and said in a gentle whisper, "I always keep my promises."

"You promised to e-mail me when your period started. I've been concerned."

"I would have kept the promise, but it didn't start. I'm at least five days late. That's never happened before. I'm pregnant." She closed her eyes and added, "I haven't had sex with another man for several years, so you can feel assured the child is yours."

He didn't reply. He released her breasts. She felt his arms tighten around her. He kissed both of her closed eyes, the tip of her nose, and then ever so gently, her lips. Neither spoke. Her ear was against his chest. She could hear him breathing. Minutes passed. She didn't love him but his being there was wonderful. The father of her first child was holding her. She reveled in the warmth of his body. More minutes passed.

Linda had wildly mixed emotions about carrying the baby. She was elated with the idea of becoming a mother, but profoundly heartbroken that it wasn't Murdock's. But it *was* Jack's. And he was here. His compassionate understanding calmed the turbulent waves of confusion in her mind. *The baby does complicate things,* she thought. *But I won't let it tonight. Tonight must be uncomplicated because right now I need what Jack is giving me.* She broke the silence and said, "Jack, I'm so glad you're here."

"I know. So am I."

Then, with a practiced ease, he morphed into a mischievous little boy who had found his toys and eagerly began to play with them. She felt his hardness pressing against her leg. She moved ever so slightly until it pressed where she wanted it to. Presently his play stopped. He reached for her penlight and sat there for what seemed like several minutes, feasting his eyes on the beauty her breasts—utterly entranced by the power of the moment. He commanded her to stand. Unbuttoning her white silk pants, he let them and her underpants fall to the floor.

She wondered what Murdock would say if he could see her now. She closed her mind to it. While he was engaged in boyish exploring, she wondered how Jack got past the guards inside and outside the wall. She wasn't sure that she wanted to know.

Still exhausted from the long day, she drifted between valleys of sleep and crests of pleasure. One crest was aroused by the little boy deciding to play rough with his toys. Suddenly and vigorously he combined aggressive manual with even more aggressive oral stimulation. The pain delighted her. She involuntarily whimpered, inflaming his passion even more. Hers rose to meet his. His left hand possessed pure artistry. She felt it nimbly massaging her stomach, inching its way ever so gently and slowly downward, cleverly stimulating; skillfully arousing anticipation, inch by wonderful inch; then taking command of her most female part, maneuvering, firmly dominating and preparing her. Euphoria made her blood boil. *Ah,* she said to herself. *This old man intuitively knows how to satisfy. My God, I've almost forgotten those sensations. They haven't had the emotional cash to buy time on my agenda.* She sensed them now, boiling to the surface from deep within her. She purred as two fingers penetrated her. By his unrelenting and total confiscation of her body, he stirred responses that she would be powerless to withhold if she'd wanted to.

She slipped off his lap and took that which earlier had been pressing against her and made love to it—driving him so crazy that he let loose his toys and she heard him groan in agony—precisely the punishment she'd decided upon. He decided to get her into bed before he lost control too soon. He picked her up, carried her to the bed, and inelegantly dropped her on it. She regretted that she'd allowed herself so few experiences like this. She feigned resistance. She thought to herself, humorously, *Isn't that what a girl is supposed to do? Make him feel like he's conquering you? Let him dream!*

Conquest was fast upon her. Parting her legs apart, he pinned her hard to the bed so she couldn't move and could barely breathe. Briefly studying her eyes, he hesitated, took a deep breath, and then rudely forced himself into her. He was out of control like a run-away-train on a fast track free-wheeling downhill without brakes. His grunt of victory told her his moment had come far too soon. But he had stamina. He didn't stop. He wouldn't cheat her. Nor would she cheat him. When the old man got a tad winded and withdrew from the skirmish, Linda rolled over on top and took command. With newly discovered talent, she compelled the dimension of time to totally surrender to the dimension of passion. She made her baby's father forget that any world, any universe, or any other obligation existed outside that bed.

* * *

Later, when they were both exhausted, they reclined naked on the two lounge chairs on the balcony. Linda marveled. If the guys on that boat were really scoping them with the infrared, Jack didn't seem to care anymore. She didn't either. They could eat their hearts out. It would be obvious Jack had made his conquest. That's the way men think. Those guys wouldn't dream that she'd made hers double. When he'd gotten out of bed, Jack's legs were rubber.

Linda felt her life changing. *Maybe the loss of my position with Enrique wouldn't be so bad. Maybe I have lost touch with Linda—the woman. Maybe I've become a plastic Linda and the real Linda imprisoned within me needs to be free. Maybe that's what Jack is trying to do—set me free from the plastic mould. My girlfriends have been trying to tell me what I've been missing. Maybe I should listen.*

But what about Jack? Jack had spent two nights now convincing her that deep down inside she's a passionate woman. She was still certain that she wasn't *in love* with him. She was reasonably confident that Murdock would soon smoke out the truth about the Weidner's, and that Enrique's horror would soon end. She resolved that then she must make Murdock more important than her career. There wasn't one piece of paper in all of her files that could give her what she now desperately wanted—love, marriage, and children. However, there was the inconvenience of Jack's child. Thoughts churned through her mind. *In spite of the child, why did I let him make love to me again tonight? Have I lost my self control? I just let him walk in and do it. Surely he can't hold me to a rash promise made in the jungle after a life-threatening escape. I'm in love with Murdock. I've already endangered a future with him.* She thought better of it. *No, I haven't. He's made no commitment to me; or I to him. I let Jack make love to me because I needed it. I did make a commitment in the jungle. Am I a prisoner of a promise? Am I not free to abrogate that promise? Tonight I had no desire to abrogate. Necessity is not exactly the opposite of freedom, but it is close.* She shook her head unconsciously. *Semantics! I don't need to define motives. I simply am what I do.* The last statement seemed logical. She didn't understand why she was still confused. She played with the question of whether an artist might illustrate her relationship with Jack in red and purple or in soft pastels. She decided that examining a pleasure too closely destroys it.

Jack asked, "What are you thinking?"

Staring casually up at the stars she replied, "I'm thinking that my defense of Señor Perez-Krieger may soon take a positive turn."

Jack leaned over close to her. In almost a whisper, he said, "Linda, I tell you this in absolute confidence. I trust Murdock. You may share it with him. I have evidence that would free Enrique but I'm not at liberty to disclose it. You can't count on it. I may not be at liberty to give it to you until it's too late. I'm sorry. There are things I can't control. That's all I can say. Boss-servant privilege. One thing I *can* control. You can't imagine how much I hate to say this, but you have my consent to abort the baby, if that's what you want to do. I can make arrangements."

She stared at him silently. Then, breaking the silence, she said softly, "Jack, I can't do that. The baby is mine. It could be my father's only grandchild; ever. Hopefully Murdock will realize that he's desperately in love with me; so much so that your baby won't make a difference." She smiled. "I'll help him realize that he feels that way."

Jack laughed. "Romantic, idealized love can't be forced to happen. Force creates anxiety. All any of us have is *now*. The mind can remember the past and anticipate the future, but we can live in neither. You've got to take the bull by the horns. I agree that an airplane marriage between you and Murdock won't work, but there *are* simple alternatives."

Her eyes searched his.

Jack added, "I don't mean to preach, but I am old enough to be your father. Hardly anyone follows free advice, but I'll try. First, avoid memories that only reinforce regret. Second, avoid obsessive self-sufficiency. Third, remember that love never means subservience. Fourth, the world's at your feet. You have great power. If the world doesn't suit you, change it. You're an extraordinarily intelligent woman. You must see what has to be done. Do it."

"I'm not sure that I do, Jack. You mentioned a simple solution."

"Listen. Hopefully, we'll get Enrique acquitted. He really likes you. I don't mean romantically. He likes you and respects you as a person. He owes you a great deal. In the last twelve years, you've contributed more to expanding his financial empire than he has. He really doesn't need to buy Veritus, too. I know he withdrew his offer, but if he's acquitted, he'll tell you to go after it again. If he succeeds, Murdock would be one of your lower level managers. Go after Veritus, but not for him. I presume that you have a healthy nest egg and that you'll inherit and can borrow from that old mossback in Calgary. Murdock received over a million dollars in proceeds from life insurance upon Karen's death. The two of you could buy Veritus if Enrique would back off. You could operate it together from wherever you chose. From what I've heard, the owner might be more willing to sell to you two than anyone else. He might even leverage the buyout. I don't think that money is most important to him. He wants to be free of it."

"Does one man own it? Why is money not so important to him?"

"He's a monk in Bavaria. He inherited Veritus from his father. He never wanted it. He has great respect for Murdock. I'm sure he'd have great respect for you too, if he met you."

"Is his name Brother Martin?"

"Yes."

"Why didn't Murdock tell me?"

"He's sworn to secrecy. Brother Martin doesn't want the world to know. That's why I'm telling you. I think you two have a good shot at buying it. Go for it."

Jack amazed her. *He wants to be my lover, but he also wants me to marry Murdock and be happy. He's even working on overcoming objections. He's right. Murdock and I could buy Veritus. But,* she thought, *there is you, Jack.* Deep down within her, at that place where she never kidded herself, she knew that the mutual desire she and Jack shared grew out of genuine affection—a deep and abiding bond that had raised the promise that she made in the jungle to the dignity of a serious commitment. Tonight they'd shared that simple, sheer, unashamed joy of making love. Theirs was a relationship without emotional baggage. She confessed to herself that she reveled in the shameless beauty of it. Nevertheless, she had to ask. "What about us, Jack?"

Neither spoke for several minutes. Then Jack said, "There must always be *us*."

He arose, went into the bathroom, and returned wearing his bathing suit, and said, "The guys on the boat have probably snapped all the photos the camera will hold. My time is up. They're expecting me back on the ship within ten minutes."

"Where are you going?"

"I'll be on Little Cayman Island for a couple days."

Linda smiled and said, "I could meet you there tomorrow night."

Jack's eyes met hers. She read a moment of confusion, but he quickly recovered. He said, "That wouldn't be a good idea. Now listen carefully. I have three things I'd like you to do. Each is very important."

Linda arose to kiss him goodbye. "What are they, my mentor?"

"Number one, fire the security guard on the north wall. He took a bribe. Number two, tell Murdock that I talked to Susan the day she disappeared and that neither I nor my people have her. Number three, warn Murdock that very little is what it appears to be."

The moon had risen. He kissed her full on the lips, and then moved toward the north end of the balcony which was shaded from the light of the newly risen moon. He picked up the coil of rope, looped it over the wrought iron railing, and lowered it. As he prepared to put one leg over it, the moonlight illuminated Linda on the veranda. He noticed an awkward expression on her face. Perhaps it was confusion. Her eyes met his. She said, "I have one rather important thing to mention in case you haven't noticed."

"What's that?"

"Surely, Jack, you've been trained to observe. Something has just happened."

"What did I miss?"

"If you look closely, you'll notice that I'm not pregnant."

He stared at the incontrovertible proof; his expression was at first blank, and then sad. Without saying a word, he walked over to her, wrapped his arms around her in a bear hug, and tenderly kissed her again on the lips. Then, silently stepping back into the shadow of a tall royal palm, he lifted his legs over the railing and descended from view.

Linda stood staring out to sea. She noticed that the men on the ship had sent a small boat to pick up a swimmer. *Which,* she wondered, *had been his primary purpose: to make love to me, or to deliver the message?* Impulsively, she shrugged. The answer was unknowable. Of one thing Linda was certain. Her state of mind was much more tranquil than before Jack had arrived.

A tear ran down her cheek. She wiped it with the back of her hand. *Was it a tear of regret because of the baby that I'd taken into my heart? Or was it a tear of relief?* That answer, too, was unknowable to any reasonable degree of certainty.

She could've had the pomegranate martinis.

Becoming conscious of her nakedness, she turned her back to the sea and went inside to tend to her necessity.

36

Saint Luke's Monastery
Tuesday June 20, 8:01 a.m.

The mountain air was cool. The monastery was located far up the slope at the tree line. Below were tall pines and deciduous trees, mostly beech mixed with oak and sycamore. Upward from the monastery were short pines; beyond them were dwarf shrubs and tiny mountain wild flowers that bravely peeked through the snow.

Enclosed within the cloister was a garden. Four pathways, one from each cardinal point, led to four elegantly hand-carved oak benches which encircled a delightful fountain. Murdock and Grace seated themselves together on one. The sun shone through the clear high altitude air and warmed them. The garden was alive with the vivid colors of spring flowers. Brother Martin joined them.

"Aren't they exquisite?" he asked. "The red ones nearest the fountain are rusty-leaved Alpenrose, which some call Rhododendron ferrugineum. The tiny blue ones are stemless gentian. Those with the large white petals that look like daises are Alpine pasque-flower. Those with the smaller white petals are glacier buttercup." Pointing to the rear of the garden along the tall outside wall, he said, "Those are the edelweiss. They won't bloom until September. That big bird circling overhead is a golden eagle."

Murdock was totally distracted. He was listening but he wasn't hearing. Linda was on his mind. He'd noticed the stress in her voice yesterday during both phone calls. *Everyone has a breaking point*, he thought. *How close is she to hers?* He hoped that she'd had a good night's sleep. He had no clue that Jack had seen to that.

Grace noticed his inattention. From the moment they had met this morning in the lobby of the Zugspitze Hof Hotel, she sensed that his mind was elsewhere. She sensed that Brother Martin was unsettled, too. The

261

verbal tour of the flower garden was a pleasant diversion, but a diversion nonetheless. After an awkward moment of silence, she stepped close to Brother Martin and said, "You know I'm not a religious person, but I *am* curious. Would you please clear up something for me?"

Brother Martin's eyes, which today seemed very tired, fixed on hers. "I shall try."

Grace's eyes met his. "If God came down to earth and became a human for thirty-three years like you guys claim, who was left up there to run heaven and all of the universes?"

It worked. She smiled inwardly as the tiredness in his eyes turned to a twinkle.

"That's a very good question. I wish more people would ask it. I believe that God doesn't have a timeline like we do. He, being eternal, lives in yesterday, today, and tomorrow at the same time. We were not begotten by God as Christ was; we were made by him. He made us children of time. Time leads obstinately to death. Our perspective is not eternal. It's fatal. That's a major difference between us and God."

"That's cute, Marty, but it does seem pointless."

"That's a legitimate observation, too, Grace, and very perceptive. Countless millions share your skepticism. I see it this way. God became human so that he could make us a promise in an idiom that we could understand. The promise is this—if we just believe that Jesus is the Christ, our savior, we become united with God the Father. If we're united with God, how can we help but live forever?"

Grace grinned.

He continued, "Our goal at Saint Luke's Monastery is to see the world for what it is and to speak to it as scientists and businessmen with moral clarity."

Grace frowned. "Okay. When I was with the Michigan State Police, I killed another human being. It was not in self-defense in any traditional sense. How can a person of no faith like me find absolution for taking that life?"

Before he answered, Brother Martin's eyes searched hers. He was tempted to take her hand but he thought better of it. He said, "Grace, if there is no god and no savior, you must learn to absolve yourself."

Murdock came out of his funk and realized Grace had been making conversation to protect him. He chimed in, "While we're asking religious questions, I've often wondered why this open area is called a cloister."

Brother Martin smiled judiciously. "A Latin word, *clausura*, literally translates *to shut up*. Since early Christian times, monks have shut themselves off from the world within cloisters. Historically, they were not free to leave without their abbot's permission; nor was anyone free to enter. If a monk left without permission during the night, he could be excommunicated; thus condemned to hell. We've retained the name, not the restrictions. Often, the enclosed walkway that surrounds the garden is called the cloister." He paused, and studied the expression on Murdock's face. He inquired, "What's troubling you, Murdock?"

Murdock was silent for several seconds, and then said, "I'm sorry, sir. I'm deeply concerned about Linda DiStefano."

Brother Martin asked, "Is she Señor Perez-Krieger's chief operating officer?"

"Yes. But she's acting as his criminal defense attorney, too. She's young—in her mid to late thirties. But she's under immense pressure. I'm concerned that she's bitten off more than she can chew."

Grace injected, "You may be underestimating that woman."

Brother Martin added, "We're all showing strain. It's natural. Do we have the moral high ground? Are we absolutely certain that Señor Perez-Krieger is innocent?"

"There's little absolute assurance this side of heaven, but I'm confident that I haven't misjudged his character. Linda, likewise, is confident."

Brother Martin stared at the eagle, still circling overhead. Returning his gaze to Murdock, he said, "Give me an assessment of her. What makes her tick?"

"I might be biased."

Grace injected, "He's fallen in love with her. If they ever get their act together, they'll marry."

A broad smile crept across Brother Martin's face. "Good," he said. "That alone gives me more confidence in her opinions. I'm very pleased to hear that, Murdock. You've mourned Karen long enough. You need to move on. We need to move on, too, and resolve this case so that Señor Perez-Krieger is cleared. Miss DiStefano's life needs to be restored to a sane schedule. Mrs. Ling must be found and returned to her husband. These Traction people must be exposed and prosecuted. You can engage Miss DiStefano, and I can sell Veritus before my top execs bail out."

Grace asked, "Have any left?"

"Not yet. Rumors suggest that several of my senior staff in Chicago are job searching. I heard they're concerned that that rascal Boris Romanovsky is going to buy it. He isn't. I won't sell to him, but I don't want that fact to get out. It won't be long before the media learns that I own it. From that point, you know the drill. Our enemies will float innuendos to a willfully gullible media. They'll enthusiastically believe the worst and will work our ill-informed public into a lather. TV commentators always seem to be armed with more facts than there are. I'll be connected to Perez-Krieger by his offer to purchase Veritus, even though he withdrew it. The monastery and our brothers will be tarred by innuendo. Much of the public will believe the worst and come to the conclusion that we're a dangerous cult serving as a secretive meeting place for doers of dark deeds. I've never involved myself in the running of Veritus, but from here on in, I want you to report to me directly. Grace, you are assigned to Murdock. Until the conclusion of this case, you are not to report to Ernst Müller. I've notified our head office in Chicago. They'll notify Ernst. Now, what's the status of our investigation?"

Murdock nodded toward Grace and said, "She's come up with some fascinating information."

Grace was pleased that he gave her the credit and the opportunity, rather than taking it himself as her superior. She turned toward Brother Martin. "I'm almost positive that Josef Weidner and Ernesto Flavio are the same person. Working on that assumption, I charmed one of Boris Romanovsky's bank managers and learned that Flavio is connected to a corporation called Pleiades Transshipments. That's a Liechtenstein corporation. It owns five seagoing cargo ships. It had owned a ship named the Selena, but records show that it was lost at sea off the mouth of the Columbia River over a year ago."

Martin's eyes met Murdock's as he asked, "Isn't that the ship on which you met the green woman who used the name Selena?"

"Yes, but apparently it wasn't lost."

Grace continued. "Pleiades has its main office in Málaga, Spain. I hung around the bars near the docks in Málaga. After buying a few drinks for a longshoreman and stirring in a touch of tease, he told me that he recently saw a ship named the MS Purple Star that was the twin sister of the MS Selena. They must have been identical twins that aged identically. He said that even the rust spots were the same. Apparently companies often change the names of ships and their countries of registration."

"Why?" Brother Martin asked.

"I understand it's done for various reasons, few are forthright."

"Please continue."

"I checked the corporate registrations in Liechtenstein. Pleiades was incorporated six years ago. Flavio is shown as its present secretary-treasurer. The president is our disappearing linguist, Claude V. Mitchell."

Brother Martin's eyes brightened. "He's the man that Brother Gustav met—the one who claimed that the drawings on the Peruvian plateau were made by alien visitors and that the ancients mistook them for gods and goddesses."

Grace nodded. "Yes. Pleiades is a closed corporation. It has only three shareholders. Flavio and Mitchell are two of them. I'm still working on the third. I took a guess but my source assured me that I was wrong."

Murdock asked, "Who did you think it might be?"

"Boris Romanovsky. Their main account is in one of his institutions—the Eastern Mediterranean Bank."

"Are you positive that he isn't?"

"No, Boss. Like you said, it's hard to be positive in this murky game."

Brother Martin added, "The names of the shareholders wouldn't be in the corporate papers filed in Liechtenstein. Where did you get your info?"

"From one of the oldest and most reliable sources known to investigators—the chief financial officer's mistress. After I talked to her, I worked my way into a cocktail party and introduced myself to his wife. I learned from her that Pleiades has a bizjet registered in Germany. Its registration letters are D-XHGG. I've talked to air traffic controllers in Málaga. Its pilots have frequently filed flight plans to both Aruba and Casablanca in Morocco."

Brother Martin asked, "Doesn't Boris Romanovsky own a bank and a villa on Aruba?"

"Yes," she said and then nodded toward Murdock.

Murdock added, "Our office on Aruba informed me that the plane almost always refuels there and the passengers usually play the tables and stay overnight. From there, they file a flight plan to La Ceiba on the Caribbean coast of Honduras. A few weeks ago, Linda DiStefano was kidnapped and taken upriver into the jungle of Honduras. That river flows into the Caribbean about eighty miles east of La Ceiba. I've told you about the malevolent ceremony that I witnessed there. Susan Ling could be a prisoner there if she's still alive. You've read the e-mail I sent you in regard to that cosmologist, Paul West, who wants to meet the Green Lady. Perhaps he and I should go into that jungle and have a look."

Brother Martin said, "One of the greatest sins of scientists is their refusal to believe in the existence of evil. Perhaps if you two go, Dr. West will change his opinion. It's the Old Evil One that we need to overcome."

Grace suggested, "It's hard to overcome what doesn't exist, Marty."

Brother Martin smiled. "I hope you're right—that it or he doesn't exist—but I wouldn't bet my life on it." He turned toward Murdock and asked, "Would you set up a search party?"

"Yes. I'm acquainted with Fernando Millán, a colonel in the Honduran National Police. I trust him. He saved my life in the jungle last year. I expect that he'd work with me."

Brother Martin's eyes locked on his. "There are a lot of folks in that jungle who don't trust the National Police. Years ago I was a missionary there. I'm still in contact with some old parishioners among the Miskito Indians. I know my way around large parts of that jungle. People change but topography doesn't. If you go in, I'm going in with you."

Murdock said, "That could be dangerous."

Brother Martin's eyes met his. "*Could* is not the word I'd use. It *will* be dangerous. Do you have any more for me?"

"I think that's all we have for now."

Brother Martin stood and offered his hand to Murdock and Grace. They shook. After the polite goodbyes, he left.

Murdock and Grace had ridden in on horseback. After they exited the monastery and mounted, Murdock asked, "Do you know what the 'V' stands for in Claude V. Mitchell's name?"

"No. Is it important?"

"It could be. See if you can get it. What was your impression of our meeting?"

Grace frowned. "I'm amazed that Marty, an intelligent, obviously well-educated man, actually believes that 'Old Evil One' stuff."

"My wife, Karen, did, too."

"Wow. People here in Europe are actually institutionalizing atheism. They're moving from passive indifference to God into zealous unbelief. Secular societies are being formed. They hold meetings. Atheists take the pulpit and debunk religion. Converts from Christianity receive certificates of de-baptism. Their main message is simply 'We don't believe.'"

"Have you joined them?"

Grace grinned. "I don't join much of anything. There's something else, Boss. Greta Himmelreich is getting much friendlier all of a sudden. She e-mailed me yesterday and urged me to meet with her and Dr. Lore Fritz at the Mädchenhaus Café at nine in the morning on Saturday, July 1 and asked me to confirm that I'd be there. I did. I've had women cozy up to me because they thought I was gay, so I've learned to recognize hits. I'm convinced that this liaison is not sexually motivated."

"It's strange that she's setting it up so far in advance. Is the café open on Saturday mornings?"

"No."

"Won't you see her some evening before that?"

"I presume so."

"It sounds like she's scheduling someone else to be there, too."

Grace smiled. "That *is* what it sounds like."

37

Little Cayman Island
Wednesday, June 21, 7:45 p.m.

Denise stepped out of the shower, took a towel, and dried herself. At ten o'clock she had to take over the front desk at the Lost Flamingo. She'd tired of working nights. It wouldn't last much longer. She sensed that Jack's project was nearing completion and then they'd either buy the place or she'd move on.

Jack had arrived at 3:30 that afternoon and made love to her immediately. But, unlike any time in the past, it had been like a scene from a second rate silent movie. He avoided the delightful word games they usually played. Sweet nothings had gone unspoken. Warm conversation had been skipped. Wherever his mind had been, it hadn't been with her. Had it been on business, or on some woman who had captivated his roaming soul last night? Denise didn't know, but she hadn't complained. He'd made up for everything in the vigor of his performance and the power with which he'd commanded her. She loved being dominated by him. He'd not merely taken her; he'd all but consumed her. She'd blissfully submitted to wave after wave of undulating passion. She'd screamed and clawed like he loved her to. Then, like a toy boat bobbing adrift uncontrollably on angry waves, she had been sucked into the vortex of his whirlpool of uncontrollable passion, happily drowning in the madness of climactic ecstasy. When he'd suddenly disengaged, she'd had to catch her breath. He'd acted like a man afraid that he was making love for the last time and wanted to make the most of it.

As she hung up her towel, she wondered who had inspired this delightful erotic madness. Whoever it was, she must have exhausted him. Jack had fallen asleep immediately after disconnection.

She hung the bath towel, put on her robe, and returned to her bedroom. Jack had awakened and was sitting on the edge of the bed. Denise's eyes met his. She asked, "Is she special to you?"

Jack cocked his head and stared at her. "Who?"

"I'm talking about the woman who mesmerized you last night. The one you were thinking about when you were making love to me."

"Denise, I—"

"Save it, baby. It's okay. Denise understands. We've exchanged no promises. Are you committed for dinner?"

"I'm taking the guys to Grand Turtle Inn. By the way, they'll be moving out first thing tomorrow morning. That'll free up six rooms for you."

"We don't need them freed this time of year. Are you picking up the check for a dozen guys?"

"I have an expense account, Denise."

"They've been here three days doing nothing. What the hell do they do? They don't look like common laborers."

"Let's say they're security guards, Denise. They've been here for three days because some damn bureaucrat didn't ship their uniforms. The uniforms arrived on Grand Cayman this morning. I brought them over here. The guys are checking to see if they fit. I hope to hell they do before someone gets hurt."

"Who's going to get hurt? Are you running a security guard business?"

"You know better than to ask so many questions, Denise. The more answers you have, the less safe you are."

"Are you leaving with them?"

"I'm leaving, but we're going in different directions. Something unforeseen came up suddenly—an opportunity to help a friend and service my contract at the same time. I'll be in North Africa tonight. That's all I can tell you. Here's a check for their rooms. If all goes well, I'll be back in a week or two. But let's sit down in the kitchen for a minute. I have a question."

Denise seated herself at her kitchen table. He poured coffee for both and joined her. As she sipped the steaming liquid, Jack said, "In a few simple words that a layman can understand, can you explain to me what neuroplasticity means?"

Denise smiled. She never knew what to expect from this man. She took another sip and said, "I did a research paper on it a few years ago, but I'm by no means an expert. We've learned recently that the human brain isn't hardwired. It can change both its structure and its function during a person's life. Experiences can alter it. Brain injuries can cause it to reroute its communications network. Things like aging and the affect of hormones and drugs can physically change it, too."

She studied his face. She read a look of consternation she hadn't seen there before. Her eyes met his. "Is her time getting close?" He nodded. "You need to make a move soon, don't you?"

He pressed her hand and said, "Study up, just in case. By the time you see her, I'm afraid she may have some really serious problems."

"Can you tell me when she'll arrive?"

"As soon as we can extract her." He gave her a quick kiss. "I've got to join the guys. Goodbye, Denise."

"Goodbye, Jack. Thanks for the ride. Come again soon."

As he walked out, he looked over his shoulder and solemnly said, "Oh, I shall, my dear. God willing, I shall."

38

The magnificent summer morning tempted Grace to set out for a day of sailing on the Chiemsee, her favorite lake nestled in the foothills of the Bavarian Alps. Duty and curiosity drew her elsewhere. She walked the few blocks from her apartment to the beautiful gardens of the Gärtnerplatz. The few gay bars located in that conservative city were located near there. From Gärtnerplatz she could easily walk the short distance to the Mädchenhaus Café.

The cleaning woman had propped open the front door. Grace walked in. Dr. Lore Fritz was seated at a table just inside the door. She motioned for Grace to join her. She did. As Dr. Fritz was offering the usual polite greetings, Grace noticed a man seated at the bar talking to Greta. He was a handsome fellow, indeed—an older man with a gray moustache and beard. His jaunty blue sport coat over an open collar golf shirt, royal blue slacks, and a white Greek captain's hat suggested that this was no ordinary fellow. His eyes were worldly wise. Grace felt her face flush as Lore asked, "Does he turn you on?"

Grace looked at her warily. "If he were thirty years younger, I'd sure like to meet him. Who is he?"

"We call him Jack. Are you bisexual?"

"I'll make that decision when I grow up."

"Okay. It's none of my business. He's the man who directed us to invite you here this morning."

Grace studied his face. Then turning to Dr. Fritz she exclaimed, "He *directed* you?" There was a long pause. Dr. Fritz didn't reply. Grace took a shot in the dark and asked, "Is he the man who furnished the money to buy this place?"

There was another long pause. Lore's eyes met hers, then turned toward the bar and said, "Greta's motioning for you to join them in the office. I'll remain here by the door. If, when you grow up, you decide that you *are* bisexual, please remember me."

"I'm sure that I'll never forget you. You're a very attractive woman. Someday I may give you an opportunity to convince me."

An affectionate smile crossed Lore's face. Grace returned it with a smile somewhat less ardent, then turned away and joined the other two in the office. It was a dingy room without windows. Grace didn't care for rooms with no windows. She didn't care for this office especially. It was small, poorly lighted, and overcrowded with discolored furniture. The walls and ceiling were paneled with grubby acoustical tiles. The smell of stale cigarette smoke or worse permeated the acrid air. They seated themselves around a shabby desk that fit the décor perfectly. Jack sat behind it in the catbird chair, obviously considering his opening gambit.

Grace said, "Okay, Mr. Jack, or whoever you are, why am I here?"

Jack, obviously pleased that she had taken the initiative to open the conversation, said, "You're here, Grace, because Greta says you can be trusted. My superiors prohibit me from talking to your boss, Murdock McCabe. He'd recognize me as someone else—someone my superiors want everyone to think is dead. I trust Murdock, but I'm not authorized to trust him. I'm taking a gamble with you because a life hangs in the balance."

"I must report that to him. He'll certainly guess who you are."

"Don't report anything except the life hanging in the balance, at least not before July 16. It would endanger my life."

"Will Jack fade out of existence on that date?"

"You may take nothing for granted other than what I tell you. I'm going to give you valuable information. Your keeping secrets is my *quid pro quo*. When you finally tell him, Murdock will acknowledge that you did the right thing by holding back. Also, in return for the information, you must not disclose this meeting ever to the Bavarian State Police; especially not to Rudi Benzinger. In the fullness of time, I shall tell him. If they're watching the place, the police didn't see me arrive. They won't see me leave. Nor will they come inside. If they ask why you came here on a Saturday morning, say you were just visiting your friends, Greta and Lore. If they push, tell them you had sex in the office. Most cops have dirty minds. They like to believe things like that. The original reason that I had Greta set up this meeting is that I've obtained the declassification of certain information in our secret files. I'll give you copies, but first let me give you a heads-up. One night several weeks ago one of my agents snuck into the Veritus office in Portland, Oregon. He downloaded some files from Susan Ling's computer."

"How could your agent sneak past our night clerk?"

"Please don't feign naïveté. You're a big girl. I don't have much time. On the day Susan disappeared, she had been researching German-speaking actresses; fishing for someone who might be playing Gretchen. Among the women who belonged to the Frankfurt Thespian Association was Hilde Müller. Susan researched her background. That research was interrupted by a luncheon date with Proteus."

"Who is he?"

"Who knows? We suspect that he works for some special branch of our CIA. Personally, I believe he works for Traction, too. My contract coordinator doesn't buy that. He refuses to push my idea upward through the acronyms and share with the other intelligence branches like the law requires. Most of it is still stove piped. Other branches never see it. My guess is that Proteus is a double agent whose true loyalty lies with Traction. I suspect that Susan, being somewhat incautious, asked him about this Müller woman. If Müller was in fact Gretchen, then Traction would consider Susan's possession of that information extremely threatening. Their whole trumped-up story about Señor Perez-Krieger would unwind. Their power over other prominent people would dissolve. Proteus probably lured her into his apartment with a promise of sex, drugged her, put her on a bizjet, and took her to where they could torture her and determine how much Veritus knows."

"That sounds horrible. I hope you're wrong about the torture. Is Hilde Müller really Gretchen?"

"We needed to know, too. One of my agents located a girlfriend of Hilde's. She and Hilde were both members of the Frankfort Thespian Association. The girlfriend says that in August of last year Hilde travelled to Vienna by train. She had an appointment to meet a producer at the Kaiserin Elisabeth Hotel. That was the last time her friend heard from her."

"That's about the time that the Weidner's first appeared in Europe, allegedly from Paraguay. They stayed at that hotel."

"Yes. All of that is detailed in this file." He handed her a CD. "As the lawyers say, this is *some* evidence. Obviously it's not *conclusive* evidence. You folks are going to have to tie the loose ends and prove that Hilde was Gretchen. Even then, that doesn't exonerate Señor Perez-Krieger. The woman *is* dead. Somebody killed her."

She tucked the CD into her handbag. Jack was certainly an interesting new character in this slowly unfolding drama. Grace liked him. She said, "Thanks for the information. I'm indebted to you. The info about Hilde may buy us more time. The attorney general is under some pressure to make this case move. By the way, are you familiar with a man called Ernesto Flavio?"

"Even if we thought that was another alias for Josef Weidner, I couldn't tell you."

"Gotcha. You said that this was the original reason for bringing me here. Is there another?"

"Greta, would you please keep Lore company and close the door behind you?"

"Of course." Greta arose, walked to the door, then turned and said, "By the way, Grace, I think Lore is in love with you. She'd do anything for you. I don't mind sharing, so it wouldn't offend me."

Sharing? What's to share? Grace thought. She smiled with feigned appreciation. "Thank you," she said and then turned to Jack. Sitting next to this handsome, tough-minded, smartly dressed, worldly man who exuded male magnetism, Lore had little attraction for her. She thought, *Maybe Jack doesn't have to be thirty years younger.* When Greta closed the door, Jack came around the desk, moved Greta's chair closer to hers, sat on it, leaned close to Grace and almost in a whisper, asked, "Does *Purple Star* mean anything to you?"

Grace, amused by the cloak and dagger mood of it all, nodded and whispered back, "Yes. It's an ocean-going freighter owned by Pleiades Transshipping. It might be the MS Selena renamed. That's the ship on which my boss was held prisoner off the coast of Oregon last year."

"Yes, and I was, too. It *is* the Selena. Do you know who owns Pleiades?"

"Ernest Flavio and Claude V. Mitchell are two of them. The third I haven't been able to identify, yet. Do you know?"

"It's a woman who goes by various aliases. Her real name is Patricia Romanovsky."

"My God!" she exclaimed, not hiding her astonishment. She thought, *Boris proposed marriage to Linda DiStefano and he already has a wife.* Her eyes met Jack's as she said, "Patricia isn't a Russian name but may I assume she *is* Boris's wife?"

"She's his American trophy wife. The trouble with marrying trophy wives is that sometimes a guy bites off more than he can chew. She's a mouthful."

Grace's initial amusement turned to repugnance. Had Boris been playing Linda for a chump when he'd offered her marriage? *Have I misjudged Boris? His offer sounded like a sincere business arrangement. If he'd made the offer to me, would I have accepted it?* She couldn't answer. Murdock would decide whether to tell Linda. Grace asked, "Are they still married?"

"I don't know." He glanced at his wrist watch. "My time is running out. I can't stay here much longer."

Grace's eyes locked on his. "You mentioned a matter of life and death."

"Yes. This you must share with Murdock immediately. Two days ago we located Susan Ling. She's still alive. I don't know why. I've missed something. She had to have outlived her usefulness a month ago. The Traction people are holding her in a fortified villa in the Atlas Mountains of Morocco. We want to know what she's learned about them. Yesterday, we did some discrete air surveillance. She was outdoors in the courtyard with her ankle chained to a stake. Last night one of my guys got one of the security guards drunk in the village. He says that Susan is chained there every day from 10:00 to 11:00 a.m. Why, he didn't know."

"Are you going after her?"

"I can't. We're just common spies. My contract prohibits me or my people from taking any aggressive action. I'd be in deep do-do. That would go double in the Kingdom of Morocco. Give this map to Murdock. He'll get her out. He should move quickly. Whatever is charming her existence may not last forever. He shouldn't notify the Moroccan police. The proper people have been bribed. If they know you're coming, Susan will never be seen again."

"I'll contact him immediately."

"Go with him. You're both experienced with guns. You'd better be armed to the teeth and have a chain cutter. You'll need a chopper. Contact Miguel Gonzales. Miguel is a semi-retired mercenary that I've worked with several times. He's the best. He owns a chopper. He's based at the airport outside Málaga, Spain, which isn't too far from the Atlas Mountains. Here's his card. He's handy with a gun, too. I don't know whether he'll risk his life and his chopper unless you have big dollars available. If you do, it's important that *you* talk to Miguel; not Murdock. Money isn't everything to him. You've got what it takes to convince him. Murdock doesn't. You understand the world. Now I must go."

They both arose. Jack walked over to her, wrapped her in a tight bear hug, kissed her hard and long on the mouth, his tongue exploring hers, then released her and disappeared through the door. Plopping herself on the edge of Greta's desk, she caught her breath.

An eminently handsome and debonair man, she thought, *and obviously younger than I'd guessed.* His charm lingered on.

39

The sheer depth of the dust, both on and under the furniture, impressed Grace. It was so evenly distributed that it looked as if it were there by design. Toward the far corner of the room and under the dust, was a desk. The well-worn wooden relic looked as if it had taken a few rounds of machine gun fire during the Spanish civil war back in the 1930s. It must have been old then, too. Most of the varnish had been a victim of time. Grace stood next to it. She noticed a rickety chair across the room, but she was hesitant to test it.

The door opened. In walked a rather short, olive-skinned man with a round face, heavy head of black hair, piercing dark eyes, enormous muscular arms, and an engaging smile. He spoke loudly.

"I am Miguel Pedro Juanito Gonzalez. My friends call me Miguel. You are Grace. My friend Jack told me about you. He said that you are stunning and that you have gorgeous knockers. He didn't exaggerate. Jack seldom does. He also tells me that you're not married, but that's not important right this minute."

Miguel seated himself on another rickety chair behind his desk, tipped it back to a perilous angle, and put both feet on top the desk. He didn't invite Grace to be seated. She sensed that by standing, he could better feast his eyes on her. She patiently let him. She tried not to laugh. It was like loading ammunition in her arsenal. After his eyes had delighted in every detail, he said, "Fifty-thousand American dollars is not enough if they start shooting at me, and those bastards will. They could damage my chopper, me, or both. Who'd support my wife and children?"

"Who mentioned fifty-thousand, Miguel?"

"Jack."

"How many children do you have, Miguel?"

He laughed. "Five by my wife and I'm not sure how many by my five mistresses in the village." He shrugged and then scanned her body again, more thoughtfully. Grace smiled. "Yes, I know. Men tell me I'm built to have children. Forty-thousand." Elevating his inspection to her face, their eyes met. With a boyish smile he said, "One-hundred-thousand U.S. dollars. Like I said, if I lose my chopper, how can I make a living? Who will feed my wife, my mistresses and my children?" With a faux girlish smile, Grace replied, "If you lose your chopper, none of us will *need* to make a living. I examined your chopper, Miguel. That bucket of bolts was ancient on the day I was born. Let's quit haggling. I can't go more than sixty-thousand. That's the limit of my authority."

She had chosen a tight sweater to maximize her advantages. His eyes fixated on the gorgeous ones. He met her eyes again. Grinning, he said, "Get authority from your superiors."

"Miguel, I have tried. The money isn't in the budget, so neither my station chief nor his superior can authorize it. If you can't handle it for that price, I'll try someone else."

"Who?" Another boyish grin expanded across his face. "Okay. Jack says you're good people and Mrs. Ling needs saving from those bastards. Sixty-five thousand. I know you can do that. That settles the money, but the total consideration needs to be sweetened." He stared at her crotch. "You're a big girl. You know how to sweeten the deal."

She feigned a dramatic hesitation, shrugged her shoulders, sighed, and then submissively declared, "You can have me once."

Visibly surprised and clearly thrilled by the effortlessness of his success, he boldly retorted, "Twice. Once each way."

She shrugged again, sighed dramatically, and then locked her eyes firmly onto his. "Agreed. You go once around the world and then never again. Now, can you focus enough on business for us to finalize our plans?"

"It would be best to do *it* now. I will brush the dust off the top of this desk. After we have done it both ways, then I can focus on our plans."

"Not a chance, *hombre*. First *you* perform; then *I* perform."

With a feigned sad expression like that of a little boy who's been denied his favorite toy, he said, "Okay, Grace, first we make war. Jack has provided me with aerial photos of the compound and a navigation chart for northern Morocco. When do you wish to recover this Susan Ling and who is going to help you?"

"A man by the name of Murdock McCabe will arrive from the states later today. If weather permits, we'd like to do it tomorrow. I expect that she'll be chained to a stake outside from 10:00 to 11:00 a.m. Jack assures me that you're brave, strong, reliable, and a skilled chopper pilot. We'll be depending on you. Don't go chicken on us. If you abandon us there, Jack will come after you." Jack hadn't said that, but judging by the alarmed look on his face, it was a helpful little white lie.

Miguel replied, "Grace, you can count on Miguel. Now here is what we'll do. You two must both be here by 5:00 a.m. sharp. The chopper will be fueled and ready to go. We'll depart when I say so. Our flight will take us in a southeasterly direction, across the Mediterranean Sea. We will stop for refueling at Melilla. That's a Spanish enclave on the north coast of Africa. We will wait there. The police will be bribed to not ask questions. My friends will deliver to us four AK-47s with sufficient ammunition. Can this Susan fire a gun?"

"I've heard that she's an excellent shot."

"You don't need excellence with an AK-47. You just spray the bastards with bullets. Anyway, we can't wait until we're sure she's outside. We must anticipate. If the wind and weather are right, we'll proceed below the Moroccan radar into the mountains. We'll be too low for radio navigation. The river valley will lead to our target. Just in case a Moroccan air traffic controller does pick us up on radar, the man in charge of the radar facility has been bribed to protect us. This little hand-held radio is tuned to Jack's frequency. Either he'll be somewhere on the mountain where he can see into the compound, or he may use a drone airplane. Otherwise, he may have access to live satellite photos. He hasn't let me know for sure. Just before we come within sight of it, Jack will tell us whether she's accessible. If not, and before they see us, we turn back and try again the next day. The money for bribes, guns, and ammunition will be billed as costs, in addition to the $65,000 and your body. By the way, you be careful. If you get yourself killed, I'll really be pissed."

Grace smiled and said, "Believe me; I don't want to piss you off."

"Remember, when we move in, we'll have one shot at it. We'll sneak in low, climb when we get very close, then drop out of the sky suddenly and confuse the guards. It's best that we shoot first so they can't shoot back. When we hit the ground, you and I will cover Murdock. He will exit the chopper, hand her an AK-47, and free her from the chain. They will join us in the chopper and we'll get the hell out of there. It shouldn't take more than a minute. If it does, we're in deep ca-ca."

"What's the flip side of the coin?"

Miguel's eyes fixed on hers. "The *issues* as you Americans say? First, we could follow a wrong tributary by mistake and get lost in the valley. Second, some trigger-happy kid in the Moroccan air force could take us out. Third, there's a helicopter landing pad next to the villa. If we use it, we'd have to scale the walls by hand. We'd all be shot either going in or trying to get out. So, we must land inside the walls. Fourth, there's not much room. Fifth, while we're in route, a wind could come up that would make it dangerous or impossible to land in a tight space."

Grace frowned and said bravely, "Gosh. That sounds exciting."

"It's not funny, and that's not the worst of it. Have you ever heard of vortex ring effects or of ground resonance?"

Grace nodded in the negative.

"When we're landing and get close to the ground, the spinning rotor presses wind downward against the ground. That ground-effect wind can create a circular vortex around the turning blades. Sometimes this vortex combines with terrain, wind, or rain, and causes the blades to lose most of their lift. When that happens, we bang hard against the ground; sometimes hard enough to create shock waves that can seriously damage the aircraft. Terrain is our issue—namely the walls surrounding the villa. The downward wind will deflect off them, buffet us, and invite trouble."

"And ground resonance?"

"To put it simply, in a four-bladed chopper like mine, if we land too hard, the shock can pass upward to the rotor disk and cause an imbalance in the rotor system. That can result in violent oscillations and catastrophic damage to the airframe. Sometimes immediate takeoff can restore the balance, but that would mean we'd leave without Mrs. Ling."

"Murdock and I would take a dim view of leaving without her. Besides, if you and I are ever going to do something on top of that desk, you've got to find a way of avoiding that happenstance."

"Could you get someone to move the walls? Seriously, that's why Jack recommended me. I'm expert and cool. I can't guarantee success, but I'll get you in and out when no one else can. That raises another question, Señorita. What happens after we've beaten the bastards and we have this woman safely here?"

"Mr. McCabe will take her away in a waiting bizjet. I'll stay behind long enough to keep my promise. If you're good at *it*, maybe we could make it could happen again. I get to Málaga occasionally."

"Ah, Señorita, I shall bring you back alive, and even dust off the desk for you. My wife and five women in the village can tell you that I *am* good at *it*."

279

"At dusting? That remains to be seen." Grace grinned; and then turned and headed out the door. Looking over her shoulder she said, "See you in the morning, lover boy."

40

Over the Mediterranean Sea
Tuesday, July 4, 5:35 a.m.

It was a cool bright morning—not a cloud in the sky. Crossing the Guadalmedina River, the chopper proceeded over the busy port city of Málaga. Miguel Pedro Juanito Gonzales nudged Murdock, pointed down, and shouted over the noise of engines and rotor blades.

"That seaport was begun by the Phoenicians over 3,000 years ago. Next to Barcelona, it's the second leading Spanish port on the Mediterranean."

Murdock smiled and nodded in appreciation. He watched Miguel. The man handled the controls as if they were second nature to him. In a few hours, they would be flying into an extremely dangerous situation, but Miguel appeared totally composed—cool as a block of ice. He had told Murdock that he'd hired out as a mercenary in two of the Congo rebellions, in the Liberian civil war, and the most recent revolt in the Ivory Coast. He had flown in combat, fired weapons, and killed. Miguel was no stranger to danger.

As the chopper crossed the shoreline, Spain's famous *Costa del Sol* disappeared behind them. Below, in every direction, lay the deep blue waters of the Mediterranean Sea. No one spoke. Grace was seated in the left rear seat. Murdock was impressed by the way she had taken charge of arrangements and negotiated with Miguel. The rental of the helicopter, the weapons, and the munitions would be billed separately, but with the death-defying nature of the flight, Miguel's $65,000 was a good price. Miguel could lose his life—they could all lose their lives on this venture.

Murdock looked over his shoulder at Grace and smiled. She returned the smile. She, too, was composed. He would never have ordered her to accompany him. Reckless rescues are not part of her job description.

She didn't even get hazardous duty pay. Grace came of her own accord, without question. She barely knew Susan. She barely knew him. Yet there she sat, lazily gazing out the window at the ships and pleasure boats below on the morning of what could be the last day of her life. Murdock didn't know what made this woman tick. Her telling Brother Martin that he was in love with Linda DiStefano had come from the clear blue. He wasn't too happy about the remark, but he hadn't said anything to Grace.

Murdock also had come without question. He searched for a word to best describe Susan. He settled on vivacious. In the year that he had come to know her well, she had become invaluable to him. Her absolute genius for research was priceless. They had worked so closely and so well together, that she had become his doppelganger—his mirror image. Susan was to him what Linda is to Jose Enrique Perez-Krieger. But even forgetting all of that, the woman was a human being involuntarily held in a horrific situation.

He hoped that Susan might be able to throw some light on Enrique's case. The investigation had been going on for too long with a mere modicum of progress. Although Grace's revelation about Pleiades Transshipping and the one-third interest of Patricia Romanovsky was interesting, it didn't move the investigation substantially in terms of hard evidence that Linda and Mike could use in court. Murdock's frustration was heightened because Enrique had been permanently scarred. Murdock remembered the old adage, "If you throw enough manure on a man, the odor will linger on even if none of the manure sticks."

It bothered Murdock that he couldn't tell Rudi the truth about the Mädchenhaus Café. He had a duty to tell him. He also had a duty to keep Grace's promise to Jack. And Jack was an item by himself. In retrospect, it seemed likely that Jack's meeting with Enrique at Hemmingway's had not been a chance meeting. Murdock was convinced that the purpose of the meeting was to worm his way onto Enrique's boat for the sail to Little Cayman Island. It didn't make sense unless Jack was involved in some way with the murder. Denise wasn't telling all she knew. Murdock was certain of that. He was chagrinned that he'd not asked the right questions. What are the right questions when you're dealing with something as obscure as Traction? *Opaque,* he thought, *might be a better word.* He decided that there was more to Denise than meets the eye. He'd need to come up with something that would convince her to help him. However, that could waste more time. She might simply be what she claims to be.

Perhaps the even bigger question is how and why Jack controls Greta Himmelreich and the Mädchenhaus Café. Is Jack wealthy? If so, why is there no evidence of him in public records? If it wasn't his money that set up Greta, whose was it? Is he a government agent? Does the United States Government own and operate a lesbian bar in Munich? He chuckled to himself. *Anything's possible in the cloak-and-dagger world.* He hoped that someday Rudi would understand why he had to keep Grace's promise.

Miguel leaned over to him and shouted over the engine noise, "In twenty minutes we'll be landing at Melilla, the Spanish enclave on the north coast of Africa." Murdock smiled and nodded. He lowered his head and thought of Linda. The bravado that had brought him here was tempered by his concern for her. If they failed today, and if he didn't return, the consequences for Linda would be tragic. She was in love with him. He also understood the full measure of respect that she had for Enrique. Losing his case would deeply disturb her. If she had to cope with losing both himself and Enrique, that might be more than she could manage. They *had* to succeed.

Murdock looked up. The shoreline of North Africa had appeared on the southern horizon. He glanced at Miguel. He was adjusting the dial on the omni receiver—an avionic by which he navigated electronically. By centering the needle, Miguel could follow a radio beam directly to the airport. Murdock was a multi-engine and instrumented pilot, but he'd never flown a chopper. He had a friend who did, so Murdock was well aware of what could go wrong when they set down within a tight space.

He admitted to himself that he'd become uncommonly fond of Linda. If it wasn't love, it was a darn close substitute. But he didn't feel the same burning desire that Karen had stirred in him. Linda was different. Hers was an infectious magnetism that came on unhurriedly, matured, and now drew him in taut. *Maybe,* he thought, *love for two different women isn't the same.* The more he thought about it, the more he realized that it didn't take a rocket scientist to figure it out. *Could she find it in her heart to overlook my undying love for Karen and live with the chance that, whenever we're making love, I could be thinking of Karen?* It seemed to him very un-womanlike. *Can a man have more than one true love in a lifetime?* Right now, he desperately wanted to believe it was possible. If not—well, a love-marriage takes two. He knew that if he lived to the end of this day, he had to pull his thoughts together. It was only fair to put the questions honestly and forthrightly to Linda. He had to know what she could tolerate.

He shook his head. Why was he here? No superior in Veritus ordered him to come. He could risk his life but did he have a right to put Linda's sanity in danger? That was a moot question. He could never live with himself if he sacrificed Susan. Unless he at least tried to rescue her, he would be forever haunted by cowardice. He felt confident that Linda understood.

He looked over his shoulder again at Grace. She was still staring at the water below.

* * *

The refueling stop at Melilla had run smoothly. The Guardia car arrived at the same time as the gas truck. The police quickly loaded the automatic weapons and ammunition into the chopper. Miguel explained that they were *renting* from the police chief, and that no receipt would be available. Reimbursement would have to be made without one. Murdock smiled knowingly.

They sat on the ground until shortly before nine o'clock. If Susan were on schedule, she would be chained to the stake by 10:00. Miguel didn't want to approach the compound too early.

After lifting off, they flew back out to sea. For several minutes, they maintained a westward direction more or less parallel to the uneven Moroccan coast. Miguel studied his chart, which had been marked by Jack, and he identified points on shore. Presently, he made a sharp left turn. The Atlas Mountains appeared imposingly before them. Miguel identified the river valley that he wanted and they proceeded upriver.

Grace felt keyed up and more alive than she'd ever felt. She'd heard that this sometimes happens when a person is facing almost certain death. She admitted to herself that she almost certainly was. If the guards didn't kill them, the chopper itself might.

She watched the dark green water of the river emptying into lighter green surf of the Mediterranean Sea. Cream-colored houses with red roofs checkered the shoreline and crowded the river bank. Horses were pulling carts. Farmers waved as they passed over. There were few cars. The granite slopes of the mountains on both sides of the river were narrowing—gradually closing in on the chopper. What she did not see, and for which she was thankful, was a chopper owned by the Royal Moroccan *Gendarmerie*. She wondered whether Miguel would present a bill for bribes paid to them; without a receipt.

She took a deep breath. Slipping a clip into the AK-47, she checked that the safety was on. She hadn't been able to test fire it. She hoped it would work. If it jammed—well, best not to think about that, but she had to. The Guardia chief could have pawned off worthless weapons upon them, maybe figuring they'd get killed anyway. Miguel had assured them that the chief had no idea where they were going.

Grace wondered what her children might have looked like. Never before had she thought about children. She vowed that if she came out of this alive, she'd no longer like to live alone. What would it be? Home, marriage, family, or merely a relationship with a man or a woman? Whenever men had shown an interest in her, she'd let slip a flippant remark that would turn them off. It was her most effective defense. However, if that man in the right front seat took an interest in her, she might react quite differently. Whether *he* knew it or not, Grace was certain that he was in love with Linda DiStefano. In fact, he's in love with two women—one of them dead. There was no room for Grace in his life, as far as she could see. If she had to die next to a man, she'd prefer that it be Murdock McCabe. That idea, strangely, stimulated an erotic delight.

Was there some romantic liaison between him and Susan? They were like two peas in a pod. Had they lain in a pod together? She doubted it. Murdock was too much in control of himself. She liked Susan. They were in the process of becoming friends when Susan disappeared. Grace admitted to herself that she didn't like her well enough to endanger her life for her. *Am I here out of a sense of duty*, she asked herself, *Or am I here to impress Murdock? Or is it just for the thrills and excitement? Or am I just proving that I'm equal to the men? What the hell's the difference?*

The valley was becoming significantly narrower. Their forward motion stopped. Miguel hovered, studying at his chart. Below them lay a confluence of two rivers. One would lead to their target. He pointed to the tributary on the left and said, "We must wait here until we hear from Jack. If we go further, the enemy will see or hear us prematurely."

"How long do we wait?"

"If I could find a place to safely set down, we could wait for hours. Hovering, we can wait for an hour. It's ten o'clock now. Our intelligence says that she's chained outside from 10:00 to 11:00."

A green light flashed on the hand-held radio. A voice said, "No joy."

Miguel said, "He will report every ten minutes; immediately if she appears. We will not acknowledge. Look at the smokestack on that house."

Murdock knew what it meant. As the sun became higher in the sky, a wind was coming up. The smoke showed the wind direction. An experienced pilot could estimate the speed by the angle of the smoke leaving the stack—about ten knots Murdock guessed. If that same wind is blowing at the villa, it will complicate the landing. If it becomes much stronger, problems with vortices and ground resonance increase.

Miguel again leaned close to him and said, "The canyon will be narrower than this. That, plus the wind whipping around the villa's security walls, will make it too reckless to land if the wind exceeds seventeen knots. If the wind is coming down slope, it must be under fourteen knots.

Otherwise we shall return to Melilla and try tomorrow. Right now I'll retrace our course. If one of the enemies is travelling on that road down there, our hovering here would be suspicious. We need the advantage of surprise."

After retreating a few miles down the valley, Miguel hovered again. The green light flashed again. "No joy."

Murdock looked at his watch. It was nearly 10:15. He turned and looked at Grace. She raised both hands as if to say "What else can we do but wait?"

Time stood still. Murdock watched the fuel gauge. Miguel scanned the ground, looking for a spot where they might put down. There was none. He studied the fuel gauge, too.

The green light flashed again. "Still no joy."

There was no smokestack within view at this location. From the effort it took to keep the chopper hovering over the same ground position, Miguel estimated that the wind had increased. He estimated fifteen knots. But this wasn't the target. The wind could be quite different up there. And the wind speed would be determined by his best guess. Murdock realized that, too. The situation was fluid.

Grace spoke a silent prayer, "God, I'm not convinced that you exist, but if you do, it would be really nice if you could be supportive right now." She recalled the old army saying that there are no atheists in the trenches.

Ten-thirty passed. It had gotten hot. Grace really needed a ladies room. They just don't hang them in the sky. Realizing that she was under more stress than she had thought, she calmed herself by dreaming about a cold pomegranate martini in a delightfully air-conditioned cocktail lounge back on the Costa del Sol. She wished she'd had one for breakfast.

The green light flashed again. "No joy."

Miguel glanced at Murdock and tapped on the fuel gauge. The green light flashed again. "Joy. We have joy."

Miguel advanced the collective pitch lever, adjusting the angle of attack. The chopper tilted, began climbing, and rapidly accelerated forward. "Three minutes from target," Miguel yelled over the engine noise. Murdock and Grace checked their weapons, plus the weapons they had prepared for Miguel and Susan.

Murdock leaned over to Miguel. "Susan is sharp. When she sees us approaching, she'll know that we'll have a weapon for her."

"I sure as hell hope you're right. When I drop this sucker in, we're going to need all the firepower we can get. Shit! Look at that damn smoke."

"Does it look like it's over our limits?"

"Yeah."

Murdock searched up stream. "What are you going to do?"

Miguel yelled, "Do either of you have any plans for the rest of your life?"

"Go," Grace hollered.

"Go," Murdock added.

"We're into the shit now," Miguel shouted. "See those litchen-sploched twelve-foot high gray stone walls? That's our target. By now those sons-a-bitches know we're coming." He pointed and screamed over the engine noise, "There's one on top the wall."

They came up on him fast. Grace kicked the door open, stuck her weapon out, and fired. The man keeled over and fell forward to the ground. Another got on top of the wall, looked at them, threw his gun down, leapt to the ground outside, and limped away. Susan came into view. Next to her was a man with an automatic weapon. Surprised, he momentarily stared at them. Susan whacked him hard on the ankle with her chain. Shocked, he dropped the weapon and grabbed his ankle. That was the last mistake he made. Susan grabbed his weapon and fired. He dropped, falling against her legs and knocking her to the ground with him on top of her. She struggled to get out from under him, but the chain restrained her.

Meanwhile, Miguel gingerly lowered the chopper inside the wall, preparing to touch down about thirty feet from Susan. Murdock, hanging out the right door, saw two men exiting a door on the north side of the main house. They looked bewildered. As they raised their weapons, Murdock fired. Both fell. The chopper was struck by two rounds coming from the east wall. One nicked Grace's shoulder—just a flesh wound. Her rapid reaction eliminated the shooter. As the chopper came within a few feet of the ground, Murdock slipped through the door and positioned himself on the right skid. His assignment was to free Susan from her chains. Just as the chopper was about to settle onto the ground, vagrant gusts of wind jumped the walls from two directions; unsettling it; stealing lift from the rotators; causing the aircraft to strike the ground and bounce hard several times. Murdock fell off. The shock from the ground strikes reverberated upward through the airframe, shaking both engine and rotors. The chopper quivered violently. Instantly recognizing ground resonance, Miguel applied full power. After two violent shudders, the aircraft began ascending. Grace was thrown against her seatbelt, hanging halfway out the door. A new man on the wall shot at her. She wet her pants, but that didn't affect her aim. The man would never fire another shot. Once in the air and well above the top of the walls, the chopper corrected itself. The vibrations stopped. Miguel quickly moved the aircraft well out of firing range. He couldn't go back. It wasn't possible to land inside the walls, and his gas gauge indicated that he had only enough fuel to return to Melilla. As they gained altitude, Grace watched the villa disappear in the distance behind them.

Murdock was not badly hurt. Susan, chancing a ricochet, fired on her own chain and freed herself. Dragging what remained of her chain, still attached to the ankle cuff, she motioned for Murdock to follow. Crouched over, they ran for about thirty feet, dropped behind a three-foot high garden wall, and lay on their stomachs. The wall, with a thicket of shrubs eight feet behind it, provided a defensive position. Susan pointed to the shrubs and said, "There's a gate through the wall about forty feet beyond those shrubs. It's not the main gate. It has a simple padlock. We can shoot it off, but they'll expect us to make for it. We need a plan, Boss."

Murdock peered over the wall. No one else had come out of the house. He slid over close to Susan and said, "The chopper won't come back. It would be suicide. We're on our own. There's a meadow north of here about 2,000 feet. The chopper could touch down there, but we've got to move quickly. Miguel is low on fuel. Unless we're in that meadow within ten minutes, he'll have to leave us. For all I know, he's already left us. I think Grace is wounded. She needs medical attention."

"Even assuming that we can get out of the gate, Boss, 2,000 feet will seem like two miles. I don't hear any chopper sound, do you?"

"No. About a half mile north of the meadow, there's a road. It leads down the valley toward the coast, west of Melilla. Do you have any idea how many security people we're up against?"

"There's probably a dozen left alive. They're not too brave. It looks like they're hiding inside, Boss. If they see us run, I think they'll run after us."

"Or else, in the confusion, they may think we've already escaped in the chopper. No one seems to be making an effort to locate us."

"Boss, there are dogs, really mean dogs. They're killers."

"What breed of dogs?"

"I don't know, Boss. The only thing I know about dogs is which end you feed."

"You look like you're in pretty good physical shape, Susan. Are you?"

"Yes, Boss."

"Did they harm you, Susan?"

"At first they tortured information out of me; not very accurate information, I'm afraid. Then the woman who runs this place wanted to kill me, but Mr. Proteus has some influence here. He adopted me as his woman. I was placed in a solitary cell next to his room. He insisted that they feed me well and put me out to pasture every morning at 10:00. When he was here, he saw to it himself. When I wasn't being watched, I exercised."

"So, if we make a run for it, you can physically handle it?

"I can run like a filly, Boss. But when we shoot that lock off, they're going to know where we are, and those dogs can run faster than either of us."

"When the chopper pulled away, did the sound of the rotors seem strange to you?"

"Yeah, Boss. You're right. It seemed strange when the guns fired, too. There's a loud echo in this valley."

Murdock peeked over the three-foot wall again. He saw no one. Turning to Susan, he said, "After dark, we can crawl on our bellies over to that door and shoot the lock off. With the echo, they won't know where the shot came from, unless by chance they see the flash."

Susan's eyes met his. "It's a long time until dark, Boss."

He looked at her. It was the first time he'd taken a hard look. Her clothing was filthy. Evidently she had worn the same clothes since she was kidnapped. The buttons on her blouse had been torn off. Her slacks were ripped in the front and held together with one safety pin. She obviously was braless. A wound to the side of the head had begun to heal. He assumed that they had used her, as wicked men will use an attractive woman before they killed her. Yet her eyes looked fresh and eager. They had beaten her physically, but they hadn't conquered her spirit. If it came to a shoot-out, Murdock was convinced that she'd be an aggressive warrior.

They were in a really miserable position laying there in the dirt, waiting for the next shoe to drop. In an ideal world, he could have phoned the local police and reported a kidnapped woman being held in the villa. Unfortunately, that ideal world didn't exist for them. The Traction folks had big money. It took only one sour cop to pass the warning. Before the cavalry charged the walls, Susan would have been dead and buried.

* * *

Murdock's wristwatch had shattered when he'd fallen off the skid. They had been lying on their bellies in the dirt for a long time. He guessed that it was about 12:30 p.m. Still no one had challenged them. One guard had come out of the house. He'd cautiously circuited the property, not looking too hard. Apparently, neither bravery nor attention to duty was among his qualities.

From their prone position, they searched the west ridge of the mountains. Several times Murdock thought he'd seen a flash of reflected sunlight. If Jack or his people saw Susan earlier, maybe they were still there and could see their present predicament. If they had a view from a satellite, then they surely could.

He hoped that Miguel had found medical attention for Grace. As he was about to mention it to Susan, there was a horrendously loud explosion near them and a dazzling flash of light. Its echo slammed against one mountain wall, and then crashed against the other; then back and forth with a horrid gut-rending resonance. Dirt fell on them, getting in their hair, their ears, their nostrils, and their mouths.

"Jesus Christ," Murdock exclaimed. "They must be using a grenade launcher on us." They could hear windows shattering in the main house and glass falling upon pavement. They both cupped their hands over their ears in anticipation of the next round. The bushes which had formed their protection to the rear were decimated. Murdock turned, looked at them, grabbed Susan's arm, and pulled her right hand from her ear.

He said, "Come on, Susan, run like hell. Someone's blown the door from the wall. The cat's out of the bag."

Susan added, "Those damn dogs won't be far behind."

In seconds, they were both on their feet running. At full bore they vaulted over what was left of the shrubs, leapt over the burning door, and through a vastly expanded opening in the wall. As they cleared it, what remained of the twelve-foot wall collapsed. Now enveloped in a cloud of black smoke, they became confused—couldn't tell which way to go. A voice hollered, "This way." Friend or foe, they didn't know. In a split second, they bet on friend. It paid off. Outside the smoke was Miguel. From behind the cloud of smoke, they could hear barking dogs. Miguel raised his AK-47 and sprayed several rounds into the smoke. A man screamed. The barking stopped. As the smoke lifted, they saw a man lying among three dogs; none a threat anymore. Nevertheless they ran. They continued running until they came to the road. A rickety pickup truck was parked there. Following Miguel's lead, they jumped inside. Miguel started the engine. As they sped away, he explained, "I put the chopper down in a farmer's field. The old man asked $200.00 to borrow this pickup for an hour. That was a hell-of-a-deal, so I paid him. He'd never seen that much money at one time. I didn't get a receipt."

"How is Grace?" Murdock asked.

"Grace has gonads. She just got nicked. She's bleeding some. I left her guarding the chopper. We have enough fuel to reach Melilla, but just barely. If the Royal Moroccan *Gendarmerie* gets on our ass, and chases us too far off course, we'll have to put down and take our chances."

Murdock asked, "Haven't you bribed them, too?"

"Of course, but the enemy may have paid them more. If they shoot at us, we'll know. It's best that we shoot them down if they look menacing. We don't belong here. We're illegal—without a clearance. Besides, we've already shot up a fair number of their citizens."

"Christ, Miguel, I don't want to start a war."

"It would only be a tiny one, Señor."

Miguel pulled off the road and alongside the chopper. Grace was standing next to it talking to the old man who owned the truck, her shoulder bleeding. The farmer got out of the way as the four entered it. In minutes, they were in the air. As they flew northward, the valley widened. Murdock made out the shore of the Mediterranean. Miguel descended to a few feet above river level and said, "Air traffic control radar can't pick us up at this altitude."

Murdock looked over his shoulder. Susan had discovered a first aid kit in the pocket behind the pilot's seat. She was dressing Grace's wound. In minutes, they crossed the shoreline outbound. When Miguel was convinced that he was over international waters, he made a sharp turn to the right. Flying eastward, he soon re-entered Spanish airspace near Melilla. He made another sharp right and aimed the aircraft toward the airport.

Murdock stared at the gas gauge. A red needle was riding slightly to the wrong side of a big E. He tapped the gauge. It wasn't stuck. He pointed it out to Miguel. Miguel grinned as he leaned over to him and said, "It must be wrong. We're still flying."

Murdock saw another chopper approaching from the right, still a fair distance away. It looked military. Miguel noticed it, too. He said, "Those are the bastards from the Royal Moroccan *Gendarmerie*. We're okay. They won't fly into Spanish territory. If they'd caught up with us three minutes ago, you would have had your war."

Murdock asked, "If we should have another hard landing and get wacked by ground resonance, will you have enough fuel to recover?"

Miguel turned his head toward him and smiled.

They were low over the city now. Murdock listened intently to the sound of the engines. If he heard the engine cough, they'd make an awful mess in the neighborhood below. But there was no cough. In minutes, they were safely on the ground.

* * *

The refueling at Melilla and the trip back across the Mediterranean were both uneventful. Grace had appreciated Susan's help in dressing her wound, and she appreciated the fact that her pants had dried, too. At the airport at Málaga, a bizjet was waiting for them. They would make the short trip to Munich where Grace had arranged for Dr. Lore Fritz to meet Susan and provide private medical attention. Murdock would accompany them as far as Munich, meet with Rudi, and then proceed to Portland, Oregon. Grace would debrief Susan after the medical exam. Since Jack had given them Susan's location, Grace had promised that Greta could debrief Susan, too.

When the chopper landed, the women freshened up in the ladies room at the fixed base operation—the terminal for privately-owned aircraft. They joined Murdock outside Miguel's office. He gave Miguel's check to Grace. She wanted to personally pay Miguel.

Murdock and Susan boarded the bizjet. Grace disappeared into Miguel's office. She handed him the check and asked for a receipt. He complied, with a grin creeping crossing his face. Then, reaching for her hand, he said, "We can use the couch in my waiting room, Señorita. It is not as hard as the desk."

She asked naïvely, "For what?"

"Why Señorita, surely you remember that part of our arrangement was that I could enjoy the use of your lovely body."

Grace's eyes sparkled as they met his. "Surely a wise and experienced man-of-the-world like yourself didn't believe that a fine upstanding woman like myself would really do such a thing, did you?"

Manuel grinned and asked, "Did you believe my story about the five mistresses in the village?"

"Not for one minute."

"Ah, Señorita, maybe you and I, we have a liar's draw, but we told delightful lies. I learned long ago that you don't get if you don't ask, and sometimes you get when you least expect it. I will make the couch clean and comfortable in the hope that you will return and give your favors to the brave and handsome pilot who saved your life and the lives of your friends."

"You *are* handsome and you *are* brave, Miguel. We all *do* owe our lives to you. Unfortunately, I must be in the air in a few minutes. I do want to return and see whether the couch is really clean. I hope to do so as soon as possible. Meanwhile, *Hasta la vista, mi amigo.*"

He pulled her close to him, bear-hugged her, and planted a kiss full upon her lips. "Until me meet again, Señorita."

41

Munich, Bavaria, Germany
Thursday, July 6, 2:11 p.m.

After a brief social meeting with Ernst Müller, the station chief at the Munich office of Veritus, Murdock walked the familiar few blocks to the headquarters of the Bavarian State Police. As Murdock entered the building, he was met by a woman in a neatly pressed brown uniform. Her name tag read, "Ingrid."

"You're Murdock McCabe," Ingrid said. "We met briefly two years ago when you worked with us in a murder investigation."

"You have a good memory."

"Thank you, Mr. McCabe. Actually, I keep good records. You probably remember the drill. We take this elevator to the fifth floor. I understand that you and Herr Benzinger are good friends. We all have a great admiration for him. We will be sorry to see him go."

If he had decided to go, he must have made up his mind in the last few days. Murdock hadn't heard. He said, "That day will come for each of us, if we live long enough. He's too young to retire completely. Perhaps he'll move on to something else."

They exited the elevator into the anteroom. "Ingrid smiled calculatingly and said, "Perhaps he will, Mr. McCabe."

Ingrid left him with the exceedingly large woman who was seated behind the hefty oak desk—a woman whose name he desperately wanted to remember, but which his mind had blocked. She hadn't changed in two years. Her dirty-blonde hair was still braided and knotted into a tight bun. Her cold gray eyes were fixed on him. Herr Benzinger was busy on the phone. Without another word, the woman waved her hand in the direction of a chair. Murdock, amused, seated himself.

He had spent yesterday evening with Susan and Grace at her apartment. Susan had been examined by Dr. Lore Fritz at her office. She was in reasonably good health and fit for travel. Susan and Murdock would fly back to Portland after Murdock had completed his meeting with Rudi Benzinger and after Susan had been debriefed by Greta.

While in captivity, Susan had heard a rumor about a major operation scheduled to take place soon. She believed that it would be launched from Traction's compound in Honduras.

The double doors to Rudi's office opened. Murdock arose. As Rudi entered the anteroom, he greeted Murdock warmly. The Amazon stared; unimpressed. As they entered the office, Rudi told the woman that he would take no interruptions. An officer closed the double doors firmly behind them. After Rudi poured a rich Colombian coffee for both, Murdock said, "I just learned that you're planning to retire."

"Yes. I made the decision two days ago. Word travels fast. I plan to leave on August 4th. If I continued working, I'd be working for 40 percent of my salary because I can retire and draw 60 percent for doing nothing. I understand that Ernst Müller is looking for a transfer. Do you think I'd have a shot at station chief for Veritus here in Munich?"

"I think you should be more ambitious than that. I say that cautiously. You know that Veritus is on the market."

"Yes. I've heard that Boris Romanovsky is one of the bidders. I wouldn't be interested in a position if he or someone of his ilk were the successful bidder."

"I can assure you that he won't be. I'd like to put together a consortium of investors and take a shot at it. It would have to be a leveraged buy-out, but that's not uncommon. Would that interest you?"

Rudi frowned. "I'm sorry, Murdock. I wouldn't bet my state pension on it."

"I understand."

"My friend, I'm informed that Greta Himmelreich and Susan are presently together in Grace's apartment. Tell me what's going on at the Mädchenhaus Café."

"Of course, I've never been there. If I did know the answer to that question, it might be part of an information package, that for a short time, I have a commitment not to disclose."

Rudi smiled. "That was a somewhat convoluted answer, Murdock. Is the information temporarily unknowable because of some duty that arose out of your being able to rescue Susan Ling?"

"Many things are reasonably possible."

"Are the activities that might be going on at the Mädchenhaus Café criminally threatening to the state of Bavaria?"

"To the best of my knowledge, they aren't a threat. However, what's going on in the highlands of Honduras might very well be. Susan heard parts of conversations that are alarming. You remember Brother Stephen's chip and schematics? They have plans for a barrage of attacks. These plans may be in an advanced state of readiness. One is directed against Professor Amy Gallagher at Cascadia College in Washington State. Another is against the monks at St. Luke's. Their purpose hasn't changed. They want all of Brother Stephen's work, including his notes and ledgers. They've already murdered twice, and attempted a third. I'm convinced they set up Enrique and killed Gretchen, too. I'm also convinced that the only way to stop them and free Enrique is to go after them in their lair. Their leader might be the woman whom you convicted of murder two years ago—the one who escaped. I don't have any hard evidence that she committed a crime in Honduras. If I mount a posse, I could use someone from your department to work with Fernando Millán of the Honduran National Police. Your warrant for the escapee would legally justify the raid. Otherwise, we might be treated by the authorities as a bunch of brigands."

"When do you intend to do this?"

"Hopefully in a couple weeks. I don't have authority yet from Top Dog. I'll solicit volunteers from people I know throughout the agency. Susan also heard Proteus arguing with someone over the DAX."

"You mean the stock exchange in Berlin?"

"That's what Susan assumed. She didn't catch the entire substance of the conversation. Maybe Proteus's only connection to the DAX is merely as an investor, but I'd expect it to be more sinister."

* * *

After Greta departed Grace's apartment, Grace poured a hot cup of cocoa for both. Susan hadn't felt uncomfortable with Greta. She didn't like being debriefed by a stranger, but Murdock had approved.

It was necessary for Grace to prepare a report for Veritus so that Susan could draw her salary for the time she was in captivity. Susan felt comfortable talking to her. Grace asked, "What motivated the Traction people to kidnap you?"

"I thought from the beginning that Gretchen was a fake. On May 1, I spent the morning researching German actresses who might be playing her. I had a luncheon appointment with Mr. Proteus. Just before I was about to leave, I came up with the name Hilde Müller. She was a thespian from Frankfurt. She hadn't had any part in plays for over nine months. I suspected she might be acting the part of Gretchen. I planned to check further when I got back from lunch. When I arrived at the restaurant, I was met by a man who called himself Jack. I'd met him a year earlier. At that time, he used another name. He confirmed my suspicion about Hilde Müller. When Mr. Proteus arrived, I made the mistake of asking him whether he'd heard that name. Without replying, he suddenly decided that he wanted sex instead of lunch. I preferred sex to food myself. We went to his apartment. He offered me a drink. Sipping it was the last thing I remembered until I woke up lying on the floor of a bizjet with Mr. Proteus on top of me. He likes rough sex. I didn't complain about that, but I sure as hell complained about being on that airplane.

"There was an insolent older woman on board. It turned out that she was my jailor. As I tried to get up, she helped him hold me down. Mr. Proteus did me a second time—or a third for all I know. He said, 'Susan, my little fortune cookie, relax and enjoy. I suspect that you're going to be with us for a long time.' The woman laughed as he took his pleasure, and continued laughing until he was satisfied. Without thanking me—I don't know why I expected him to—he stood up, pulled up his pants and went forward into a compartment that looked like an office. What the woman did after he left was humiliating, but she didn't harm anything but my pride. She also told me we'd stopped on Aruba to refuel, and that we were on our way to Morocco.

We landed at an airstrip somewhere in Morocco and transferred to a chopper which took us to their compound in the Atlas Mountains. When we arrived there, I was chained to the wall of a dark cell below ground. They wanted information on Amy Gallagher, Paul West, and what I knew about the deceased monk. I refused, so I was tortured. For three days, I was deprived of food, water and sleep. The third day I was whipped. I have a fetish—sadomasochism, so I could handle myself pretty well. I faked that the pain was excruciating. The fourth day I pretended to cave in. I'm a skillful liar when I need to be. I crafted some plausible stories. They seemed to satisfy them. That bought me time, but eventually they caught on."

"Then what did they do to you?"

"My jailor designed the torture. She started with a hose that applied very hot water to selective parts of my body several times a day. After each, my head was held under cold water until I passed out. The next week my jailor began applying every imaginable medieval tool that inflicted physical pain. Again, having participated in sadomasochism, I was accustomed to both the tools and the pain. After a couple weeks, Mr. Proteus persuaded her to stop torture and suggested that she use truth-inducing drugs, instead. She consented. A few days later, he acquired both the drugs and a professional who was trained to apply them. I'm sure I gave up Jack, but fortunately, I didn't know much about him. I doubt they'll be able to identify him from my description and I don't know what he's up to. When I came out from under the drug, my jailor informed me that a person she called *La Señora* had phoned from Honduras and ordered me killed. For over twelve hours, I sat on a concrete floor, chained to the wall, unable to move, with no toilet facilities, and awaited death. I could face death because it would be a relief, but I was disturbed that neither Murdock nor my husband would ever know how I died or where my body was buried. That evening a man came into my cell armed with a 45-caliber pistol. As he checked the clip, Mr. Proteus came in and told him that *La Señora* had countermanded the death order. He had convinced her to give me to him as his woman. Being chained all day, there was nowhere I could go so she let him have me. I can't describe how elated I was. He warned me that her indulgence wouldn't last any longer than she thought was necessary."

"I'm surprised that they kept you alive after they'd gotten what they wanted. How were you still useful to *La Señora*?"

"I wasn't. I was useful to Mr. Proteus and he was useful to her. Mr. Proteus made up a story that I was pregnant with his child. They couldn't put me to death without killing his supposed child. He saved my life. They moved me into a cell close to Mr. Proteus's bedroom. Although I was still chained, I had a comfortable cot and a bathroom within chain's length. I felt more secure there. However, even when he used me, I remained chained. Thankfully, he had great influence over *La Señora*. He insisted that I be taken into the courtyard every day at 10:00 a.m. and be allowed to sit in the sun for an hour.

"My jailor said that Mr. Proteus and *La Señora* argued over me on the phone. Eventually, *La Señora* convinced Mr. Proteus to accept another woman in my place. However, before my jailor learned about that, she reported to Mr. Proteus that I was really pregnant."

"Were you?"

"My jailor and I both knew that my period was two weeks late. Mr. Proteus was the only one who had known me—in the Biblical sense. He's never had children. Determined to have this child, he convinced *La Señora* to let me live until the baby was born and I finished nursing. Mr. Proteus confided in me that then he'd plead for a second child.

After he learned that he'd really impregnated me, he began to handle me differently. His violent sexual attacks ended. He actually became affectionate. Whenever he was present in the villa, we engaged in tender love-making twice daily—I, in an attempt to stay alive, he for whatever reason men have."

"Good grief," Grace said. "Either a period or a miscarriage would have done you in."

"The way my jailor punched me and beat me when Mr. Proteus wasn't around, I supposed that a miscarriage was her plan."

Grace was overwhelmed with empathy. She'd had a generous dose of the real world with the Michigan State Police, but she still found it difficult to accept the enormity of man's inhumanity to man—or worse, a woman's to another woman. She was tough, but Susan's story nearly brought her to tears. "How were you emotionally?" she asked.

"Sometimes I felt overwhelmed by a desperate longing to be free. My jailor insisted my situation was hopeless. If anything happened to Proteus, or if *La Señora* didn't need him any longer, the death sentence would instantly be carried out. She also said that she regretted telling Proteus that I was pregnant because she wanted to watch me die slowly."

"How did you maintain your sanity?"

"I prayed a little. That gave me hope. I believe that God exists but I've seen little evidence that he takes any interest in the universe he created. Talking to him was like talking to a wall, but every once in awhile, I do it anyway. I knew that only a miracle could save me. Now I wonder if I've been wrong about God's disinterest."

"I doubt it. How do you feel about Mr. Proteus?"

"I don't understand him. I'm reasonably certain that he's a double agent. I wished God would inspire the flip side of his double agency so that Mr. Proteus would find a way to bail me out."

"Do you believe God sent us?"

"How did Jack learn where I was? Why did Proteus help me before he knew I was pregnant with his child?"

Grace shook her head. "Susan, I don't know. I confess that I don't understand Mr. Proteus either. He reminds me of the classical Roman god by the same name."

"There was a Roman god by that name?"

"Proteus was a minor sea god. When he came out of the sea, he would change forms. Sometimes he appeared as a lion, a swine, a serpent, a leopard, or even a tree. The English word *protean* means easily taking many shapes; easily changing. Proteus is often mentioned in literature. If

I recall correctly, in Shakespeare's *Richard III,*[2] Richard, the king-soon-to-be says,

> *I can add colors to the chameleon,*
> *Change shapes with Proteus for advantages ..."*

Susan smiled, her eyes meeting Grace's. "Whatever else the guy is, he became a gentleman determined to save my life. I hoped that before I had anymore of his children, Murdock would find me and set me free. He did. You came, too. And I can't forget about that nice Spaniard, Miguel. I don't know how I can begin to thank you all."

"There's no need. Now, in my report to the company, I'll say that you were raped in the line of duty. Veritus should pay the expenses of the abortion or the confinement, plus an indemnity."

Susan shook her head. "I'm not sure it was ever rape. I needed someone on my side. He was the only someone I had. I freely gave him what he wanted, including, fortunately, a life-saving pregnancy. Was it rape? Where do you draw the line?"

Grace smiled. "I just drew it. For the purpose of this report, it was rape. It's financially foolish to call it anything else."

The phone rang. Grace answered it. After a brief conversation, she hung up and turned to Susan. "That was Dr. Fritz. She confirmed that you're pregnant. As I see it, you've got three options. First, abortions are illegal in this state, but I can get Lore to do one in her office and your husband need never know."

"And Murdock need never know?"

"Right. Second, have the baby and tell your husband it's his. Mothers have been doing that since babies were invented. Or third, tell him the truth and do whatever he wants you to do. You needn't make that decision today. The baby isn't far along. You've at least a month to think about it. If it were my decision, I'd choose the first and have Lore do it today."

Susan didn't respond.

---

[2] *Richard III,* Act III, Scene ii.

42

Murdock walked through the door of the Gross Knödel, one of the many excellent restaurants in Dornbirn. The restaurant was overcrowded. Fortunately, Murdock's friend, Werner Gerber, had made reservations for two. An attractive woman, slight, breastless, with contrasting dark black eyes, and long blonde braided hair, with cheeks expertly rouged, and her lipstick slightly overdone, was playing the zither on a small stage. The music was clearly crowd-pleasing. It was also clear that the woman enjoyed both the music and the polite applause of the diners. Murdock recognized the ever-popular "Third Man Theme."

Werner is a detective with the provincial police in Dornbirn. Murdock had met him several years ago when Murdock had been assigned by the FBI to investigate a criminal conspiracy. The Bureau suspected that its tentacles reached from central Europe into the United States. He and Werner had worked closely and confidently together and had become close personal friends.

Murdock had arrived early. The *maitre'd* escorted him to a table next to the stage. Within seconds, a waitress presented herself to take his drink order. He ordered a VO Manhattan-on-the-rocks. It had been a long frustrating day of mostly running into dead ends. He took a deep breath and hoped it wouldn't be too long before the drink arrived.

At 5:30 a.m., Grace had driven him to the airport at Munich to catch a 6:30 flight to Vienna with a connection to Dornbirn. Grace had left her car there and caught a later flight to Lisbon, Portugal. She had spent the day checking on the Portuguese roots of Ernesto Flavio—assuming that such roots existed. Tomorrow, if Dr. Lore Fritz approved, Susan would

300

return to Portland. Among the restaurants in Dornbirn, the Gross Knödel had a richly deserved reputation for comfortable, relaxed, family-oriented ambiance. By the time his drink arrived, Murdock had already begun to relax. He had spent the day hunting records and chasing leads. By noon, he had found a parish church record of the baptism of a baby girl, Hilde Meier, who had been born on August 25, 1959. That conformed to the testimony elicited by Linda from Frau Hilde Weidner at the deposition on June 12. After a quick lunch, he phoned every number listed under the name Meier. None had heard of Hilde, except one. She was a far-removed cousin who believed that Hilde and her parents had moved to somewhere in South America several years ago. She had no family photographs that might include Hilde. He found no school records, hence, no class pictures.

Grace had phoned. She had found a record of an Emilio Flavio. He had served in the Portuguese diplomatic service fifty years ago. For several years he had been stationed in Berlin. There he had met a young German woman who worked in the Foreign Service. They courted, married, transferred to Athens, and had two sons and a daughter. Her source did not know the children's names. She was pursuing that lead by tracking down retired diplomats who may have known Emilio. She had also phoned Greta to see whether her group had any inroads into the German Foreign Office. They did.

His admiration for Grace grew by the day. He liked the way she handled herself. She needed little direction. Like Susan, she anticipated his requests. She even anticipated requests that he hadn't thought of until after they had talked or e-mailed. He sensed that Linda sensed something. Electricity had developed between him and Grace. It energized him. Had it become obvious? Grace was an idea person. She aroused his mind and stirred his thinking. Linda was an idea person, too. He was not trying to make Linda jealous. Besides, a person couldn't be jealous unless they felt insecure, but he couldn't deny the electricity. It wasn't romantic. He'd not been turned on by Grace sexually. It was professional—on his part. What about Grace? He wasn't sure. Why had she been so eager to follow him into Morocco?

To be honest with himself, he had to admit that his interest in Grace was more than professional. He liked her as a person. He enjoyed her company—the little personal chats they had about trivial things; her straightforward attitude toward life; her pragmatic real-world points of view; her always constructive criticism; and her unidealistic approach to everything. If they didn't remain friends after the investigation was completed, there would definitely be an empty spot in his life. That was true of man-friends, too. Rudi came to mind. Werner, too—the man who would join him for dinner. There would be a hole in his life if he lost any friend.

He wondered how Linda would feel if Grace became a close friend? How would Karen have felt? How would he feel if Karen or Linda had a close, personal, man-friend? He guessed that it would depend on how close and how personal. He'd loved Karen unequivocally and completely. If she'd needed another close man-friend to make her happy without lessening her love for him, if that were possible, he could have handled that. Or so he speculated.

After speaking to Grace, Murdock had talked briefly with Werner by phone. It was then that they had set up this dinner meeting.

Murdock checked his phone for new messages. There were none. When he looked up, Werner was standing next to the table. Murdock arose. They shook hands. After they were seated and the small-talk passed, Werner said, "I've reviewed your e-mail. Thanks for the heads-up. What progress did you make today?"

"It's likely that Hilde Meier, born on August 25, 1959 here in Dornbirn, is the person I'm looking for. Apparently she and her family moved to Paraguay several years after her birth. Her distant cousin guessed that Hilde was about eight when they moved. She must have been in school here, but the school records don't list her name. Paraguayan records of their presence have been conveniently destroyed by fire."

"Perhaps she went to a parochial school. I'll have my people check it out. We'll also check government records in Vienna for a passport photo. Unfortunately, computer records don't go back that far. It may take time. I know you don't have much of that, but we'll see if we can push them."

A waitress came. Werner ordered a local beer.

"There's one other thing, Werner. My source also heard a rumor that Hilde had returned from South America a couple years ago. If she's here, she doesn't have a telephone. Nor does she have an account with the electric service or with a bank."

"Perhaps she's married."

"A woman claiming to be her is using the married name Weidner. I don't believe she's really the Hilde I'm looking for. Have any unidentified female bodies been found over the past two years?"

"No. Not in this province. I do remember hearing about one being discovered some time ago across the border in the Swiss Alps. To my knowledge, it's never been identified. Tomorrow I'll tell the Swiss your story. Even if she is the one, I don't know how they could possibly prove it. If I can get a morgue photo, I could get it into our local newspaper. If it's she, somebody here must have known her. You mentioned that you had another mystery."

"I do, but you can't be of help on that one."

"Satisfy a policeman's curiosity."

"The last time we met, I told you about the two murders in Bavaria."

"The monk and the American professor?"

"Yes. The professor had a daughter, Amy Gallagher, who's a professor of astrophysics at a college in Washington State. The professor set up a trust fund which went to Amy upon his death. That fund financed her work in the search for extraterrestrial intelligence. Another professor, Dr. Roy West, from the University of New South Wales, has joined her in that research. He told us that he was on assignment from his dean to collaborate with Professor Gallagher. He claimed that his salary and expenses were being paid by the Australian university. He also claimed to be an American from Detroit. As a matter of routine, I requested our Detroit and Sydney offices to check him out. They confirmed that he is a genuine astrophysicist and that he was born and raised in Detroit. The past few years he has been involved in research and teaching at the University of New South Wales, but his dean did not assign him to work with Professor Gallagher. At the end of the last semester, some friend from the United States visited him. The unlikely name he gave was John Smith."

"There are many people that have that name, Murdock."

"You're right, of course, but the day after John Smith departed Australia, Dr. West asked for a year's leave of absence. It was granted, apparently because he didn't leave them much choice. The university is not paying his salary or expenses."

"Has he any record of criminal activity?"

"We've found none. But he *is* being dishonest with Professor Gallagher and with us. He's covering up something. He pushes us for information on Traction and the Green Lady that I mentioned in the e-mail."

"It may be wise, then, not to let him know that you know. We've heard rumors about a criminal organization called Traction. Keep me up to speed."

"Will do. I've requested that our Sydney office seal the report. I hesitate jumping to a conclusion. Do you remember my talking about the monastery where the murdered monk had lived?"

"Yes. Saint Luke's on the slope of the Zugspitze."

"The abbot, Brother Martin, repeating a quote from a source he'd long-forgotten, advised me, 'It's best to judge no one until God brings to light things hidden in the darkness. Much of which appears evil is merely borne of despair.'"

"That may be good advice, Murdock, but at times it's difficult to follow. I'm curious, too, about this Green Lady. Your e-mail said that you personally saw her walk on air."

"That's what she appeared to do. I haven't received any satisfactory explanation from physicists I've spoken to. She had hundreds of superstitious followers in a drug-induced trance. They danced around bonfires and wildly and indiscriminately copulated. It was either great theatre or something really strange."

"I'm Roman Catholic, as you know. Our church believes in demons and other evil spirits—fallen angels. They can take possession of people. We have a procedure to drive them away."

"Exorcism?"

"Precisely. The church doesn't make a big thing of it. I had lunch yesterday with an acquaintance of mine who's a spiritualist. She read your e-mail and suggested that this green woman could be an evil spirit that has morphed over and achieved human form. She wondered if Brother Stephen's chip generated some signal capable of cutting through the chaos that separates our four-dimensional world from a spiritual existence in the seventh or some other dimension. Perhaps, she said, the spirit interpreted the signal as an invitation to follow it to its source."

"That's really far out, Werner."

"I agree. I found our luncheon conversation interesting, but I wouldn't devote much time to that theory."

Murdock didn't believe in spiritualists, but he respected their right to entertain unusual opinions. "Please thank your friend for me, Werner. When we resolve this matter, I'll e-mail you and you can pass it on to her. In the meantime, I'll try to keep an open mind."

43

Grand Cayman Island
Monday, July 10, 5:12 p.m.

Owen Roberts International Airport was busy. One flight had just arrived from Tampa; another from Miami. There was a crush getting through customs. While Murdock was waiting in line, Linda phoned. She had just left the office of Robert Grayson, the attorney general, and was on her way to pick him up.

At a late afternoon pre-trial conference, Grayson had not been unsympathetic to her need for more time, but the government in London was taking more heat internationally over the delay. "When the media are determined to fry the prime minister, the fact that the Cayman Islands have an autonomous government is conveniently ignored," he'd explained. She was thankful that Grayson was a strong player. He had listened intently as she explained Susan's Internet search for a missing actress identified as Hilde Müller. Grace was in Frankfurt searching for her friends. "If it were true that Hilde played Gretchen," the attorney general had observed, "who arranged this farce, and why?" Linda had explained their suspicions. He agreed to keep the information confidential until Grace completed her investigation. If she produced hard evidence, he admitted that it might justify reopening the police investigation. However, even if all were true, it wouldn't exonerate Enrique. Somebody murdered Gretchen, or Hilde. He would still be the prime suspect. He would have had a motive if he believed the threat to his son was genuine. The attorney general also admitted that there was sufficient evidence to justify dragging his feet a little longer. However, he would have to set a trial date for August.

As she pulled up to the curb just outside customs, Murdock was standing at the curb. He threw his travel bag into the back seat and joined her in the front. As she pulled out of the passenger pick-up area, he leaned

305

over and planted a kiss on her cheek. Pleased, she smiled and headed for Seven Mile Beach Drive. It was the road to Hemmingway's. The windows were down. They enjoyed the cool sea breeze and the clean smell of the salt water. Murdock told her about his investigation in Dornbirn and his meeting with Werner Gerber. In less than ten minutes, they were seating themselves at the cocktail lounge. Both enjoyed having cocktails at the bar before dinner. Without need for inquiry, the bartender delivered one Pomegranate Martini and one Manhattan-on-the-rocks. After both had taken a deep breath and a sip, they worked at letting their worlds slow down. Linda said, "I phoned Susan this morning. I shared with her how pleased I was that she was safe. I insisted that she fill me in on her rescue, but insisting wasn't necessary. She treated me as if I had a right to know. From what she described, you, she and Grace are lucky to be alive."

He smiled and added, "Miguel, our pilot, too."

Linda stared out to sea and said, "Last night I got a call from my most aggressive suitor."

Boris?"

"Yes. Before he could renew his offer of marriage, I accused him of proposing while he already had a wife. He actually became flustered. He begged me to believe that he and Patricia had been divorced in the Dominican Republic five years ago. But I'm digressing." She lifted her cocktail glass as if she were offering toast. Her eyes met his as she said, "In case you haven't noticed, I'm in love with you, Murdock McCabe."

After a brief but awkward silence, Murdock raised his glass and said, "I was thinking about you almost constantly as we went into Morocco. I was determined to come back alive because I was in love with you. I'd never told you because it seemed so unfair to you."

"Because of Karen?"

"Yes."

Linda's eyes mellowed, and then beaming, she touched her glass against his and said, "I think we have a charming meeting of the minds. Let's celebrate. To us and to our future together." They raised and touched their glasses, and then sipped. After the toast, she raised her glass again and added, "And to Veritus."

Instead of raising his glass, he leaned over and planted a long kiss on her lips. They had never kissed before—not like that. She spilled her drink. "Good grief," she said. "I feel like a giddy schoolgirl."

The bartender, having overhead, leaned over the bar, winked, and said, "I can get you two a room fast and at a hell-of-a discount."

They all laughed. The bartender announced that the next round was on him.

After thanking him, Murdock turned to Linda and said, "I hate to talk business right now, but it's best to get it past us so we can enjoy the remainder of the evening. How did the pre-trial conference with the attorney general go?"

"Quite well. I brought him up to speed and suggested that there was reason to hope that exonerating evidence could be found within the next several weeks."

"We believe the Traction folks have some major movement afoot. I can't put my finger on it. Has anything unusual happened here? Maybe something you've not thought of mentioning? Anything at all?"

Linda pondered. "The only thing I can think of is that the quality of our security guards changed. We're using the same agency, but a couple weeks ago they replaced every man. The new guys are more polite and more professional. They're armed to the teeth."

"Had you requested the change?"

"Not really. I'd had reason to believe that one of our former guards had taken a bribe. I asked to have him replaced. He was. Several days later they all were."

"Was the change in quality like the difference between militia and regular army?"

Linda thought for a moment. "That would describe it perfectly. Their chief seems to be a rather educated and dignified fellow—much more so than one might expect in an average security company. He's called Mac. I invited Mac to lunch a few days ago. Not only was he good company, he was quite candid. The crew now serving us had been brought together for the first time about three weeks ago. They'd all met at the Lost Flamingo Hotel on Little Cayman Island. Mac was impressed by the quality of the men he'd been given. His boss has a new contract with the agency that's been servicing our account for three years."

"Did you have any forewarning of the mass replacement?"

"No. I presumed that it was an over-reaction to my complaint."

"If you can reach Mac by phone, ask him if he had any contact with a Denise Perkins at the Lost Flamingo Hotel and listen closely for the tone of his answer."

Linda extracted her phone from her handbag, punched in a quick-dial number, and waited. The chief answered. As they spoke, she turned to Murdock and said, "Mac says that she is the night manager. He'd been introduced to her by his boss, but he hadn't gotten to know her."

"Please ask him who the man was who introduced her."

Linda posed the question. Her face flushed. Her eyes met Murdock's. "He said that it was a man he knew only as Jack."

Murdock noticed the flush. "Tell him thank you."

Linda terminated the call, turned toward Murdock, and asked, "Who is Denise Perkins?"

"She's exactly who Mac said she is."

"Is she important?"

"Every woman is important to someone. What was his tone?"

"Matter-of-fact. No shock or surprise."

"Good. Moving on, as you know, Grace is in Frankfort. It's six hours later there. I hope to hear from her soon. She's hunting for friends of Hilde Müller who might have a snapshot or a publicly photo of her. If she succeeds, she should be e-mailing them to you shortly."

"Good. The crown prosecutor who handled the rape case will be helpful. He interviewed Gretchen. If he identifies Hilde as Gretchen, that might buy us even more time, but we need a motive. Why Enrique? Or his son? Why not frame someone else? Why was it necessary to kill her?"

"I suspect we'll have an answer to that soon. To shift the subject a tad, I talked with Brother Martin last night. He's the abbot at Saint Luke's Monastery in Bavaria."

"I'm familiar with the name. He's the owner of Veritus."

Murdock paused thoughtfully. "Did I tell you that?"

"No. I have sources. What did he say?"

"He told me that one of the brothers at Saint Luke's, a fellow by the name of Brother Antonio, disappeared. Foul play is unlikely. Antonio simply took his possessions and departed. He's important because he was a close associate of the murdered monk, Brother Stephen. He kept and controlled Stephen's archives. Brother Martin doesn't know whether anything is missing. Brother Antonio was the only one who knew them well."

"Do you think that his "gone missing" status could be linked to our problems?"

"I suspect so. Grace will look into it as soon as I can spring her loose from Frankfort."

They ordered their second drinks. Linda took a good look at Murdock. He'd obviously bought a new light blue sport coat and fawn slacks for the occasion. She thought the shoes were new, too. He was not a man prone to recklessly buy new clothes. Obviously, to Murdock, tonight was a special occasion. She raised her glass in another toast, "To good memories. We need to produce some soon."

"I have a month's vacation accumulated. When I close this case, I'd like to spend it with you."

She was surprised. Just thinking about it relieved her and injected joy into a life that daily seemed to become bleaker. The concerns that had held her in their tense grip for weeks became suddenly less important. She was a big girl. She knew nothing had been solved, but for tonight, at least, she could turn over a page. With what Murdock later described as a million-dollar smile, she said, "Believe me, Murdock McCabe, that's the best news I've heard in a long time."

He learned over and hugged her.

"Twenty percent off-season discount," the bartender said, grinning. Murdock added, "Pretty soon he's going to offer a deal we can't refuse." They all laughed.

When they regained their composure, Linda turned serious and asked, "What did you learn from debriefing Susan?"

"Susan overheard several conversations. One was between Mr. Proteus and an unnamed individual. The individual told Proteus that there will be a media leak in Indianapolis suggesting that the witness, William Banter, is on a hit list. It will be made to appear that Enrique hires assassins. But it could be the real thing. In either event, we've passed it on to the local police. Susan also overheard talk about a plan to kidnap Professor Amy Gallagher and take her to their lair in Honduras. That's made us both rather curious. Why hadn't they tried that sooner? Amy's been vulnerable. She's a sitting duck. Her house at Cannon Beach, Oregon is easily accessible. The small city is loaded with tourists every day. Kidnappers could blend into the crowd and strike at their leisure. Her office building complex at the college is open to the public. If they've wanted her, why haven't they taken her?"

"Have you an explanation?"

"I have a suspicion. Maybe the chip and schematics are not so important to them anymore. Maybe their interest now is mere curiosity. Maybe they would take her to gain bargaining power for some reason."

"Maybe ransom?"

"Perhaps. The disappearance of Brother Antonio without saying a word to Brother Martin reinforces our suspicion that something's afoot. Maybe they're only planning on faking an attempt to take her in order to throw us off track. Your friend Jack, who seems to avoid me, is a person of intense interest. Why has he put together a cabal of professional guards to protect you? How did he happen to be in the jungle of the Mosquito Coast of Honduras when you were kidnapped? How did he learn where Susan was being held? He seems to get a hell of a lot of things right. He told you to warn me that nothing is what it appears to be. I need to rethink everything."

Linda leaned forward to push a basket of pretzels closer to them. She said, "I'm impressed with Grace. She's made some real progress tracking down that Pleiades Transshipping bunch."

Murdock nodded in agreement. "I don't mean to take anything away from Grace, but she admitted herself that the info came almost too easily. Greta's lesbian network in Munich is well-connected and amazingly efficient. She and I both wonder whether they're flying a false flag. Has Traction invited us to play a game we can't lose? Maybe they're orchestrating our every step. That's an uncomfortable thought."

"They weren't playing when they kidnapped me and dragged me off to Honduras."

"You've got a point there, but maybe they lost control of the people they hired. Do they have as much control as we give them credit for? Maybe the bums on the river boat let it get out of hand. Maybe Jack was programmed to save you. Do you think Jack is the genuine article?"

"Unequivocally, yes."

Surprise crossed Murdock's face. "Unequivocally? That's pretty strong."

Linda smiled. "You can make book on it."

Murdock cocked his head thoughtfully and said, "Okay, if you say so. I don't know how you know him well enough to be *that* certain, but your judgments are usually on target. Let's move on. Please tell me about Enrique's corporations. How is the stock structured? I understand that not all shares are closely held by the family; that some are listed on the DAX Stock Exchange in Berlin and the New York Stock Exchange. Those are held by the general public. If that's true, how does Enrique maintain control?"

Linda sipped her martini. "Almost all of his corporations have two classes of common shares designated A and B. The A shares are voting shares. They are all held by the family; Enrique holds a majority. These shares are subject to a stock redemption agreement. If a family member wishes to sell A shares, the corporation has a right of first refusal. Thus no A shares can be sold to the general public unless the corporation declines to buy them. That won't happen. The B shares are listed on the stock exchanges. Those shares can vote only on fundamental changes to the bylaws or the Articles of Incorporation. They can't vote on members of the board of directors or influence general business decisions. A dividend preference is given to the B shares. This system allows Enrique to raise capital easily without his control being threatened."

"Has the market value of the B shares taken a whack over the last several months?"

"Oh, yes. They've lost over 50 percent of their market value. The scandal has hurt them, but the institutional investors—the really big investors—know that I'll be gone if Estrelita takes over. When they made their investments, they counted on the serendipity that flows from Enrique and me working as a team." She paused, and then said, "Good God, are you thinking what I'm thinking?"

"When market value of the B shares fell, were there buyers willing to pick up shares on the cheap?"

"There always are. There are bottom-feeders who are not adverse to risk. Punters can make big money in a down market, or fall flat on their faces. There's more money made gambling on Wall Street than there is in Las Vegas."

"That's true especially when the punters can control the risk. If we're to listen to unequivocal Jack, we need to start thinking outside the box. What if, instead of trying to destroy the economy, the Traction people are merely massaging it for their own benefit?" He paused thoughtfully, and then added, "Susan needs to have access to your corporate stock records and the assistance of those of your people who know them best. If manipulating risk is their game, they may be using agents buying for them as undisclosed principals. Maybe Susan can find a pattern. If they suspect that we're on to them, they'll become extremely dangerous."

His phone rang. After a brief conversation, he said, "That was Grace. She doesn't have photos of Hilde yet, but she's been given the address of a young man who dated Hilde. He's supposed to have a few dozen. If he hasn't chucked them, Grace will e-mail copies to us tomorrow. I asked her to find a middle initial for Patricia Romanovsky. It's D. She's checking to see whether that stands for her maiden name. If it does, I met a disreputable gal a couple years ago who used the name Patti Dale. She was quite active at the same lesbian bar that Grace mines for information."

"I doubt that a lesbian would have married Boris Romanovsky."

"She could be bisexual, but let's not waste time on diversions. Let's concentrate on us."

With cocktails, dinner, and soft shadows from candlelight, the evening passed. Having dinner together was not new, but tonight their relationship was new. Both felt they were in the process of committing their lives to one another. They were perfectly delighted to be alone in a crowd. Within themselves they discovered a new excitement—an excitement like one has at the beginning of a long anticipated adventure. As the evening passed, each observed in the other pleasant traits barely noticed before. They shared dreams never dreamt before. Murdock marveled how much Linda was like Karen. *She has the same glow, the enthusiasm, the realism, the intelligence, the compassion, the strength, and the zest for life that Karen had. Maybe Linda has just a little added edge on each.*

Linda marveled that he was so unlike any man she'd ever known. *I've not met a man who's had the strength of conviction, the rugged determination to succeed against enormous odds, the brutal honesty, the concern for people, the intellect, and the wholesome good looks of Murdock McCabe.*

When it was nearly midnight, his eyes met hers as he said, "They're holding the room for me. I'd better check in and get some sleep."

Linda's eyes glittered in the candlelight. "I don't think either is a good idea. Stay in my apartment tonight."

"But you don't have an extra—"

She interrupted. "No, I don't, silly man. Who cares? Tonight, no one exists except us. Can you buy that delusion, Murdock McCabe?"

He cocked his head as a wry grin crept across his face. "It's bought."

* * *

As they passed Old Robin Point and turned off the Queen's Highway, they drove up to the gate of the compound. Linda was stopped by a guard. "Sorry, miss," he said. "I just needed to take a closer look. They make pretty good theatrical masks these days. We can't let any imitations get by." He saluted and opened the gate. She thanked him for his diligence, drove through and parked at the main entrance to the villa. Hand in hand they walked through the open door and took the elevator to her private apartment on the third floor. The door was unlocked. They entered, walked past the kitchenette, and into the great room. Linda opened the French doors to the balcony. The cool sea breeze floated in. She invited him to join her on a love seat just inside the doors which had a view of the Caribbean. Colored ground lights pointing upward lit the tall palmettos and reflected off the security wall to provide just enough light to enhance romance. An armed guard was visibly patrolling along the inside of that wall.

Linda disappeared into the kitchenette, fixed two hot chocolates, and then joined him on the loveseat. Snuggling close together they shared the enjoyment of the warm mugs of sweet liquid. When both mugs had been placed on the end table, she put her head on his shoulder. He put his arm firmly around her. The rest of the world had gone to sleep. They alone were awake. The night was their private dominion.

"Linda."

"What?"

"Have you ever thought of pooling our assets and putting in an offer to Brother Martin?"

"To buy Veritus?"

"Yes. Grace told him that you and I are an item. He'd like to meet you. Once he does, I think he'd be pleased to receive an offer from us. We could leverage it, or he might sell on an installment contract. You would leave Enrique. We could keep the present staff and continue to run it out of Chicago. We could live wherever we wanted."

"Why, Mr. Murdock McCabe, you've read my mind. I've thought exactly of doing that. The market for Veritus is under stress because of the bad publicity. The sooner we strike, the better. Let's talk to him together."

"Excellent idea. I'll phone him in the morning."

Linda chided," We may need to get some sleep in the morning."

Murdock smiled. "Right." He hugged her a little tighter.

"Murdock, there are some issues we need to face. I know you're still in love with Karen. I know that you remember when you made love to Karen the first time. I know that you'll think of her tonight. You may often think of her when we're just living our daily lives. I've searched my heart to discover whether I can compete with that kind of nostalgia."

Murdock released his arm around her ever so slightly. "What did you decide?"

Linda's eyes met his. "It's not necessary to compete. I'd be thrilled to marry a man who had a happy first marriage. I wish I'd known Karen. She sounds like a truly astonishing woman. I accept her as a part of you without hesitation or reservation. She was a wonderful part of your life and the memory of her tragic ending will never leave you. That's all part of the pageant of our lives together. She becomes a wonderful part of us. She always will be, and we will be happy."

"Linda, I don't know what to say. You understand so completely. Thank you."

As he went to hug her more tightly, she pulled away. In the half light reflected inside from the security wall, he saw her eyes fix seriously on his. She said, "I have a more serious problem. His name is Jack."

This is not what he wanted to hear. "Ah, the mysterious unequivocal Jack. Did you make a pact with him after he saved your life in the jungle?"

Linda took his left hand and squeezed it. Speaking in a hushed tone, she said, "No fair. You've been reading my mind when I wasn't looking."

"Well, if Jack is who I think he is, after he rescued you, I'm sure the two of you made love."

"Passionately and frequently until we fell asleep exhausted. Who do you think he is?"

"He reminds me of a man I once knew as Smokey. At that time, he posed as a barfly in Cannon Beach, Oregon." Murdock decided not to mention Denise or Susan Ling. "Are you in love with him?"

"No, not *in love*, but the fact of Jack could be a discomfort to you. I don't apologize for that fact, and I certainly don't wish to make you uncomfortable. He killed two men to free me. He risked his life all day by leading me through the dense jungle where violent men were searching for us. They would have killed him to get me. You can imagine the horror of what they wanted to do to me. He led me to a tribal village where he had friends and we were safe. He violated a contract to do it. His friends loaned us a hut where there was one bed. What we did was only human under the circumstances. I'm not proud of it. I'm not ashamed of it. It was something that I hadn't done for a long, long time. You and I had no commitment. The most horrible day of my life ended up with a pleasurable memory."

In the soft reflected light, Murdock's eyes searched hers. "Thanks for the heads-up dose of reality. Honesty sometimes requires courage. I admire that courage. Are you going to see Jack again?"

"Murdock, we had faced death all day. An intense bonding happened that night. We both knew that it couldn't end there. Jack sincerely believes that you and I should marry. He wants us to be happy. He truly doesn't want to upset our marriage, but we made a pledge to each other—that we would see each other from time to time. Unless he releases me, I feel bound by that pledge. I don't want it to happen behind your back. He's sixty-nine. He could live another twenty years or more. I honestly don't know whether I can bring myself to ask him to release me. I'm not sure I want him to. I do want to see him again. We're not in love, nor do I think we ever will be, but there was that bonding. What we experienced that night was physical and unforgettable."

Murdock stared out to sea. After seconds that seemed like minutes to Linda, he said quietly, "I agree that there's nothing to be ashamed of, either then or now. I can live with your pledge. It's more natural for you to bond with a live man than I to a dead woman. You need never ask him to release you on my account. I think Shakespeare said it best, 'There is nothing either good or bad, but thinking makes it so.'"[3]

---

[3] *Hamlet, Act II, Scene ii*

"I don't want to mislead. Jack could be a wound in our marriage that may not heal during his lifetime." Linda arose and excused herself to go to the powder room. After taking a few steps, she turned and said, "You do understand what *seeing him* involves, don't you?" With that, she left him to his thoughts.

Murdock was aware that she had created a diplomatic pause. She had asked him point-blank whether he could tolerate what most husbands would consider intolerable. Or rather, she had asked him whether he loved her enough to tolerate the intolerable. Or did she simply ask whether the intolerable is tolerable? Were they distinctions without a difference? Whichever, she had been plainspoken and unambiguous.

He was concerned for her. She had been raised Roman Catholic. He knew that she attended mass only once or twice a year, but the church would consider her seeing Jack a sin. Would that come to haunt her? He believed in God, generally, but his parents had not been churchgoers. Karen had been a Christian. She had explained to him that Christ came to earth for sinners, not for saints. Karen believed that Jesus' death on the cross dissolved all sins if a person believed in him and was baptized. "Our sins were not only forgiven," Karen had said, "but forgotten in God's eyes." *For Linda's sake and perhaps for mine, too, I hope that Karen was right.*

Linda sat in front of the mirror for several minutes touching up her makeup. This moment was, perhaps, the most important of her life. Jack had awakened her to her personal needs and emboldened her to face them and share them with Murdock. Yet, Jack himself was the problem. *Unless I've misjudged him, Murdock is not a shallow, unsophisticated, naïve man. Nor is he unsure or uncomfortable with who he is. He understands how I feel about Jack, and he understands why. He understands that he can't talk me out of it. If he needs time to think about it, the answer is no. But he won't need it. He'll make a firm decision and we'll live with it—together or separately.* It was time. She put her tools down, arose, and headed for Murdock.

Murdock was standing at the railing of the balcony, looking out to sea. She joined him. Without turning toward her, he said, "I know that you love me, Linda. I know that I love you. We may not love everything the other does. To expect that would be shallow. When a person makes a cake, many ingredients are brought together with a delightful result. Many ingredients make up a marriage, too." He turned toward her, took her hand, and said, "Jack and Karen will both be ingredients in our marriage. They're both a wonderful part of *us*. We'll be happy because our marriage will be open and honest, and because we both want the other to be happy."

For several minutes neither spoke. They stood looking out to sea, with the evening breeze in their hair. The sound of people celebrating something drifted in from small boats offshore. Linda broke the silence.

"Murdock, it will never diminish my love for you. He admits to having an interest in several other women, so as to frequency—"

"Stop," he insisted. "It's better that some things remain unsaid. Let's just say that we'll both be faithful to each other—each with one exception." He paused again thoughtfully, and then asked, "Do you need more than one exception?"

Without hesitation, Linda replied, "No. Except for Jack, I promise that I'll never have sex outside of marriage without your consent, which I assume will be seldom if ever given. I presume you'll promise the same unless you need an exception for Grace or Susan, or both."

Murdock kissed her on the cheek and said, "I do not." Then, grinning, he added, "I promise that my consent will never be unreasonably withheld."

"Nor mine."

Linda frowned, and then looking up, her eyes meeting his. She said hesitatingly, "That was the easy part. Will you be able to live with the realism when Jack happens?"

Murdock went silent. After several seconds, his eyes met hers. He formed his sentence cautiously, saying, "Yes. If I met Jack today, I could shake his hand and consider him a friend." Then, after several more silent seconds, he added, "You can invite him to our wedding." Having said that, he hoped that he could handle it. He was certain that that was what she needed to hear.

A delighted smile crossed her face as she said, "I think he'll come." Her expression changed to one of curiosity as she asked, "Is Denise Perkins another of Jack's women?"

"Jack who?"

After a moment of silence, Linda chuckled and said, "You're right. I think we've talked quite enough about Jack."

She laid her head on his shoulder again. He put his arm around her again. They stared out to sea again, letting the fresh sea air kiss their faces. Far in the distance, the lights of a ship bobbed on the horizon and then disappeared. Nearer shore a fishing boat was putting out. The sky was cloudless. They could hear the soft sounds of gentle waves licking the sandy shore. They listened to each other breathing. For long minutes, the quietness in both spoke to the quietness in the other.

Why, he puzzled, *had he been so disposed to share the enchanting woman?* The answers to some questions are obscure, especially to the questioner.

She took his hand and led him into the bedroom. As they sat on the edge of the bed, Linda slowly unbuttoned her blouse. Words weren't necessary. The invitation was not lost on Murdock. He slipped it off her shoulders and dropped it onto the bed. He ran a hand over her bra, delighted by her hardened nipples. Reaching behind her with both hands, he unfastened her bra, but before he slipped the straps off her shoulders, he hesitated. He'd heard a sound that didn't belong. Was it a door latch closing? Had there been a flash or light from the outside corridor? Someone had entered. Murdock released the bra, arose, fists clenched, and stood to confront the intruder. He saw a shadow of a man. Light reflecting off the outside security wall briefly caught the man's face. As Murdock was about to throw a left, Linda lunged forward, and with both hands restrained him, exclaiming, "Please don't. It's Jack!"

44

Grand Cayman Island
Tuesday, July 11, 1:18 a.m.

Jack seated himself on the love seat across from Murdock and Linda. After a moment of awkward silence he said, "It's good to see the two of you putting some common sense into your relationship. Careers aren't everything. You have so much to offer each other. I regret having to interrupt." He turned toward her and said, "You may want to cover yourself, Linda. We have a lot to talk about and we've got to do it now—before morning."

Murdock picked up her bra and blouse and handed them to her. "I know this man, Linda. We met a year ago under a different guise."

Jack's eyes met Murdock's. "Do you trust me?" Murdock glanced at Linda who had fastened her bra and was reaching for her blouse. He turned to Jack and replied, "Unequivocally."

"And I trust the two of you. What I'm about to say is highly confidential. We need each other. You need evidence to exonerate Enrique. I have it. I need to rescue a woman. I need help and I don't have it. Let me explain. I am a private subcontractor in the international intelligence business. I work for a general contractor who works for an intelligence agency of the United States Government. The government agency must go unnamed. Over the last two years, I've become an expert on Traction. Those folks are both a short- and long-term threat to the United States, and to civil society everywhere. You've already learned that their avowed goal is to destabilize the economic and political establishments of the civilized world."

Murdock interrupted. "That's their avowed goal, but I suspect that their real goal is the opposite, is it not?"

318

"Yes. Very observant, my friend. We should go into business together. My superiors see them as simple drug runners. They *are* drug runners, but they're not simple. This whole Caribbean area is drifting into chaos. Kidnapping, burglary, hijacking and rape are rapidly increasing. Linda can testify to that. She avoided rape by mere chance that I happened to be there. Violent crime has become so omnipresent on most islands, especially Jamaica, that it's chasing tourists away. The sea lanes of the Caribbean carry so many narcotics that the street value of their illegal economy exceeds the value of the entire legal economy. The Traction people are leading movers. Governments are being corrupted. Billions of U.S. dollars buy many political friends with ease."

Murdock asked, "Are they also a religious cult?"

"Yes. They use their mysterious green woman to produce fear and superstition, and to terrorize their mules. Their faithful young women are sold into prostitution. Their faithful men become mules to carry drugs across our southern border. The older women process drugs, but drugs are not their endgame." His eyes met Murdock's. "Have you figured out what it is?"

"They've forced down the market value of the shares of all of Enrique's corporations. My guess is that they're buying as many as they can get. But if that's true, they can't get control. They're buying B shares; the A shares have the vote. The family holds them."

"Okay," Jack said. "Then I'll add my guess. They don't need control. They don't want it. When Enrique goes to trial there will be more cheap shares on the market. They'll buy them. Then—bingo. The exculpatory DVD is mailed to the attorney general's office. The attorney general will have a duty to expose the exculpatory evidence. It will create more than a reasonable doubt. The AG will dismiss the charges against Perez-Krieger. The media will plaster every TV screen in the world with the video. All of a sudden the shares in Enrique's corporations start hitting new heights." Turning to Murdock, he said, "Thanks in no small measure to Linda, his businesses are very profitable." His eyes met Linda's. "Has the falling market value affected profits?"

Linda shook her head. "Not much. Some of our companies have lost some sales but their customers can't get a better price or more reliable service elsewhere. They come back."

Jack smiled. "The eureka moment will come. Enrique will be free. The shares bought in the down market by Traction will leap in value. The Traction people are taking sour money and turning it sweet. My guess is that they're buying your B shares in every stock market worldwide where they're available. Enrique was the first target because he's the biggest. New corporate scandals make the news weekly. Big money buys big secrets or creates big rumors. It's like the old saying, 'It's not what you know. It's not who you know. It's what you know about who you know.' They'll manipulate the market. Unless or until drugs are legalized and political villainy is marginalized, Traction and their ilk will buy up the world."

Linda asked, "What can *we* do, Jack?"

"This bunch has an Achilles heel. They have this Green Lady, as Murdock has called her. They have made her an object of worship. They claim that she's from some other world in this universe or another. Rumors about her have spread throughout Central America. Her stature grows. When these rumors hit the media, all hell will break loose. Murdock saw her in the jungle of Honduras. She appears to have supernatural powers. Supernatural powers scare people. If they figure how to best exploit her, the possibilities are chilling. So, between cooking people's brains with drugs, selling young women into sexual slavery, buying up shares in leading corporations, and offering an ancient green goddess for modern consumption, they're a major threat."

Murdock asked, "What's our government doing about it?"

"Not a damn thing."

Linda exclaimed, "Why not?"

"Intelligence is gathered by many thousands of people. I'm one. Some gatherers work for the government directly. I don't. I'm a subcontractor. I report to my contractor who's inclined to listen to me. He reports to some woman in the government. She thinks I'm nuts. She won't go to her supervisor with a cockamamie story about a green goddess from fairyland. Besides, her department is into homeland security, and not into drugs. She doesn't see a threat to the homeland from fairyland. She's at a lower level making a huge decision. Even if I could bypass her, there's little hope. The whole system of intelligence gathering is of Dickensian complexity. Even Dickens wouldn't believe it. The left hand of the CIA doesn't know what the left hand of the FBI is doing. They won't talk to each other. Under the Justice department rules, they *can't* talk to each other. There's no way my report can reach a level where it could be acted upon. One bureaucrat would have to pass it to another. By the time critical information works its way up through the acronyms, the important stuff and the trivia, the factual stuff and the whimsical, all are so intermixed they can't be differentiated. All that really counts is that we produce pages of reports. We're paid for reports. The more different reports that come to a particular bureaucrat from the more different subordinate bureaucrats, the more important that particular bureaucrat is and the larger his salary is. It's government by mandarin. Paperwork is the indispensible and ever-devouring demon. No one in the government bureaus is eager to look too hard at altering the status quo because too many bureaucrats' and politicians' toes might get stepped on. Any political decision maker, including the president, who relies only upon the reports of career staff, is irresponsible."

Murdock asked, "Do you believe she's a green goddess from fairyland?"

"I believe it's critically important that we find out. That's why I hired Professor West and brought him up here from Australia—to study the monk Stephen's work that Professor Amy Gallagher has in her possession, and won't give to the government."

"Does Amy Gallagher know that he's your man?"

"No. I didn't think that would be helpful."

"To whom?"

"To me. Anyway, Amy's about to find out."

"I presume we're talking about the woman that I met as Diana in Germany and as Selena in Oregon."

"Selena, yes; Diana, possibly. She may have been put in as a substitute one evening when you were on a dinner date at the Zugspitze Hof Hotel in the Bavarian Alps."

"The eyes—I would swear the two were the same woman."

"That remains to be seen." Jack moved to the edge of the love seat and leaned forward until he was close to both of them. His eyes locked onto Murdock's as he said, "We need to focus on several things. First, we infiltrated the cottage on Little Cayman Island where the unfortunate actress died. We had a fortuitous catch. My men and I expected something important was going down. Traction had had it bugged with video and sound. One of my men snuck in and wired it to a transmitter. We parked a van a few doors down the street, and intercepted the transmission. I have a copy of what they have on their DVD. It shows a man from behind putting on a mask with Enrique's likeness—the mask that the witness from Indiana saw. He killed Hilde Müller, who had played Gretchen. The sooner I can give it to you, the sooner we can stop Enrique's market value from falling. That will cut off Traction's ability to buy any more shares at bargain basement prices. But I have a problem. My contractor won't permit me to give you that DVD until I have freed the Green Lady from Traction and placed her under our protection. He feels that, if we can confirm that she's from fairyland, that will swiftly stovepipe all the way up to the White House and we're in for a huge bonus."

Murdock injected, "By 'free' do you mean making her your prisoner?"

"Temporarily."

"But?" Linda asked.

"But our contract doesn't permit us to use our employees on a pseudo military expedition into Honduras to kidnap her. Traction's compound is in the hills that rise just west of the Mosquito Coast."

Linda pushed, "So why did you come here, Jack? Was it business or pleasure?"

"It's a pleasure seeing you two but Murdock is so experienced at rescuing women that I thought maybe he and I could put a plan together." He turned to Murdock and added, "I located Susan for you. What do you say?"

"I say that I have a few questions. First, what do you know about Mr. Proteus?"

"He's one of our guys. He wanted Susan freed. After discovering who I was, he got the information to me."

"So he's a friend who kidnapped Susan and raped her repeatedly? He is some friend."

"He's one of them, too. It's not too difficult to know whose friend a double agent really is. Loyalty usually follows the cash. The government's budget for his pay is far below what Traction can pay him. That makes him dangerous. I don't know how much he knows about me, or about what I'm up to. That can't be too much because right now I'm not sure myself. It depends largely on you."

Murdock said, "I ran into Proteus on Little Cayman a month or so ago. He allegedly was advising Boris Romanovsky on the purchase of a boat."

"I believe that to be true. I have a safe house there for me and my operatives. I don't think he caught onto it. He never met Denise."

"Who *is* Denise, really?" Linda asked.

Murdock said, "You remember. We asked Mac. She's the night manager at the Lost Flamingo Hotel on Little Cayman Island—where your security guards congregated before they came here."

Jack appreciated that Murdock didn't mention that he and Denise were lovers. His eyes met Murdock's and said thank you. He wondered if Murdock knew about him and Linda. *If so,* Jack thought, *he's being a remarkable gentleman.*

Murdock said, "If you're looking for my opinion, here it is. I'll phone my friend Rudi Benzinger of the Bavarian State Police. He's about to retire. He'd like a position with Veritus. That should motivate him to help. I'll ask him to join us and bring a warrant for the arrest of one Patti Dale, an escaped convict."

"She was married to Boris Romanovsky."

"So I've heard. That will give us some legal justification to go in there and take her. Next, I'll phone Major Fernando Millán."

"*Colonel* Millán now. I know him, too. He knows what I'm up to. The National Police aren't popular along the Mosquito Coast, nor in the hills that drop down into it. It would be a warning to Traction if they got involved. Even the colonel doesn't trust his lower-ranking officers."

"Do you know exactly where Traction's lair is?"

"Not exactly. I posed as a tourist and thought I was getting close, but when I had to liberate Linda, I blew my cover."

Murdock said, "Brother Martin was a missionary there years ago. He still has contacts among the Miskito Indians. If I go in, he insists on going in with me. We can get Grace on the team, too. Susan is an expert with a .38 caliber. The four of us could pose as husband and wife tourists and get pretty darn close before they get wise."

Jack pondered the proposal. "It sounds good. When Brother Martin finds their location, I could approach from the Nicaraguan side of the border. No one knows me there. Miguel Gonzales will join us. I have a chopper for him. When we're ready to move in on the ground, he'll zero in on my radio. He and one of his buddies can mount one hell of a two-man air assault, if we need it. The chopper will be large enough that as soon as we have the Green Lady, he'll zoom in and take us all out."

Linda ventured, "This all sounds sort of reckless. How many people do they have to protect them? What kind of firepower do they have? Will she want to come?"

"I don't know the numbers. I've heard rumors that they're light on protection right now. Dr. West believes that the Green Lady's in love with Murdock. He thinks she'd follow him. Let's hope he's right. The rest I don't know until we get there. If we return with the Green Lady, I can release the DVD. It'll set Enrique free."

"You two are so casual about this. You sound like two little boys organizing a sand lot baseball game. Neither of you is asking my opinion. You two men are important to me and you're talking about two women that I respect very much. You could all end up dead. It's foolhardy for so few of you fooling with those Traction people. I'm not sure the devil himself would walk into the den of that wolf pack. What happens if you both get killed and the people with the DVD get killed, too? How does that help Enrique?"

Jack remarked, "Denise has a copy. She's been instructed to deliver it to the attorney general if I'm killed. Many of our own people would like to see me dead. Life in this business is always tenuous. For all I know, someone in Washington has directed Proteus to kill me. He'd collect from both sides. We have one big advantage. We'll have surprise on our side."

Linda observed, "This Denise sounds more important than a night manager at a hotel. There's something you guys aren't telling me, like what does Denise do with this Green Lady if she's delivered to the Lost Flamingo Hotel?

"That's a fair question, Linda. I've arranged for Miguel to fly both the Green Lady and Murdock to Denise. She is a psychotherapist. She's expecting her and knows what to do. I don't want any government, either our Dickensian clowns or any others, to lay a hand on her until after we know where her mind is."

Murdock nodded. "That should be interesting."

Jack urged, "There isn't time for niceties. Linda, you arrange bizjets for tomorrow. We need one to go to Oregon and pick up Dr. West, Dr. Gallagher and Susan. I've already talked to West and Gallagher. When they get her, Dr. West and Dr. Gallagher will split off and fly to Little Cayman Island to join Denise at the Lost Flamingo. Come morning, I'll phone Colonel Millán. I need him to bring in the cavalry at the last minute as a diversion. Murdock, you phone Susan. She knows my part in her rescue. She'll want to come. Murdock, right now folks are getting out of bed in Europe. You can phone Rudi, Grace, and Brother Martin. Linda, wake up your pilots and send a jet within the hour to Germany to pick them up. We'll all meet tomorrow in Linda's office." Jack stared at the two of them and asked, "Does that sound like a plan?"

Murdock quipped, "I can't think of a better one."

Murdock headed for Linda's office to start making phone calls. Linda sat down next to Jack and took his hand. She said, "I want to come along, too."

Jack shook his head. "That's unwise. I'm confident that Murdock would agree. Everyone else has had experience in law enforcement. We're comfortable with weapons and danger."

"Brother Martin hasn't had experience with weapons."

"We need him as an interlocutor. His Miskito friends can serve as guides. Grace and Murdock worked well together in Morocco. Susan and Martin will make a team. She's the sharpshooter. She can protect him. You'd have to go with me along the Nicaraguan route. Believe me, I'd feel safer if I didn't have to be concerned about you. You need to stay here. If we don't come back, you need to make sure that Denise delivers the DVD to the attorney general."

"I suspect Denise can do it without my help. I presume you've trained her. I insist upon going."

He squeezed her hand and with command in his voice, said firmly, "Stay here, Linda."

45

Grand Cayman Island
Wednesday, July 12, 1:00 p.m.

The first bands of a hurricane, which had brewed off the West African coast, had now reached the West Indies. All forecasts predicted that it would spill onto the Caribbean Sea tomorrow. A blocking high pressure area parked just south of Aruba, which seldom is struck by a hurricane, is forecasted to force it up toward the Cayman Islands and Honduras. It was also forecasted to reach category five before it got to either. The meteorologists who assign names had dubbed this one Hurricane Gilberto. The weather man on Grand Cayman Island didn't sign on to its Spanish name. He labeled it Apophis, the Greek name for the Egyptian god of destruction.

The building code in the Cayman Islands requires that all structures be built to withstand 200 mph winds. Enrique's compound complied. Linda had put the maintenance crew on the alert. If the storm turned toward them, all shutters must be bolted down and antennas retracted. Today it was raining. Dark clouds masked the sunlight and made midday seem like evening. The clouds were not directly connected with the approaching storm. To Linda, they seemed to be an ominous foreshadowing of what was to come—both weather-wise and in regard to Jack and Murdock's plan. Apophis was one more issue at a time when issues were overly abundant.

The conference room adjacent to Linda's office was brightly lit; offsetting the pervasive gloom outside. In the center of the room was a twelve-foot long mahogany conference table set with napkins and flatware. A sideboard contained a smorgasbord fit for a king. No kings were present, but there were several hungry people in attendance. After obtaining their food, the group seated themselves at the conference table. As they ate, Murdock spoke.

"You all may have gotten acquainted in the last few minutes, but it's important that it be perfectly clear exactly who we are and why each of us is here. Three of us are agents of Veritus Investigations International. Seated on my left is Susan Ling, my assistant station chief in Portland. On my right is Grace Bauer from our Munich office. Veritus has been retained by Miss Linda DiStefano, sitting at the far end of this table, to determine who framed Señor Perez-Krieger for the murder of a young woman who called herself Gretchen. Everyone here has heard of Traction. We believe that the people who run it are the culprits. We haven't been able to prove it. We believe that they not only staged a murder, but they also fabricated a rape and framed Enrique's son. The combination of rape, murder, and one of the wealthiest men in the world is so perfectly tuned to the outrage frequency of irresponsible media quacks that it has resonated around the world. Jack, sitting next to Susan, has evidence that will exonerate Enrique. We have been operating on the theory that the mysterious Green Lady is the head of Traction. Jack thinks not. His cloak-and-dagger masters won't permit him to release it unless he captures the Green Lady."

Jack interrupted, "I'd choose the word *liberate* rather than *capture*."

Murdock smiled. "Your objection is noted. Jack believes that the Green Lady is located in Traction's compound in the highlands of Honduras where they drop onto the area called Mosquitia. His sources indicate that she's going to be moved to a location where she'll be less accessible. If she is to be liberated, it must be done now. Jack's problem is that he has no troops. Even if he did, his contract with his cloak and dagger masters prohibit him from leading an expedition into a foreign country, even if that country consents. It's not the usual fare of Veritus, either. I've received authority from the owner of Veritus to lead such an expedition. However, Jack, Susan, Grace, and I can't do it alone." He nodded toward Jack.

Jack arose and said, "Our plan is daunting and bold—so bold that the Traction folks are unlikely to anticipate it. I'm counting on surprise. If the Traction people know when and why we're coming, we'd have no chance of success. Nothing must go out of this room. We need your cooperation and your help.

"On the wall you'll notice a map. It illustrates a huge savannah on the north coast of Honduras known as Mosquitia, and also the adjoining central highlands. The savannah is the least populated and most undeveloped part of the country. Brother Martin is reasonably familiar with the area. He served as a missionary there a decade ago. Brother Martin..."

Brother Martin arose, walked over to it, and said, "It's been almost ten years since I've been there, but geography doesn't change. The same tribes inhabit it, too. Last night I talked by phone with a Miskito Indian contact whom I trust. He and I agreed as to where the most likely location of the Traction compound would be. He'd heard stories of a ranch there with fortifications being built around it. I've circled it here with a red felt-point. Please notice that this circle charts a flat-floored valley between two mountains and that it's near where the central highlands drop off to the tall grasslands of the tropical savannah. There are copies of the map in front of you on the conference table." He reseated himself.

Jack arose and said, "I've obtained satellite photos of the area. Scrutiny of those photos confirms some admittedly spotty intelligence that I've received. The satellite photo is next to the map and copies are also in front of you. Notice a compound walled-in on three sides. The walls appear low—possibly still under construction. The east wall is the least constructed; almost nonexistent. It looks like a temporary spit-rail fence. It should be easily breached. Within the compound is a main house near the west wall, and several detached cabins—four, I believe—stretching from the main house toward the east wall. I believe the Green Lady is in one of those. Please notice that between the main house and the west wall there's a helicopter pad." He nodded toward Murdock.

Murdock said, "Jack and I have worked out a plan. If everyone is willing, we'll divide into five groups. Brother Martin and Susan will be the first group. They'll fly to Houston by bizjet tomorrow. There, posing as husband and wife tourists, they'll pick up tickets from a travel agency which has booked them by commercial jet to Tegucigalpa, the capital of Honduras. A propeller-driven aircraft operated by Isleña Airlines and small enough to handle a short runway will take them to Puerto Lempira on the coast of Mosquitia. There they will stay overnight at the North Coast Hotel, ostensibly awaiting professional guides to take them through the savannah and into the highlands. The guides will actually be Miskito Indians who are friends of Brother Martin from his missionary days."

Jack added, "The second group will consist of Murdock and Grace Bauer. Tomorrow they'll fly by bizjet to Miami. They'll also pose as husband and wife tourists. A tourist agent will provide them with tickets on a commercial flight to Tegucigalpa. From there a small commercial plane operated by Sosa Airlines will take them to Puerto Lempira. They will also stay at the North Coast Hotel. In the early evening, they will chance-meet in the cocktail lounge and get acquainted with Martin and Susan. They'll all discover that they'll be taking the same guides on the same trip the next day. Hopefully any Traction spies in Puerto Lempira will be suckered by the ruse. The next day they will take a taxi up an excuse for a road and into the flooded savannah to a point where they will meet Brother Martin's Miskito friends. The Miskitos will take the two couples through the tall grass of the savannah by flat-bottom boats. When they reach the edge of the highlands, they'll leave the boats and hike several miles to a point near the Traction compound. Brother Martin and Susan will split off and ostensibly lose their Indian guides and fellow travelers. They'll approach the Traction compound and beg the Traction people to take them in for the night. They'll seem no threat, so I'm betting that they'll succeed. During the night, they'll find the Green Lady and tell her that Murdock is waiting for her and that he'll be coming to extricate her in the morning."

Murdock said, "It's daring, but we think it'll work."

Susan said, "If Proteus is in the compound, he'll recognize me."

Murdock nodded in agreement. "If we're unfortunate and Proteus is in the compound, I will substitute Grace for you."

Susan said, "There's at least a twenty-year age difference between Brother Martin and me."

Jack suggested, "Polish your engagement and wedding rings so they look new. When you two are in public, act like newlyweds on a honeymoon. People will think you're his trophy bride."

Susan nodded in agreement.

Murdock explained, "Jack and Miguel Gonzalez are the third group. Miguel is sitting next to Grace. Tonight Jack will fly to Managua, Nicaragua. Tomorrow he will move northward by low-flying chopper and cross the Coco River into Honduras. He will approach on foot from the south. Meanwhile, Miguel will pick up a rented chopper in Tegucigalpa. He will standby there, awaiting a radio signal from Jack. If Jack confirms that he has identified the Traction compound, he will radio Miguel and give the exact global positioning coordinates. Upon Jack's command, Miguel and a well-armed mercenary that he's worked with in Africa will fly into the general area, find a spot to set down, and hold his position. Upon Jack's second command, Miguel will pick up Grace or Susan and me. We'll be hiding in brush near the east wall. Then he'll sweep around to the west wall, fly over it and into the compound. He'll land on the chopper pad. Brother Martin, Susan or Grace, and the Green Lady will be waiting, and will run for the chopper. Grace and I and the mercenary will pin down the enemy with gunfire and cover you. Once we're all on board, Miguel will fly us to Puerto Lempira. From there, a bizjet will fly the Green Lady and us to Little Cayman Island."

Jack added, "The fourth group will be Rudi Benzinger who is seated next to me, and Colonel Fernando Millán of the Honduran National Police seated next to him. Rudi has an escapee warrant for the arrest of Patricia Dale Romanovsky. Tonight, Rudi and Fernando will fly to Tegucigalpa. The colonel will arrange a police chopper and a few well-armed, well-trained, and well-trusted policemen who will think they're bodyguards for the visiting dignitary from Bavaria. When Miguel receives his signal to move, he will communicate it to Colonel Millán. The colonel will order his chopper to move toward the compound for the purpose of arresting Patricia. He will coordinate with Miguel so that the police arrive just as Miguel is lifting us out of there. As Miguel is making our escape, the police will land with guns blazing, if necessary. The arrest legitimizes the plan, legally. Colonel Millán also appreciates our desire to keep the Green Lady secret until we know more about her."

Grace asked, "Suppose Patti Dale is merely masquerading as a Green Lady, or that there's a real Green Lady who doesn't wish to come?"

Jack replied, "In either case, we've given it our best shot. Martin, Susan, and I would run for Miguel's chopper and hopefully we'll all get the hell out of there."

Grace asked, "Where will you be coming from?"

"As Miguel is approaching the chopper pad near the west wall, I'll come across the east wall on foot, firing an automatic weapon as a diversion from the rest of you. That'll be at the same time Miguel's chopper will land with Murdock, Grace, and the mercenary firing. The National Police chopper will be overhead, preparing to land. All of this activity should create enough disruption and confusion that we, who have a plan, should be able to execute it and get out of there in one piece."

Colonel Millán arose and said, "I am not familiar with the area into which we are going. It is dangerous for police to go there. We seldom do. The area is largely lawless or tribal law applies. You could meet bandits along the way. Be prepared. If you run into men who are armed—well—you've heard the old axiom, 'Shoot first and ask questions later.'"

Grace looked at Jack and said, "You weren't exaggerating when you said the plan was daunting."

Murdock arose and continued, "The fifth group consists of Dr. Amy Gallagher, who is seated on Miss DiStefano's right, Dr. Roy West, seated on Miss DiStefano's left, and Denise Perkins. Denise is the night manager of the Lost Flamingo Hotel on Little Cayman Island. She's a psychologist and an undercover associate of Jack's. Obviously, she's not here." He looked around the table. No one had raised a hand. He said, "If there are no further questions, that's it."

Over coffee they studied the map and satellite photos. Several questions were handled by Murdock and Jack, but in the end, everyone bought into the plan. When they broke up, Jack invited Rudi into Linda's private office. He handed him a document containing a list. "Do you know what this list represents?" Jack asked.

Rudi examined them wide-eyed. His eyes met Jack's. Rudi said, "This is a list of anonymous tips that we've received over the last year about terrorist groups in Bavaria."

"Did they turn out to be accurate?"

"Yes, but we've kept them secret. How do you know about them?"

"I and my people are your anonymous source. You've been putting heat on the Mädchenhaus Café. That's been one of our most useful listening posts. There's no threat to the State of Bavaria or to Germany there. We've always helped you; never hurt you. Please count your blessings and call off your dogs. My contract is expiring in a couple days. We're shutting down. Greta will be listing it for sale. We'd at least like to get back what we invested in it. If you hassle us, it could depress the sale price."

Rudi shook his head, smiled and said, "Thank you. Perhaps I can express my appreciation better at another time. I'll make a phone call to call off the dogs right away—just in case I'm not able to after our adventure in Honduras."

Jack smiled and thanked him. As Rudi left the office, Linda came in and seated herself on the edge of her desk. The phone rang. She answered and after several seconds said, "Thank you," and hung up. Her eyes fixed on Jack. She asked, "Is the timing of the plan important?"

"Yes," Jack assured her. "From information I've received, I believe the plan must be executed immediately or it may be too late to extricate the Green Lady. Why do you ask?"

"That was Mac. A hurricane warning has been issued for the Cayman Islands and Honduras. It looks like we and your plan are going to take a direct hit."

46

The airport at Puerto Lempira, Honduras
Friday, July 14, 7:14 p.m.

The area around and inland from Puerto Lempira, Honduras consists of countless square miles of tall grass. The tropical savannah is punctuated by swamps and mangrove. It has one season—the rainy season. When the rain is particularly heavy, shallow water covers much of the savannah. Today was no exception.

Through the heavy black clouds to the north, a bright white light appeared in the sky. It signaled the approach of the daily Isleña Airlines commercial flight from the capital, Tegucigalpa. Presently the aircraft touched down, rolled out, turned off the runway onto the taxiway, and taxied to the ramp. It came to a stop in front of the administration building. When the cabin door opened, stairs were lowered to the ground. Passengers exited into the pouring rain. The last two were American tourists, a tall distinguished older man and a petite younger woman companion. They could have been father and daughter, except her wedding ring and the familiarities taken with one another that suggested otherwise. Neither had an umbrella. In seconds they were soaked to the skin. The cab they had ordered was waiting. The man gathered their luggage as the woman got into the cab. The cabbie took the bags from him, so he joined the woman in the cab. Before they could dry, they arrived at the North Coast Hotel. It had no canopy. They got soaked again, assuming they could get wetter, between the cab and the entrance doors. Workmen were boarding up the windows of the first floor, preparing for the hurricane. After checking in, the couple promptly went to their room, showered, and put on dry clothing. It had been a very long day. Brother Martin and Susan made their way to the cocktail lounge.

They found tables that were outdoors but under cover. An air-conditioned venue inside would have been preferable, but there was none. The approach of evening combined with the heavy cloud cover, made the area rather dark. Candles burning on each table created a romantic setting—ideal for a couple on their honeymoon. She looked into his eyes as if he were the king of the world; and he into hers as if she were a beautiful goddess. Any beholder had to envy them.

The central feature of the lounge was a circular swimming pool open to the rain. Colored lights embedded below the water level created a fantasy of enchantment. Tall palmettos surrounded it. Colored lights at their base shone upward into their fronds. Next to their table an attractively arranged garden of tropical flowers caught their attention. There was no breeze—perhaps the lull before the storm. It was hot. A cheerful waitress breezily took their order for gin and quinines and hot snacks. When she reappeared with their drinks, Brother Martin and Susan were holding hands. The waitress gave a wink and a knowing smile. "The hot snacks," she said, "will take a little longer."

They sipped their drinks, obviously worshipping each other and engaging in the small talk of lovers. The lounge was less than half full. They had chosen their table because it was isolated from other customers. After a half hour, Brother Martin glanced across the pool. Murdock and Grace were seated at a table also posing as husband and wife. When the waitress served the hot snacks, Brother Martin gave her a tip and requested that she invite the American couple on the other side of the pool to join them. Several minutes later, Murdock and Grace came around the pool and introduced themselves. The two couples pretended they were meeting for the first time. Murdock and Grace seated themselves. No one else was within hearing distance. Still holding Susan's hand, in a low voice, Brother Martin said, "In the morning, we'll first travel through the savannah by road. The trip will be rough. Large parts of the road are unpaved and uneven. After about thirty miles, we'll meet my Indian friends. They'll take us across the flooded area of the savannah in two flat bottom boats. The savannah is always hot and humid. Nothing ever quite dries. Everything, even the flat bottom boats, will smell a little rotten. Tall grasses make the savannah practically featureless. Within several miles of our target area, the boats will become useless. From there we'll proceed on foot climbing into the highlands. I'm not familiar with the particular trails we'll be using, but often trails are so rough that they'd be daunting for a goat. Be certain that the batteries in your global positioning devices are fully charged. If Miguel is unable to retrieve any of us, we'll need to escape on foot and those devices will be critical for orientation. In a panic retreat, there are many caves in which we can hide—caves like the Green Lady used when Murdock saw her last year."

After a few drinks and small talk, the conversation turned to Jack. Brother Martin asked Murdock how well he knew him.

"I met him a little over a year ago on the coast of Oregon. He seemed a harmless barfly. But once, slightly out of character, I saw him rescue a woman in a barroom from an uncomfortable situation. While I was with the FBI, I'd had some experience doing covert work. My familiarity with it cautioned me to the possibility that he was more than he seemed to be. When Susan checked him out, he didn't seem to exist. That reinforced my assumption. There came a time when I desperately needed a boat to take me out onto the Pacific Ocean to rescue a kidnapped friend. A raging storm was pounding the mouth of the Columbia River—the most dangerous river mouth in the country. Jack blew his cover and came through. He risked his life to help me. Not too long ago he risked his life again to rescue Linda DiStefano right here in Honduras. So…I don't know him well, but the few times I've run into him, he always does the honorable thing. That's more than I can say for a lot of men."

Brother Martin remarked, "We're accepting what he's told us and betting our lives on his promises."

"In my judgment," Murdock said, "it's a safe bet that what he told us—he believes to be true."

Brother Martin smiled and asked, "Who is this Denise woman? I got the impression from some of Jack's remarks that he's a womanizer. Is this Denise his paramour?"

Murdock felt a tinge of agitation. His eyes met Brother Martin's. "I'd rather not make that judgment. He's a healthy, vigorous, courageous and eminently handsome man. Women naturally would be attracted to him. He mentioned to me that Denise was assigned by his general contractor. If something's happened between them, I wouldn't be surprised, nor would I be concerned. I've met Denise twice. She has credentials in forensic psychology and in psychotherapy. We've talked at some length. I've had experience with forensic psychologists. She's solid. I can't believe that any romantic entanglement between them would diminish Denise's usefulness. Jack, being the man he is, probably has several woman friends."

Susan's eyes met his.

Brother Martin asked, "Who's paying his freight?"

"My guess is United States Naval Intelligence. If anyone doesn't share my confidence in Jack, it's best to pull out right now. I'd need time to revise the plan."

"I'm satisfied," Brother Martin said. No one else spoke.

After an awkward silence, Grace asked, "When Miguel arrives at the Traction compound , what if there's a chopper already parked on the pad?"

"There's room for Miguel to land next to it, but if it's on wheels, it would be better for Martin and Susan to push it off the pad, if that's possible time-wise. I don't want Miguel to have to hover and try to force the Green Lady up a rope ladder, especially if people are shooting at us."

Brother Martin said, "Judging from the satellite photo, it looks like an old military chopper sitting on the pad. Before I went into the ministry, I flew that model for the Green Berets in Vietnam. I should be able to fly it, if necessary."

Murdock said, "If it's still there, it might be best to just move it off the pad, if you can. If you tried to fly it, the excitement of the skirmish might cause Miguel and his sidekick to mistake you for an enemy and shoot you down."

Brother Martin nodded. "Good point."

Susan asked, "What if Brother Martin and I get up to the stockade gate and they won't take us in?"

Murdock smiled. "You need to convince them."

Susan continued. "They'll be suspicious. If they hesitate, we'll need to make them more suspicious. That way they'll be afraid to not take us in. If Patti Dale is not the Green Lady and if the Green Lady is a prisoner, as Jack suspects, we might get lucky and be imprisoned with her. We could prepare her for the rescue."

"This plan is pretty fluid," Grace observed. "We'll need to depend on our wits."

Susan said, "Everyone here is good at that. Jack is probably an expert."

Murdock agreed and said, "Until Miguel picks us up, Grace and I will be observing. We'll know which building they've put you in. If you don't appear in the morning, we'll assume that you're prisoners and we have to set you free. As a last resort, we'll wait for the police to stir themselves into the situation. However, Jack would rather have the Green Lady out of there before they arrive. He wants as little publicity for her as possible. But the bottom line is that we do what we have to do. I think that's it, unless someone has more questions."

There were none.

Martin and Susan excused themselves and returned to their room. Anyone watching, they hoped, would have thought them tourist couples. And people were watching. Americans here don't pass unnoticed, especially off-season. Only the most adventurous would chance a summer journey into the featureless savannah; and only those who could afford such a trip. That was the other problem. Money attracts hoodlums. Traveling inland away from civilization and into the faceless savannah, invites them.

When they were back in their room, Susan asked, "How much faith do you have in our Miskito Indian guides?"

"I've known these two men and their families since they were boys. I trust them implicitly. I'd bet my life on them."

"Good. We are. I've heard of the Miskito Indian tribe, but I don't know much about them. As a born researcher, I'm curious."

"I don't know when they first appeared on this coast or where they came from. Since the British and Spanish arrived in the sixteenth and seventeenth centuries, Miskito culture has been heavily influenced by theirs. As a Christian missionary, I found them challenging. They live close to superstition. Most are primitive farmers. Cassava is their staple crop. Many keep poultry and cattle, too. During the eighteenth and nineteenth centuries, the English imported many Africans as slaves. They intermarried with the Miskitos."

"Did many become Christians?"

"I wasn't particularly successful as a missionary, but I made many lasting friends. By the way, they call this province *Gracias a Dios* which means thanks to God."

Susan felt a bit uncomfortable. She was alone in a hotel room with a clergyman. They were pretending to be husband and wife, and they would be spending the night together. She said, somewhat awkwardly, "I believe in God."

Brother Martin sensed her discomfort. He was uncomfortable, too. To make conversation he asked, "Do you consider yourself a Christian?"

Susan grinned and said, "I suppose there are a lot like me who casually think of themselves as Christians without forming any clear opinion of what precisely a Christian is. Some of us aren't sure that we want to know for fear of exclusion. We define ourselves by what we're not. We're not Muslims, nor Jews, nor Buddhists, and so forth, so we must be Christians."

"Well, Susan, in a sense, religion and even the Bible are like a fine work of art. They mean all things to all people. Within the Christian religion there are literally hundreds of denominations. They arose out of the disputes of theologians. We don't agree with one another on points of detail, but in general most of us agree on the gospel of forgiveness."

"So," Susan said, grinning again, "The devil *is* in the detail."

Brother Martin chuckled. "Most folks would agree with you."

335

After a prolonged and awkward silence, during which both considered undressing for bed, Susan asked, "May I ask you a religious question?"

"Of course."

"Do you think that God would even forgive a woman for aborting her child?"

Brother Martin's eyes searched hers. After another awkward silence, he said gently, "The question isn't academic, is it?"

"No. During those two months that I was held prisoner in Morocco, I was impregnated by Mr. Proteus. Have you heard of him?"

"He's the alleged double agent. I've heard that you were raped repeatedly."

Susan's eyes met his hard on. "Honestly, Reverend, that would be difficult. I love sex. I especially love rough sex. Rape requires lack of consent. With me, that's nearly impossible. Fortunately, my husband has always loved me enough to accept that. He's free to have dalliances, too, but he won't accept the baby. He's given me the choice of aborting the baby or aborting the marriage. Unless the baby is aborted by the end of the month, he'll file for divorce."

"Do you love your husband?"

After a thoughtful pause, Susan said, "Yes, I think so. It depends on how one defines love. I feel comfortable with him. I like to be with him most of the time. I really don't play around that often. I don't think he does, either, but everything's different now. That living being growing inside me is *my* baby—my own flesh and blood. I'm facing a life or death question. But I see his viewpoint, too. Would it be an unforgiveable sin to kill my baby?"

Brother Martin's eyes softened. "I think you state it more harshly than most women would. That tells me your concern is deeply felt. I believe that human life begins at conception. Killing a human is a sin. Killing a defenseless human is especially repugnant to me, but unforgiveable by God? No."

"You would forgive me?"

"It's unimportant whether people forgive you. I don't believe that God sent his Son to earth for the benefit of saints; he sent him for the benefit of sinners. It's what's in *your* heart that matters. If the constraints in your life demand its death—then pray for forgiveness. Our Lord said that whoever lives and believes in him will never die; and whoever dies believing in him will live forever. I think it's the believing that counts. You and your husband need to pray over this together."

She frowned and said, "He's not a praying man."

Susan wasn't satisfied with his answer. She would have felt better if she had been scolded. She wished her mother were still alive. That woman knew how to scold. Her mother believed that wives should never submit unless forced. Her father was a meek man. He never stood up for his marital rights. She wondered where her almost uninhibited passion came from.

Susan said, "It's only a matter of time before Mr. Proteus comes looking for me. I'm not looking forward to that. I need to make a decision."

"Are you sure your husband meant what he said?"

"I'm sure. Would it be improper to pray for a miscarriage?" No sooner had she gotten the question out, she was sorry. *It's awful even to think of that little baby bailing out its mother by dying of its own accord.*

"Pray. Submit it to God's will. If you think that's the way out of your problem, pray for that. It might be well, however, to follow Jesus' example and pray, 'but your will, not mine be done.' That way it's squarely in the hands of God."

There followed a long silence. Changing the subject, Susan asked, "Do you know what you're getting into tomorrow, Reverend?"

Brother Martin frowned and said, "Unfortunately, yes."

"People may die. People died when Murdock, Grace, and Miguel flew into Morocco to set me free. You'll be carrying a weapon. You may need to use it. If we're going to beat the bad guys, we must all be willing to use our weapons in defense of one another."

"In defending one's life and the lives of one's friends, sometimes deadly force must be used. I believe our cause is just."

Susan's eyes locked onto his. "It's not the cause. It's us. If it turns into a skirmish, we fight to protect our buddies and to achieve our objective. We won't be in church. It'll be like being back in Vietnam again. You can't hesitate. Hesitation can cause friends to die. It's an old saw, but it's still true—the best defense is an offense. In Morocco, if Murdock and Grace had waited for the guards to shoot first, I doubt that the three of us would have been enjoying cocktails today. I know you're Top Dog. I know you own the outfit I work for. I know, too, that this should be a more just world, but right now we can't afford to think about that. Tomorrow those sons-of-bitches are going to be shooting at us. We must shoot to kill the bastards; not to convert them."

Brother Martin's eyes searched hers. He said, "I really was a Green Beret. I know what we're doing. If we kill tomorrow, that can't be justified by weak human logic. But I say again, God forgives. Christ died for all our sins."

337

Susan thought that achieving moral high ground had to be more complicated than that. "It must be nice to be so confident," she said. She did feel better about him. In her mind, the weakest link had perhaps become the strongest. Now she faced only one other major problem. They needed to get some sleep and there was only one bed.

* * *

Murdock and Grace lingered in the lounge. Grace enjoyed this man. She struggled not to admit it, but she'd fallen in love with him during the Moroccan campaign. The experience was a marvelous phenomenon. She'd never been in love with a man before—or for that matter, a woman, either. She resisted silly schoolgirl instincts. She remembered how some of her giddy girlfriends had pined over some undeserving characters to which she'd never given a glance. But Murdock McCabe was everything a man should be. Now, sitting next to him in candlelight, fantasizing that she was his wife, thinking about another life-threatening adventure that awaited them tomorrow, she wanted to make love. She wanted it in the worst way. They would be sleeping in the same bedroom. Would she have to ask? Or would he think of it himself?

Murdock said, "Our two Indian guides will be carrying side arms. Brother Martin doesn't know how proficient they are. He also doesn't know how brave they'll be if the going gets tough. They both have families. We need to assume they'll cave in."

"And if they do, they'll be in our way. We don't need them for our escape. Miguel is reliable."

"That's true. If Jack gives him the proper coordinates, he'll show up when he's supposed to. Jack feels that they have a soft underbelly because their defenses are still under construction. I trust Jack, but he's made it clear that that's merely his opinion. What if he's wrong? What if they have ground-to-air missiles and know how to use them? Back-tracking through that featureless flooded savannah would be challenging without the Indians and their flat-bottom boats. Our threat is not only from Traction. Crime is a factor. Roads are dangerous. We could be waylaid by highwaymen before we ever get there. The Indian guides will use their weapons to defend themselves, but we can't expect them to attack Traction. When we come within sight of Traction's lair, we need to tell the Indians to wait for us at some point, in case we have to retreat on foot."

"Was the ceremony you saw last year located at their compound?"

"No. I believe it was several miles west of there."

Grace wondered whether she should offer to make love. *It's Morocco all over again*, she thought. *We could both die tomorrow, but he's practically engaged to be married. I'd be inviting him to be unfaithful to Linda DiStefano. But he isn't married yet. Linda could be making out with someone else. Murdock could have one last fling before the final knot is tied.* But when she thought of all the married men who had propositioned her, the final knot didn't seem so final. *Maybe he's sitting over there thinking about the same thing, but too shy to mention it. I think Murdock is genuinely in love with Linda. He'd regret having sex with me. Worse, he might be disgusted if I even hinted at it. I'd better control my desire for his sake. Only recriminations might follow.* She rethought her position. *That's silly. After tomorrow, nothing may follow.*

Murdock asked, "Would you like another drink?" She gladly accepted. He sighed. "I wish I knew how loyal their paid goons are. The biggest question is the Green Lady. If she is someone other than Patti Dale, I hope she wants to be rescued. She seems to be integrally involved in their crimes. Jack feels she's an unwilling tool who doesn't understand their evil designs. Once again that's merely his opinion. We can't take it to the bank."

"Yes, but Dr. West is convinced that she's in love with you. If that's true, she should come willingly." Grace thought, *If the Green Lady loves Murdock, at least says something positive about her character.*

"Well, Grace, you couldn't prove it by me. She was too strange. I couldn't tell where she was coming from. Both Jack and Roy West believe it's possible that she could actually be an extraterrestrial, or extrauniversal, to coin a word. If she is, that might explain her off-and-on green complexion. Both times that I saw her she seemed to disappear. However, Dr. West thinks her walking on air is fakery."

"How does he think she faked it?"

"He believes that Traction has an accomplished physicist. He hasn't been able to identify him, yet. With Jack's encouragement, I did some reading about 'light.' Have you delved into that, Grace?"

"I know that light is made up of electromagnetic waves of photons. Their different frequencies striking our eyes are interpreted by our brains as different colors."

"Right. How they interact with matter involves some complicated mathematics, which are beyond me. However, physicists have used sophisticated math to figure out how to paint it with a material that deflects the light rays that strike an object, bend them around it, and return them to their original trajectory on the other side. They call it metamaterial. Apparently the secret is to use materials that have an atomic structure smaller than the wavelength of the radiated light. Wearing a cloak made of the material theoretically would make a person invisible. The material hasn't been perfected yet unless Traction's man perfected it."

* * *

Brother Martin stood by the window looking out. Night had fallen. Dark figures were moving about below on poorly lighted streets. An old man pushed a cart with vegetables that he hadn't been able to sell at the market. A woman and child with tattered clothing came out of a store and into the soaking rain. A taxicab passed them, with one headlight out. Brother Martin closed the shutter and then turned to Susan.

He said, "Sometimes, when I press my ear close to God's good earth, I hear the unending notes that sadness sings."

Susan said, "I think I know what you mean, but I couldn't have put it in such a beautiful metaphor. It's bedtime. Sadly we both feel awkward. If we're really going to play husband and wife, we should make love. Being a reverend and the owner of Veritus which employs me, you must think it improper. In my mind, impropriety has nothing to do with it. You own the stock in the company, but you don't run it. You have a whole chain of command that does. Besides, you're in the process of selling it. I'd like you to make love to me. It has nothing to do with my job. You have no obligation to get me promoted or my salary increased. You're a handsome, mature man. I'm a most willing woman. Unless I miss my guess, you'd like to do it, but you feel it's morally wrong. No one will ever know except God, and as you so eloquently pointed out, he will forgive you."

"Susan, I really want to, but I'm afraid that I've had very little experience. I might not be very good at it."

"Believe me, Brother Martin, I'm good enough at it for both of us, and we certainly don't have to worry about my getting pregnant."

Without further talk, Susan began undressing. As he watched her, he realized that this could be the last time in her lifetime that she could make love. Or in his lifetime, too. She wasn't showing yet. Her trim naked body looked stunning as she climbed into bed. *She's a brave and attractive young woman,* he thought. *It would be cruel to disappoint her.*

* * *

Murdock and Grace ordered still another drink. Murdock didn't really want it. He was stalling. When they returned to their room, they'd be alone for the night. A decision would be made. He was buying time.

As he searched her eyes in the candlelight, for the first time he saw the eyes of a strikingly attractive woman. Had she changed? Was she wearing more alluring makeup? *No,* he thought, *it's probably the same that she always wears and I've never noticed. The candlelight just makes her look more intriguing. But she* is *intriguing. She followed me into Morocco and she's following me again into the wilds of Honduras. Should I have one last fling before marriage? Linda has Jack. But that's different. He hasn't pledged to marry her. How can I have a last fling when I haven't had a first one?*

But he had that rule. Never diddle a subordinate, even if she wants to be diddled. Grace wasn't coming on to him but he sensed that it wouldn't take much. *Is she in love with me?* he wondered. *I'm not sure I could handle that right now. She certainly must know that I'm totally committed to Linda. Even if we made love tonight, it could never lead to anything. Maybe she doesn't care whether it could. Maybe she'd be pleased if we shared a memory. More likely, she doesn't feel that way about me at all and she'd be offended if I came on to her. Why am I even thinking about it? That isn't me. Besides, I have too much respect for Grace. I wouldn't want to insult her by propositioning her.*

Grace stared over at the bar for no particular reason except not to meet Murdock's glance. She noticed that he wasn't any more attentive to his drink than she was to hers. *He's ill at ease, too. I need to put him at ease. To do that, which way do I go?*

Murdock, making conversation, said, "Jack thinks that Traction made a DVD of Gretchen's murder so that they could exonerate him. He thinks they've been buying up the depressed stock in Enrique's many corporations. When he's exonerated, those stocks will leap in value. They'll make billions."

Grace, becoming red-faced, swallowed hard and said, "Yes, he mentioned that. We've talked about it before. That's motive enough to kill the poor girl. Money makes people funny. What do you think?"

"If they are, they're using the agent for an undisclosed principal vehicle. In fact, they could be using any number of agents. We can't tell. Let's take our drinks back to the room. We need to get some sleep." As they arose from their chairs, he added, "I'll take the couch. You can have the bed."

Grace bit her lip.

47

Grand Cayman Island,
Tuesday, July 12, 4:56 a.m.

Linda had had a fitful night's sleep. During most of it she was awake playing *what if.* What if the Traction people have already seen through their ruse? What if Brother Martin was wrong about the location of the Traction compound? What if they couldn't connect with Jack? What if Miguel Gonzales was not positioned in Tegucigalpa awaiting Jack's signal? What if Jack is wrong about the Green Lady? What if the compound is defended more vigorously than Jack suspects? What if the plan blows up, or if someone gets killed? The crack of dawn came as a relief. She was out of bed at first light. Honduras is in the same time zone. The two couples would begin moving inland in about an hour. She wished she could phone Murdock, but her instructions were to make no contact. Even more, she wished she could be with him. Sure, she had no law enforcement experience, but she had fired guns in target practice.

She decided to cook herself a hearty breakfast. Eggs, bacon and cottage fries would do the job. The act of cooking would occupy her mind. Almost everything she held near and dear was at stake. It wouldn't do to start the day without a proper meal. It would relax her, or so she thought.

While Murdock and Grace were playing husband and wife last night, she hoped that the night had been uneventful. Or if it was eventful, she hoped that it had been both a beginning and an end. In either event, she hoped Murdock would have a good breakfast.

Late yesterday afternoon she had met with Robert Grayson, the attorney general. Under a promise of strictest confidence, she had brought him up to speed. He had heard of both Rudi Benzinger and Colonel Millán. That was good. It lent legitimacy. She needed his help. If Jack was

342

right, and if Murdock arrived on Little Cayman Island as planned with the Green Lady, she wouldn't have a passport. Linda obtained the promise that the attorney general would waive the passport requirement without giving too much information to the immigration agents. Linda promised that he would be kept up to speed as long as the Green Lady was in the Cayman Islands.

As she ate breakfast, she thought about her almost romantic interlude with Murdock. Before Jack's unexpected arrival, she had felt none of the desperate urgency that had propelled her first love-making with Jack. She had felt at ease with Murdock. She felt love. The anticipation was marvelous. She'd never experienced sex with a man she loved—not the way she loved Murdock. Then, just as it was about to happen, Jack had popped in. The frustration was almost uncontainable; but there hadn't been time to wallow in it. Jack had convinced them that time was critical.

At 7:30 a.m., her phone rang. It was George Waller, her chief pilot. He said, "I'm sorry to call so early, Miss DiStefano, but I thought you'd want to know. Your bizjet had a 100-hour inspection yesterday. A failed O-ring was detected on a server that controls the rudder. The replacement part could be here tomorrow morning, but that hurricane could close the airport and delay it. Meanwhile, the plane is grounded. I could obtain another aircraft, but I couldn't get one here until about eight o'clock tonight; and then only if the airport isn't closed."

"Thank you, George. That won't be necessary. I'm not planning on going anywhere."

No sooner had she hung up than her phone rang again. It was the gate. A car had pulled up. Inside was a man named Boris Romanovsky. He was asking to speak to her immediately. Intensely suspicious, she wondered why Boris appeared unannounced at the very hour that the two couples were departing Puerto Lempira for the Traction compound in the interior of Honduras. There was only one good way to find out.

After several minutes, a security guard knocked on her apartment door. Boris had insisted upon coming directly to her apartment, rather than waiting in her office. Linda, still in her robe, nodded okay. Boris entered.

"Have you had breakfast?" she asked as she ushered him through the apartment and invited him to sit at the table on the balcony.

"No, kind lady. Boris has not taken time."

"Would sweet rolls and coffee suffice? Or shall I make bacon and eggs?"

"Boris would enjoy sweet rolls and coffee, please, kind lady."

Linda noticed Boris's eyes fixated on the front of her robe. She hadn't belted it tightly and she was nude under it. She excused herself, went into her bedroom and hastily dressed. That done, she obtained coffee from the kitchen and rejoined Boris on the balcony.

She forced a smile. "I wasn't expecting you, Mr. Romanovsky. You've made me most curious. Why have you appeared so suddenly and so early in the morning?"

"Boris wishes to repeat offer of marriage."

Linda stared at him in disbelief. She cocked her head and asked, "So you take off in the middle of the night, fly to Grand Cayman Island, drive up to our compound, arrive at 7:30 a.m. just so you can propose to me again. Really?"

"You are quite correct, kind lady, but there is more. Boris does not know what is going on here since Jack has chosen security guards that Boris has been unable to bribe. Obviously, Jack has taken interest in kind lady since he saved your life. Before he changed security guards, my people reported that you gave Jack rights that Boris would like. Boris knows what future wife is doing. Boris will marry you to get same rights. But Boris is surprised. Jack is too old for you. He has too many women like you and too little money. To be honest, Boris expects you are maybe his special one. Perhaps Boris has too many women, too. But so, when you are married to Boris, you may still use Boris's friend Jack, but you must not have children by Jack until you have given four to Boris. That should not be difficult to control."

Linda smiled brightly. "Might we compromise at two?"

Boris chuckled under his breath. "Perhaps we talk about that when nice lady gets serious." He laughed. "By the time you have even two, my friend Jack may be too old; or too dead."

Some friend, she thought. "You would permit me to continue seeing Jack?" she asked quizzically.

"What else can gentleman do? None of us lives in sexual vacuum. Boris will keep his women, too."

Linda stepped inside, obtained the sweet rolls and more coffee, and then returned to the balcony. After putting them on the table, she tipped the umbrella to shade them from the early morning sun. She said, "You mentioned that Jack was your friend. He's never mentioned your name."

Boris looked down at the table, tore off a piece of sweet roll, dunked it in his coffee, and ate it—all the while chuckling under his breath. When he looked up again, he said, "You have spent little time with Jack. Besides, kind lady, when man is on top of woman, he does not discuss other men. He puts whole mind to what woman expects." He looked down at his meal again and snickered under his breath. Linda thought his remarks were disgusting, but he was both disgusting and right. She hesitated to respond; then concluded it was better not to. Instead, she stared out to sea and in her peripheral vision watched him dunk and eat.

Presently he looked up again and said, "Boris is here because Linda and Boris need each other. Forget marriage for now. Boris and Linda must talk. Linda must listen carefully to Boris and trust what Boris says. Boris will share secrets so that Linda *can* trust Boris. Until yesterday Boris had contract with Jack. You have heard of Traction. They do billions in precursors for methamphetamines. Most of billions are washed clean through Pleiades Transshipping Company and some other companies. Boris knows. They use Boris's banks in Cyprus and Aruba."

"So you are involved with Traction."

"Boris is businessman—a banker among other things. She uses Boris's banks. She has used them since Boris and she were married."

"Who is this *she*?"

"Diana and Selena and Hecate are some of her pseudonyms; Patricia Dale Romanovsky is her autonym. She is evil genius of Traction. Do you believe in existence of pure evil, kind lady?"

Linda smiled. "No, not really. I think most people who are honest with themselves don't. Calling someone *evil* is judgmental. In this day and age most people try not to be judgmental."

"You mean weak people who need to be politically correct. Boris prefers hypocrites. They know difference between right and wrong. Hitler murdered six million people and Stalin twenty-four million. They were evil. If you substitute therapeutic words for moral words, maybe word *wicked* would be closer to political correctness. But Boris's ex-wife is more than wicked. She is possessed by pure evil. Boris learned right after marriage. Boris would not have children by her. Her children would be devils. Boris paid priests to pray for Boris every day until divorce was final. Boris wants children by you. You are holy."

"I am *holy*?"

"Holy means not evil. Many people today are relativists, but they are hypocrites. They are relativists only when they are trying to prove your standards wrong."

Linda's eyes met his. She had never heard Boris wax so philosophical. He had more depth than she had anticipated. "Perhaps seeing evil in others could intoxicate one into being blind to his or her own faults. But we were talking about Jack. You claimed he is your friend."

"Jack has made mistake. He believes that Patricia has brought down Enrique so that she could buy up stock in his companies for song; then raise him up again and profit. She is not buying. Boris is buying because Boris knows that Jack has DVD made from stolen signals. It shows man putting on mask with Enrique's likeness after man has killed young woman. It is same man who pretends to be young woman's father. My ex-wife does not know Jack has it."

"If Jack is your friend, why haven't you told him that you're the one buying the shares? Maybe he needs to know that."

"Boris tells Jack everything that Boris has contracted to tell Jack—like money moved by Pleiades. Sometimes Boris tells more—when it is in Boris's best interest. Enough of that. Listen to Boris carefully. Thursday big meeting was held here. Boris knows who was here, but not why or what happened. Boris also knows that last night Jack was discovered on foot in mountains of southern Honduras by Traction people."

Linda's eyes widened. "What do you mean?"

"Boris means what Boris says. Jack is in compound of evil Patricia. You must trust Boris. Are Veritus people in Honduras counting on Jack for anything?"

But she *didn't* trust Boris, and she wasn't inclined to reveal the plan. But she was fully aware that Jack was vital to the plan. If Boris is telling the truth, the plan was in serious jeopardy. Miguel would be in Tegucigalpa now, refueling the chopper and awaiting Jack's command. No command; no rescue. The plan was daring. Now it seemed foolhardy. The Honduran National Police might still fly in, but their purpose was to affect an arrest; not to bail out the Veritus people. Besides, they're awaiting Jack's signal, too. She decided to act as if the news were unimportant. She said, "You mentioned precursors. What's that all about?"

"Precursors, especially ephedrine, come by ship from Hong Kong triads to South Africa. From there they are flown to Congo where planes are changed. Second plane flies them to Morocco. Ship takes them to the coast of Honduras. They are transported overland by human mules. They are simple superstitious people who believe in magical powers of green woman and fear her more than they fear arrest. They risk their lives to carry precursor to northern states of Mexico where labs cook them into methamphetamine for United States market."

"I thought that cocaine and heroin were the main drugs smuggled into the United States."

"Methamphetamine is more popular than cocaine and heroin combined. People smoke it. They get surge of euphoria and libido and feeling of security."

"I've heard that it causes permanent psychological damage."

"Only if used for long time, kind lady. One and one-half million Americans use it. It is big cash cow for Traction. Traction uses cash to invest in stocks, but not Enrique's. They invest in companies in United States that are involved in homeland security. Traction has big plan to threaten United States with biological weapons. They want to weaken America by forcing it to spend huge sums on homeland security. Traction will profit at same time. Boris does not know end game. But Boris's ex-wife is very dangerous and very evil."

"Is Herr Weidner in their top echelon?"

"He is man of many names. He changes appearance as easily as you change clothes. He had a German mother and a Portuguese father. He easily poses as either Weidner or Flavio. Patricia has the DVD showing him from behind putting on an Enrique mask before he kills poor actress girl. On the day before trial of Señor Perez-Krieger begins, they will offer DVD to you for billions of dollars."

That's a switch from Jack's theory, she thought.

Boris continued, "So, not only is Jack wrong about stocks, but now he appears to have fallen into their trap. Or was that his plan? Was that his way of getting inside their compound?"

She thought, *Jack's no fool. He always seems to have it together.* She was convinced that Boris had no knowledge of the plan. Why did Boris want to know it? One thing was for sure. She needed to warn Murdock. If it were Jack's plan to be captured, she was convinced he hadn't shared it with Murdock. Were the two couples falling into a trap? Is Jack the man she thought he was? Is he a mere opportunist? She shuddered to think that that's all he is and that he was just another man who had merely used her again. But tactically she decided to continue the pretense that his information was unimportant. She asked, "Do you still maintain the same level of financial services for Traction?"

Boris smiled enigmatically. "There has been inflection in Boris's policy toward Pleiades Transshipping."

"What does that mean?"

"You are wasting precious time, kind lady. Murdock McCabe and Susan Ling have not been in Portland for several days. Professor Amy Gallagher and Roy West, have not been at Cascadia College. My friend Grace Bauer seems to be nowhere in Europe. Rudi Benzinger is not in his office. All, plus Colonel Millán of the Honduran National Police, were within this compound a few days ago. Boris is not fool. Boris knows you do not trust."

"Enrique nearly got murdered on your Cypriot estate a couple years ago. I got kidnapped from your boat. You do business with Traction and a mysterious character who calls himself Mr. Proteus. I doubt that Grace Bauer is your friend. I am not your friend. I'm searching for the true motive that brought you here. Can you help me?"

Boris finished the last bite of his sweet roll and poured coffee for both of them from the carafe Linda had placed on the table. He took a sip of coffee, then smiled and said, "Boris doubles financial arrangements in marriage offer."

Linda smiled brightly and said, "Please pay close attention. Linda is *not* going to marry Boris; Boris."

Boris gingerly took another sip of the steaming coffee, grinned and said, "Never close doors, kind lady. Another man was here. Do you think Boris does not know? His name is Miguel Gonzales. He is from Málaga, Spain. He is mercenary with contract from Jack. Last week he worked for Murdock McCabe who took friend Grace on reckless mission to Morocco. They think they were lucky. It was not luck. Boris asked king to hold off Moroccan Air Force. Military just watched."

That was surprising news, if it were true. "Was Murdock aware that you did that?"

"Jack knew. He asked Boris to use influence. Not even kings want to screw with Russian bankers."

After a long, pregnant silence during which Linda was struggling to accurately assess the situation, she asked calmly, "Have you had enough to eat?"

"Yes. Thank you, kind lady. Hours ago Boris was sleeping on flight from Aruba to Houston when Boris's spies reported Jack's capture. Boris immediately ordered pilot to divert flight to Grand Cayman Island. Yesterday Boris's spy at the airport reported that your plane was down for service. Boris thought you might need to get to Honduras. Boris's plane has been refueled and it awaits you, kind lady, but you must decide quickly before storm causes airport to close."

Linda asked thoughtfully, "Did your person at the airport have anything to do with my plane being down?"

"Kind lady, how can you ask such question? Boris is gentleman, a prince, and descendent of Tsars. No. We have more important things to talk about. When Patricia was married to Boris, a large sum of money was channeled though Boris's bank on Cyprus to her. The source of the funds was Saint Petersburg."

"The one in Russia or Florida?"

"Russia. She used this money to start Traction. Boris didn't like that. Many things Boris does not like. Boris makes money from Traction's accounts in Boris's banks. Boris likes that. Boris's contract with Jack has expired. Boris doesn't like that. Jack is Boris's friend. Boris likes that. Boris likes kind lady. If kind lady wants friends to have chance to live, kind lady must trust Boris. Boris will fly wherever you need to go. If you do nothing, then people both Boris and you like may die."

The man sounded sincere. But his happenstance of being there was too convenient; too much of a coincidence. She thought, *if I'm taken prisoner, too, that would make the situation even more unworkable for Murdock. But how would he even know? It couldn't make the adventure more daring than it already is. If Boris is trying to kidnap me, that would push down stock in Enrique's companies. Boris would benefit by acquiring more at a lower price.* What should she do? What *could* she do? She had met Miguel. Maybe he would listen to her. Colonel Millán had met her, too. But she wasn't an actor in the plan. However, the plan had already come apart. She sized up Boris. She decided to push for one more bit of information to see if it rang true. She asked, "Are you intimating that the Russian government is behind all this—that all of Traction's activities are for the benefit of Mother Russia?"

"Kind lady, nothing is for benefit of Mother Russia. Russian government is irrational. Ruling elite say to hell with Russian people. Feed them sops that make them happy with their miserable lives. Power protects supremacy and wealth of ruling oligarchy. They live like princes in world of illusion. They create more illusion. They have tentacles into Russian mafia and mafia has tentacles into them. Traction could be branch of Russian mafia."

"So this Green Lady is illusion?"

"She, kind lady, puzzles Boris, too. Maybe Patricia plays Green Lady. Maybe she has something to do with strange monk. Boris's spies in Traction compound get inconveniently killed. Spies' body parts are always mailed to Boris."

"If your ex-wife discovers that you're helping me, won't she try to kill you?"

"Yes. Boris should know better. Boris became fool when Boris fell in love with you, kind lady."

Linda hesitated; thought hard; then said hesitatingly, "Are you asking me to believe that you're willing to risk your life because you're in love with me, even after I've assured you that I'll never marry you?"

"Boris is telling you that Boris wants to help. Boris is telling you that *never* never means never."

I'm a gambler, she thought. *I've gambled in many business negotiations, and usually came out on top, but this was different. I'd be gambling my life in what might be a futile attempt to save Murdock's and Jack's lives;*

and the others. Has Boris ever lied to me? I can't say that he has. I can't say that he hasn't. I don't believe he's ever told the whole truth, either. I don't know whether Miguel will listen to me and ignore Jack's orders to wait for his signal. Maybe they had a back-up plan. For all I know, Boris would carry me off to be his sex slave like Proteus did to Susan Ling. What shall I do? He's right about one thing. Doing nothing is doing something, and I'd have to live with the thought of what I might have done. She asked, "Will you fly me to Tegucigalpa, Honduras immediately?"

"Boris will give order to pilot as soon as you give a time."

"Ten o'clock. One hour from now."

* * *

Meanwhile, at that same hour, the airport coffee shop at Tegucigalpa was cool and not crowded. Miguel's third cup of coffee lay on the table, fresh and steaming. He cleaned the last of the egg yolk from his plate with the last piece of toast. The rented chopper was in reasonably good working order. He'd checked it out personally. At that moment it was being refueled. As he washed down the toast with coffee, he felt sorry for the kid out there in the heat of the morning sniffing gasoline fumes from the hundred octane aviation fuel. He remembered when he'd been a kid doing the same thing. He lit a cigar. No one complained about the smoke. Noise from the air conditioner was unpleasant. Choppers are noisy, but when Miguel was relaxing, he liked it quiet. The attractive young woman at the far end of the lunch counter looked like she might be available for a price. Miguel shook off the idea—for now. Not this early in the morning. His immediate problem was that Jack had not made the prearranged communications check at 8:00 a.m. That was troubling. Once a plan was agreed upon, Jack meticulously followed it. There was a backup plan, but he didn't like it. It was too dangerous. *Reckless,* he thought, *would be a better word.* Because he didn't like it, he and Jack had agreed that it was optional. His option was to abandon the project and return to Spain.

He knew the project was important to Jack. The last item of Jack's contract with the prime contractor was to deliver some woman in Honduras to another woman on Little Cayman Island. Miguel didn't know why. He didn't need to know why. The less he knew the better. Miguel had been a mercenary most of his life. Most of the time, he and his group had contracts with governments and almost-governments in central Africa. When push came to shove, it wasn't the contract that mattered. It was covering the ass of your buddies, and their covering yours. You fought for each other.

When the action started, money was an afterthought. Right now he and Jack were the group, and he didn't know where Jack was.

Jack had been unhappy with his subcontract. He'd told Miguel that the prime contractor was working for government bureaucrats that were, as Jack had put it, too institutionally dim-witted to recognize a threat to the United States when they saw one. Jack had lined up a new contract—one with United States Naval Intelligence where he would be the prime contractor. Miguel hoped there would be a job in it for him, too. He'd already worked with Jack on four different projects and through three of Jack's different disguises. Miguel felt he was getting too old for Central Africa, but he liked working with Jack.

When he'd first started hiring out to mercenary armies, Miguel felt that the causes he was being paid to fight for were just. He outgrew that. Thin lines separate civil wars from pure banditry. He'd crossed them. His buddies had crossed them. Old governments had crossed them. New governments crossed them with impunity. If he reached a point where he killed for the enjoyment of it, he'd quit. There were few just causes to fight for. He'd just fly the chopper—maybe shoot a few people if he had to. He thought about those Traction people and laughed inwardly. *When they're defeated and utterly destroyed, that'll create opportunities for new people, probably more sinister. That's not Jack's intention, but that's all Jack's doing.*

The clock read 8:30. Jack would never be that late. He wasn't free. This project may have become too reckless, but he had nothing better to do. He'd wait until noon.

* * *

Linda looked down upon the waters of the Caribbean Sea more than 20,000 feet below. It was near noon. From the position of the sun, she couldn't be certain whether they were flying southeast or southwest. She stared at Boris who was sitting across the aisle from her.

Boris grinned and said, "Boris must make decision, kind lady. Shall Boris tell pilot to turn toward Aruba where Boris and Linda will consummate marriage tonight. Linda would become one of wealthiest women in world, or shall Boris have him continue toward Honduras where Linda will witness tragedy and possibly lose her life? Boris prefers life and marriage."

Linda's face went blank. For a moment, her self-confidence hiccupped. She caught hold of herself and asked, "Are you thinking out loud or is that my choice to make?"

Boris's facial expression turned hard. "You should not have come with Boris, kind lady. That was reckless. You should know better. Boris can do with you as Boris wishes."

Linda, sounding much more self-assured than she was, said, "But you are a prince; a descendent of Tsars."

Boris shook his head from side to side. "Tsars were bad people, kind lady. In Russia, power is always abused. When Boris was young man in Soviet government, Boris's superiors ordered him to collect bribes and to extort. Sometimes, when government boss ordered Boris to collect from difficult citizen, Boris had to use brute force. When Boris used brute force, if citizen was not too healthy, he or she died. But always Boris stole share of extortion money before it got to government boss. Government boss expected that. A Russian does not expect a Russian to be honest. That is how everything works in Russia. Boris stole and saved big money. When Soviet state fell, Boris bought state assets for song and sold for huge profit. Boris became oligarch. Boris used profit to get the hell out of Russia and start banks in Cyprus and Aruba. Many foolish oligarchs stayed in Russia and were imprisoned or murdered. Boris has stayed alive. If you walk into mouth of female devil in Honduras, you will be gang-raped and murdered while ex-wife watches with pleasure. Boris knows how to take care of nice lady. You must come to Aruba where Boris can protect you."

Linda forced a smile. "Am I your prisoner?"

"Unfortunately, kind and most beautiful lady, Boris could make anyone a prisoner except you. Boris uses word *unfortunately* because Boris fears that kind lady will make wrong decision. Boris and Linda should begin making beautiful children rather than flying into nest of female rat."

Linda turned her head away from him and toward the window. "I know the routine. Make love, not war. I didn't ask for this war. It was handed to me. I can't let my future husband and his friends fight it with their hands tied behind their backs. I need to find Miguel Gonzales. Maybe he will have some idea. Please turn toward Tegucigalpa now."

Boris sighed. "Boris was bluffing. Pilot is already beginning descent into Tegucigalpa. Boris hoped you change your mind. You are good woman. Maybe best woman ever."

The intercom buzzed. Boris picked it up, listened, and then turned toward Linda. "Co-pilot has made contact with Miguel Gonzales. He waits in coffee shop."

* * *

352

The clock read almost noon. Miguel was getting hungry again. He picked up the luncheon menu. In the mirror behind the lunch counter he saw the outside door open. The kid who had fueled the chopper walked in and handed Miguel the charge sheet. Behind him a well-dressed woman also entered. He recognized her. Jack had introduced them two days ago. It was Linda DiStefano. He didn't like it at all. He signed for the gasoline, put his cigar down, and rose to greet her. She wasn't supposed to be here. Surprises were seldom good in his business. She wasn't part of the plan. He thought, *no one must suspect that I'm doing anything but soliciting tourists who want to fly to the offshore islands.* Speaking rather loudly to Linda, he said, "When do you wish to leave for the islands, Señora?"

"Señorita," she responded, instantly picking up on the subterfuge. "I can leave as soon as it's convenient for you. I assume that you accept credit cards."

"*Sí, Señorita.*"

Boris walked in the door, paused, saw them and walked over to them. Miguel asked, "Is your man friend travelling with you, Señorita?"

"We aren't together. We just happened to be on the same tour. He doesn't like to fly, so he'll be staying behind."

"But my dear lady," Boris said, "You should not go alone in a strange land. Your travelling companion shall not desert you now. The islands have a reputation for being quite beautiful but they can be dangerous for a woman travelling by herself."

"But you get airsick. That bothers me. I've hired this man and I shall go alone. You can hire another, if you wish."

Miguel didn't like the looks of Boris. He instantly mistrusted him. His eyes met Boris's and he said, "The *Señorita* wishes to travel alone, Señor. She has hired me as her guide. I, Miguel Gonzales, will protect her. If you wish to go to the islands, please find another pilot."

"Then Boris shall indeed do that, Señor."

48

The morning had been blistering hot since before the sun rose. For nearly two hours Murdock, Brother Martin, Susan and Grace had travelled in a rickety van without air-conditioning down a bone-jarring dusty road. They were dressed as tourists. Brother Martin was wearing a colorful shirt and Bermuda shorts; Murdock a camouflage shirt and shorts; the women flowered tops, khaki slacks, and large brimmed hats. Their clothing was soaked with perspiration. Each carried a backpack containing food for three meals plus drinking water, salt, global positioning devices, satellite phones, back-up batteries, long sleeve shirts, insect repellant, field glasses, ammunition, and a sidearm. Happily they had arrived at the point where they would meet the Indian guides. They exited the van, happy to be free of the jostling from poor suspension and rough roads. Murdock asked the driver to wait, to make sure the boats would show up. He refused. Immediately wheeling the van around, and without even an *hasta la vista,* he pointed the vehicle toward Puerto Lempira, leaving them coughing in a cloud of dust.

A fugitive sun was hiding above a low overcast. If the overcast returned tomorrow morning, it would be difficult for the choppers to be of any help. The alternate plan was to put everything on hold until the sky cleared. That option would become more tenuous as the winds of Apophis moved closer.

Their wait wasn't long. Two flat-bottom motor boats parted the tall grasses and beached where they were waiting. Brother Martin knew one of the boatmen. He introduced him as Jorge. The second introduced himself as Juan. For several minutes, Brother Martin spoke amiably to them in

354

a local dialect. Satisfied that everything was going according to plan, Brother Martin turned to Murdock and said, "Jorge speaks English well. Juan does not. They are comfortable with our plan. As you can see, they are armed and will fight bandits, if necessary. When we reach the mountains, Juan will remain with the boats. Jorge will lead us to a prominence which overlooks the compound. He will not follow us into what they call the valley of the Evil Green Spirit. I recommend that we proceed now. Each boat can handle two people plus their gear and the operator."

Murdock assigned Brother Martin and Susan to one; he and Grace would ride in the other. In minutes, they were proceeding westward through the savannah—nothing visible other than tall grass and the sky.

As Murdock watched the grass passing on either side, he thought about his fellow adventurers. *I'm always amazed that there is a rare breed of people like these—people willing to give up all their tomorrows, if necessary, to play their small part in protecting a world from what they see as evil.* He recalled his English lit class in college when he'd read Shakespeare's *Henry V,* particularly the lines where the king addresses his army before the Battle of Agincourt. The English were outnumbered by a French army four times their size. King Henry says, "We few, we happy few, we band of brothers; for he today that sheds his blood with me shall be my brother." *And that's what we are—a band of brothers and sisters that sees Traction for what it is—a cult of death and drugs that devastate people's brains. They employed an innocent young actress yearning for a job and with impunity murdered her. They took Susan captive and spared her life only because one of them raped and impregnated her.*

Murdock hoped that any Indians they might encounter would be friendly. His recollection of Linda and Jack's experience wasn't encouraging. He was well aware that this was the lawless area the colonel had described. Colonel Millán had told him that the hills into which the four were headed had dozens of airstrips and chopper pads, many used by Traction and other smugglers. Even if the police were willing to go in, the Honduran government often couldn't afford to buy enough fuel for choppers. American aid money for that purpose often evaporated mysteriously. Colonel Millán was one of the good guys. Murdock hoped the colonel would be able to follow through on his promise to bring Rudi and some troops tomorrow morning.

Murdock was amazed at how willingly people chose to follow him. In the Boy Scouts, he had been chosen a patrol leader. In high school, he had been elected a class officer. The college basketball team had chosen him captain. His law school frat, Sigma Nu Phi, had elected him president of the local chapter. In the FBI, his agent-in-charge had assigned him numerous complex investigations. Veritus had moved him up to station chief in two short years. Now, today, he has three Veritus people who chose to risk their lives by following his orders, plus the owner of Veritus. It was humbling. Murdock was not a praying man, but today he prayed that they had chosen wisely, and he asked God for guidance and strength of purpose.

He was thankful that Linda was safe—330 miles away on Grand Cayman Island.

Jorge indicated that they'd be at the beginning of the high country trail in another hour. Yesterday Jack had received intelligence that reported that one of the outbuildings was used as a prison. Security guards with dogs patrolled it. Jack had believed that the guards were even less committed than the Moroccans who had been afraid to show their heads when the shooting started. But, Jack warned, the guards had a reputation for being deadly dangerous when they thought they had the upper hand. Murdock resolved to make certain that that didn't happen.

Grace was sitting next to him. She knew her life was on the line again. Only eleven days ago she'd gone into Morocco with this man. She had volunteered to go on that one, and she had volunteered to go on this one. She recognized the nature of the same evil that she'd fought against during her years with the Michigan State Police. Evil had no religious connotation. It consisted of any act that she felt demeaned the human spirit. *Besides,* she thought, *I'd be bored in a quiet neighborhood, waiting for my husband to come home, or driving myself to work each day to toil within the cells of a little office. I'd suffocate in a tiny world. I need to be alive in an extravagant larger-than-life world. I need to be one of a thousand women doing a thousand daring things; exploring a thousand possibilities and imagining more; chancing a thousand dangers; meeting one brave man. Reality isn't enough. I need to transcend myself and laugh in the face of God.*

Had she become a crusader? *Nothing that noble,* she thought, glancing at Murdock. She'd found that one brave man. *He's the real reason I'm here. I've fallen in love with this man who faces peril with dignity because he has a deep sense of honor and duty. These are rare traits judging by the bums I've known. I wonder if he ever thinks about such things. I doubt it. It's inborn. Does he have any idea of his extraordinariness? Does he have any clue as to how desperately I wanted to climb in bed with him last night? Does he have a clue that I love him? That I've never loved any man before him? Is there even a chance that he could realize that I'd make him a better wife than that cold queen of business? If it weren't for Linda, I'm sure he'd notice me as a woman. But Linda is safe, probably sitting in* her office on Grand Cayman Island—managing the world. If Linda were here facing the same perils as we, then God, if he exists and had a mind to, or plain dumb luck if he doesn't, could sort us out. But even if it weren't Linda, would it be Susan? She thought not. But she wasn't sure why.

Grace felt comfortable with the new experience of being in love. It defined her to herself. She decided that she wasn't bisexual. Last night she'd slept with him in the same bedroom; he on the couch; she in the bed. If tomorrow isn't the end of time, she desperately wanted to sleep with him again, but she wanted it to be different. In the mean time, she would do whatever she could to help him live to see more tomorrows.

Grace glanced over to the boat beside them. Susan smiled. She thrived on high adventure, although it was usually in bed. Last night in the hotel she had been in a bedroom with the older man sitting next to her, Brother Martin. He had wanted to make love, but even though she'd insisted it would please her, the poor man couldn't bring himself to bed another man's wife. She'd met very few men with that issue before. Most had solved it differently.

Susan picked up her backpack and placed it on her lap. Reaching inside she checked again to make certain there was a full clip in the pistol. She thoroughly enjoyed daring-do. Researching with a computer keyboard was a challenge. She enjoyed that. But moving through the tall grass of a Honduran savannah and facing danger with people she respected and trusted, was a hell-of-a-lot more fun. She knew firsthand how evil the Traction people were. Happy would be her day if they were destroyed. *Someone in the government intelligence—some boss of Jack's, must know we're here. We must be their pawns,* she thought. *If we screw up, the Honduran government can't criticize the United States. No one in Washington will be red-faced. After all, Veritus is an international organization. Its headquarters just happen to be in the United States.* Susan smiled inwardly. *Polite fictions rule the world.*

She frowned. When She had volunteered for this escapade, she hadn't stopped to think about her baby. She simply wasn't accustomed to being pregnant. Nor had she decided whether she wanted to be. As she stared at the mountains now visible in the distance, it came home to her that she was risking two lives. *Did I have a right to do that? Stupid question,* she thought. *I can't get out of the boat and walk back.* But she did make a decision. If she and the baby survived tomorrow, she would do nothing to harm the child.

Brother Martin saw fear in the eyes of both Indian guides. He knew why. The sense of impending evil was almost palpable. He'd felt it in Vietnam. There, relentless fear and suspicion ruled. Even civilians and children had to be treated as probable enemy combatants. They often were. But he'd found a good side. Somewhere in that holocaust of death and destruction he had seen the face of God. And in God's eyes Martin had read an enormous sadness. He had interpreted it as God mourning the modern world where science and secularism were scarring people's souls and blinding their eyes to the eternal. He had resolved that, when the war ended and he returned to civilian life, he would study for the ministry and become a missionary.

As the heat of the day became more intense, Brother Martin's thoughts turned to Brother Antonio. He had never gone missing before. Three years ago, when Brother Antonio first came to Saint Luke's, he had insisted on becoming Brother Stephen's collaborator. He wondered whether Brother Antonio had had an ulterior motive. Antonio and his associates in Spain had built the prototype of the hardware that made Brother Stephen's chip useable. Martin still didn't know precisely what its use was. He understood that it was highly advanced leading-edge technology; however he had a theologian's mind. He could parse words but not electrons. Brother Antonio had never been able to explain it to him so that he could understand it. Now Martin hoped that Brother Antonio hadn't had a part in Brother Stephen's murder.

When Martin discovered Antonio was missing, he had contacted his family in Seville. They are a noble family descended from Spanish royalty, although they had dropped all titles. Antonio is a not-too-distant relative of the present king of Spain. The family owns several profitable businesses. Antonio could afford to go anywhere and do almost anything. He had a gentle, exacting mind. He travelled frequently; often to destinations that Brother Martin thought curious. But this time, not even the family knew where he was. He'd always kept his abbot informed. *Perhaps he has been kidnapped. I should have seen it coming,* he thought, scolding himself. *Traction has put pressure on Professor Amy Gallagher to get information on Brother Stephen's chip and schematics. It's ludicrous that they didn't go after Brother Antonio instead. He would have been a better pick. Why didn't they?*

As soon as he completed that thought, a reason came to mind. He frowned, looked over at Murdock and Grace in the other boat, shook his head, and then rejected it.

* * *

When they ran out of flooded savannah, they exited the boats and put on their backpacks. Jorge explained that the trail over the mountain and into the canyon would be treacherous. The approach from the west would have been much easier in terms of terrain but there was little cover. The folks at the ranch would not expect anyone other than an Indian to enter from the east.

Brother Martin suggested that he say a prayer. Following his lead, they all bowed their heads except Grace who was amazed at the spectacle. He prayed, "Lord, we have not been your most faithful servants. More often than not we've ignored you, often pretending that you're merely an outdated idea of no consequence. But you never ignored us. Forgive our arrogance. We're about to walk into the valley of the shadow of death. We do fear the evil because our faith is weak. If our cause is just, be our strong right arm. If we stumble and fall, lift us up. If you are with us, even death loses its sting. Hear our prayer for Jesus' sake, but your will, not ours, be done." When the prayer was finished, he glanced at Grace.

She smiled and said, "Nice thoughts, Marty. If your boss is really up there, I hope he listened."

* * *

By 3:00 p.m., they had been climbing for more than an hour. They came upon what appeared to be a pass. It was a rugged outcropping of rocks, some of them loose, and some of them sharp and unfriendly. Cautiously they ascended up the unstable mess. Loose rocks rolled down, endangering those climbers below. Murdock made a mental note. If they'd have to escape by foot, hurrying down this slope could cause a disastrous rock slide. Hopefully Jack's choppers would be on schedule and escape by foot wouldn't be necessary. However, Murdock had great respect for Murphy's Law.

As they crossed the crest they faced a deep ravine—the beginning of a rather narrow but deep canyon. The map showed that, in a mile, it widened and descended into a meadow. That's where Brother Martin calculated that Traction's ranch was located. At this point the slope was too steep for climbing down. Anyway, Murdock didn't want to. He wanted to get atop the ridge above the ranch and familiarize himself with both the topography and the layout of the buildings. They needed to get there before sunset. On their right lay a narrow ledge along a sheer ridge—the ledge measured thirteen inches in width, more or less. On their left was a sheer drop. The right was their only option. As they peered down into the chasm, Murdock said, "It looks like a drop of least seventy-five feet."

Susan agreed and added, "Along the trail on the right the wall looks like sturdy weeds growing out of the cracks. Hopefully they have deep roots. That's all we have to hang onto."

Grace added, pointing upward, "Those look like rain clouds. If we'd have to retreat this way on foot, I hope the trail along the ledge won't be wet. It'd be too dangerous. I'd sure like to know where the leading bands of the hurricane will be tomorrow morning."

Brother Martin agreed. "Hopefully surprise will totally confuse them, our plan will work, and the choppers will bail us all out."

Jorge assured them, "The ledge is all rock. None of it is loose. It was cut out by my tribe over a century ago. No one knows why."

Murdock said, "Thank you, Jorge. It's good to know that it's firm. I think we have close to a hundred treacherous feet to manage." Steeling his nerve, Murdock volunteered, "I'll go first."

He began inching along the ledge followed by Grace, Susan, Jorge, and Brother Martin. No one looked down. To the relief of everyone, the passage was uneventful. Past the ledge, the trail divided. Jorge indicated that the branch to the left would take them to a promontory from which they could look down upon the target ranch over a hundred feet below. The trail was poor. Thickets of underbrush nearly obliterated it in places. Some vines had sharp spikes which would tear at their clothing and skin. Jorge, who wielded a sharp machete, hacked at the thick underbrush and widened the trail.

Presently they came upon the promised vantage point. Lying on their bellies, they inched through the brush, poked their heads over the side, and peered down upon their goal. Each made a mental map. After a few minutes, when they'd backed away from the edge and re-grouped, Murdock said, "The ranch house is about three times larger than I imagined. It looks like the interior might be complicated. I counted four outbuildings as the satellite photos indicated. Judging from the men sitting around it, the one next to the ranch house looks like a barracks for the security guards. One is coming out of the next one with a weapon. It may be their armory."

They all agreed.

Jorge said, "The third from the big house is where the twin woman is kept."

They all stared at him. "What twin woman?" Grace asked.

"The one with the evil magic. The twin of the woman in the big house."

Murdock asked, "Have you seen the one with the evil magic?"

"Oh, yes, Señor. My son brought me up here a month ago. He is very brave. Everyone is afraid of her—the one who turns green in the night. If she has so much evil power, why does she live in the little house while her sister lives in the big one?"

Susan asked, "Why do you say they are twins?"

"Because they look very much alike, Señora, but my son tells me that the one who lives in the big house does not turn green. It is very curious. I am not superstitious. My son is afraid not to be. No one goes down there. If you go, I will not go with you. It isn't because I'm superstitious. It's because I am wise. I don't know what you will do down there, but I know you all have guns. Down there they have bigger guns. I don't like guns. I especially don't like guns when they're fired at me."

Murdock agreed that was a good idea for him to wait here.

Jorge said, "The trail which leads down is 500 feet west of here. It is almost grown over so those people down there won't see you descending if you avoid shaking the tall plants."

Murdock said, "It's going to be a little tough to avoid that. Jack was correct. It looks like an innocent ranch. The chopper pad looks to be about 200 feet from the house. I saw two armed security guards in a Humvee near that dirt road that approaches from the west."

Grace added, "I saw a security person go into the outbuilding next to the barracks and exchange one rifle for another. I agree that that's their armory. If we can get into it, we might be able to confuse and distract them with a really spectacular fireworks display. Of course it might blow up the whole operation, including us."

"Right," Murdock said. "But we'd better be conscious of the fact that they, too, could blow it up if it was to their advantage. It would wipe out any chopper on the pad."

Brother Martin injected, "Just to the left of the ranch house and partially hidden in shrubs is a ground-to-air missile launcher. It's capable of taking down a chopper. If I can get my hands on it, I can neutralize it, but there could be more in the armory."

The fact that Susan had complained of car-sickness on the bus that morning, and had been sick yesterday morning too, had not been lost on Murdock. *During her prolonged captivity in Morocco, they certainly didn't furnish her with birth control pills*, he thought. He said, "We need to switch partners. The Traction people know me. If any of them were at their Moroccan operation, they might recognize Susan. We can't tell if Proteus is in the ranch house. It'll be safer if Brother Martin and Grace go down the trail and approach the ranch as we planned. Hopefully they will take you in, either so the ranch doesn't blow its cover, or out of curiosity. Before morning, locate the Green Lady; convince her that I'm coming for her in the morning. Urge her that she must escape with me. If she's really one of them, and not a prisoner as Jack thinks, you'll become prisoners. Either way, prepare yourselves for the surprise attack in the morning. We'll get you two out with or without her. Hopefully Rudi and the Honduran police will recover his escaped convict, too.

Grace inched up to the edge again, and after several seconds, motioned for the others to join her. They put their field glasses on the veranda of the ranch house. Jack was seated, apparently speaking comfortably to a man. When they re-gathered away from the edge, Murdock said, "That's the man I met on the ship off the Oregon coast last year—the man who called himself Mr. Verbius."

Grace added, "In the Dianic legends, Verbius was a minor Roman god. He's said to be the first priest of the Diana cult. Some traditions say that he was the god of portals and doorways." She turned to Murdock and asked, "Do you think Jack is one of them?"

Murdock shook his head in frustration. "That's a good question. Has he duped us and sucked us into a trap?"

He wondered if Linda's kidnapping had been a ruse so that Jack could rescue her and then sucker them into this trap. He read the eyes of the others. They were as confused as he.

Brother Martin spoke first. "It's possible that they caught him near their property but they don't know who he is. It doesn't make sense that he'd set us up."

Grace added, "We're small fry. I agree."

Susan said, "If the Green Lady is in control and Paul West is correct about her being in love with Murdock, the trap idea might make some sense."

Jorge added, "My son thinks she is in control, Señora. I do not think she is in control. I think she is being controlled, but I do not understand how. My people say she comes from the stars. My people also say she has magic." He glanced at Brother Martin and assured him, "Pastor Martin, I usually do not believe in magic, but sometimes, like my son, I, too, am afraid not to."

Brother Martin smiled.

"It's decision time," Murdock said. "Do we believe in Jack?"

He looked around the circle. Jorge stepped out of it. Susan nodded affirmatively. Brother Martin joined her. Grace said, "The information that he gave us about Susan in Morocco was right on. I believe him."

Murdock said, "That means that we have to rescue him, too, before they find out who he is. He knows the plan. That's half the battle."

"Good," Susan said. "I don't see his transmitter attached to his belt. He can't send the attack signal to Miguel without it."

Murdock frowned and said, "You've got a point. However, if he knew he was about to be discovered, he would have dropped it, so they wouldn't ask questions."

Susan stressed, "The plan requires Miguel to get you two and the Green Lady out before the Hondurans come in shooting. If Miguel doesn't receive a signal, will he come in on his own? If so, when? Would he take the initiative to coordinate with the police? If not, how do we avoid the cops shooting us by mistake?"

Murdock urged, "Susan's right. We're between a rock and a hard place, but I can't see retreating. If we're right about Jack, he will find a way to help execute what's left of the plan. We can't tell whether Proteus is there. Grace, please replace Susan. You and Martin need to leave now. If nothing happens by way of choppers by ten o'clock tomorrow morning, Susan and I will create one hell of a fuss at the east gate. Hopefully Jack will take the cue and bust into the armory. If Miguel doesn't come and all hell breaks loose, Martin and Grace should forget the Green Lady and head for the armory. We'll need all the firepower we can get. If God's listened to Martin's prayer, we could sure use him for back-up. All who agree that we should commit, raise your right hand."

Except for Jorge, all hands were raised.

Leaving their weapons with Murdock, Brother Martin and Grace started down the trail toward the Traction compound. Grace frowned. She was with the wrong man.

49

Traction Compound in Honduras
Sunday, July 16, 2:38 a.m.

Grace glanced at her watch. Nervous energy had kept her mind racing all night. From time to time she'd fallen into a fitful sleep, but now she was wide awake.

Yesterday evening she and Brother Martin had walked up to the main gate of the Traction compound. They had told the guard that they'd gotten separated from their spouses and that their Indian guide had deserted them. They needed sanctuary for the night. The guard contacted someone, whereupon they had been taken to the porch of the ranch house. A man who stood at least six-foot-four met them there. He introduced himself as Professor Claude V. Mitchell. He explained that he was a linguist who was studying Indian dialects. He had asked Martin whether they had met before, but Martin had said that he thought not. Mitchell had then escorted them to the cabin in which they would sleep. It had four small bedrooms and a dining area. One of the bedrooms was occupied by Jack.

Mitchell had introduced Jack as a fellow wanderer who would leave with them in the morning. A light meal had been provided. During the evening, they had been free to move about, but they were not to disturb the woman in the next building—the cabin between them and the armory. They were also prohibited from going outside their cabin from sunset to sunrise. Security guards might shoot them, mistaking them for bandits.

The evening had passed calmly. Jack had become friendly with Mitchell. After a light meal was delivered to their cabin, he had joined Mitchell on the porch of the ranch house. Grace and Martin thought it best not to get too close to either Jack or Mitchell, so they had brought chairs outside their cabin and sat next to the door where Murdock and Susan could see them. They were in the mouth of the lioness but at least they would sleep more comfortably than Murdock and Susan who would be on the ground with who knows how many visitors of the insect and animal variety. Before dark, they had moved inside. When Jack, accompanied by a guard, returned shortly before midnight, they had all decided to get some sleep. The three were the only ones billeted in the cabin.

It would be morning in a couple hours. Grace awoke the other two. They congregated in the dining area.

Jack said, "The plan is dead. Mitchell has been very friendly, but the Patricia woman doesn't trust me. She ordered the security guards to seize my radio. I can't give the attack order to Miguel. He won't move without it. The police won't move until he does. Obviously, Murdock and Susan have figured that out. What does Murdock plan to do?"

Grace explained, "If the choppers don't come, Murdock and Susan will make a fuss in the underbrush outside the split rail fence on the east at 10:00 a.m. That'll be our signal to raid the armory, get bigger firepower, and shoot our way out of here, with or without the Green Lady."

Brother Martin said, "I'd like to propose an alternate plan. That chopper on the pad is a military type that I flew in Vietnam. At daybreak, we grab the Green Lady, quietly make our way to it, and take off before our enemy figures out what's happening. It would mean flying on cold engines, which isn't recommended, but if I warm it up first we'd probably have people shooting at us before we got off the ground. If we can pull it off, it'll avoid putting Murdock and Susan in danger."

Jack asked, "Has it been refueled?"

"No, and I don't see any facility for doing that. I assume that it came in with enough fuel to return to where it came from."

Grace reached out in the darkness to feel where Jack was. He was next to her. She whispered, "I agree with Marty. The chopper is our best shot."

Jack said, "I agree. That's Plan Two unless that hurricane gets here by morning."

"If it does," Grace said, "it should create enough confusion that we'll be able to make it on the run over the split rail and join Murdock and Susan on the trail."

"Good," Brother Martin said. "That's Plan Three. The fact that the chopper's still here suggests that the hurricane can't be too close. They would've flown it out. The winds would destroy it sitting where it is."

Conspiring in whispers, Jack suggested that one of them must make contact with the Green Lady. "We need to know if my theory is correct.

Is she a prisoner who would like to escape? Can she be trusted with the knowledge of our plans?"

Grace offered, "That may be difficult for her to decide on such short notice."

Brother Martin said, "We're going to have to choose between the plans on short notice, too. We just have to chance it. I think you should go, Grace—woman to woman. You have good intuition. If you think it's safe, brief her on our plans. Stress that Murdock is part of the team and that he's waiting for her."

Jack said, "Meeting with the Green Lady—even trying to get into her cabin without being shot by security—is dangerous as hell. We should flip coins."

Grace insisted, "No. Even if we could see the coins, we shouldn't flip. It's better that I go. She'll feel less threatened if her nighttime intruder is a woman."

Jack warned, "There are two elevated platforms about fifty yards south used by security. All cabin doors face south. The guards can see almost every square foot. Search lights aren't turned on unless they hear something, or see something in the moonlight. The moon will rise in about an hour. If they see you, they may shoot. Are you sure that you want to do this, Grace?"

Grace, who had been sitting cross-legged, uncrossed her legs, arose and said, "This is a Veritus project to obtain exculpatory evidence that will free our client, José Enrique Perez-Krieger. I'm the only Veritus employee here, so I guess it's my call. I'll see you guys later."

Jack urged, "Slither on your belly."

She thanked him for the advice, passed through the open door, and casually walked the thirty-some feet to the next building. No floodlight came on. She tried the door handle. It wasn't locked. She quietly opened it and slipped in. Looking down a narrow hallway, she saw what she assumed to be a dim greenish nightlight. Pressing her back against the wall, she inched her way cautiously toward it. She sensed that there was no security guard. She hoped she was right. It was then that she realized she hadn't put her shoes on. *That's a blessing. My bare feet don't make any noise.* She came to a doorway; the door was partly open. She stopped. The greenish light was coming from that room. Ever so slowly, she inched into a position where she could peek into the room. A woman, who appeared to be about her age, was sleeping on a cot. Grace was unprepared for what she saw. There was no night light. A green luminescence was irradiating from the sleeping woman. Its soft glow filled the room. Grace was shocked. She hesitated. From the stories she had heard about the Green Lady, she had assumed fakery. This wasn't fakery. She was witnessing something extraordinary.

Unsure of herself, she guardedly walked over to the green woman. Grace placed her hand gently over the woman's mouth. The woman awoke, startled. Her eyes opened wide and locked onto Grace's—so much so that Grace felt ill at ease. The woman neither struggled nor attempted to push her hand aside. Collecting her wits, Grace whispered calmly, "My name is Grace Bauer. I work for Murdock McCabe, whom you've met. He and I are both employed by Veritus Investigations International. We're investigating an incident about which you may have some knowledge. A woman was murdered. We think that the people in the ranch house did it and framed our client. Do you understand me?"

The green woman nodded once in the affirmative.

"Good. In the next cabin are two men who are also friends of Murdock McCabe. One is a monk called Brother Martin; the other Jack Hastings. Murdock is not far from here. Don't be afraid. We've come to rescue you. I'm going to release my hand from your mouth. When I do, hopefully you won't make any noise. If you do, I could be shot. If you will not make any noise, please blink your eyes."

She blinked.

Grace removed her hand and said, "Do you wish to talk to me—girl to girl?"

A very soft and unassuming voice replied, "Yes. I think I do."

"Okay," Grace said. "I sure hope you're on our side or I'm a dead woman."

The woman questioned, "Why are you rescuing me? Am I a prisoner?"

Grace was unsure of how to respond. Jack believed she was a prisoner. Speaking in a confident tone, Grace said, "Murdock believes you are."

The woman smiled brightly and gently protested, "But I have lived quite comfortably in this delightful cabin. Since my existence was re-created here, Mr. Verbius has taught me your language. I speak quite well, do I not?"

"You do, indeed. I don't believe that you had a part in the crimes that the people in the ranch house committed. Unfortunately, your innocence has been misused for evil purposes. They've used you to create nasty illusions and frighten people. We believe they're about to take you away from this cottage. Why or where, we don't know. I do hope you'll come with us instead. If you do, an innocent man will not have to spend the rest of his life in prison. Murdock and I will take you to a safe-house where you'll meet caring people. Two of them are astrophysicists. One is a psychologist. They're all looking forward to meeting you."

Grace hesitated to tell her how tentative their plans had become. Even if Murdock and Susan caused an effective distraction, it wasn't a safe bet that they could escape with this woman on foot, especially if they were being chased over the treacherous trail ledge. If the cops showed up while they were still there and started shooting, how would they know the good guys from the bad guys?

The woman asked, "Must I leave before I talk to the quiet one? He and Mr. Proteus will arrive shortly after daybreak."

Grace drew a blank. She asked, "Who is the quiet one?"

"He is the one who made it possible for me to come to the earth."

"May I know his name?"

"I have heard Mr. Proteus call him the Spaniard gook. I do not understand 'gook.' Mr. Verbius laughed when I asked him. The quiet one calls himself Antonio."

If it's Brother Antonio, he would recognize her. She knew the name Proteus from Susan, but she hadn't met him. The green woman renewed her bright smile and said, "I think you are a friend, Grace. Why is Murdock not here?"

"The people in the ranch house know him. They feel threatened by him. They'd kill him."

The green woman frowned. Nervously she asked, "How will you take me to him?"

Conscious that time was running out, Grace, as patiently as possible, explained the three plans and their contingencies. When she finished, the green woman was silent. Grace waited for her response. Blandly the green woman asked, "Will you stay with me tonight?"

Grace took a deep breath of relief. Their gamble appeared to be paying off. "No. That wouldn't be wise. If the people in the ranch house find me here, they'll know that we're not just hikers lost in the mountains and our lives will be endangered. I need you to trust me. Can you do that?"

A puzzled look crossed the green woman's face. She asked, "Do you like Murdock?"

"Yes. He's a fine boss."

The green woman reached out and gripped Grace's hand. "Antonio told me about women and men. Do you like him as women like men?"

Grace returned the grip. "I find him quite appealing."

The green woman tightened her grip. "Have you seen him naked?"

Grace smiled kindly. "No. Nor has he seen me naked."

"Is Murdock in love with you?"

Grace was thankful that she'd put the question that way rather than the reverse. She squeezed the green woman's hand and said, "I'm confident that he isn't."

"Is he in love with anyone?"

Grace felt trapped and perplexed. If the green woman knew about Linda—if she became the woman scorned—she might turn on them. But Grace feared that if she lied, the woman might see through a false answer and lose confidence in her entire story. Grace gambled. She leaned over close to the woman's ear and whispered as if in confidence, "He's never told *me* if he is."

"Good. What shall we do?"

"When the time is right, I or one of the men will come for you. A chopper will enter the compound and land. We will run for the chopper. If all goes well, Murdock will be in it. If that chopper doesn't come, we will run for the chopper that's on the pad now. The monk will fly us out of here to meet Murdock. Please wait here, if you can. If you can't, please try to find us when unusual things start happening. Until either event, please be patient. I must go now. The moon will rise soon. I don't want the guards to see me. I hope you and I can talk more when you're free. I want to get to know you better. We'll be friends. Would you like that?"

The woman said, "Yes, I think so. Thank you, Grace, for informing me that I am not free. Please thank your men, too. I fear that it may be too dangerous for me ever to be truly free. Will I be able to speak with people who have scientific minds?"

"Yes. Does no one here have a scientific mind?"

"The Spaniard does, and Mr. Verbius to a certain extent. I don't know how educated Patricia is. She's an enigma. I learned that word from a book yesterday. An enigma is like a mystery, and there is so much that I don't understand about Patricia. She looks like me. Mr. Verbius says we are twin sisters but I don't see how that's possible. It is confusing, is it not?"

Grace smiled broadly. "That's for sure."

"There's knowledge I must share. You see, my existence has travelled a long distance from a place that's very close."

Grace remembered the moon. She released her grip. "Moonlight may appear any minute. The guards will be able to see me. I must leave. I'll see you after sunrise. Good night."

"When Antonio leaves me, he always says, 'God be with you' so I say it to you. God be with you, Grace."

Grace cocked her head and asked, "What god?"

"Don't be silly, Grace. I'm not sure what the word means. Good night."

369

Grace retreated through the door, and then froze. A dull orange sliver of a moon was hanging just above the eastern horizon. A security guard with an automatic weapon was no more than twenty feet from her; his back toward her. Sidestepping, she inched her way toward the building where Martin and Jack awaited. Halfway in between, the guard started to turn toward her. She nearly wet her pants. Inspired, she dropped them to her ankles and squatted. The guard, startled, pointed the weapon at her head and a flashlight at her exposed female part and in broken English demanded in a gruff whisper, "What you doing there, Señora?"

Grace grinned sheepishly. "I had to pee. There's only one toilet and a man is on it. I couldn't wait. I didn't want to pee on the floor."

Fortunately, a trickle of urine glistened in the light. He had not anticipated such delightful entertainment. He came closer. He was a slightly overweight homely man dressed in a uniform that desperately needed a seamstress and a launderer. She finished and arose, leaving her panties and slacks around her ankles. The hand holding his flashlight shook. He had the look of a curious ten-year-old boy who'd not seen a naked woman before. At least while he was staring, he wasn't shooting.

"Don't move," he ordered as he clicked on the weapon's safety.

Smiling innocently, she said, "I'm finished. May I bend over to pull up my panties and slacks?"

He lowered his weapon, slid the tip under her slacks, and lifted both panties and slacks. She grabbed them. He removed the weapon. She brought an end to the show and then pulled up her slacks. He grinned, then clicked his flashlight off and slid it into a holster. Wrapping his arms her, he gave her a bear hug, and hard kissed her lips. Then in a whisper, he said, "Next time, Señora, if man on toilet, piss in sink. If partner saw you, he shoot you. Is no good for you out here in dark. If partner sees us now, I must shoot you. Go inside, Señora." As she turned to go, he grinned and added, "*y gracias á usted.*"

Zipping her slacks as she walked, she looked over her shoulder and answered, "*de nada.*"

Martin and Jack eagerly listened to her whispered report. In conclusion, she said, "I think she's confused by all the contingencies, but so are we. None of them may work and we'll have to wing it."

Both men agreed. Moonlight coming in through the window lit Brother Martin's face. In the eerie half darkness, he whispered, "God doesn't let too many things happen that can overpower us."

Grace said to Jack, "If Brother Antonio shows up, my cover and Marty's are blown." She wondered to herself if it were already blown. Whose side was Jack on? She turned toward Brother Martin and said,

"I hope to hell you're right, Marty, about what God doesn't do. If any good fortune is going to come of this, we'd better not count on God. Let's review our scripts again and make sure we've covered all contingencies."

Jack urged, "First we need to know more about this Spaniard. The Green Lady didn't mention that he was a monk. We can't make intelligent choices until we know whether he's that Brother Antonio character that you two know. Could you go back to the Green Lady and get a description of him?"

Frustrated, she answered, "Sure, Jack. All I'm risking is rape and death in either order."

"I hear thunder," Brother Martin said. "It could be the outer bands of the hurricane, or it could be just a local instability storm."

Grace walked to the doorway, opened it, and studied the sky. Dark storm clouds had hidden the moon. Without further hesitation, she raced in a crouched position toward the Green Lady's cabin. She stopped, froze, and fell flat on her belly. A man was standing near the Green Lady's cabin door. Two men. The other was a few feet beyond it. An unfamiliar voice speaking good English lamented, "I'd sure like to get in the pants of that tourist woman. I'd make her forget her husband." The other, in a voice more familiar and speaking in broken English scoffed, "She's prime stuff. She not give you any." In a flash of lightning, Grace saw the other put his hand on his holstered pistol. The first said, "This sucker is my ticket, man. If she doesn't want to be nice, this'll convince her." The other voice replied, "Husband might show up tomorrow; he not like that. Besides, she Mizz Dale's guest." The first said, "Yeah. Well, I'd like to have a piece of Mizz Dale, too." The second replied, "That's not smart, man. It's like screwing a viper. That bitch is evil. Just thinking about her scares shit out of me."

The two walked off together in the opposite direction. Grace waited until they had gone a fair distance. Then she got up off the ground and walked cautiously into the Green Lady's cabin. The Green Lady was awake, standing by a window, marveling at the lightning in the fast approaching storm. She was smiling. Grace asked for the description of the Spaniard. The Green Lady said, "He is a handsome man—elegant, regal, about thirty-five, skin like copper, dark brown eyes, narrow nose, thin lips, dark black hair, and black chevron moustache, about five-foot-seven. He is a kind, considerate man. He listens with patience and understanding when I try to explain my existence. He is compassionate when I am sad. I would not like to leave without saying farewell to him. You would like him, Grace."

Yeah, Grace thought. *I did.* "Has he ever mentioned that he was a monk?"

"No. He didn't say he wasn't, either. He doesn't talk about himself. He is always interested in me. He sometimes wears something unusual like a long coat with no buttons in the front and a hood that he puts over his head when it rains."

Grace thanked her and retreated to the doorway. The storm was hard at it. Torrential rain pelted the ground creating muddy ponds. Clouds fired jagged bolts of lightning at each other, and aimed a few at the ground. The air was electric. Grace waited. The light display was awesome, but it wasn't light that she needed. Her odds of being shot were greater than the odds of being hit by lightning. Neither appealed to her. Grace was still the only Veritus employee inside the compound. She had decisions to make. She wondered when Brother Antonio would arrive and blow their cover. There were no lights on the chopper pad so he wouldn't arrive before sunrise. She needed to make *some* move early.

After twenty minutes, the sky became tamer. Lightning bolts were still visible in the far west, but they shed little light on that dangerous space between the two cabins. Storm clouds hid the moon. Poking her head out the door, she searched the darkness. She thanked the god she didn't believe in for little favors and started across the mottled ground. She hadn't gone five yards before she was struck from behind by a large man who knocked her over. She lay on her belly in muddy water, with the man on top of her. His large right hand covered her mouth; his left arm twisted hers into a painful hammer-lock. With the weight of his body, he pinned her to the ground. Briefly she struggled. He tightened the hammer-lock. His full weight pressed on top of her and immobilized her. Struggling was futile. She alternated between gasping for air and moaning in pain. A voice some distance away asked, "Did you find something?" The man on top replied, "Nothing here. How about you?" The answer came back, "No. Nothing."

Grace couldn't move. She could barely breathe. He shifted his weight slightly. She breathed easier. He eased up somewhat on the hammer-lock, lessening the pain. Several minutes passed. His hand was still hard upon her mouth. Presently he arose; his hand still pressed tight across her mouth. Suddenly he released the hammer-lock, grabbed her around the waist, dragged her the remaining distance into her cabin, rudely dropped her onto the floor, and disappeared into the night.

Martin and Jack were stunned. Jack asked, "Why the hell did he do that? Where's the damn *quid pro quo*?"

Grace, mud from head to toe but grateful to be alive, grinned and said, "The man is satisfied with simple pleasures. Just before he dropped me, he groped my right tit. Oh. Sorry Marty. Breast. But it's a tit to most guys."

Brother Martin smiled kindly. "I'm familiar with the term. When I was younger, I groped a few tits myself. What do we do now, folks?"

* * *

At the top of the mountain, Murdock and Susan were drenched. The clouds hammered each other with thunder and lightning. Neither slept. The sun wouldn't rise for two hours. Just before midnight, his satellite phone had beeped with a text message from Rudi. It read, "Ant and Prot dep 7 30 for ranch." Murdock had replied, "u dep 7 15. Tel Mig dep 7 40."

A reply came at 12:30 a.m. The message read, "Col ok. Mig not w o Jack ord."

He and Susan discussed the exchange of messages and explored alternative plans. Shortly after 3:00 a.m., Murdock noticed that Susan was bent over with the dry heaves. It jolted him. He needed her badly. She noticed him staring and said, "Sorry, Boss. I'm pregnant and this *is* morning. It'll pass. What's important is whether Jack can signal Miguel. Maybe his radio is in that cabin."

Murdock's eyes locked onto hers. "Christ, Susan. If I'd known you were pregnant, I wouldn't have permitted you to come. Remain here with Jorge. I'll take your weapon when I start down the trail. I can make as much noise as the two of us. Can I rely on you to do that?"

"Whatever you say, Boss."

"You don't sound sincere, Susan. You've always followed my instructions. I insist that you follow them now. I want your promise that you'll remain here."

Looking haggard, she replied, "Okay, Boss. You've got it."

They sat there quietly for several minutes, Jorge off by himself. Murdock took out a granola bar and munched on it. Susan glanced at it and turned a little green. Neither spoke for several minutes. Then Susan asked, "What's bothering you, Boss?"

Murdock shook his head in disgust. "It's ludicrous. Here we are—a preacher, a cloak-and-dagger agent, one pregnant Veritus agent, one non-pregnant female agent and me. The cloak-and-dagger agent has talked us into fighting his own little war to save the world. We shouldn't need to. The U.S. government along with the Hondurans should be doing this.

If they'd stopped these people a year ago when they should've, Enrique wouldn't be in deep do-do now and we wouldn't be here."

Susan reflected for a moment and then said, "Yeah, Jack has his own agenda but the governments *didn't* do it. We're here doing it for Enrique, Boss. I only hope Jack *is* working for the boys in Washington. If he is, they probably know we're here. I don't think Jack's told us everything. Those types never do. The Washington boys are busy covering their asses. If we succeed, Jack will be lionized in the agency. In public media the politicos will take the credit. If we fail and get killed, we never existed."

Murdock crawled over to Susan, planted a kiss on her forehead, picked up her weapon and his own, arose, and silently started down the trail.

50

Tegucigalpa Airport, Honduras
Sunday, July 16, 6:15 a.m.

Linda met Miguel at the chopper. The aircraft was parked less than a hundred feet from the door of the all-night coffee shop. Miguel looked disheveled. She wondered whether he'd spent the night there. He turned on the radio equipment and began monitoring the frequency that Jack had assigned. Linda insisted that they become airborne so that he could respond more quickly when he received the signal. Miguel declined. "Señorita," he said, "when Jack gives the signal, there will be plenty of time. It makes no sense to be burning fuel unnecessarily. I might urgently need it later. Besides, my mercenary soldier is not here yet. I need his firepower. You must be patient, Señorita. Please wait in the coffee shop or go over to your room in the airport hotel."

"I'm going with you."

"If Jack signals, you mustn't go with me. It will be too dangerous. You are a gentle woman. You are not cut out for this. Besides, I will need space to evacuate Jack, Murdock, Brother Martin, Grace, and the green woman. You would add needless weight in both directions. Weight burns fuel. Please listen to Miguel."

"I can help haul them aboard. I don't wish to stay behind."

"Señorita, a man has come out of the coffee shop and he is walking toward you. I believe it is the man called Boris that we talked to yesterday."

Linda turned to face him. *He keeps coming up like a bad penny,* she thought. His timing was inconvenient. She wanted to keep Miguel focused. Boris was frowning.

"Good morning, nice lady. Boris is surprised to see you here so early. You must wish to be in the islands for breakfast." Glancing into the chopper, he said to Miguel, "That is interesting radio equipment that you have. It appears too sophisticated for flights from the capital to the islands. It must have been very expensive. Boris is interested in radio. Tell me about it."

Linda said, "Maybe he can do that some other time. Why are you here?"

"Nice lady, Boris gave you wrong information yesterday. Boris's spy reports that Jack is not a prisoner. He saw Jack sitting on the porch at my ex-wife's ranch—you know—that one in the mountain canyon that you wish to explore today." He half turned to leave. "Join Boris for coffee, nice lady. Is not healthy where you go. Hurricane may overtake you. They may close airport here after noon. You could not return. Boris thinks is not smart to try to go there. What can Boris do to protect you? Tell Boris and Boris will do it."

"I'd like to join you for coffee, Mr. Romanovsky, but this man and I have business to discuss. Perhaps when I return."

"If you return." He turned and walked into the coffee shop.

Linda and Miguel stared at each other. Miguel said, "I don't trust this Boris. Was he telling the truth yesterday, or is he telling it now? Even if he received misinformation, was it misinformation yesterday or today?"

"We need to assume the worst and hope for the best. If Jack is one of them—well, I'd be extremely disappointed. My gut feelings are usually accurate. I'm going to bet the farm that the Traction folks don't know who he is."

"I hope it's a small farm, Señorita."

She feared for Murdock, and for Susan, Grace, and Martin. *They must have seen Jack. How did they interpret his presence? The plan is in tatters. Everyone is winging it. I've got to convince this Spanish oaf to go in without Jack's orders.* She asked, "What *is* this radio equipment all about? Why was Boris so interested?"

Miguel cocked his head, grinned, and said, "Señorita DiStefano, This chopper is rented but the avionics—the radio stuff by which I navigate—that's GI. I don't know how Jack gets it, but it's highly accurate military equipment."

"What does GI mean?"

"Government issue. This piece of global positioning equipment will give me Jack's precise location within inches of his transmitter. I've monitored it for over an hour. It has not moved. It is highly unlikely that Jack would stay in one exact location that long."

"What does that suggest to you?"

"It suggests, Señorita DiStefano that Jack has abandoned his radio or someone has taken it from him."

"What if it stops transmitting?"

"It would make no difference. I have the coordinates."

"Does that mean you can fly directly to that location now?"

"Yes, Señorita. But my instructions from Jack are not to fly anywhere near that area without his specific instruction."

"If he's been taken prisoner, we need to move. Your friend could be in serious trouble. His life may be in danger right now."

"But Señorita, I don't *know* that he's been captured. I have worked for Jack many times. When he orders me to wait in position, he means it. He would be very disturbed if I move. The conflicting information that man Boris gave you is useless. I know Jack. He can take care of himself. My impression of that Boris is that he is *un embaucador;* in English I think you say a trickster. Do you dare trust him? Do I dare disobey Jack? If I do, more people may get hurt. Behind you, two more men are coming toward us. I think it is the two policemen."

Linda turned. Rudi Benzinger and Colonel Millán were walking toward them. Miguel stepped forward and offered his hand. Linda offered hers. They shook and after the pleasantries, Rudi said, "I'm surprised to see you here, Miss DiStefano."

"Yesterday I was informed that Jack had been taken prisoner, which blew the plan. I'm trying to inform Murdock."

Rudi responded, "I've exchanged text messages with him. He's aware that Brother Antonio and Proteus have a chopper on this field somewhere. They're scheduled to depart here at 7:30 a.m. I bet they're going to the Traction ranch. Murdock, Colonel Millán, and I agreed that we would leave here at sunrise to get there before they do."

It was obvious that that hadn't happened.

Colonel Millán injected, "However, Señorita DiStefano, as you Americans say, Murphy's Law intervened."

"I'm Canadian. What's Murphy done?"

"Our chopper's engines didn't check out. I have requested a replacement from the air force. The air force colonel promised to awaken a pilot and send one over as soon as possible. Once he gets here, I'll use my pilot. I trust him."

Linda glanced at Rudi. "Does Murdock know about this issue?"

"I sent him another text message a short time ago. Susan replied that Murdock had already headed down the trail. He's planning on Miguel picking him up as originally planned."

Colonel Millán's eyes met Miguel's. "Murdock wanted you to fly in after us but we could be very late. I think it's important that you show up before the chopper carrying this Brother Antonio and Mr. Proteus. Don't wait. It may be another hour before we get out of here. The air force is never swift. Now if you'll excuse us, we best get over to the location where the air force chopper will land. Maybe by some miracle we can still get aloft before 7:30."

As they walked away, Linda's eyes met Miguel's. "You heard the colonel. Let's get cracking."

Miguel frowned and shook his head from side to side. "He's not my colonel, Señorita. Jack's my boss. I must hold my position and await his order."

Linda glared at him. Thrusting her face within inches of his, she said firmly, "Miguel—read my lips. Jack is assisting Veritus so *you* are indirectly working for Veritus. Veritus is working for *me. I* will write the check that pays you. Jack and I are *very* close. Quite honestly, a man and a woman couldn't get closer than Jack and I have been. I know what Jack wants you to do. Normally I'm a reasonably well-behaved and dignified woman. When the world was young and political correctness had not yet infected it, I might have been called a *lady.* But my patience has run out. Pay close attention. I'm going to speak in the vernacular so you can't misunderstand. Get this fucking machine in the air NOW!"

51

Murdock paused, crouched low in the underbrush. Kneeling, he checked his pistol. The clip was full. He shoved the weapon into his belt. Grace and Brother Martin's side arms were in his backpack. He checked their clips, too. Taking a deep breath, he mulled the unanswered questions. Was Jack who he claimed to be? During the first tame light of dawn, do the security guards patrol the fence on foot? He'd searched as far as he could see. A first hint of the rising sun was low against the eastern horizon. No guards were visible. Is a guard posted outside the cabin where Grace and Martin are? He couldn't see from that angle. He would have to move laterally to his left. Could he blow up the armory without killing everyone? It was dangerous to speculate without first getting inside and assessing it. Is Miguel coming? He couldn't count on him. Can the Honduran police be relied upon? If so, their chopper should be in the air shortly with Rudi, Colonel Millán and some other police officers on board. They'd better arrive before the Traction chopper arrives with Mr. Proteus and Brother Antonio. Are the folks in the ranch house cautious? Hopefully they have a false sense of security. Will Grace and Martin be able to convince the Green Lady to follow us? God only knows. Will Susan obey orders and stay behind? When things start popping, he didn't need a pregnant woman in the mix. If we must retreat by land, would Jorge be there to assist? Brother Martin trusts Jorge. Would that narrow ledge be too rain-soaked and slippery to navigate? If Jack isn't straight, if he's misused Linda, how would she react? At least she's safe back on Grand Cayman Island and I don't have to tell her everything right away.

379

So much has gone wrong with our plan already, he thought. *It's become disorganized like the FBI raid that resulted in Karen's death. Our situation is impossible so it'll require persistence and skill.*

Remaining in a crouched position, he moved cautiously toward the fence at the unfinished eastern wall. If there is a guard patrolling, would he be inside or outside the perimeter? The answer came swiftly—movement in the underbrush to his left. Dropping silently to the ground on his belly, he froze. The movement froze, too. He barely breathed. Nothing. No sound. Had he imagined it? Still nothing. Minutes passed. Daylight was getting brighter and shadows shorter. How long could he afford to lay and wait? Was he mistaken? Is a guard playing cat and mouse? He felt a stone next to his right hand. Picking it up, he flung it backhanded about twenty feet. Nothing. Then a stone landed near his head. He rolled over onto his back. A heavy boot slammed against his chest. The cold steel barrel of an AK-47 pressed hard against his forehead. He heard the safety release. A husky ugly grinning man was standing over him. In a gruff voice the man said, "You're dead, *hombre.*"

Murdock closed his eyes. The barrel slid off his forehead. Immediately he reopened them. The man, bleeding profusely from his throat, caved into a dead heap next to him.

"I'm sorry, Boss," Susan said, wiping blood off her knife with a leaf. "I couldn't find Jorge, and I couldn't stay back there alone. I'm afraid of wild animals."

Murdock swallowed a laugh. Pulling her down on top of him, he took her head in both hands and firmly planted a kiss upon her forehead. She grinned, then took his head firmly in both hands, planted a kiss hard upon his lips, and rolled off him.

She said, "Besides, Boss, you need all the troops you can get."

Restraining another laugh at the irony of the understatement, he replied, "Right. While we still have some long shadows for cover, we'd better make a run for their cabin. I hope he was the only guard in this sector. If I'm wrong—"

"Wrong isn't an option, Boss. Let's run like hell. You lead."

They sprinted up to a split log fence and ducked under it. Within a hundred feet of their goal, Susan grabbed Murdock's right arm and pulled him down. They lay there huddled close; barely breathing. No words passed. A guard was standing near the target cabin. Was that his post? Or was he just passing by? Are Grace and Brother Martin still in that cabin? Where's Jack? Susan reached for her switchblade. Murdock grabbed her wrist. The guard was at the edge of a shadow and becoming easier to see.

Fortunately, his back was to them, but his AK-47 was un-slung and ready for action. The guard began moving away.

In the half light, Murdock saw a face in the cabin window. He couldn't identify it. Was it another guard? If so, in seconds they would be in deep do-do. But he saw no choice. Arising and throwing caution to the wind, they sprinted for the cabin door. As they raced through it into the cabin, they came face-to-face with Jack.

* * *

Hovering 2,000 feet over ridges and trees, Miguel pointed to a river in the near distance and said, "That is *el Río Coco*. Jack's transmitter has moved. It's on the other side. It shouldn't be. When I got the fix on it, it was north of here."

"Then why are we hovering? Let's find it."

"His transmitter is moving. There is little point in finding it."

"Why not?"

"That river is the border with Nicaragua, Señorita. We do not have a clearance to fly into Nicaragua. They might shoot at us. Besides, the suspected ranch is not in Nicaragua. I can't believe Jack is moving away from the compound. Someone other than Jack has the instrument. They're not taking any chances. They may be moving it around just in case someone may be honing in on it. They must suspect Jack. Our target is behind us. I saw a canyon a few miles back that fit Brother Martin's description."

"Could there be many canyons around here that fit his description?"

"I can't say, Señorita. My chart suggests that there are. But Jack's plan to cross the river near here leads me to believe that it may be the canyon with the creek less than ten miles back. Even if I'm wrong, we can't be too far off the mark. It's in the general area that Brother Martin marked on the chart. I'm going back to look."

"How will you know for certain?"

"I won't, Señorita. But please remember, it was not my idea to make this flight."

* * *

Within the cabin, Jack gave Murdock and Susan a heads-up on the ranch house. "There's a great room as you enter the front door. Six bedrooms are aligned along either side of a hallway which forms a T with the great room. An elementary kitchen is in the southwest corner of the great room with a breakfast bar and stools. Yesterday evening I heard

381

that Mr. Proteus, Brother Antonio, and a third man will arrive by chopper sometime this morning. Mitchell didn't mention the name of the third man and I couldn't ask without raising suspicion.

Grace interrupted. Pointing out the window, she exclaimed, "Claude Mitchell is coming this way. He's carrying food."

Murdock pointed toward a small closet. Susan and he hurriedly squeezed into it and closed the door. "I'm glad I'm only two months," she whispered.

"Me, too." Murdock affirmed.

Mitchell stepped into the cabin with a meal of dry toast and coffee. As he left, Brother Martin grabbed a piece of toast and stepped outside with him. They talked for several minutes. When Brother Martin rejoined the group, he said, "They're still buying our story about being lost tourists. Mitchell says that a storm is coming. In about an hour, the chopper is flying to Tegucigalpa so it can be put into a hangar. They'll take the three of us on that flight. The chopper has been pushed off the landing pad for now because the other chopper will drop off the three passengers shortly."

Murdock's eyes met Brother Martin's. "If we steal that chopper they're pushing off the pad, are you certain that you can fly it?"

"I'll give it my best shot."

"Good," Murdock said. "Without Miguel, it's the only way to escape with the Green Lady. We'll need to move quickly and deliberately. As soon as the new chopper arrives and the passengers go into the ranch house, Grace and I will go next door and get the Green Lady. Martin, you and Susan will head for the chopper that you're familiar with. Jack, you'll head for the armory, grab some automatic weapons and ammo, and then start shooting toward the guard tower. Take it down if you can. That should distract them. As soon as Brother Martin has started the chopper engines, we all run for it with our weapons drawn. We'll jump on board and Martin will fly us out of here. Does that sound like a plan?"

Jack said, "I can't think of a better one, assuming the Green Lady is still in her cabin."

Murdock stressed, "We'll be wide open and exposed, Jack. You'll be the only one with real firepower." Murdock thought, *He'd better be committed to our side.* His eyes met Susan's.

She nodded her head affirmatively. "It's the best we can do, Boss."

Brother Martin injected, "Remember, we *are* the good guys. God *is* on our side."

Grace asked, "What if God decided to test our metal and doesn't let those damn engines start?"

"Good point," Murdock replied. "If Martin can't start the engines, we wait for Jack to start shooting. Grace and I will grab the Green Lady. We all make a dash for the east fence, jump it or get under it, and dash up the mountain trail. When we've gathered at the top, we'll back-track to the savannah. Hopefully the boats will be there."

Grace asked, "What if we're cut off from the east fence?"

"We gather here, or wherever we can, and hold our ground. We keep firing until our ammo is gone, or, like an old western movie, Colonel Millán and his cavalry arrive in the nick of time."

"If they don't," Susan said, "I'm going to ask for a refund on my ticket."

Time passed slowly. Fortunately no guard disturbed them. It was nearly 9:00 a.m. when Susan thought she heard engines. In seconds, a chopper appeared from over the mountain, hovered overhead, and settled gently onto the chopper pad. Three men exited. Martin, Murdock and Grace recognized the first as Brother Antonio. The second man Murdock and Susan recognized as Mr. Proteus. No one recognized the third man. Proteus and the third man walked directly to the ranch house. Brother Antonio headed directly toward the cabin of the Green Lady.

Grace exclaimed, "This is our first 'oh shit.' What will she tell him about us?"

Murdock replied, "We can't give her a chance. As soon as he gets inside, you and I will make a dash for her cabin. Martin, change shirts with me. Hopefully the guards won't notice that I'm a stranger."

"It's better if I go myself," Brother Martin urged. "No one knows Brother Antonio better than I."

Murdock shook his head in the negative. "But the woman doesn't know you. I don't want a strange face in there yet. She's the reason we're here."

* * *

Linda was impatient. A half hour ago Miguel had pointed to a gauge and declared that the oil temperature was too high. After landing the chopper in a clearing, he said, "This damn rented equipment. You never know whether they've done the required maintenance. This oil filter hasn't been changed for years. It's plugged with sludge. I'm going to bypass it. It's illegal, but renting the aircraft without performing required maintenance is illegal, too. Fortunately there's a tool kit under my seat. I'll bet I'm not the first one who's needed it. I hope the bypass works."

"Me, too."

* * *

Murdock, dressed in Martin's shirt, along with Grace, entered the Green Lady's cabin, their side arms hidden so as not to frighten her. She and Brother Antonio were seated near a window. Antonio leapt to his feet, shocked. Showing the bulge under his shirt to Antonio, Murdock threatened, "Don't raise an alarm. It wouldn't be wise."

"How did you get here?" Antonio demanded. "What are you doing here?"

The Green Lady explained, "They say that they've come to set me free from my captors, Patti Dale and Mr. Verbius. But Patti and Mr. Verbius are the only friends that I have, except for you, of course. You are my dearest friend Antonio. Only you understand me."

Brother Antonio took both her hands in his and locked his eyes on hers. "Patti Dale and Mr. Verbius are *not* your friends. They are evil people who have misled you and misused both you and me. They have threatened the lives of my family in Spain if I didn't cooperate. I'm not proud of what I've done. In fact, I'm ashamed. Murdock and Grace are your friends. Go with them."

The Green Lady looked puzzled. She sighed and said to him, "You must come with us."

"I can't, my dear one. That viper would have my sister murdered." His eyes turned to Murdock and Grace. "I must go to the ranch house so they'll not think I'm part of your plot. You can trust me. I won't betray you. I too want this woman free—if she ever can be in this world."

Brother Antonio arose to leave but Murdock blocked his way. "How can we trust you? You were the associate of Brother Stephen. Your acquaintances murdered him. For all we know, you were an accessory to his murder. You pledged loyalty to your Abbott, Brother Martin. Now it appears that you were a spy in the monastery."

The Green Lady stared at Murdock, her mouth open. Brother Antonio frowned. "Be careful. You're disturbing our lady. Things are not as they appear. We live in an age where science fiction quickly ceases to be fiction. Stephen believed that there is a parallel universe only an atom's width apart from ours. He believed that life forms there may be trying to burrow into our own. He, with my assistance, designed a microchip with highly specialized circuitry. Our goal was to transmit signals through the chaos that separates us from them by using negative energy in the dark matter. Simply put, our purpose was to create what he called a hot-spot of invitation.

"Stephen wished to give the schematics to a friendly government that would invest the money to build the necessary transmitter and antenna system. He considered NASA. Several years back, at a conference in

Vienna, I mentioned our project to Professor Claude Mitchell who now fancies himself as the god, Verbius. He's the one who had a theory about extraterrestrials coming to ancient Peru and made huge geometric etchings in a rock plateau. He introduced me to Patti Romanovsky. At that time, she was divorcing her husband and cornering huge swaths of his wealth. She agreed to fund our project privately and keep it secret from politicians. The hot-spot was constructed and activated. I believe that we succeeded in drawing this lady's existence into our universe. She apparently took the form of the first person she came in contact with—the iniquitous Patricia Dale Romanovsky. Patti named her Diana. I visit here because I'm interested in Diana's welfare."

Murdock asked, "Were you culpable in the death of Brother Stephen?"

"No. I would never have harmed him. He was my friend. Brother Stephen was murdered to prevent his giving the schematics to anyone else." His eyes locked onto Murdock's. He asked, "Are you two alone? Oh. Sorry. Of course you wouldn't tell me. May I go now?"

Murdock glanced at Grace who had been observing without speaking. She said, "His body language says he's playing us straight. I'd put my money on him."

Turning to Brother Antonio, Murdock said, "We're betting our lives on you. Go. Pretend nothing has happened."

"They're expecting me to bring her to the ranch house."

Grace suggested, "She isn't feeling well. Tell them you'll come after her in an hour."

Antonio looked at Murdock. He nodded in agreement. Without another word, Brother Antonio exited the cabin and walked toward the ranch house. As he did, they heard the sound of another helicopter. Murdock looked out the window toward the ranch house. Judging by the confusion on the porch, it was unexpected. No one was rolling the first chopper off the only landing pad to make room for it. As it drew nearer, three security guards appeared from their cabin with automatic weapons drawn. Murdock's eyes met Grace's.

"If they open fire," he said, "no one in that chopper is going to survive."

* * *

Earlier, at the airport in Tegucigalpa, the air force pilot and Colonel Millán had argued for a half hour. The air force would not attack a ranch within their country. Finally, Millán had reached the pilot's commanding officer and obtained authority for his own police pilot to fly the aircraft.

Rudi and the colonel had climbed aboard the chopper with five well-armed police officers. One had knowledge of the general area that Brother Martin had indicated. He studied it as they departed. Pointing to a canyon, he suggested that the pilot set his coordinates for that location. The pilot did. "We should be there in less than an hour," the pilot said.

As they gained altitude, Rudi felt uncomfortable. A week ago he'd been sitting in a comfortable office in Munich contemplating retirement. Now he was on a reckless mission into the mountains of Honduras. But his friend, Murdock, needed him. He might have felt more comfortable if the colonel had more troops, but budget problems made it impossible. Rudi could understand that. *Well,* he thought soothing his anxiety, *Jack believes the Traction folks are a paper tiger.* But Jack's opinion was little solace.

* * *

Confusion reigned at the Traction ranch house as the unexpected chopper descended. Brother Martin, Jack and Susan took advantage of the security guards' distraction. They ran to the Green Lady's cabin and joined Murdock and Grace. All five peered out the window. Brother Antonio, Patti Dale and Claude Mitchell were standing on the porch. Patti waved her hand, apparently giving a command. The guards lowered their weapons. As the chopper settled onto the grass about a hundred feet from the ranch house, she walked out to meet it. A man exited. No sooner had he exited than the chopper pilot slammed the door shut, revved up the engines, and lifted off. The passenger turned and shook his fist at the pilot.

"The pilot's gun-shy," Murdock said. "He's clearing out of here."

As the passenger walked toward the porch, Grace recognized him. "It's Boris Romanovsky."

"Where's the pilot of the first chopper that arrived?" Brother Martin wondered out loud.

Susan responded, "I saw him walk into the cabin where the security guards live. When those folks go into the ranch house, we could all run for the chopper that you know how to fly."

Grace pointed to the porch. "Look. Brother Antonio is on the porch looking straight at us."

Martin's eyes met Murdock's. Murdock asked, "Does anyone have a reason we should wait?" No one spoke. "Then this is it. MOVE!"

Murdock took the Green Lady's hand, yanked her to her feet, and said, "Look. Your friend Antonio is signaling for us to run."

They exited the cabin and, except for Jack, raced toward the porch because the chopper was on the other side of the ranch house. Jack ran toward the armory. Murdock and the Green Lady ran behind Grace and Martin. As they were about to pass the porch, three security guards armed with automatic weapons stepped in front of them. They stopped. The guards' firepower was superior to theirs. They dropped their weapons. As one of the guards retrieved them, the others herded them into the ranch house. Murdock hoped that Jack was still operational. Brother Antonio watched, but remained outside.

Inside, the guards lined them up in the great room. Patti was sitting on a stool at the kitchen counter. Mr. Proteus was next to her. Claude Mitchell, with a shocked look on his face, was standing next to a coffee pot. The third man who had arrived on the chopper, sometimes known as Flavio, other times as Weidner, was sitting on the table next to it. Also shocked as he came out of the bathroom, was Boris Romanovsky. Patti calmly lit a cigarette, sneered, and asked, "Where is the man called Jack? I don't see him." The three guards looked at each other.

She nodded to the two guards standing just inside the door. "Go find him and bring him to me. If he resists, kill him." Turning her attention to the Green Lady, she commanded, "Diana, you come over here, my dear." Staring scornfully at Susan she asked, "Are you that Asian bitch that our Proteus knocked-up in Morocco?"

Susan smiled and said politely, "My name is Susan Ling. Mr. Proteus was quite dedicated to the project. It could have happened on the trip over to Morocco. I understand that you couldn't get knocked-up after poor Mr. Romanovsky spent many months trying."

Patti stood up, her face twisted in rage. "You impertinent little yellow slant-eyed slut. You're a mouthy little bitch, aren't you?" Turning to the remaining security guard, she ordered, "Take them outside and kill them. Shoot the slut first."

A blank look crossed the guard's face. He replied, "I'm sorry, ma'am, but I ain't likely to do that."

Patti's face flushed. Scornfully she demanded, "Are you the bastard who's been spying for my ex-husband?"

"If I was, ma'am, he'd likely not want me to tell."

Murdock gambled. Catching the guard's attention, with his fist closed and his thumb pointed up, he motioned toward the ceiling. The guard grinnded a toothless grin, laughed, then raised his weapon and started strafing the ceiling. Plaster and woodchips flew wildly around the room.

Verbius was hit on the head by a good sized chunk. He fell dazed to the floor. Murdock lunged forward and threw a shoulder block into Patti's stomach. She dropped her weapon and lay splayed on the floor. Her weapon slid near Grace's feet. Grace slumped onto the floor and grabbed it. The Green Lady was wide-eyed and frozen in place. Brother Martin grabbed her by her left hand and dragged her outside. On the porch, Brother Antonio grasped her right hand. They ran toward the chopper. Security guards, reacting to the gunfire within, ignored them as they ran into the ranch house. When the three reached the chopper, Brother Martin released the Green Lady's hand, opened the door of the aircraft, climbed inside and immediately seated himself behind the controls. Antonio pushed the Green Lady inside but didn't follow her. He slammed the door closed behind her. Martin found the controls familiar. He threw a few switches. In seconds, he'd started the engines.

As the gang of security guards ran in the front door, Murdock and Susan grabbed weapons. The three ran down the hallway and out the back door. Racing around the west end of the house, they sprinted toward the chopper. Another chopper was approaching from the canyon to the west. Ignoring it, they ran toward Martin's, with Susan trailing behind. Murdock realized Martin's rotors were at close to flying speed. The guards that had followed them would appear in seconds with weapons capable of shooting it down. They might have surface-to-air missiles. The Green Lady was onboard. He grabbed Grace, stopped her, and gave the thumbs-up signal to Martin. Seeing the signal, Brother Martin instantly assessed the situation, and lifted the machine off the ground. Barely clearing the west wall, he retreated down the valley, buying distance as he gained altitude. Guards arrived from out the back door and fired at the chopper. Either they were bad shots or the chopper was out of range. As Murdock and Grace dropped onto their stomachs in offensive positions, he was pleased that the Green Lady was safe.

But Susan wasn't safe. She had stumbled and fallen. Proteus was standing about ten feet from her. She got up. Flavio was running toward her. As he reached her and grabbed her, he saw Patti on the porch pointing a pistol at Susan. Flavio released her and ran. Susan froze. Proteus bolted in her direction as Patti fired, throwing himself in front of her, knocking her down and falling next to her. Patti, holding her breath to steady the second shot, took aim at Susan again. A shot came from just inside the door, striking Patti in the spine. Her pistol fired into the air. She spun off the porch, and slumped to the ground. She breathed no more. Murdock saw her lying there. He thought, *When she was alive she wanted to rule the world and kill anyone who got in her way. Now her lifeless body claims a few square feet of Honduran dirt. Now she either knows the wrath of God, or she doesn't know anything anymore.* Standing in the doorway with a pistol in his hand was her ex-husband, Boris Romanovsky. Boris walked over to the edge of the porch and fired another shot into her lifeless body.

Confusion reigned. Flavio, seeing a threatening helicopter approaching, shouted a command to the guards to join him at the armory.

Susan got up on her knees. Mr. Proteus lay next to her. Blood was gushing from his chest, his wound obviously fatal. Susan put her hand under his head and held it off the ground. She cried. In a spontaneous moment, he had saved her life and the life of their child. Grasping her forearm, he pulled her close to him. His lips moved. She couldn't hear. His eyes pleaded. She put her ear close to his lips. Struggling for enough breath to form words, he asked desperately, "Are you still carrying my child?"

As his breathing stopped, she said, "Yes. It's my child, too." She would have said *yes* even if it weren't true. Did he hear her answer? The melancholy truth is that she'd never know.

* * *

Miguel, following his instincts, had found the valley that Brother Martin described. As he and Linda approached barely thirty feet above the ground, they saw the action. As Martin's chopper cleared the wall westbound, Miguel passed it, and headed for the landing pad. He could see that not all of the good guys escaped with Martin. As Miguel busied himself with landing the aircraft, Linda noticed a woman lying next to the front porch apparently dead, and Susan kneeling over a man on the ground. They passed over Boris running toward another man who was also lying on the ground near the helicopter pad. The other man's chest was saturated with blood. Linda recognized him. It was Jack.

As soon as they touched down, Linda pushed the door open, jumped out of the chopper, and ran over to Jack. Boris, who was now kneeling over him, shouted, "He needs immediate medical attention." Miguel joined them. He took one look at his friend and nodded in agreement. Both looked at Linda. It seemed obvious to her they were right. But where were Murdock and Grace? They would be trapped if Miguel didn't wait for them.

Miguel said, "I've given the coordinates to Colonel Millán, Señorita. The police are very close. It's becoming dangerously windy. We must leave."

Jack was semiconscious. Miguel and Boris lifted him and put his arms around their shoulders. They dragged him to the aircraft, shoved him on board and then got on board themselves. Miguel shouted to Linda, "Get onboard, Señorita. Jack will want you to be with him. Be fast, now."

Linda ran to the aircraft's open door. Her eyes met Miguel's. "Hand me your weapon," she commanded. "I'm staying here. You get Jack to the hospital. Do it NOW."

He threw her a pistol. "Do you know how to use it, Señorita?"

"I used to trap-shoot with my father. Dammit, get out of here."

Miguel pushed the throttles forward and shouted, "Okay, Señorita. It's your funeral."

As Linda watched, Miguel lifted off. She saw Boris inside trying to deal with the bleeding.

Murdock, running to help Susan, stopped abruptly when to his surprise he saw Linda. Mitchell, who called himself Verbius, was stretched out flat on his stomach on the porch. He held a weapon in his right hand. Seeing Murdock standing still, he took aim and fired. Murdock spun around, fell to the ground, and rolled over onto his hands and knees. Grace leaped on top of him, flattening him. Linda, not too many feet away from Mitchell, raised her pistol and fired. The bullet entered the top of his head. His weapon dropped out of his hand. Grace, in the confusion of the moment and not knowing who had fired, rolled off Murdock, leapt to her feet gun in hand, and confronted Linda. Grace froze, staring in disbelief. Had her unspoken prayer to the nonexistent god been answered? Her rival was right here in the thick of battle. Recovering from the shock, Grace bent over to assess Murdock's wound.

Getting to his feet, Murdock assured her, "It's a flesh wound. I'm fine." The enormity of her spontaneous act to protect his life didn't strike him until later. It struck Linda.

In all the commotion, no one had noticed still another chopper approaching the landing pad that Miguel's had just vacated.

* * *

Rudi had seen the ranch first and pointed it out to the pilot. Colonel Millán ordered his men to check their weapons. As the police chopper crossed over the north wall, Rudi saw Murdock and Grace lying on the ground. Another man was lying not too far away with a weapon in his hand. At the edge of the scene, Linda was standing, with her feet wide apart, apparently bewildered. He noticed men in security uniforms at a cabin door. Weapons were being handed out including a surface-to-air missile. Rudi forced open the chopper's door and climbed out on a runner. Before it touched the ground, he leapt off. As he ran toward Murdock, he heard Colonel Millán scream, "Missiles. Get out of here."

The chopper's engines roared. After barely touching the ground, it lifted off again and backed over the north wall, keeping close to the ground. A missile roared low over the wall, missing the chopper, and exploded on the side of the north mountain. A second struck the north wall of the compound and blasted a gaping hole through it. The police chopper reappeared rising over the south wall. Police fired from the aircraft, felling the man with the launcher and a few others.

Murdock saw that Linda, Grace and Rudi were on their feet and that Flavio and his men were pinned down by the police. He motioned to them and to the guard who had spared their lives and shouted, "Follow me. There's safety in the underbrush until the cops clear the area."

And so there was, but the cops didn't clear the area. The winds from the outer bands of the hurricane had become too strong. They couldn't land. Murdock understood that it was fast becoming too dangerous to remain in the air. He saw the colonel shrug as the pilot turned west to outrun the storm.

* * *

When they reached the promontory, Jorge was waiting. Murdock looked back over the edge. Flavio and some of his men had decided there was safety in the underbrush, too.

Grace suggested, "We wouldn't want that bunch to catch up with us. They've got a hell of a lot more firepower than we do. That guy, who's leading them, was the third man on the chopper with Antonio and Proteus. Who is he?"

"I recognize him," Linda said. "He was in the courtroom on Grand Cayman posing as Herr Weidner."

Grace added, "Then he's Flavio, too."

Murdock said, "He murdered the actress, Hilde Müller. Jack captured that on the DVD that we're trying to get."

Jorge suggested, "They're coming fast, Señor. They have big guns. Let's run like hell."

Murdock was still bleeding. Linda took a clean handkerchief from her slacks to clean the wound.

"There isn't time," Murdock said.

391

They headed eastward along the trail, retreating in the direction of the savannah. Jorge led, followed by Rudi, Susan, Murdock, Linda, the guard, and Grace. Rudi, with his weapon drawn, brought up the rear."

Moving easily all seemed quiet behind them. There was no telling where Flavio and his goons were, whether they were gaining on them, or even whether they were following them. They couldn't even be sure that Flavio had seen them. Presently they came upon the clearing that preceded the ledge. The wind was whipping up dust, but there was no rain as yet.

Murdock said, "If they catch up with us while we're crossing the ledge, we'll be sitting ducks. The wind will be blowing dirt in our eyes. It must be gusting to at least fifty miles per hour. It's impossible. Does everyone agree that we stop here and hold our ground?"

No one wanted to attempt the ledge. If anyone was tempted, heavy rain started pelting them, wetting the ledge and making it slippery. Rivulets of water were running down the slope, pooling on the ledge, crossing it, and in dozens of miniature waterfalls, dropping seventy feet into the canyon. Jorge motioned for them to follow. He led them into dense underbrush. After about fifty feet, Jorge stopped. He pushed his way through a group of dwarf palmetto. There, low to the ground, and hidden by the palmetto, was the mouth of a cave. Jorge motioned for them to drop to their bellies and slither in. They obeyed. Once inside, he turned on his flashlight. The cave rapidly expanded so that they could stand erect. Except for a rivulet of water running down one side, the cave was dry and cool. Rudi, the last one in, gave the silence signal. Jorge turned off his light. Outside, several men were speaking. One said, "They must-a got across the ledge, or they took the other freeken trail at the fork." "Naw. They wouldn't do that. Shit. That'd just take them higher into the damn mountains." "Maybe that's what they wanted." "I don't think so. They crossed the freeken ledge." "It's too damn miserable here to wait around. They probably had some freeken boats waiting on the flooded savannah." "Yeah, Flavio. Those bastards are gone." "Maybe. Maybe not." "Maybe the storm will pass over by morning. Let's get back to the ranch." "I guess Traction is yours now, Flavio. The rest are dead." "Yeah. Maybe."

The voices faded and were gone. In a whisper, Murdock suggested that they still remain quiet. Flavio may be listening for them.

Hours passed. By late afternoon, Murdock decided to reconnoiter. He slithered outside, with Rudi close behind. No one was in sight. The wind had died down. The sun had dried the trail along the ledge. He called for the others to come out. When they had gathered he said, "Either the hurricane took a sharp turn north and we just caught the edge of it, or we're in the eye. Judging from the clouds, I'd say it turned north. Let's cross the ledge before Flavio and his goons come back."

They all agreed except the guard. He was afraid of the ledge and chose instead to follow a back trail that went off to the north. They all thanked him for saving their lives. Grace put both her arms around him, pressed hard against him, and gave him a kiss on the lips that he would remember. His face reddened. Then, wishing them all good luck, he disappeared into the tall foliage.

Footing on the ledge was by no means sure. Linda confessed, "I'm afraid of heights."

"You'll be okay," Murdock assured her. "Stay close behind me. Put your right hand on my left shoulder. Use your left to grab onto the weeds that look secure. Sidestep. Don't look down."

Jorge led, followed by Susan. Murdock followed close behind her. Linda didn't move. Grace stared at her and said reassuringly, "You've got to go. There's no choice. We'd better get across before the bad guys come back. There's safety on the other side."

Linda nodded bravely. Placing her hand on Murdock's shoulder, she started with Grace close behind. Rudi hesitated, searching the back trail.

As they passed the halfway point, a singing bullet ricocheted off the rock wall just above Linda. Dirt, dust, and rock chips fell in her hair and face. Reflexively, she removed her hand from Murdock's shoulder to protect her eyes, but in doing so, she lost her balance. Moving her right foot in an attempt to regain it, she stepped off the ledge and fell, sliding on her stomach over the edge. She slowed herself momentarily as she grabbed hold of a weed growing out of a crevice and her right forearm caught the trail. Still sliding, she looked down. The floor of the canyon was at least seventy feet below. When Linda's hand let loose from Murdock's shoulder, he instinctively looked behind him. He saw no one between him and Rudi. In near panic, he looked down.

After a split second's indecision, Grace had dropped onto her stomach, her cheek hard against the ledge rock, her body pressing down on top of Linda's forearm. She could feel it slipping under her. Reaching as far over the side as she could, Grace grasped the belt on Linda's slacks, and looped her fingers around it. The weed was tearing from its roots. Linda, with nothing to hang onto, slid a few more inches, pulling Grace to the very edge of the trail, her head and right shoulder over the side. Grace was losing her grip. She couldn't hold Linda without going over herself. *Without Linda I'd be...* But Grace couldn't live with letting her fall.

At the same moment, the man who had fired stood in the clearing, and was taking aim again. Rudi took aim first and fired. The man slumped to the ground. Two men with him dropped their weapons and ran back down the trail.

Rudi turned, saw the situation, dropped onto Grace's legs, pinning her to the ledge with all his weight. Murdock squatted down, his back hard against the rock wall, and grasped Linda's arm as it slipped from under Grace. Susan steadied Murdock. Jorge wrapped both his arms around Susan's waist. As Murdock pulled Linda up several inches, Grace let go of Linda's belt and locked her right arm around Linda's upper thigh. Murdock and Grace lifted her as far as they could. Rudi, reaching from above Grace, grabbed Grace's right arm at the elbow and helped her pull Linda. Linda bent her leg so that Rudi was able to grasp her left ankle. He pulled until her left knee was over Grace's head and on the trail. Linda bent her right leg at the knee. Rudi grabbed that, too. Murdock took both her arms and raised her off of Grace and Rudi and onto her knees. Rudi eased back and helped Grace onto her feet.

Murdock's eyes met Linda's. "Get on your feet," he urged softly. Cautiously, Linda arose and stood tenuously on the narrow ledge. Murdock continued, "Now we'll sidestep again. We have less than fifty yards to go. The floor of the canyon is rising to meet us. The danger diminishes with every step." He searched her eyes. The horror he had seen in them seconds earlier had retreated. They were calm.

Another ten minutes brought them beyond the abyss. There were still dangerous loose rocks on the down slope. Murdock gave a signal to stop. They surveyed it. Murdock said, "The wind and heavy rain haven't helped. It looks even more unstable than it was yesterday. Any one of us could cause a rockslide that could kill anyone below them. We need to spread out so that no one is in front of anyone."

Jorge added, "If you see a loose rock in front of you, kick it down. It will take other loose rocks with it."

"Stay alert," Murdock added.

The descent was uneventful. When they reached the level ground below, they heard a roar of engines behind them and getting louder fast. The sound came from the direction of the Traction compound. "Those are chopper engines," Murdock said. There was nowhere to hide. As the aircraft crested the mountain, its forward motion stopped. It hovered over them at about 500 feet. Murdock made out the face of Brother Antonio. He also made out its markings which identified it as Honduran Air Force. After several seconds of hovering, it descended to the bottom of the rocks and landed fifty yards from them at the edge of the flooded savannah. The door opened and Colonel Millán exited followed by Brother Antonio.

Colonel Millán walked over to Rudi and asked, "Has this Antonio fellow been involved in any criminal activity in your jurisdiction?"

Rudi shrugged and said, "I have no warrant for him."

The colonel turned to the others. "We picked this man up in the Traction compound. Have any of you seen him commit a crime in Honduras?"

All replied in the negative.

He smiled and turned to Brother Antonio. "Well, Antonio, perhaps your sister is safe now. You're a free man."

Linda turned to Grace, hugged her, and said, "Thank you for saving my life. I'll never forget you."

Grace smiled awkwardly. "Nor shall I forget you, Ms. DiStefano."

Murdock remembered that Grace had fallen on him during the shooting. He wrapped both arms around her in a bear hug and said, "That goes for me, too. You were brave and self-sacrificing far beyond the call of duty. You may have saved my life." Releasing the hug, his eyes locked onto hers and he added, "I can't begin to thank you enough. We need more courageous people like you in Veritus. There's a fine future for you with the company. I hope you'll stay with us."

Linda had watched Grace melt in his arms.

When Murdock released her, Grace quickly recovered, turned to Linda and said unassumingly, "Actually, on the ledge, I slipped and fell and you just happened to break my fall."

Linda smiled and suggested, "You just happened to grab the belt on my slacks to steady yourself, and you just happened to trip and fall on top Murdock when he went down during the fire-fight."

For several seconds, no one spoke. Then Linda, with a tear meandering down her cheek, walked over to Grace. She put her arm around her again, hugged her again, and tenderly kissed her cheek.

After an awkward silence, Colonel Millán suggested, "Why don't we all squeeze into the chopper and go get some lunch?"

52

Portland, Oregon
Friday, July 21, 8:30 a.m.

So much had ended and so much had just begun.

Murdock McCabe sat alone in his office. Before getting on the elevator, he'd bought pipe tobacco for the first time in years. Exiting the elevator, he'd waved to Susan, entered his office, closed the door behind him, and seated himself on his desk chair. He retrieved his old pipe from his desk drawer and packed it. Resting his right elbow on the chair's arm, he held the pipe with his right hand and lit it. The aroma of vanilla drifted across the room. He sat back, pleased.

Susan had waved back, but not with her usual verve. She was a more circumspect Susan. As if being pregnant by a dead man wasn't enough, her marriage was flaming out into dying embers. She loved her husband. She loved her unborn baby, too. He had given her a clear choice. She couldn't keep both. Hence the embers.

To make things worse, her favorite boss, ever, was leaving.

Murdock drew on the aromatic tobacco and turned things over in his mind. He was pleased that the raid had exonerated Enrique and eliminated the evil perpetrators. He regretted that three people had paid with their lives, *but,* he thought, *they'd paid in their own coin.* In an hour, there would be a debriefing in the conference room.

Only ten days had passed since the day Jack and he had formed the plan to free the Green Lady. That evening, in a lonesome corner at Hemingway's, he and Jack had had several drinks. Being gentlemen, neither had mentioned Linda. Jack had been intent on bringing Murdock up to speed on several issues. As he did, Murdock began to realize what Jack had meant when he'd told Linda that things weren't what they appeared to be. Jack was a retired United States Naval officer. His last duty post had been Naval Intelligence. Subsequent to retirement, he had contracted with Naval Intelligence as a consultant and a freelancer. Both the navy and he understood that he had a private agenda, too. It didn't matter to the navy. He was too valuable.

Jack had a noteworthy asset which was all too obvious to Murdock. He was a lady's man. He confessed that his love of attractive women had been frequently and splendidly reciprocated. His affairs had shaped, as serendipity, an intelligence network of clever and gifted women devoted to him. He had been caring enough never to give any woman the impression that she was his only love. Each, like Denise, had admired him enough, and had been sophisticated enough, and had been comfortable enough with whom *she* was, that she didn't need to be.

Murdock reminisced about the first time he'd met Jack a year ago. Jack had a contract with the United States Coast Guard to assist in the investigation of a rumored threat to homeland security on the Pacific Coast. Jack was disguised as a barfly called Smokey. The rumor asserted that a murky organization calling itself Traction was poised to launch an anthrax attack by water on either Longview, Washington, a city upstream on the Colombia River, or on Portland, Oregon, on a tributary of the Columbia. The rumor also suggested that Traction had a second agenda in that area. It involved some sort of bizarre computer chip allegedly in the possession of an astrophysicist named Professor Amy Gallagher.

Murdock took a drag on his pipe as a smile crossed his face. Jack had particularly welcomed that contract. Professor Amy Gallagher and he had been lovers for several years. Like most of his liaisons, it was a well-kept secret. Because Linda knew Amy, Jack had requested that Murdock not mention it to Linda as long as he was still alive. Murdock understood. He decided never to mention it. No good could come of it. It might embarrass them both.

When Murdock had assisted Rudi two years ago in the investigation of Brother Stephen's death, he had met Brother Antonio. He had learned that Brother Antonio had a sister named Maria Rosita. Years ago she had been a college roommate of Patti Dale. Unfortunately she had innocently mentioned their work to Patti. Patti saw an opportunity. She and her Traction crew awaited their chance. When the chip was completed and Brother Stephen thought he'd received an extraterrestrial response, they killed him. Shortly thereafter they killed Amy's father, Professor Klugman. Both Brother Stephen and Professor Klugman had planned on giving it to NASA. They compelled Brother Antonio to give them a copy of the chip and its schematics by threatening Maria Rosita's life and the lives of their parents, With Antonio's reluctant help, they created what Jack had described as a "hot spot" that had amazingly attracted the Green Lady to them.

Having succeeded, Patti wished to protect her success. Was Amy Gallagher a threat? How much information did Amy have? Did she realize its potential? Could Amy duplicate their success? Would she share the information with NASA?

Given all that, Murdock had asked what Jack had done to protect Amy. Jack had admitted that he had feared for Amy's safety. His friend and sometimes collaborator, Boris Romanovsky, offered to protect Amy if she would come to Aruba. Jack knew what that would involve and he wasn't too enthused. He never made exclusive claims on his women, but he didn't like to share them with his friends. Besides, there was no foolproof way to protect her. Traction had to be kept at bay until its evil masters could be destroyed.

Murdock had told Jack the story of his experience with the Green Lady in the jungle of Honduras. Jack had suspected that she might be genuine. The knowledge that she would possess would be invaluable. Jack didn't want Traction to have it. Navy intelligence had scoffed at the idea of a green woman arriving from somewhere in space. Their contact man said it sounded like something out of a C. S. Lewis novel.

Jack had met with Brother Antonio who confirmed his suspicion. In addition to his concern for Amy, Jack became deeply concerned for Brother Antonio, Maria Rosita and their parents. He convinced Antonio that they could never truly be safe until Traction was destroyed. With a mixture of hope and trepidation, Antonio agreed to collaborate and become Jack's mole inside Traction.

Jack and Amy had decided to involve Dr. Roy West. West had recently written a learnèd paper on the theory of parallel universes and their likely proximity to ours. Jack had consulted with West several times over more than a few years. They'd become fast friends. Amy had been impressed with West's credentials.

Murdock took another drag on his pipe. He was troubled. If any government gets a hold of the Green Lady, she probably wouldn't experience a moment of freedom for the rest of her life. If Dr. West was on the government payroll, he'd have to report her. Jack had assured him that West was not on the government payroll. He was on Jack's. Jack had appeared to be just as concerned as Murdock. He'd made Murdock promise that if he, Jack, were killed in the operation, Murdock would protect her. Now Jack was clinging to life in a Honduran hospital.

Murdock felt comfortable with the conference this morning. It would bring together a conspiracy of protectors, not the least of which was Linda DiStefano. Linda had arranged for the Green Lady to enter the Cayman Islands legally. She and Robert Grayson, the attorney general, had gotten to know and trust each another. She felt that Grayson was an honest and dedicated lawyer—not a politician. She had extracted a promise of confidentiality. Upon leveling with him, he had raised an interesting legal question. If this Green Lady is what she appears to be, she may technically not be human. If she isn't, she may not enjoy the protection of justice under the law. Grayson had agreed that until she could decide for herself what she wanted to do, it would be best to lose her somewhere in the United States. He arranged for a Cayman passport so she could enter the country.

Murdock glanced at his watch. The conference was scheduled to start in less than a half hour. Susan called on the intercom. Linda and Brother Martin had arrived. The three were setting up the conference room. Susan was making the coffee. She never delegated that.

Last evening, Murdock and Linda had had dinner with Brother Martin. He had made an offer to sell and they had agreed to buy Veritus.

The intercom buzzed again. Susan reported that Boris Romanovsky was on an outside line. Murdock took a long drag on his pipe, blew out the smoke, and then rested the pipe on a saucer. He picked up the call. Boris was phoning from a hospital in Honduras. He came directly to the point.

"Jack didn't make it. He passed early this morning."

Murdock got a lump in his throat. He felt a mixture of regret and relief. Except for his liaison with Linda, Jack had earned his deep respect and admiration. "I didn't think he'd survive," he responded quietly. "There appeared to be too much loss of blood." After a period of silence, he added, "Brother Martin, Linda, and I were talking about him at dinner last night. None of us saw who shot him. Did you see?"

"No."

After several seconds of awkward silence, Murdock added, "I sincerely regret that he didn't make it. I understand he was your friend. You have my condolences. I'm sure I can speak for Linda, too."

He felt certain that Linda had loved Jack. He would have to tell her. With a sound of unanticipated compassion, Boris added, "Is best for you, Murdock McCabe, and...cough, cough...and your woman who foolishly chooses you rather than Boris." He fell silent. Murdock felt even more awkward, and didn't know what to say. *Maybe this man really does love her*, he thought. *Or at least is really desperate to have her.*

After several more seconds of silence, Boris added, "Do not mourn. What happens to Jack is part of nature. You and Boris are men of world. Men of world create reality. Our minds make illusions which spin facts into whatever dodgy dossiers we need. Unreasonable masquerades as reasonable. Jacks of world seldom *do* make it. But always world has 'Jacks.' 'Jacks' evaporate and condense again whenever furtive gods of clandestine digressions demand eloquence of their skills. Goodbye." Click.

Murdock sat dumbfounded. *What the hell did he just say? It sounded like something out of an early twentieth century Russian novel.* He picked up his pipe, re-lit it, drew on it, sat back, and, after several seconds, smiled inwardly. *Maybe I've underestimated old Boris. I didn't think old Boris was so, so erudite.*

The office door opened. Linda and Grace walked in with cups of coffee and seated themselves in front of his desk. After the greetings and small talk, Murdock said that he'd just received a phone call from Honduras about Jack. Grace, reading perplexity on his face and having guessed that Jack and Linda had done it in the jungle, excused herself and went to the powder room. Linda also read it. After Grace exited the room, she asked quietly, "Was that Boris?"

He answered sympathetically, "Yes."

Her hand shook as she took a sip of coffee, choked, coughed, and then asked, "Did Jack die?"

"Boris said that he passed away this morning. If that's true, I'm sincerely sorry. I didn't want that to happen." Murdock sensed the sadness in her soul.

She felt numb. Her heart broke. She wouldn't be alive if it hadn't been for Jack. He'd shaken her out of her executive stupor and forced her to be a woman again. He and Murdock had formed the plan that had saved Enrique. Jack had died executing that plan. However, Jack's death *did* relieve a burden upon their impending marriage—and her persistent feeling of guilt. That was a relief, but not quite a welcome one. His death added a new guilt. She'd benefited from a fine man's death. A tear ran down her cheek. She made no effort to hide it. It was an honest tear. Linda collected her thoughts. Their eyes met. "You said, 'If it's true.' Do you doubt Boris's word?" Murdock repeated Boris's final remarks as accurately as he could remember, including his surprising eloquence. He awaited her response.

Frowning and somewhat baffled, Linda's eyes lowered. Neither spoke. The silence was almost palpable. Presently Murdock picked up his pipe, relit it, and took a long drag on it. As she looked up, he met her eyes again but said nothing. Her expression softened. Then, with the merest hint of a smile, she said cautiously, "Sometimes Boris really can be a delightful man." After a thoughtful pause, she added, "He's right, of course. For men like Jack, the door closes and locks but the key is never lost. Then along comes another Jack with a different face and a different name, but the same old key to open it." Her eyes avoided Murdock's as she asked off-handedly, "Do *you* think the world can ever do without Jacks?"

Somewhat uncomfortable, he leaned back in his chair and stared out the window as he replied, "They're bigger than life; not quite real. I seriously doubt it."

After a pause, she added thoughtfully, "Let's not share Boris's last remarks with anyone. Okay?"

"Naturally."

* * *

Murdock seated himself at the head of the conference table with Susan on his left and Linda on his right. Seating themselves randomly were Brother Martin, Grace, Professor Amy Gallagher, Professor Roy West, Denise Perkins, and the Green Lady. Murdock asked Linda to give everyone a heads-up.

Linda excused herself for not standing and then said, "Two days ago Denise reported to Jack's general contractor that the Green Lady died in the shoot-out at the Traction Compound. Colonel Millán has a dead female body to support that. The general contractor authorized Denise to release the DVD to me. Yesterday, I reviewed it with Robert Grayson, the attorney general. This morning he filed a motion with the court to *nolle prosequi* which simply means that the Crown will proceed no further. Enrique is free."

That news was greeted by a round of applause.

"Enrique asked me to express his undying gratitude to each of you who made this victory possible. He's inviting each of you to what I can assure you will be a colossal party at his compound next week Saturday. If you can come, I'll arrange bizjets to pick you up and return you home." Continuing somewhat awkwardly, she added, "A little bit ago, Boris Romanovsky phoned and reported Jack didn't recover from his wounds. I'm sure we all deeply regret hearing that. He was a courageous and genuinely caring man. I think I knew him well enough to say that Jack would never want us to cancel the party out of respect for him. Minutes ago, I shared that thought with Enrique and he agreed."

Murdock observed Denise and Amy. Both, he thought, under reacted. He was convinced that Boris had phoned both of them, too.

Turning toward Denise, Linda said, "I think Denise has some information for you about our Green Lady."

Denise thanked her and said, "I do, but first I'd like to say something about Jack. I had the opportunity to work quite closely with him. I found him exceedingly intelligent and sincerely committed to the defense of his country. We need more Jack's in this world."

With a curious look on her face, Amy stared at her. After a few moments of silence, Denise changed the subject and said, "Our Green Lady has chosen to call herself Alma."

Grace brightened and remarked, "That's an interesting choice. In Spanish, *alma* means soul, or the essence of humanity; the main point; the heart of things."

Linda added, "It's a logical choice. The attorney general thought so, too. He put the name Alma Greene on her passport."

Murdock injected, "Linda and I are concerned that if any government gets control of her, she'll become a prisoner again. She'd be examined by teams of government appointed neurologists, biologists, and whatever. The bureaucrats would issue media statements. The media would confuse fact and opinion so the public could never sort out the truth. She'd be an alien invader from another world. Hounds of blind fear would be barking at an extraterrestrial moon. Politicians would do their normal routine—let the media pump fright into their constituents and then promise to pass a law and appropriate money to protect them."

Brother Martin turned to the Green Lady and asked, "Alma, how do you feel about that?"

Alma leaned forward, with her hands clasped, and her elbows resting on the conference table. She smiled and began, "First, let me say that Denise has been a real friend. She's helped me to understand those issues. Murdock and Linda want to provide a place for me out of the limelight, as Denise put it. I would like them to do that. I do wish to spend time with Professor Gallagher and Professor West. There may be much we can learn from one another. Whatever scientific knowledge I can give them, they can pass on to the scientific community under their own names. I appreciate everything that all of you have done for me. You must have questions. I'll try to answer them."

"Where are you from?" Grace asked.

"I will try to put it into your words. As best I can both remember and explain, I came from nothing—that is from no-thing—from what the two professors might call pure intellectual energy, from an endless graceful waltz in dimensions infinitely unlike yours, from musical frequencies deeply felt but never heard, from dark energy that I sense is all around you, or your universe is all around it. Your laws of physics are incalculably different from ours. I remember a sense of edgy nervousness that caused us to suspect that you and your universe existed beyond that curtain where the music and the waltz dissolve into chaos. Brother Stephen's transmission invited us to pierce that curtain. I was chosen."

Murdock turned his chair toward her, met her eyes, and inquired, "How do you feel about that?"

"I have come to live in your world where the music of a waltz can actually be heard; where I have felt both pain and joy for the first time. It is not easy to be here. At first I tried to feel what Mr. Verbius told me to feel. I was like a light bulb he could turn on and off. I came on in different colors. I don't mean colors like green or blue—I should say different moods. He taught me what he wanted me to say in each mood, and how to use each mood to advantage. I found it bewildering. Murdock observed my confusion when I was made to confront him on the ship where his friend was being held captive. After I saw him, I decided that I must make myself into a person with my own feelings. I had to decide what kind of person I am to be. Yesterday Antonio explained that the Traction people were destructive angels. He told me that the creative force gave you power to overcome them and set me free." She awaited another question.

Grace leaned forward, cocked her head slightly, and asked, "Are you human? I mean, are you a real woman? Can you conceive and have children?"

"I don't know. Señor Flavio told me there was a delightful way that he could help me find out, but Patti forbade it. That made Señor Flavio angry. I wasn't happy either. I wanted to know."

Dr. West grinned and asked, "Do you still want to know?"

"Yes, of course. There are many things I would like to know. That is one of them."

West added, "Our ancestors came into being out of compounds of carbon, hydrogen, and oxygen. How it happened is admittedly obscure. Apparently you were formed instantly out of the same compounds—and like you said, they seemed to have come out of nothing. What is the first thing you remember when that happened?"

"I remember a loud noise."

Grace interjected, "Like a rumble or a big bang?"

"Like a big bang, but I had no sense of time. I don't know whether the bang lasted a moment or millions of years."

Grace had another question. "The man you knew as Mr. Verbius thought that giants visited our planet in ancient times and that our ancestors mistook them for gods and goddesses. The ancient Romans and the modern adherents of Wicca worship a goddess they call Diana. Do you know anything about that? Does the name Diana mean anything to you?"

"Patti and Mr. Verbius, the man you called Professor Claude Mitchell, told me that my name was Diana. They also told me I am a goddess. I do not believe that I am. Your mythological gods and goddesses were not us. That doesn't mean they never existed. Nor does it mean that Mr. Verbius was wrong about the writings in Peru. It means that we didn't create either the gods or the writings. Perhaps these gods and goddesses are or were figments of conscience." She became silent and awaited another question.

Amy asked, "How old are you?"

"I don't remember ever not being, but then I wouldn't, would I."

Amy pushed, "Do you sense that you are eternal?"

"I don't know. Our dance was timeless."

Brother Martin asked, "Is there a God?"

Alma smiled. After what seemed a prolonged silence, she asked, "Don't you know?"

Brother Martin returned the smile. "We know only by faith."

Alma was silent for more than a minute. Then, carefully choosing her words, she said, "I think perhaps your universe was also created out of nothing. As I said, I am not sure that I understand the laws of your physics. Mr. Verbius told me that all things evolved by means of mutations out of things simpler—that your ancestors crawled out of the sea. I think I am capable of believing that if it is possible that something can simply evolve out of a void. Can nonexistence mutate? I do not understand."

Brother Martin smiled and said kindly, "I don't, either. One more question, please. Does Satan exist?"

Alma asked, "If there is a creative force, must there not be a destructive force? Doesn't every force in your universe have a counter force? Call it Satan, if you wish. That's the best I can understand."

Grace asked, "How were you transported from your world to ours?"

Alma shrugged and looked at Amy. Amy replied, "Until yesterday, I believed that what I'm about to say was science fiction. Dr. West and I think that Alma existed in an intelligent form outside our universe. We're not convinced the word 'transported' is appropriate, however, he and I haven't agreed on a better one. I'm inclined to say that her existence was 'transliterated.' The normal meaning of that word is to write or spell words from one alphabet in the corresponding characters of a different alphabet. You end up with the same words, but they can be read only by people familiar with the other alphabet. That might be, at best, a metaphor that clumsily sheds light on how she arrived."

Roy West added, "We believe that her existence arrived at the point where Brother Antonio, Patti Dale Romanovsky, and Claude Mitchell were transmitting an invitational signal using Brother Stephen's chip. When that existence arrived, it took a form that we could recognize, copying the likeness of Patti Dale, the only female present."

Murdock asked, "May I presume that you were a woman in this prior existence?"

"No," Alma replied. "It is best that you presume nothing. I don't remember different sexes. That doesn't mean there weren't any. I have no idea why a female form was chosen—or whomever or whatever chose it."

Denise added, "I'm not a neurologist, but from what Alma has described to me, my guess is that neuroplastic changes have been taking place in her brain. I don't think Patti's brain was copied exactly because Alma brought with her an intelligence of her own. When Murdock met her on the ship last year, her brain was still wired similar to Patti's. She spoke Patti's thoughts scrambled with her own. She used phrases that Mitchell taught her. In my opinion, Alma is daily becoming more human and less whatever she was. Her thoughts are becoming her own. She doesn't much like what they made her when she first arrived here."

After a brief period of silence, Grace said, "Alma, I feel very comfortable talking to you. Do you feel comfortable talking to us?"

"Yes. I like talking to all of you. You all want to help me. I want to help you. I'm learning what I am. Strangely, I have the feeling that I've never been this small before."

Amy's eyes searched hers. Amy said, "Sometimes you are difficult to understand—not your diction. Claude Mitchell taught you well. It's your concepts. For example, you told me that our world needs to see so many things that can't be seen. When I asked you to explain that, your face went blank and you were silent."

Alma shook her head from side to side. "I don't know how to express some concepts in your words. I can metaphase, but I must think carefully before I can paraphrase. Your idiom is difficult. I do wish to be understood correctly."

Shifting the subject, Brother Martin asked, "Where you come from, do they worship God?"

Her face became expressionless. Everyone waited patiently. Eventually she asked, "Who are *they*?"

"Your fellow beings."

Alma was silent for over a minute. Then she said, "I will need to think about translating the word "beings" into a word that I can precisely understand. I do hope you will be patient with me. By the way, Denise told me that Patti used me for evil purposes. I do understand that the word *evil* represents the destruction energy. May I assume that the word *God* represents the creation energy?"

Brother Martin smiled kindly and said, "You certainly may."

Amy reiterated, "My father searched for God most of his life and never found proof that he or she exists. He concluded that the god-myths were untrue. Do you think his conclusion was wrong?"

Alma replied kindly, "The nonexistence of proof is not the proof of nonexistence." Then, with a childish smile, she added, "Certainty and uncertainty are equal spectators. Perhaps your father was simply searching for truth rather than God specifically. I suspect that your word *truth* includes what can't be seen, and even what can't be known. I've read several of your science fiction writers. I believe some come closer to truth than many scientists do."

Dr. West nodded and said, "What we're discovering about the essence of the universe is strange beyond what science fiction writers have imagined. Brother Stephen was out distanced by his own reality. I'll go out on a limb. I believe that the circuits in his chip transmitted an unintended negative harmonic in dark energy that invited a positive response from the "someplace" that Alma came from. That's pure speculation. No one has proved that dark energy or dark matter actually exists, but I unscientifically speculate that it's the glue that holds the universe together."

Alma laughed and said, "Maybe that was my challenge—to pass through glue without getting stuck."

They all laughed.

After a moment of silence, Amy turned to Alma and said, "From the material my father sent me, I'd like to read a diary entry made by Brother Stephen." She turned to Murdock and asked, "May I share it with everyone?"

Murdock replied, "I'm sure we're all interested."

Amy read from a file on her laptop.

> *"Today, Wednesday, November 12, I had to squelch my excitement so it wouldn't overheat. My transmitter broadcasts my standard message twenty-four hours a day. My receiver listens for any replies and records them. Last night the recording disclosed what I first thought was an electronic echo of my message. After closer inspection, I concluded that it was either someone*

repeating my message back to me or passing it on to someone else. My message was pre-scripted by what I speculate was their forwarding message. Brother Gustav says it resembles no human language within his knowledge. The promptness of the response is troublesome. Traveling at the speed of light it would take at least eight years for my message to get to and a response come back from a planet around the nearest star other than the sun. It would, unless the universe is made of stranger stuff than I think. Assuming for the sake of argument that it isn't, and assuming that what I heard is a reaction to my message, they must be quite close—perhaps just outside our solar system traveling toward us. If that's true, how long have they been en route? Have they discovered a means of navigating straight lines through some wormhole in the curvature of space so that time and distance is minimized? If they're on their way, their science must be more advanced than ours. Their society would have adjusted to thousands of scientific discoveries that we have not. How will we deal with such a deluge of knowledge? Or will they not share it with us?"

Amy asked, "Are there others who are coming here besides you? And if so, how close are they?"

"My existence came alone. I have no knowledge of others coming. That doesn't mean they won't. It means that I don't expect that any will."

Dr. West asked, "How long was your journey and how fast did you travel?

"My journey lasted one instant. I was merely atoms away. To us the Big Bang was a mere pop that occurred moments ago. However, it is a very great distance for you and would take eons of time with your present technology. It would cost untold trillions of dollars. If you succeeded, at some time before your descendents arrived, they would have ceased to be human. Be happy as a human in your world instead of a swath of miscellaneous energy in mine."

Amy read from Brother Stephen's diary again.

> *"I have reached the final phase of my attempt to make contact with extraterrestrial intelligence. You may ask why a wealthy man would become a monk and then devote countless hours and millions of dollars in a search for what may not be? The answer is quixotic. It's the quest—the pure and simple passion for knowledge that my mother instilled in me—the sheer thrill of probing the unknown. My relentless need to learn transcends all pragmatic objections, fires my imagination, jerks me from the routines of life, and compels me to imagine the unimaginable. I became a monk because I believe it is God's will that my quest not be merely physical science, but also contemplative. The world will be compelled to face the moral consequences of what I find."*

Amy said, "My father was concerned about the moral consequences should succeed. Mr. Grayson put the main issue in focus."

Alma was deep in thought. After a period of silence, she said, "Maybe different *beings* are merely different arrangements of points of energy. My points of energy have rearranged themselves so that I became human-like. How did I become what I was originally? I sense a creation energy that organized my points of energy into my former existence." She was silent again for several seconds, then cocked her head and added, "That creation energy must exist because I believe it does."

Brother Martin suggested, "Searching for truth is searching for God."

Grace remarked, "One person's truth is another person's fiction, Marty." Turning to Alma she asked, "Why were you sent?"

"I do not understand, yet. Denise said that each day my brain becomes a little more human. I think that's true. When I first arrived, I could levitate—make myself lighter than air. I can't do that anymore. But each day I remember more little things from before. Perhaps I may have come from a dying universe that is discharging into nonexistence."

Linda asked, "How or why do you turn green?"

Roy West responded. "She can't explain it. I have a theory. Think of photosynthesis in plants. It's controlled by a chemical called chlorophyll. That chemical is green for a reason. It's tuned to the spectrum of the sun in such a way that it absorbs all the frequencies of sunlight in the most efficient way possible except one. The one frequency it can't absorb is green, so we see the frequency that it rejects. Something like that happens with her skin when it absorbs artificial light. That's why Alma has only looked green in dark places. She now is often able to resist the change and absorb the green frequency."

After another period of silence around the table, Murdock asked, "When was the first time that you and I met?"

"It was delightful. Shortly after I arrived, my mind and thoughts were closer to Patti's. It had only begun to differentiate. Two years ago, she was posing as a woman called Diana Crenshaw. She wanted to see if I could pass. You and she had dinner one evening at the Zugspitze Hof Restaurant on the side of that mountain in Bavaria. When she excused herself to go to the powder room, it was I who returned. You never noticed the switch. You are such a good man. That night I learned what it meant to love. You were falling in love with the woman she pretended to be. I wished that I were she and that you could love me. I still do. Now that I've met Linda, I love her, too. I want you both to be happy. I look forward to seeing you two wonderful people married. I especially look forward to meeting your children someday soon."

Murdock smiled and said, "I'm looking forward to that, too. However, there's something I need to say. In the last several days, I've gotten a quite different picture of you than I had before. I'd had the impression that you were an evil genius with the ability to cannily hold yourself out as someone innocent. Now you seem to confirm Jack's and Denise's opinion that you are blameless. Which of you is real? How can I trust that you're telling the truth now?"

Alma fidgeted. After some thought she answered, "I'm telling you what I *believe* to be true. What more can I do?"

Murdock's eyes locked onto hers. "There's an old proverb that says that truth is the daughter of time. For the present time, we need to treat you cautiously and you need to treat us cautiously as well. In time you will see that Linda and I are keeping our promise to make provision for you. If Amy and Roy become convinced that your science is genuine and that you have been honest with them, then time will have cemented a mutual trust and friendship that I hope Linda and I can share."

Alma's eyes softened, but she spoke firmly. "I will work with the two professors whenever they want. I'll work with Brother Martin, too. You talk about trust. When I first met you, Murdock McCabe, I needed to trust somebody. The only person I'd completely trusted had been Brother Antonio but my false friends kept him away from me most of the time. I decided to trust you, too, but they prevented me from seeing you. When

I did see you in Honduras a few days ago, I did what you wanted. That's the truth."

There was silence around the table.

Murdock thanked her for her confidence. At that point, he mentioned that Amy and Roy wished to meet with Alma briefly in another conference room. After they departed, Brother Martin said, "Those of us who shared our misadventure a few days ago are fortunate to be here today. I suggest that each of us in his or her own way thank God that my prayer was answered during that wild scene at the Traction compound."

Grace asked, "What makes you think it was, Marty?"

"When our situation deteriorated, there were so many things that had to go right for all of us to survive that the odds we faced were daunting. It would take a miracle for all of them to fall into place. Except for Jack, they did."

"Marty," Grace said, "Wake up, man. You're so tied up in that religious stuff that you don't recognize fortuitous coincidence when you see it."

Martin laughed jovially and asked, "Is that what you'd call it?"

Murdock announced that the meeting was over and invited them all to join him for brunch in ten minutes at the Tall Spruce, a restaurant on the top floor. As they exited the conference room, out of the corner of his eye, Murdock noticed Grace catch Brother Martin by the arm. He started to react but thought better of it. Instead, he went into his office. Standing next to the window, he looked toward Mount Hood in the distance—alone with his thoughts again. He was pleased with their purchase of Veritus. Linda had given notice to Enrique. He had turned in his resignation as station chief, effective upon the closing of the sale and purchase. They would keep the Chicago staff. He and Linda would not participate in day-to-day operations. Instead, they would enjoy acres of leisure time together.

Looking back toward the conference room, he hoped that Grace and Brother Martin were not having an argument. He deeply respected them both.

* * *

When Grace and Martin were alone, she said, "I do really like you, Brother Martin. I apologize if I've seemed rude and disrespectful. It's just my nature to be a brassy bitch. You have a right to believe in whatever you wish. When the cards were down, you came through. You were cool. You flew that chopper through a hellish storm of gunfire."

"There's no need to apologize, Grace. Don't ever shed your irreverence. It wouldn't be you. You're delightful just as you are. You compel people to think logically and see the other side of the coin. That's a rare quality. You're passionate in your disbelief. Too many people are neither hot nor cold but lukewarm. It's for their souls that I fear the most. I pray that some day you'll receive the gift of Christian faith from the Holy Spirit. If you do, I know you'll express it with just as much passion. Oh, what an apostle you'd make."

Grace cocked her head and said, "No offense, but I just can't understand how intelligent people like you in this age of reason can still believe in magic, gods, and in angels looking over their shoulders. Alma gave no sign that her point of origin had such superstitions. They can't be dumb. Whatever they are, they were smart enough to get her here."

"Perhaps it's wishful thinking, but between Alma's words, I read something else. When her memory matures, I suspect that we'll find that she and her fellow beings worshiped that 'Creative Energy.'"

"You make me wish I could believe, but your doctrines are erected on unproved suppositions. They're logical within your belief system, but only if you accept the basic premise that God exists. I can't. Most cultured people that I know don't buy that logic. I don't think Alma will."

Murdock stuck his head in the door. "Are you guys coming?

Brother Martin waved and said, "In a minute."

Murdock left them to themselves.

Brother Martin's eyes met Grace's. "I agree with you, Grace. Faith isn't supported by logic. Think of the hundreds of poor souls that believed in Patti's green goddess and Alma isn't a goddess at all. It's illogical to believe that God listens to millions of prayers at the same time, but I believe he does. So where *does* faith come from? I think it's a gift that God extrudes out of skeptical disbelief. Disbelief is rebelliousness—a denial of the yearning to believe. Disbelief is the shadow side of the human yearning for God. Of course, judging by extrinsic evidence, there's a mere fifty-fifty chance that God even exists. We have the freewill to believe or not. I choose to believe."

Grace placed her laptop in its carrying case and pushed her chair back from the conference table. "That's a good sales pitch, Marty, I mean, Brother Martin."

"Marty."

"Thanks. Marty, I respect your right to choose, but if He or She exists, conveniently hiding in some mysterious remote heaven—that doesn't cut it. God would have to pop down to earth and appear in a form that people could see, talk in a language people could understand, and toss in a few miracles to boot. Then I'd take a second look."

Brother Martin sat back in his chair, his elbow resting on the arm, his chin supported by his hand, and his eyes fixed on hers. He grinned and asked, "Really?"

Epilogue

Murdock and Linda were married in October of that same year in the church she had attended as a girl in Calgary. Enrique was the best man. Included in the wedding party were both Grace and Susan, who was visibly pregnant. Unrelenting Boris gave Linda a new bizjet as a wedding gift. He gave a case of inexpensive Scotch to Murdock. Linda had told Boris that Murdock didn't like Scotch. During the reception, Boris told her he was still hopeful that she might bear him one child.

After completing the purchase of Veritus, Murdock and Linda built a comfortable log cabin on an eastern slope of the Bitterroot Mountains of Montana, an easy trip from Calgary for Linda's father. Not far from their cabin, down a winding trail through and under some tall conifers, but within their property boundaries, is another log cabin. A woman lives there alone. She seldom goes out at night. Almost daily she is visited by Murdock and Linda, and often by a Spanish-looking gentleman. A woman physician who speaks German has been visiting recently.

On the day after Murdock and Linda's first wedding anniversary, twins were born, a girl and a boy, whom they boldly named Karen and Jack.

Shortly after they married, Linda had negotiated a contract with United States Naval Intelligence. The fees from it will pay off the purchase price for Veritus in three years. Murdock hired a dozen retired naval intelligence officers to service it. He personally supervises their secretive activities separate from Veritus. Occasionally, he spends a few days away from home for that purpose. Occasionally Linda spends a few days away from home conferring with the naval representative who got them the contract. By and large, however, Murdock and Linda spend their days happily together at home with their children and their friends.

413

Susan is now a single mother of a little girl. She has recently been appointed station chief for the Veritus office in Omaha.

Grace is assistant station chief of the Veritus office in Helena, Montana. She is a frequent visitor at Murdock and Linda's home, and often serves as a substitute mother when Linda is away.

Rudi has retired from the Bavarian State Police and has decided that he really doesn't need more excitement. He and his wife, Angelika, bought a small chalet in the Bavarian Alps where they frequently entertain Murdock, Linda, and Brother Martin for skiing weekends.

Brother Martin is content being an abbot of a rather eclectic monastery.

Boris Romanovsky has continued his success in commerce and his lack of success in love.

Miguel Pedro Juanito Gonzales considered giving up his business as a mercenary, but not too seriously. Danger to Miguel is like candy to a little boy.

Greta and Lore have made an offer to purchase the Zugspitze Hof Hotel on the slope of the mountain by the same name, not far from Saint Luke's Monastery.

Denise, with some financial help from a friend, purchased the Lost Flamingo Hotel. She changed its name to the Blue Lagoon. With some repackaging and clever advertising, she is making it a success.

So the story must end. Will Murdock and Linda live happily ever after? That great American philosopher, Yogi Berra, is reported to have said, "It's tough to make predictions, especially about the future." But I think so.

The Author

About the Author

GIL HOWARD is the pen name of Judge G. H. Zitzelsberger. Gil is a native of Buffalo, New York. He holds degrees from the University of Buffalo, Wayne University in Detroit, and Michigan State University College of Law. He was in the general practice of law, which included criminal law, in Wayne County, Michigan. He served twenty-five years as a trial court judge in that county.

Upon retiring from the bench, Gil served three years as the executive director (International Secretary) of Kiwanis International at its headquarters in Indianapolis. The Kiwanis worldwide staff reported to him. He was also the editor of *Kiwanis* magazine.

Returning to his legal career, he practiced probate law and estate planning in Bradenton, Florida, for fourteen years.

He served on various boards for the Boy Scouts of America in both the Detroit Area Council and the Crossroads of America Council. He is an Eagle Scout.

During the Korean Conflict, he served in the United States Air Force.

Gil is a multi-engine and instrument-rated pilot and has flown frequently from coast to coast in the United States and in the Caribbean. He has traveled widely in Europe, the Far East, Australia and New Zealand. He is the author of three mystery-suspense-thrillers: *The Chaos Chip* (1999), *Fury in the Shadow* (2005), and *The Price of Innocence* (2008). His stories are peppered with vivid descriptions drawn from his personal experiences.

Printed in the United States
203341BV00004BA/7-33/P

9 781434 383266